The Gilboa Iris

The Gilboa Iris

A Novel by

Zahava D. Englard

gefen
publishing house
בית הוצאה לאור
גפן
Est. 1981
JERUSALEM ◆ NEW YORK

Cover Design: Estee Kreisman
Typesetting: Irit Nachum

ISBN: 978-965-229-574-3

1 3 5 7 9 8 6 4 2

Gefen Publishing House Ltd.
6 Hatzvi Street
Jerusalem 94386, Israel
972-2-538-0247
orders@gefenpublishing.com

Gefen Books
11 Edison Place
Springfield, NJ 07081
516-593-1234
orders@gefenpublishing.com

www.gefenpublishing.com

Printed in Israel

Send for our free catalogue

Library of Congress Cataloging-in-Publication Data
Englard, Zahava.
The Gilboa Iris / Zahava D. Englard.
pages cm
ISBN 978-965-229-574-3
1. Jews, American–Israel–Fiction.   2. Kibbutzim–Fiction.
3. Soldiers–Israel–Fiction.   4. Bereavement–Fiction.
5. Terrorism–Fiction.   6. Israel–Fiction. I. Title.
PR9510.9.E54G55 2012
813'.6–dc23
2011050798

Dedicated to my daughters, Jordana and Nili,
in celebration of your spunk, your courage,
your sass and your love of life.

Jihad is our way, and death in the cause of Allah is our dream.

— Credo of the Muslim Brotherhood

The essence of optimism is that it takes not account of the present, but it is a source of inspiration, of vitality and hope where others have resigned; it enables a man to hold his head high, to claim the future for himself and not to abandon it to his enemy.

— Dietrich Bonhoeffer
Participant in the German resistance against Nazism

Hope is the thing with feathers that perches in the soul, and sings the tune without the words, and never stops at all.

— Emily Dickinson

Prologue

 *Israel, 2001*

A change of scenery is always nice, but it only works if you don't bring along the ghosts – an option to which I am not amenable. The ghosts of my children and my husband serve as my life force now. They sustain me. That and my enduring anger.

Nevertheless, a trip to the Mediterranean Sea seems like a good idea, though not much planning has gone into it. I know with certainty, however, that I must get away, if just for a short time. I have to distance myself from the feel of the battlefront, from the Judean Hills. I need water. I need to walk along the beach blasting my iPod into my head with what was my children's favorite music and lose myself in the thrashing waves of the sea. I want to know peace, if just for a moment.

Chapter 1

The Dan Accadia Hotel in Herzliya impressed me as a good choice. Perhaps I would even ask for an upgrade to a luxury suite. "Why not indulge myself?" I brooded, my dry sarcasm pervading my thoughts while I drove north on the tunnel road toward Jerusalem. Money, as it happened, was not an issue, owing to my late husband's generous life insurance policy. I scoffed as I imagined things could be worse – having a dead family *and* no money, that is. "Yeah, God is merciful," I allowed myself a sardonic smile as I stared at the sun-baked road ahead.

Above all, I would pretend that some level of escape was possible even if I had no intention of ever letting go of my wretched reality – a reality that was likewise an unreality, as I was resolute in considering myself dead. Cutting myself off from my well-meaning friends, all those I have loved and from everything that would interfere with my

1

resolve, was necessary, albeit severe. But I was determined not to lose focus. I would not allow my ghosts to dim. I did not want to *get over it.* Where I would go, they would go.

The roads were empty, unusual for this time of day. *Not good*, I thought. The quiet ride would allow me to think further about what had brought me to this point – and for the next several days I did not want to think at all. I turned onto Highway 1 from the Begin Expressway, heading toward Tel Aviv. The air conditioner was on full blast but I opened the window on my side. Something about letting my hair blow in the wind while speeding on the highway was soothing. I lit a cigarette, trying to distract myself, and turned on the radio that was tuned to Galei Tzahal, the army station. An old Israeli song played, taking me back to my days on a kibbutz, a collective agricultural community, where I volunteered for a year after graduating from high school in the States. That was before personal computers and cell phones, I mused.

Stop the celebration; stop this day, the lyrics droned.

Sixteen years had passed since those days on kibbutz, my short stab at working the land in an idealistic, socialist and communal setting – yet the memories were vivid. I turned up the volume, letting the familiar music flood the car, and I allowed the song to transport my mind back to another place in another time, many years ago.

Mount Gilboa, 1983 – Eighteen Again

The ruckus in the large communal dining hall reached its customary decibel level that evening. The greeting of friends and neighbors at the end of another workday, the clatter of dishes and the restlessness of the children were all par for the course. Married couples with their children sat at their usual tables and the singles at theirs. The long rectangular tables were the kind you would find in a school cafeteria, and the dishes and flatware likewise had an institutional flair. Austerity dominated the design motif. On the other hand, the south, east and west walls of the dining hall were encased in wall-to-wall windows, which brightened up the otherwise Spartan atmosphere. They afforded a panoramic and picturesque view of the adjacent hills and the valley of Beit She'an below – the fields, orchards and fishponds of the surrounding kibbutzim checkered in a breathtaking pattern of contrasting hues.

Prior to the Six-Day War in 1967, this kibbutz, situated on top of Mount Gilboa, served as Israel's border. Outside my room, just several yards away, stood a long and narrow foxhole. No one ever bothered to refill it with earth. After the Yom Kippur War in 1973 and later the Lebanon War in 1982, few doubted that another war would be looming around the bend. Instead of refilling it, the gardening team worked to beautify the foxhole with plants and assorted greenery.

I took in every element and every feature, as these were the final weeks of my stay and I would miss it all. While on line at the buffet tables, I smiled to myself, remembering my monthlong stint at kitchen duty. It was a grueling experience to stand over a sink day after day washing hundreds of dishes and a myriad of grease-caked pots. But at the same time I was grateful for the short reprieve from working in the fields in the heat of the summer, when 110°F was the norm as the Middle Eastern sun reached its peak.

Of course, working in the kitchen was not without its own hazards. My mind wandered to the day when Orli, the head of the kitchen, ordered me – to my horror – to gut scores of fresh fish for that day's lunch. Some of them were still twitching in the crates. But no one ever dared cross Orli. She was petite in stature, though quite fearsome in demeanor. I would never forget the wry smile she wore when ordering me about. In her eyes, I was just another overly pampered American teenager. I never balked though, at least not outwardly, and after a month under her tutelage I proved myself worthy of her respect. This was no small feat, as the burliest of men on the kibbutz feared her.

Out of my reverie I felt a strong hand wrap gently around my arm. Roni bent down to whisper in my ear to come sit next to him. After nearly a year, I still had goose bumps from his simple touch. As soon as I turned my head to face him, he was already off securing two seats at one of the tables to beat the dinner crowd onslaught. *Hmm...didn't he have guard duty this evening?* I wanted to spend whatever time I had left in Israel with Roni, but I sensed that our dinner banter was not going to be lighthearted, and I suspected that it would not end well. He must have traded shifts with someone with the intention of catching me before I headed out with some friends to Sachna, the nearby watering hole, a popular nighttime hangout for singles from the neighboring towns and kibbutzim.

Roni didn't want me returning to the States, even for just the first year of college, and for several months he had staged a zealous campaign to change my mind. With just a handful of weeks left before my flight back home, the air between us had become tense. It was not that I wanted to leave, but rather, I had little choice in the matter, and he had a difficult time accepting that.

I lost my appetite and put down my plate without filling it from the buffet, electing to munch on only some pita and hummus, routinely laid out on each dinner table. Taking a deep breath, I measured my steps as I neared Roni, his gripping gaze searing into me. I had an urge to turn up the air-conditioning.

Roni had extraordinary, luminous eyes that resembled crystal. If not for a slight tint of ice-blue, one could imagine staring straight through a prism. His chiseled features – a strong jaw and flawless Greek nose – contributed to the severe intensity he imparted. He was above-average height and very athletic looking – lean yet muscular with dependable, solid shoulders. His loose, silky-blond curls – grown out since his army service and incongruous with his stern posture – fell with casual allure, framing a tanned face. His infectious smile had a way of creasing his eyes into slits. That is, on the rare occasions when he did smile. He was a brooder, and his full lips would almost always be pursed in a sensuous frown. Any young woman's dream, let alone a naive, idealistic American teen.

I noticed him right away during my first week as a volunteer. Who wouldn't? Yet, he gave off an aloof and unapproachable demeanor. I had heard that during the Lebanon War the previous summer, he was in the bloody battle of Sultan Yacoub, where eighteen of his fellow soldiers were killed in a Syrian ambush. Lebanese Hezbollah captured three soldiers: Zachary Baumel, Yehuda Katz and Zvi Feldman. These three soldiers remain unaccounted for, but according to reports, their Arab captors paraded them through Damascus on top of their captured tank. Roni never spoke of what happened at Sultan Yacoub, though it was always there, just below the surface.

I sat down on one of two chairs that Roni pulled to the edge of the table in an attempt to afford us some privacy from the others sitting nearby. In a way, the din in the dining hall offered us a unique type of solitude. I smiled as cheerful a smile as I could muster under the circumstances and reached out to hold his hand. He furrowed his brows and enveloped my hand in both of his. He had a way of making me feel delicate and fragile when next to him. Because he radiated such strength, it pained me even more that I might be chipping away at his steely facade.

"Dara, I've decided to leave the kibbutz," he said in a low, soft tone. "I'm going to Jerusalem." My eyes widened in confusion. "Your last day here will also be mine," he continued. "There isn't anything here for me anymore, and besides, what I do here I can do anywhere – and get paid for it," he said with a half smile.

Roni was the kibbutz mechanic. Any given time of day, one could find him beneath a huge tractor tinkering away. He was happiest when fiddling with parts of an engine – they didn't talk back, as he would explain. They might sputter a bit of oil and grease from time to time, but at least he didn't have to deal with the social amenities necessary when working alongside other people. He loathed small talk, valued his independence and enjoyed his quiet time alone on the job.

"Jerusalem? But Roni, I thought you had…other plans."

"They weren't definite," he said in haste, avoiding the subject. "Look, Dara," he explained, "my father has a friend who owns an auto repair shop in the industrial center in Jerusalem, and over the years it's been quite lucrative for him. The good news is," he went on to say, brandishing his exquisite smile, "he's looking to retire in the near future and has agreed to take me on until I can pay him off. It's a good opportunity." There was an eagerness in his eyes, trying almost too hard to convince me.

Knowing what I knew about Roni, I responded with caution, "I don't understand. I mean…I'm glad you're taking steps toward your future, but is this the right move for you?"

Roni recoiled as if he had just been stung. "*Our* future, Dara! I'm not giving up on you. *I won't lose you, too.*" His last words pierced straight through me. I knew he was thinking about the friends he had lost in battle – this twenty-two-year-old whose youth was gone forever.

"Roni," I leaned closer to him, "we've been over this. You know my parents are adamant about me returning to the States. And you know why. They won't bankroll my stay here in Israel, and I'm just about down to my last dollar. Besides," I sighed, "I just can't walk out on them."

"What about *you*? What about *us*? Listen to what you're saying, Dara."

I shook my head, not wanting to listen to reason. "In spite of everything, I'm their only child. They're depending on me."

"*Depending on you?* The way they treat you is obscene."

"Still, I gave them my word, and I can't renege on it. I can't undermine my father's position with the Defense Department."

"Dara, you know that's irrational."

"Is it? I'm involved with an officer in the Israeli army. What if they're right? What if my father's loyalty is questioned? I don't want that."

"I thought you wanted *me*."

"I *do* want you. I love you. Don't you see how it's tearing me apart to leave you? But, I'll tell you what I don't want, Roni," I continued. "I don't want you to turn your back on who you are and on what *you* really want...on what you feel you need to do. And I know it's not owning an auto repair shop. My hands are tied, but yours are not."

"What I want is you, Dara. Getting that job will help pay for your university tuition here in Israel."

"If it was just about the money, there wouldn't be an issue."

"You don't have to go back there – not for an entire year. Knowing your parents, they'll push all the right buttons and guilt you into staying longer. I don't trust them. They're using you. Why can't you see that?"

But I couldn't see that. I wouldn't. The complexities of our circumstances weighed heavily upon me. I tried to control the trembling inside of me, but it seemed to be taking on a life of its own. "Perhaps it's unfair of me to ask you to wait for me when I'm on the other side of the world – when I can't even promise *when* I'd be able to get back to Israel at all."

Disregarding my last comment, Roni noted, "You have other choices, Dara."

"None that I can live with."

"But you would choose to live without me." He didn't ask. He just said it as a statement of fact.

"That's not fair." I looked down, barely whispering. "You won't leave Israel, you won't leave your family, you..."

"No, I won't." Roni cut me off before I could finish. "It's different for me, Dara. I thought you understood that. It's like abandoning your fellow soldiers on the battlefield."

"But we're not at war now. It would just be temporary."

"Dara," he murmured, sadness enveloping his eyes, "we are always at war."

I slumped back in my chair and exhaled noisily, knowing his words were true.

The idea of being apart from him for so long was unbearable, and I had consciously pushed such thoughts out of my mind. Now with this exchange – less than two months away from my departure – all my feelings drew to a head, and the control over my emotions I thought I had frittered away. I tried to swallow and felt an enormous lump in my throat; the tenseness in my chest tightened, rigid as a metal chain. The noise in the dining room seemed to grow in volume, and I couldn't take it anymore. "Roni," I breathed, "I need air." I was going to be sick. It was good that I hadn't eaten any dinner.

Feeling desperate and lacking any better idea, I flew from the dining hall to the outside lawn. Rather than take a moment to collect myself before returning to Roni, I continued running toward the edge of the mountain, darting up the path, past my room toward the foxhole. This was where I would go to think. This was my spot to be alone, to meditate. It was the very lip of the mountain, and at night the lights from down below in the valley were mesmerizing.

I looked up to the sky, which was especially black tonight and swathed in a blanket of stars, as if I could find a solution etched in its intricate pattern. But there was no solution – none that I could see. Uninvited tears welled in my eyes and fell to my cheeks. I hated hurting Roni. The thought of leaving him was killing me inside.

Why did I always have to be "the good daughter"? So dependable! So loyal! What if I didn't return to the States? And what if I disregarded my parents' fears and ignored their emotional blackmail? My thoughts reeled into one another. My parents would be furious if I told them I wasn't returning. My father, a top physicist for the US Defense Department, and my mother, a professor of art and an artist in her own right, had always put great emphasis on the value of higher education. They allowed me to take a year off to go to Israel with the sole understanding that I would return in time for the fall semester. They were relentless and very selective when it came to education, and after I was accepted to an Ivy League university in the States, there was no way they would agree to me attending university in Israel. I heard my mother saying, "You're only eighteen. You're too young and you're too naive to know what you want."

To be sure, I *wanted* to go to college. There was much I still wished to experience, and much I wanted to accomplish. I had been accepted to Columbia University, for God's sake! Even so, I was ready to give up the Ivy League, but I couldn't; my parents saw to that by threatening to disown me. My education, however, was not the only factor in play. They had other reasons for their severity. My immigrating to Israel diametrically opposed their worldview and their own aspirations in American society.

Harsh as their threat was, they were the only family I had.

Yet I didn't want to give up Roni. I was not too naive to know how deeply I loved him. *What is wrong with me? How can I walk away from him?* I yearned to live in Israel, but my parents held my father's position with the government over my head, weighing me down with an impossible yoke of guilt. Succumbing to that guilt meant leaving Roni. Just thinking about it made me hyperventilate.

I offered as a compromise to transfer to a university in Israel after one year at Columbia, but my parents refused to consider it and vowed to cut me off when I told them about Roni. They were immovable and they were serious. If I remained in Israel, I would lose the only family I had.

I wanted to try to work it out with my parents, and that required flying back to the States and dealing with them face-to-face. Roni feared they would attempt to manipulate me further. He detested my parents for the way they treated me and could not fathom why I hated to disappoint them when they were so willing to disown me.

I didn't turn around to face him when I heard him walk up behind me. Taking several deep breaths, I worked at calming myself down while wiping away my tears. In my heart, I knew I was being unreasonable. How could I expect him to put his life on hold for me? I had to end it. I was not going to be selfish – not with Roni. *Okay, Dara, grow up and get control of yourself.* There was no use in prolonging the inevitable.

I felt Roni snuggle up from behind me, his arms winding around my waist. He crouched slightly forward, nestling his head against the side of my face, and together we gazed at the stars. My breathing veered in harmony with his as I felt the up and down movement of his chest against my back. We stood like this in silence for several moments.

As soon as I could trust my own voice, I turned my head to speak, yet before I could utter a word his lips were on mine. It started out tender and soothing, but soon his kiss grew more potent, his passion dispelling all other thoughts from my mind. He grabbed hold of my arms, as his lips trailed up the side of my face. His voice, tempered with desire, took on a husky tone. "No decision will be made tonight." And I surrendered to the overriding passion that his touch stirred within me. He turned me around to face him, capturing my lips again, this time with more force, and we fell to the ground still bound to one another.

Chapter 2

The first time Roni and I met face-to-face was quite by chance and not too pleasant. The members of the kibbutz were open and welcoming to the volunteers that came from all over the world to contribute to working the land. Some, like me, did it for idealistic reasons, and others, for the adventure of a unique experience. By the end of the first week, there wasn't a member of the community that hadn't introduced themselves to us and offered their friendship, save for one – Aharon Ben-Ari. His friends called him Roni.

Roni kept his distance, and I assumed that he – like many Israelis at the time – considered all Americans spoiled, held little faith that we could handle the tough physical labor that kibbutz life entailed and saw us as little more than annoyances. I was certain that was how he regarded me. It would not have been so maddening if he merely ignored me, but often I would catch him glaring at me from a distance, as if I had the audacity to intrude into his little space in his corner of the world. With chronic consistency, he acted irritated whenever I would socialize with any of his friends, and I would swear he went out of his way to make me feel ill at ease. There were times when he left the room as soon as I entered. It could not have been coincidental. And, while he was clearly not verbose in general, he would at least grunt hello to the other female volunteers from time to time. It was obvious that he had a problem with me, and I couldn't understand why. I was determined, however, to shake his unpleasant countenance from my mind and not allow him to get to me.

After two months on the kibbutz, I found myself assigned to a group delegated to assembling irrigation pipes across the vast cotton fields. Before the onset of dawn, the field workers gathered at the top of the mountain where the members and volunteers of the kibbutz resided. There, they waited for the ride down the sharp and winding road to the valley below. Depending on what our work detail was for the day, the drivers would drop us off either at the orchard groves, the fishponds or the *radrah*. The *radrah* was what they dubbed the kibbutz field center, which had various functions. It was located on what appeared to be an isolated strip of land, but in close proximity to all the fields. The kibbutz kept all its equipment there, including a large garage that housed the trucks, tractors and assorted farming machinery and an immense array of tools. There was also a kitchen and a makeshift dining area to service the field workers during the day.

When I arrived, Roni was standing outside the entrance of the *radrah*. *Is he frowning at me? No*, I quickly surmised, *it's just his usual disposition*. Minutes later, however, I heard him arguing with one of the regulars, a short, powerfully built man named Moti, who supervised all the field work. Although I was well versed in Hebrew and had no trouble conversing in it, I didn't understand the content of the argument — at least not right away. Roni rattled off his words with such speed that I didn't pay attention, nor was I interested in any case.

Despite my indifference, I couldn't help but notice him gesturing toward me – and about me, I realized – his golden mane dancing around his face as his argument became more animated. It was then that I discerned the words *frying omelets in the kitchen*! Moti's response was inaudible, but Roni stormed away jabbering in what sounded surprisingly like fluid Arabic.

It was impossible to grasp that this was purely about me! I wasn't the only female volunteer and I didn't understand what his problem was. Why was he singling me out? And why wasn't his face under some truck or tractor? I soon gathered that when there were no machines or engines that required fixing or maintenance, Roni would lend a hand wherever it was needed. This morning he would be helping in the fields.

Evidently, he lost the argument, since Moti didn't relegate me to kitchen duty. They were shorthanded in the fields and needed every volunteer. *This was going to be a splendid day.* Grim as it seemed, I was determined to be upbeat, despite Roni.

As chance would have it, there was no room for me in the regular vehicle transporting the workers to the cotton fields, and Moti instructed me to ride in the front cab of the pickup truck carrying the irrigation pipes. A moment later, to my consternation, Roni opened the driver's side door and his stunning, sparkling eyes widened in surprise to see me sitting in the front of his truck.

This was the first time I saw him up close, since he took pains to avoid me like the plague. It was obvious that he was handsome, but whoa! I wasn't prepared for the full-scale view of those eyes in such close proximity. They were…staggering. The cliché of one's heart skipping a beat had new meaning for me. Mine, however, more like trotted right out of my chest. My knee-jerk reaction unsettled me. I didn't want to give him a second thought, and yet some emotion inside me flashed a different signal, which was decidedly vexing.

Clenching his jaw, Roni jumped into the driver's seat, unlatched the hand brake and brought the engine to a roar. He didn't hide his irritation at my presence, muttering something in Hebrew under his breath that sounded like he called me a chirping bird. *I must have heard wrong*, I thought, since I hadn't uttered a syllable. We rode in silence the entire way.

An agonizing ten minutes later we reached the cotton fields, and I grabbed the door handle to scoot out of the cab. It was stuck. *Great.* As I fiddled with the handle, a surge of heat rose up to my face, as if it wasn't already hot enough in the Beit She'an Valley. I was not prone to blushing, but I could sense I turned beet red, more out of annoyance than anything else. I already knew what Roni thought about me working in the fields, and this little glitch was not helping my case. With what looked like another one of his customary scowls, Roni leaned over me and jerked the car door open. He met my eyes with a forbidding gaze, his face just inches from mine. I was unfamiliar with the tumult raging inside of me when the curl of his lips parted long enough for me to feel his breath against me. Unnerved, I mumbled a thank-you and jumped down from the truck, his muted, arrogant laughter wafting behind me.

Resolved to focus on the job at hand, I joined the others in removing the irrigation pipes from the back of the truck. They were not heavy, just cumbersome. I was determined to carry my weight, confident that I could sail through anything that came my way. *I'll show Mr. Greek God*; I would prove to the macho male chauvinist that he was wrong about me. As delicate as I seemed, I could hold my own and didn't shy away from physical labor.

The early morning sun in Beit She'an during the summer season was oppressive, and someone passed around a jerry can filled with ice-cold water. It was just about an hour past dawn; still, one could already tell that the heat promised to be unforgiving. I took a moment to tighten my ponytail, lift and twirl it into a loose bun. It was then that

I looked up and caught Roni staring at me, appraising me from head to toe in the annoying standard male ritual. I often ignored this practice, but his gaze lingered several seconds too long, making me feel self-conscious. My breathing, which I never gave any thought to before, became disturbingly uneven. Why was I letting him get to me?

C'mon, Dara, keep it together. Pay no attention to him, I told myself. *Or, at the very least, get angry!* With a slight slant to my head, I stood in a questioning stance and met Roni's eyes once they rose from my body back to my face, as if to ask, *So? Do I pass?* In an abrupt move, he turned his attention to the cotton plants, pretending to examine them.

I knew I was attractive to men but took caution not to flaunt it. In the last year or so, I shed my tomboyish posture. As a child and up until recently, I felt awkward and lanky and found that I was most comfortable when climbing trees. In my seventeenth year, I blossomed. I was thin, but in a feminine way, more shapely now – rounded in all the right places, as some would say. My mother was quite striking, and to my surprise I grew into her spitting image, although I catered to it with a sense of detachment. No longer feeling lanky, I stood at a pleasing height. My skin tone was very pale, and its translucency was particularly profound against my jet-black hair, which fell sleekly past my shoulders. Back home, friends affectionately nicknamed me Cleo, after Cleopatra. I had just one physical feature from my father – his eyes. They were for the most part a medium blue, yet turned gray when I was tired or upset.

This womanly body along with my more mature face was still new to me, and I was not yet comfortable with it. I found men's stares to be more irksome than flattering. Yet, in spite of this, Roni's gaze threw me off-balance and made me feel altogether flustered. It was a struggle to keep my pulse in check.

I directed my interest to two girls that I had befriended in my initial weeks on the kibbutz: my roommates Jenny and Alana, both my age and, like me, volunteers from America. We engaged in small talk while waiting to receive our instructions, and two young men from Australia, Ben and Joey, joined in. Up to that point, we all had experienced several weeks of field work, but were new to assembling irrigation systems. Meanwhile, Roni had completed "examining" the cotton plants and busied himself with divvying up the pipes, tool belts, pliers, spigots and items I didn't know the name for into separate piles. He laid everything out in a meticulous fashion on the dirt road that separated two massive cotton fields.

Against my better judgment, I found myself stealing looks at him. Roni's mannerism was confident and disciplined, and my eyes drifted, drawn to his toned arms, whose muscles appeared to dance to his every movement, and then fixated on the T-shirt that fit snuggly around his strong physique. Just then, he looked up and noticed me watching him. Although embarrassed, I stopped myself from turning away in reflex and giving him any satisfaction. His expression was as stony as his features, and he shifted his attention back to his task.

When he finished, he stood with his hands on his hips, legs spread slightly apart, his M16 casually slung over his shoulder, and called us to attention, similar to an officer commanding a platoon, I imagined. Roni then demonstrated how to assemble all the pieces before attaching the spigots, spitting out the instructions with impatience, and charged us to lay the irrigation system throughout both fields. He split us up into two groups. There were five girls and four guys, and he divided us up according to gender and assigned a field to each group. *Is he actually going to make this a race between the sexes?* Jenny, Alana and I shared an incredulous look among ourselves. Roni seemed to find humor in this and with a patronizing sneer informed us that he would be back at ten o'clock to check on our progress. He jumped back into his truck and drove away, trudging up a cloud of dirt behind him.

The guy-group was already busy at work. I shrugged and grabbed a tool belt, loaded it up and snatched a bundle of pipes onto my arms.

I headed into the lush leafy growth, sliding past Jenny, Alana and two other girls, Rachel and Miri. Revealing a sly grin, I murmured to them, "We can do this." They picked up on my tone and joined right behind me.

It didn't take us long to find our own rhythm, and singing old Beatles songs as we worked helped us maintain a steady pace – our progress encouraging our swiftness. The cotton plants grew tall, some reaching to my shoulders. We removed the spigots, firmly connected new pipes to the original ones attached to the irrigation lines and fastened the spigots to the new extensions, careful not to crack the plastic with the pliers. When we exhausted our supply of pipes, we scurried back to the dirt road and loaded ourselves up with more. I couldn't say how many we did, but the field looked as if it went on forever, which lent to our exhilaration when we completed three-quarters of the task before nine o'clock. The strain, in both our lower and upper arm muscles, started to take a toll, although our collective tenacity prodded us on to finish the entire field before Roni's return. None of the girls in my group was very impressed with his condescending manner.

We were unable to see above the height of the cotton plants while sitting cross-legged on the ground in the middle of the dirt road, but we heard the roar of a truck's engine, checked our watches and guessed that it was Roni. The truck made its way around the bend and headed in our direction, stopping several feet before us. Roni vaulted out and walked toward our little circle with his now-familiar cynical frown plastered on his face. He scanned the area for the piles of pipes that he had left with us, but found none.

Weighing the scene before him, he narrowed his eyes, seeming a bit mystified, and asked where the men were. I gave a nod in the direction of the farthest end of their field. "They're finishing up," I stated matter-of-factly. I pressed my lips together and looked down to keep from laughing. Jenny and Alana bit their lips to do the same and Rachel and Miri stared down at the road pretending to amuse each other with a game of tic-tac-toe in the dirt. We wanted to play it cool.

"Dara, is it?"

My head shot up to meet his ice-blue eyes squinting at me. It startled me to hear my name roll off his tongue. I was surprised that he even knew my name. "Yes, it is," trying to sound nonchalant. I stood up from the ground and brushed the dirt off the back of my jeans. I didn't like the feeling of him standing over me as he spoke to me.

He turned his gaze from me to the rows of cotton plants. "You finished assembling all of the irrigation pipes on this entire cotton field?" Before I could even answer, he observed aloud, in disbelief, "That's impossible," as he studied the expansive area.

Since he clearly wasn't interested in hearing what I had to say, I didn't bother responding. Shrugging my shoulders, I sauntered over to the truck and leaned against its side. Then, thinking better of it, I said, "I do hope you brought us some water. The jerry can is all but empty and…we've worked up a thirst out here waiting for your return."

Still scrutinizing the span of the field and paying no attention to my harmless jab, Roni called to me over his shoulder, "Come with me," a curious tone to his simple request as he ambled toward the cotton plants. Without a word, I followed him into the foliage.

He stopped at several random pipes, testing the grip on the newly affixed parts, as well as checking for cracks. Finding nothing wrong with any of them, he moved across several rows of plants, deeper into the field, and repeated the examination, with me trailing one step behind him. After doing this a few more times, he turned around to face me with a bemused look that gradually grew into an uncharacteristic smile. I must have looked absurd, standing there wide-eyed and dazzled by him. He looked back at the greenery, raking his hand through his head of curls as if trying to solve a puzzle, and then looked once more at me – locking my eyes to his. Finally, in a soft and smooth undertone, he confessed, "I'm impressed."

I swallowed hard, tried to ignore the impossible glitter of his eyes and coolly responded, "You needn't be – it wasn't as if it were challenging."

"Hmm," he seemed to consider what I had just said. "I could always find something more demanding for you to do, perhaps even a bit more stimulating…" he trailed off.

"Don't put yourself out," I retorted, ignoring what I thought was an innuendo, although I wasn't entirely sure. Converting his Hebrew into English in my head, some things got lost in translation. His smile grew broader, creasing his eyes into glimmering slits, and I was convinced that my racing pulse just passed the sound barrier.

I was very much aware that we were alone, surrounded by the high-blossoming walls of the cotton plants. There was every reason for me to be ill at ease with him, and I felt self-conscious and didn't like it. I whirled around to head back to the dirt road, but in my haste I tripped over a stone jutting out from the earth. My right foot caught under the irrigation hose and I flew to the ground. *Just perfect!* Struggling to get my bearings, I sat upright, shoving hair off my face and fuming over my clumsiness.

Not expecting any thoughtful gesture from him, Roni surprised me by kneeling down beside me. "Are you hurt?" He sounded sincere. I was too embarrassed to answer and could only shake my head no. He held out his hand to me. I hesitated for a moment and then reluctantly grasped it, and with his other arm wrapped around the small of my back, he lifted me off the ground. His hold was strong, and his touch…spine-tingling, even dizzying – so much so that I couldn't trust my knees to hold me up. He must have assumed that my balance was off from my ground-shaking plunge, and he tightened his hold around my waist, sending an electric current pulsing right through me, so profound that I felt it quivering down my back. I prayed that my face didn't betray my thoughts and that my foolish and inexplicable feelings were not transparent. *Get a grip, Dara!* The effect Roni had on me was ridiculous.

Having pulled me to my feet, he didn't rush to let go, yet held me for a drawn-out moment as if to study my face. Lowering his eyes, he removed his arm from around my waist to take both my hands into his. He examined my palms and gently brushed away the earth. I winced, only then noticing the lacerations from my attempt to break my fall. "You're bleeding a little." He brought my hands close to his lips and blew his soothing breath over the cuts to clear the soil from them. I was undone.

"Are you sure you're all right?" He looked up from my hands with a slight smile curling up one corner of his mouth. "You look a little… unsteady."

"There's nothing unsteady about me," I managed to answer in a low huff. His eyes held mine before drifting to the various contours of my body, lingering and deliberate, and then creeping back to my eyes. So impossibly insufferable – he made my blood boil. I eased my hands out of his grasp, smoothing out my rumpled self and regaining composure before attempting the path to the dirt road once again. Piqued by his haughtiness and conflicted by my own feelings, I marched out to the clearing. Roni chuckled under his breath and followed several steps behind me.

With his truck emptied of all the irrigation pipes, the entire group had already seated themselves in the back of Roni's pickup waiting to be driven back to the *radrah*. It was time for the ten o'clock meal, a necessary repast after working since the break of dawn. I headed toward the back of the truck to join the others. It looked a little tight, but Ben, sitting close to the edge, offered his hand to help hoist me up.

While trying to gain a foothold, I suddenly felt someone grab me by the waist, pulling me back down. I gasped and stumbled backward into Roni, not at all understanding why he was doing what he was doing. He steadied me and spun me around to face him. "Where do you think you're going?" amusement still in his voice.

"Back to the *radrah*, with everyone else, and I'd appreciate it if you wouldn't manhandle me."

"Well, there isn't any more room in the back of the truck," he said, as if to justify his actions, all traces of amusement now gone. "I don't need you falling out and hurting yourself again. You'll be working in the orchards next, and I'm responsible for delivering you there in one piece. You'll sit in the front with me."

That's exactly what I wanted to avoid.

I stormed over to the front cab of the truck, jumped inside and slammed the door shut. He joined me a second later, and again we rode in silence. I could think of nothing but reaching the *radrah* and my anticipated escape from his truck.

Finally! After the longest ten minutes, I grabbed the handle and, *Oh my God, this can't be happening! Not twice in one day!* I tried to turn and twist the door handle every which way, jiggling and maneuvering in all directions, even using both hands and ignoring the sting of my cuts, but it wouldn't budge. After a prolonged minute or two of attempting to wrestle my way out of the truck, I had no choice but to abandon the struggle. I sat back in my seat and exhaled loudly – spent from my tantrum with the stubborn sliver of metal – and stared out the front window in frustration.

"Are you quite done?" Roni murmured. I glared at him as he reached over me and easily jerked the door open. I was livid. "Dara," he said, still leaning over me, too close for comfort, "do watch where you step. I won't be with you at the orchard to pick up the pieces." I bolted out of the truck, too furious to answer.

Inside the *radrah*, the Israelis commended us for our work in the fields that morning. Apparently, Roni wasn't the only one who was impressed, and it was a good feeling to gain their respect. I headed to the kitchen in the back of the *radrah* and washed my hands in a small sink just off the main preparation area.

"Damn!" I cried out as the soap burned my open cuts. Arched over in pain, I grabbed a couple of paper towels, squeezing down on my palms to stop the burning. Without warning, two bronzed hands gripped my wrists. My heart stopped. I was afraid to look up. When I did, I was prepared to see Roni's mocking glare, but that was not at all what I saw.

He lifted the paper towels and turned my palms faceup to examine them. "Come with me," he said and led me to another room off the kitchen. It was a small storage room that contained shelves of unopened boxes, canned goods, bottled water and first-aid equipment. Roni searched through the first-aid supplies purposefully and found what he was looking for. "Hold out your hands for me, Dara." I did as Roni asked and he squeezed some ointment out of a tube and dabbed it over the cuts on my hands, tenderly massaging it in until the pain ebbed. When he was done, he raised his eyes to mine, his lips curving into a slight smile, "How does that feel?"

"Better…thank you."

"Good, but I think I should bandage them for now. You'll have a hard time working in the orchard if I don't."

"Okay," I breathed, waiting for the other shoe to drop. He turned back around to the shelf, searching once again, and brought out some gauze and tape. The gentle manner in which he cradled my hands was contrary to his overall temperament, I thought, as he wrapped my palms with the gauze. "There, that should help," he said, holding each of my hands in his. "I didn't make it too tight, did I?"

"Um…no…it's fine."

"Well, I couldn't be sure. Your hands are very fragile." There was no taunting in his voice. "You might want to eat something. We'll be leaving in twenty minutes." I didn't respond. I couldn't – riveted as I was by the power of his gaze, like penetrating shards of ice…hot ice. He let go of my hands and left the room. It took a long moment for me to get back to myself. I couldn't decide whether to be in shock or if Roni was just playing with my head. So instead, I decided I was ravenous and went over to sit with Jenny and Alana at the table.

"Say, what happened to your hands?" Alana asked.

"I fell," I shrugged. "Well…actually," I admitted, rolling my eyes, "I was an absolute klutz. I tripped over an irrigation hose when Roni asked me to go with him to check on some pipes."

Alana let out a hearty laugh, her chin-length curly brown hair bobbing in rhythm. "I was wondering what happened back there. I bet Roni's never going to let you live that one down!" I smiled at her buoyant energy. Alana had a knack for finding humor in just about everything.

Just then, three young Israeli men joined our table, sitting across from us, and I was able to relax with the easy conversation. It was not before long, however, that the topic of discussion shifted. One of them, Yaniv, had just finished his turn at guard duty and would be joining us to work in the grapefruit orchard after our short break. He told us how he recently completed his army service, and he and a friend decided to join the kibbutz for a while. "You know him… Roni."

"Oh, yes, we know Roni all right!" Alana giggled.

"The problem is – he doesn't want to know us!" Jenny added. I elected to remain quiet, concentrating instead on my tomato and cheese sandwich.

Yaniv smiled at Jenny's words. His rich show of well-defined lashes adorned his kindly eyes, which rested beneath a crown of wavy, ash-brown hair. He sported a baby face, out of place on his tall, wiry frame, which afforded an easy, dimpled smile, giving off such warmth that one felt instantly comfortable with him. "Roni is a good guy," Yaniv said. "But he's been through a lot and…well, he's…*seen* a lot." Pausing for a moment, he continued. "I know that Roni can come across somewhat… severe, but try not to take it personally. He walks around carrying the burden of the world on his shoulders. Well, to be more accurate – the burden of the Jewish people. I suppose he was always like that – only… different."

"What happened to him?" Jenny asked, drawn in by Yaniv.

It seemed as if a shadow fell across his face as he furrowed his brows in thought, his eyes seeing things the rest of us could only imagine. "Roni and I were part of an elite reconnaissance unit of the paratroopers," he began. "Back in Lebanon, we were fielded with an armored brigade when we were hit with a Syrian ambush in Sultan Yacoub. Many of our friends fell that day. There was a failure in intelligence…we were surrounded, trapped for hours…and the Syrians were picking us off. It wasn't Roni's fault of course," he continued, shaking the scene out of his head, "but being that he was an officer, he took personal responsibility. He internalized it all. Every one of our fallen men ate away at him until there was nothing left – except for the anger." Then, as an afterthought, Yaniv added, "Roni used to be religious, you know, but, after Sultan Yacoub, well…now he just thinks that God is looking down and laughing at all of us."

"And you don't think the way Roni does?" Jenny asked.

"To tell you the truth, Jenny, I'm better off not thinking. That's how *I* get through it. Roni is different. He doesn't stop thinking about it. It consumes him."

Listening to Yaniv talk about Roni like that had me lost in a spiral of thoughts. Perhaps I shouldn't be so quick to judge him. I knew it was impossible to understand what he had suffered through – what so many of our men endured while trying to protect our people in our land.

A sad achiness washed over me as I contemplated this. Still, I couldn't help but feel confused by Yaniv's account. I wanted to hate Roni, and here Yaniv was giving him a soul. I was still fuming over Roni's obnoxious manner back at the cotton fields, and I was sure he was toying with me. I just didn't understand why he selected me as his prey. But then again, how could I hate someone who was hurting so deeply inside? Roni did appear to carry the burden of the world on his shoulders. He was always serious, always brooding. At my first visit to the watering hole at Sachna, I had noticed that he never laughed or joked around the way his friends did. He sat just a little bit off to the side, drawing on his cigarette, seldom allowing himself to smile. And even when he did, it was…guarded. That was the first time I saw Roni…and the first time he glowered at me.

"Yaniv!" I heard Roni's voice bellow over my head. "Two minutes, be outside – you, Ben, Joey and the five girls. We'll take the jeeps. I'm due for guard duty but I'll drop some of you off at the orchard first. *Yallah!*"

"Sure, Roni, two minutes – no problem," Yaniv winked at us and devoured the rest of his sandwich in one bite.

"*Yallah?*" Jenny scrunched her eyebrows in question.

"It's Arabic. It means 'hurry up,'" explained Yaniv. "And I think we had better – once Roni gets in this mood…well…there's nothing more freaky than a blond speaking Arabic."

We left the *radrah* and I trailed a few paces behind everyone, looking down at the ground and staring at nothing in particular, still preoccupied with what Yaniv had disclosed about Roni. I didn't even realize that everyone had already piled into the jeeps.

"Dara?"

I looked up. It was Roni, holding the front passenger door open for me. "Looks like you're my driving partner today." He eyed me with curiosity.

"Thank you," my words fell out in a hush and I slid into the seat, his M16 resting at my side.

The conversation in the back of the jeep was loud and animated during the short drive to the grapefruit orchard. Unlike the drive earlier this morning when he imparted a blatant disregard for me, I noticed Roni glance at me every now and again while he drove. We rode in silence, yet it was not irritating as before. At least he was no longer glaring at me. He also appeared to have dropped his arrogant disposition. At one point, I met his gaze and thought I detected a softness in his eyes. It was the same look as he had when he was bandaging my hands back at the *radrah. He's trying to gaslight me; there's no other explanation.*

"You've worked in the orchard before?" he asked, looking ahead at the road.

Was he making conversation with me? "Um, yes."

"It's hard work. The thorns are nasty and the grapefruit are heavy to lug around." He turned his attention from the road, trailing his eyes over me. "You're kind of delicate."

"I can handle it," I responded in a small voice, sounding too defensive. *Why do I let him get to me?* He smirked, as if I said something amusing. Feeling awkward, I turned away to look straight ahead at the road.

We arrived at a metal gate, and Roni stopped the car, got out, unlocked the gate with his set of keys and pushed its doors inward to make a wide opening for our cars to pass through. Yaniv's jeep was right behind ours. As Roni was making his way back to the jeep, he stopped and hung back – a look of concentration set in his brows gave way to wariness as the muscles in his face and neck tensed in suspicion. He turned around, his back now facing us, and cocked his head to listen.

Turning back, his eyes shot past our jeep to Yaniv. Roni trotted to the jeep and grabbed his M16. "Stay down," he commanded everyone before zipping back into the orchard. I saw Yaniv in the side-view mirror leap out of his jeep, pull the strap of his gun over his shoulder and run up to Roni. They both walked several more yards into the orchard, their M16s at the ready as they searched the area through the trees until I couldn't see them anymore.

After several drawn-out minutes, Yaniv and Roni reemerged. Yaniv turned to Roni, slapped him on the back and, with a smile, nodded for him to return to the jeep. Roni shook his head in disagreement, engaging Yaniv in what seemed a small argument. They disappeared again. Everyone in the jeep remained quiet. The waiting was tense. When they came back into view I observed Yaniv place his hand on Roni's shoulder; it appeared as if he was trying to convince him to head back to the jeep. Roni gave Yaniv a long hard look, and finally agreed.

We continued driving on a long dirt road surrounded by huge grapefruit trees on either side. I noticed that Roni's knuckles were taut around the steering wheel. I looked at his face and saw he was rigid as stone. "Roni?" I asked. "What is it – what did you think you heard back there?"

He shook his head, "Nothing, I…nothing to be concerned about… sometimes I overreact. That's all."

"Oh," I said simply, though understanding that there was much behind his restrained words. I thought it best not to press him about it and turned my attention back to the front window.

A strong citrus scent hovered in the air. I enjoyed working in the orchards and loved the shelter from the tall trees – their branches arching, protective over all who passed beneath them. This place, truly a paradise, never failed to brighten my mood.

After several more minutes, both jeeps came to a stop and everyone piled out. I turned to Roni and thanked him for the ride, my hand reaching for the door handle. He leaned over me to get it at the same time, his hand ending up clutching mine. "Force of habit," he chuckled as his eyes glistened into mine. I tried to smile casually, but I think I stopped breathing altogether. *Mental note: buy Roni sunglasses.*

"Dara?" he hesitated, turning serious. He crinkled his brows as he lifted my bandaged hand from the door handle and caressed it in his. *What was this?*

"What is it, what's wrong?" My voice was barely a whisper.

"Just…stay with the group…don't go off on your own. Besides," he abruptly changed his tone and smiled with intent, "if you should trip over your own two feet again, I'd want someone close by to catch you." I ignored his little dig and paid more attention to the words he didn't say.

"Roni, what are you not telling me? You thought you saw something or heard something back at the main gate, didn't you?"

The smile on his face quickly vanished and his chiseled features hardened, "*Izvi et zeh!* Just leave it, Dara. You're reading too much into things. I told you…I just overreacted. Let it go!"

The sudden severity in Roni's tone stunned me. Although there was instant regret in his eyes, I was unable to hide the hurt from my face. "Dara," he began, and then…he just stopped. I looked down and withdrew my hand that was still in his.

"I better go. I have some grapefruit to pick."

"Wait…look, I…I'm sorry."

"Don't worry about it. It's fine." I said flatly and turned to leave the car.

"Dara, please," he leaned closer to me, resting his arm over the back of my seat, and with his other hand he placed his fingers beneath my chin, turning my head to face him. "It was terrible of me to blow up at you like that." His tone was soft and apologetic, and he continued, "To answer your question…I didn't hear or see anything…. It was just…a feeling…that's all." He seemed unaware that his manner was impossibly seductive as he moved his hand from my chin to curve around the side of my neck. "Will you forgive me?"

He was making it very difficult to remain upset with him. But there were too many questions to Roni – too many layers to him – and a deeply embedded pain I couldn't begin to comprehend. He ran from hot to cold and from harsh to gentle; he was mystifying. Who was he? What did he want from *me*? And...why was he touching me this way? My next words seemed to slip out all on their own. "What do you want from me, Roni?"

My question caught him off guard. He clenched his jaw and stared at me with such concentration, as if I held the answers he couldn't give. Ensnared by him, I watched his gaze gradually grow softer – his tensed features relax. He looked as though he was distracted, his eyes drifting down to my lips. The space between us became smaller, and I feared that he could hear my heart pound like a jackhammer against my chest. "Roni," I breathed, not sure if I was stopping him or prodding him on. He caught himself, refocused his gaze back to my eyes and murmured, "I just want you to forgive me. That's all."

He suddenly looked sad as his thumb tenderly stroked the side of my face. I forgot how to speak. A long and tense moment hung thickly between us. My neck felt as if it were on fire from his touch, and my eyes watered from the heat. I was going to go up in flames, I just knew it. I searched his eyes for a hint of insincerity, but there was none. He was being real – so real that I was too dazed to utter a sound, let alone come up with a coherent sentence. What was clear to me at that moment was that I had to get out of the jeep before I fainted – but I couldn't trust myself to move. I was frozen and on fire all at once. *What was happening to me?*

"I suppose I can't blame you for being angry with me," he said in a muted tone when I didn't answer right away. Then, with an impish smile, "I know that I...behaved a little badly this morning. But...really, Dara," he boyishly shrugged, "I'm not so terrible." *God, he was killing me.*

"Roni, I don't think you're terrible," I managed to say at last, mindful not to betray the havoc stirring inside me.

He looked thoughtful and said, "I guess I don't deserve more than that." Lowering his eyes from mine, he let his hand fall from the side of my neck, his fingers casually moving to toy with a stray lock of my hair that fell from my ponytail onto my chest. I trembled, for a moment losing my composure. It was a moment too long. For God's sake, it was hot in the valley, and I was trembling! It was impossible for Roni not to have noticed.

His eyes flashed up to mine, narrowing at first, and then sparkled with a new energy as if he had unearthed a deep secret, his lips curling into a wicked smile. I wanted to crawl under the seat. "Hmm…can I take that to mean that you *do* forgive me?"

I died a thousand times. He pursed his outrageously sensuous lips, no doubt to hold back a triumphant grin. I had to, somehow, save face from this perfect Nordic god with his ridiculously perfect golden curls and his perfectly irritating magnificent eyes. I forced myself to find my voice. "There's nothing to forgive. You obviously can't help yourself," I said, trying to sound indifferent and failing miserably at it.

He found that amusing as well and snickered under his breath. "Well then, looks like everything is settled between us," he answered, with the wicked glint still in his eyes, his fingers still entwined in my hair. For an instant, his focus darted past me, out the side window. "Looks like your friends are very interested in our conversation."

I stole a quick look and saw them all gawking in our direction. *Great, now I would be too embarrassed to leave the jeep, and too embarrassed to remain in the jeep.* I glared back at Roni. "You may think this is amusing, but I prefer not to be the topic of hot gossip!" I shook my head, exasperated.

"I'm sorry, Dara; really, I am. I don't know why it is, but you seem to bring out the bad in me. And…about before…you may not believe me, but, I *am* sorry for snapping at you. You didn't deserve that." I was too furious to answer. He no longer bothered to suppress his smile and continued, "I have guard duty down at the other side of the fields now. Yossi, one of the kibbutz old-timers, will be guarding this end, but I'll be by later. Yaniv and I will take all of you back to the kibbutz in a couple of hours."

"Fine," I shrugged. *Like I care where he goes or what he does.* I hated him. I was sure of it. And I hated myself more for being so attracted to him. His fingers were still gingerly twisting my lock of hair when I grabbed the door handle to exit the jeep.

"You know, Dara, like I said, I'm really not so terrible."

"You know, I really don't care," I shot back – this time meaning it.

"Are you sure about that? Perhaps you might care...just a little?" He let the lock of my hair drop from his hand onto my chest, his eyes drifting again to my lips, this time taunting as he slightly parted his own lips as if he meant to kiss me, and back again to my eyes. I turned to leave but he curled his hand around my arm and whispered in my ear, "Dara, you might want to compose yourself before you go." *I definitely, without any doubt, hated him!* I opened the door and slid from beneath him, slinking out of the seat to join the others.

"What's going on with the two of you?" Alana cackled lightheartedly.

Too angry to deal with the subject, my response was curt. "Nothing."

She turned her head to Roni's jeep and then back to me. "Well, Mr. Greek god can't seem to take his eyes off of you. And frankly, sweetie," she jabbed me in the side good-naturedly, "if you couldn't feel the electric bolts flying between the two of you today, then you sure need a bit of rewiring – not to mention the fact that you two looked kind of cozy in the front of the jeep just a moment ago."

I cringed at that, still feeling mortified by Roni. "All I ever noticed about Roni is his offensive attitude," I replied, perhaps with a bit too much annoyance, as my answer caused her to laugh with gusto.

"Sure, Dara, sure – whatever you say. Like that's all any of us notice about Roni." Against my will, I broke out in a wide smile and playfully jabbed Alana back. My curiosity, however, got the best of me and I turned around to see that Roni *was* watching me just as Alana said. Only now, I saw that the scowl was back on his face. *This was maddening.* He then put his jeep in reverse, maneuvered a sharp turn and sped away.

Equipped with ladders, work gloves and large burlap sacks that we slung over our shoulders, we climbed up and began picking the fruit. Once our sacks were full, we descended the ladders and emptied the contents with caution into one of the massive bins positioned every ten or so yards along each chain of trees. We moved up and down the rows, sometimes trading stories with one another as we worked, but mostly listening to Yaniv's melodic singing as he plodded along in his cheerful manner, picking grapefruit with his rifle slung over his back. Every now and again, we heard Jenny grumble about the thorns, at times using expletives for emphasis, and Alana's laughter in response. It was backbreaking work – the sacks were heavy and bulky from the grapefruit – but I found it gratifying and enjoyed it.

After close to two hours, I noticed Alana had dozed off beneath the next tree that I had planned to work on. She looked serene as she lay there on the ground, secreted by the low branches. I chuckled to myself. She was a sweet girl and I was glad to know her. Jenny, Rachel and Miri, too. But Alana, so very good-natured, was always spreading the cheer and laughing about one thing or another, and it was fun and uplifting to be around her. Pixie-like and petite, she reminded me of Tinkerbell in the Peter Pan story. It was as if she sprinkled magic pixie dust of good spirits and jollity wherever she went.

I moved my ladder to the next tree so as not to disturb her nap. *Poor kid, she must be exhausted.* I climbed my ladder to begin at the top and work my way down. It was nearly one thirty in the afternoon and the workday was due to end in half an hour. I emptied another load of grapefruit into the bin, and it was then that I heard what at first sounded like firecrackers. Deep in my gut, though, I knew better. I never heard gunshots before, except on television and in the movies, but when the next round came, not two seconds later, it was clear – and a myriad of things transpired all at once.

"Everyone down!" Yaniv shouted from a few trees away. Hurling his semiautomatic machine gun into position, he crouched to the ground. Bullets were flying all around us, splintering the trees and ricocheting off the metal slats of the ladders. We all flew to the ground, scurrying for cover behind the trees. "Gunfire! Northeast end of the orchard, fifty meters in…" Yaniv communicated on his walkie-talkie with the local head of security. Swearing under his breath, he mumbled, "Roni was right." He laid low, staring through the sight of his M16, and fired in the direction of the bullets. At that moment, shocked out of her sleep, Alana ran out from under her tree in a panic.

I heard a frantic, high-pitched screech that pierced the air, "Nooo!" It took me a moment to realize it came from me. "Alana, get down, get down!" random cries barked from the trees. She reeled around in confusion and then jerked back and hit the ground faceup, her arms spread-eagle. Blood oozed from her lower abdomen, spilling down her side onto the earth, and all the while the bullets continued to hit the ground where she had fallen. Alana arched her head back in pain, her eyes bulging, and dug her nails into the dirt. She opened her mouth as if to scream, but no sound came out. Adrenalin took the place of logic and I propelled myself over to her, crawling low, my face scratching against the earth.

"No, Dara!" shouted Yaniv. "We get rid of the threat first!" But it was too late, and I couldn't retreat to a safer position without Alana. I wouldn't. "Don't do it! Get back!" Yaniv implored me.

"They're going to kill her!" I screamed back.

"Dammit, girl!" Yaniv continued shooting and there was suddenly an ebb in the cross fire. "One down," he muttered.

I reached Alana, grabbed her under the arms and began dragging her away from the open area. The shooting started again when I was one yard away from the tree. Just then, I felt it. A burning rip right through my leg. A howling, guttural sound of pain came out of me. I clenched my teeth, my chest rumbled with anger. With one final lunge and a gut-splitting scream, I pulled Alana under the tree.

She was unconscious, but still breathing. I didn't know what to do for her. I didn't know how to stop her bleeding. I tried putting pressure on her wound with my hands but it didn't help. I pulled off my T-shirt and used that to apply pressure, but that wasn't helping either. There was so much blood. I was scared – so scared I wanted to throw up. The burning pain in my leg was shooting in all directions, and I was drenched in Alana's blood as well as my own. *Oh, God, please help us.*

"Yaniv! On your left!" It was Roni. The next moment, I heard it – the Arab war cry, *Alahu akhbar! Alahu akhbar!* Through the gaps between the branches, I saw a lone man, eyes ablaze, his neck wrapped in a kaffiyeh, pounce into the clearing, firing indiscriminately. From Roni's position, a burst of fire, and then there was silence. The entire attack couldn't have lasted more than several minutes, though it felt like an eternity. Roni commanded us to stay where we were. *No problem there.*

We all waited in an eerie stillness. Yaniv and Roni surveyed the area for other terrorists. I heard more communication over the walkie-talkies. They found Yossi's body, the guard Roni referred to as the old-timer, though he was just fifty-three years old. The terrorists had stabbed him to death. Seconds later, the army arrived along with ambulances. The paramedics placed Alana and me on gurneys and removed us from under the tree. They first bandaged Alana, hooked her up with an IV and sped away with her in one of the ambulances. Out of the volley of voices, I heard someone say they were airlifting her to Haifa's Rambam Medical Center. One by one, everyone emerged from the trees. Jenny became hysterical when she saw me covered head to toe in blood, and Ben and Joey both tried to calm her down.

Unable to move, I remained on the ground, staring wide-eyed at the sky in a state of numbness, too shaken to utter a sound, save for gasping every now and again from the pain. Another paramedic tended to my leg wound and attached an IV to my arm. Roni knelt by my side, staring at me in silence.

Things started to look fuzzy, and I couldn't discern his expression. I expected him to be angry with me, but instead he seemed…anguished. He cupped my hand in both of his and spoke in a soft voice – almost a whisper, "You're crazy, you know that?" A rush of dizziness filled my head, and blackness took over.

Chapter 3

I woke up in Ha'Emek Hospital in Afula, a few kilometers outside of Beit She'an. Confused at first by my new surroundings, I was swiftly brought up to speed by the throbbing pain in my leg. Adding to the confusion was Roni sitting by the side of my bed. Why was *he* here? A wave of horror flashed through me, and I glanced under the blanket to check that my leg was still intact. I breathed a sigh of relief when I found that it was. Roni chuckled under his breath, obviously finding humor in my actions. *I'm so glad I could be comic relief for him.*

"Alana – how is she?" I murmured in a voice so cracked and hoarse that I barely recognized it as my own.

"She's in critical condition," he said, taking my hand into his. "Her family is flying in from the States. They should be with her in a few hours."

"Oh, my God," my heart pounded furiously. "Is there a chance she could die?"

He hesitated before answering. "I don't know. She has a serious abdominal wound. She's also lost a kidney and a lot of blood. With a wound such as hers, they also worry about infection. That's all I can tell you right now, but as soon as I hear more news on her condition, I promise I'll let you know."

"Oh my God, oh my God – not Alana…" I trailed off, my breathing becoming erratic.

"Dara, try to calm down. She's in good hands. Rambam Hospital has a lot of experience with the type of wound Alana has. Trust me…I know." He brushed my cheek with the back of his fingers. "Now you need to take care of *yourself*," he continued. "The doctors were able to remove the bullet from your leg without complications – it didn't hit any bone or major artery. Of course, it did penetrate muscle, which is bound to be painful. You could be out of here in a week or so, but you must rest."

Roni's warm tone and display of affection surprised me. I expected him, of all people, to be irate with what I did. *Did I miss something?* I decided to deal with it later. My first concern was Alana. "I don't want to wait a week," I said, shaking my head. "I have to see her."

"Dara, you've been through a major trauma. You have to give your own body time to heal."

"No. I'm fine!" I insisted. "I really need to see Alana! I have to get out of here!" I bolted up in my bed and a sudden wave of light-headedness hit me.

"Uh…I don't think so," Roni said as he took hold of my shoulders and laid me back down before I could roll over the bed's safety bar.

"You can't keep me here," I protested weakly.

He looked amused. "Dara, you took a bullet in the leg. Just where do you think you're running to?"

"I can't stay in the hospital for an entire week. I'll go mad." I then tried to appeal to him, "Look, I'll agree to behave like a good little patient for two days, and then you can spring me out of here."

"No deal," he smirked.

"I should have known better," I huffed. "I think you're actually enjoying my torment."

"Hmm. Interesting. You know, your eyes are a dead giveaway."

"What?"

"I noticed it earlier today, but I couldn't be sure. They turn gray when you're tired or...bothered. It's really quite fascinating." He pursed his lips to hold in a smile. "You probably shouldn't ever play poker," he added authoritatively.

I stared at Roni in astonishment. *He noticed that?*

"Look, Dara," he said, misinterpreting my look, "I know you need to see Alana. I'll take you to Haifa to visit her as soon as you're strong enough – I promise."

I gripped my thigh. The throbbing in my leg was getting worse. Roni pressed the buzzer for the nurse. "I think it's time for more pain medication."

"Yeah," I surrendered. "I think you're right."

"The nurse will be here soon."

"Roni?"

"Yes?"

"Why are you here?" Then quickly backtracking, "I mean, I'm glad you're here...it was nice to wake up to a...um...friendly face, but... well...I guess I was surprised to –"

"Dara," he cut me off with his low, soft voice before I could tie up my tongue any further. "As I believe the American saying goes – you've gotten under my skin." His face appeared to register as much surprise as I'm sure mine must have.

"Me? I've gotten under your skin? Um...you mean that in a...good way, right?"

"Mmm," his eyes twinkled.

"So…you're not angry with me?"

"Angry? I'm furious with you! Dara, what you did was stupid. Selfless, yes, and damn gutsy," he added with a look of amazement, "but stupid, nevertheless! You gave Yaniv a thousand heart attacks when he shouldn't have been thinking of you at the time! You could have gotten yourself killed." He looked down, rubbing his forehead and then his eyes as if to shake the image from his mind. "I don't think you realize how damn lucky you are."

I didn't answer. I knew he was right. However, I also knew that if faced with a similar situation again, I could not say that I wouldn't act in the same way.

Completely incompatible with his reproaching words, he leaned toward me and again stroked my cheek with the back of his fingers, holding my eyes with his. He was different now – no taunting. He was…genuine. I wanted to know what he was thinking, but I couldn't get my voice to work with him looking at me that way. He lowered his hand from my face and toyed with a stray lock of my hair just as he did in the jeep at the orchard. I chewed nervously on my bottom lip. I didn't want him to see the goose bumps he was causing and tried being casual about covering my arms with the blanket.

He looked like he wanted to say something more, but the nurse came in with my pain medication, and he rose from his chair and stood to the side. I felt the effects of the drug as soon as the nurse injected it into my IV, as if a curtain of fatigue was draped over me. My eyelids felt heavy, but I didn't want sleep to come just yet.

"Roni," I was barely able to whisper.

"I'm still here, Dara."

"Will…you…be…he…"

"Shhh. Sleep, Dara, I'll be here when you wake up."

My parents flew in to see me the next day. They meant to take me home as soon as I could walk, but I had made it clear: *that* wasn't happening. They didn't understand my obsession with Israel. Our home was not particularly religious – at the most, traditional, though quite laid back about it. Their work was their religion. My enthusiasm toward Israel rather stemmed from my grandfather, or Pops as I referred to him with affection. He was a World War II vet, an American air force pilot, and after the war he volunteered to fight in Israel's 1948 War of Independence.

Pops instilled in me a love for the Land of Israel and an ideology that would not waver. He saw the reestablishment of the State of Israel as the fulfillment of an ancient prophecy – and our people's destiny awaiting us there. A destiny that culminated with the coming of the Messiah, when all nations would recognize one God and live in peaceful coexistence. This would follow a great war between nations of good and evil that would ultimately take place in Jerusalem. But, he pointed out, we also believed that this war could be avoided if all people did their share in bettering the world through good deeds.

I adored my grandfather and loved losing myself in his stories. Already as a small child I dreamed of going to Israel and doing my part for our nation in our land. I was one of the few students in my Hebrew-language class that took it seriously. I'll never forget how proud my grandfather was when he learned of my plans to volunteer for a year on a kibbutz.

I did not intend to let him down. My parents stayed for three days then flew back to the States without me.

🌸

To my utter astonishment, Roni all but moved into my hospital room. After two days, when the nursing staff saw that he wasn't leaving, they provided him with a more comfortable chair that partially reclined so that he could somehow manage a few hours of sleep at night. He would only leave the hospital to do a short stint of guard duty back at the kibbutz, to take a quick shower while I dozed from the medication or to get me an ice cream from the truck that permanently parked itself across from the hospital's entrance.

On the third day of my hospital stay, I awoke to Roni holding a gift box, wrapped with an oversized pink bow. He stood over my bed looking awkward, probably for the first time in his life, I imagined. It was very early in the morning, well before my parents arrived from the bed-and-breakfast where they were staying. In fact, I saw through the window that the haze of the sun was still quite weak; it must have been just a little past dawn.

"Hi," I shyly said, rubbing my eyes. I was less groggy from painkillers this morning and was more aware of my appearance. I would have loved to wash up before seeing Roni. *Oh well, he's already seen me at my worst and hasn't yet run away screaming for cover.*

"Good morning," he answered. He looked down at his box, as if he wasn't sure what to do next. I reached for my cup of water on the bedside table, not at all sure what *I* should do next. He fidgeted as I sipped my water. I sensed that he needed a drink, a good stiff one at that. I thought to help him out.

"Is that for me?" I eyed the box in his hands.

He shrugged sheepishly and handed it to me. "Uh…yes. I got this for you."

My curiosity piqued, I still found his new attitude toward me mysterious. I placed the box on the side of my bed and tried to ease myself into a more comfortable position. My leg seemed to hurt more in the early morning and late at night, and I grimaced from the pain.

"Let me help you," Roni leaned over me, his arms wrapping around me. "Don't move, Dara, just let me lift you." I put my arms around him and let him bring me into a sitting position, taking in the scent of his skin as his soft curls brushed against my cheek. *Mmm, is that coconut-scented shampoo?*

Once I was more comfortable, I asked, "Why did you get me a gift?"

"It's not a big deal," he tried to make light of it. "I just thought you could use...well, maybe you should just open it."

I pulled the box onto my lap, untied the big pink bow and lifted the lid. Beneath the tissue paper was an exquisite antique-white silk robe accented with pearl-colored roping around the collar. My mouth dropped open. The soft fabric felt regal beneath my fingers as I brushed my hand over it.

"I thought, being in the hospital, you may feel more comfortable walking around in that," Roni gestured with his chin to the robe. He cleared his throat and attempted to speak in a more commanding tone. "You'll have to walk around a lot more now after being in bed for two full days. You need to start exercising your leg while you're still in the hospital, and well, I think we...I mean, you...should walk. I'll help you." I looked up at Roni and broke out into the biggest smile.

"Does that mean you like it?" Roni asked, getting back to himself, curling the side of his mouth into a smile.

"I love it," I said, amazed by his thoughtfulness. My eyes widened when I lifted the robe out of the box, stunned by its luxuriousness. To be sure, women on the kibbutz were not in the habit of wearing anything this grand. *This was much too expensive.* I looked back up to him and his eyes were like dancing crystals, so happy that I appreciated his gift. I didn't want to hurt his feelings, and yet, I blurted out, "Roni, it's lovely. It's...more than just lovely, but it's too much. I can't possibly accept this kind of gift from you."

"I knew you would say that," he countered in a wry tone.

"So why did you do it?"

"I didn't care," he shrugged with a smile. "Now, try it on."

I frowned.

"You're ruining my moment, Dara."

I sighed in defeat.

"Mmm, I knew I'd win."

He helped drape the robe over me as I slipped into it. It was a bit complicated with one of my arms still attached to an IV, but with deftness Roni maneuvered the tubing so that I could slide my arm through the sleeve and then eased me off the bed, bringing me to my feet. I couldn't put my full weight on my leg and had to hold on to his arms as he wrapped the robe around me and tied it snugly with the sash belt. He studied me, appraising me up and down – not in a mocking way and not in a way that made me feel uncomfortable. "You look like an angel," his voice wafted in a whisper.

It was not clear to me where all this devotion and attention was coming from, but all the same, his being there somehow felt natural. After a while, during the short intervals when Roni was not in the room with me, it was as if something were missing. I missed him, and I felt... anxious and incomplete. Once he would return, I would feel calm and whole again. It was difficult to put my finger on what was happening between us.

My parents saw much deeper into my relationship with Roni – if one could even call it a relationship. I had no clue what it was. My mother, however, regarded him with suspicion, and my father, likewise, conveyed an air of enmity toward him. They felt threatened by Roni – troubled by his constant presence, and warned me before they left not to get further involved with him.

During any lull in visitors, and if I wasn't too groggy from the pain medication, Roni spent most of the time quizzing me about my life, my likes and dislikes and about my hopes and dreams. Occasionally,

Roni allowed me to sneak in a question or two about him. I learned that his mother was French and his father German. They were Holocaust survivors and met in a displaced persons' camp in Austria after World War II, married and moved to Israel in 1948. He also had one brother and one sister, both married and living in the Galilee. Roni was the "baby" in the family. He claimed there wasn't any mystery to him; what you see is what you get, so to speak. He was steadfast about his obligation and responsibility to our land and to our people *despite the hurdles and impediments* with which God amuses Himself – he cynically interjected – by throwing them in our path. "If He is testing us," he said, "well, let's just say that I can be just as stubborn as He is." *For someone who turned away from religion, Roni sure brought up God a lot,* I thought. It was as if he had his own private war with Him. With his quiet strength, he was intent on making everyone around him feel protected; yet, the sting of his own pain was so profound that he very much needed to be freed from whatever ghosts were haunting him.

During the most recent round of questioning, he asked me what I wanted to do after my year on kibbutz, and I told him of my plans to return to the States to study toward a degree in journalism. He met my plans with a grimace and responded in an accusatory tone, "You mean you're going to leave Israel? You can't attend a university here?"

"I fully intend to return, but I already made plans to attend university back in the States – that was part of the agreement I made with my folks. And besides," I added by design, "no one in his right mind turns down an Ivy League education at Columbia University."

He wasn't impressed. "You don't belong there!" He bolted out of his chair and walked over to the window opposite my bed, his back to me.

I wasn't sure what to make of his sudden mood change. Did I miss the part where we promised something to one another? Several moments passed with an uneasy silence and then Roni turned to face me, his brooding eyes penetrating into mine. The angle of the sun through the window was such that it encircled Roni's flowing golden curls in a radiant light. I wondered if he realized his own stunning presence. He held his gaze as he drew nearer and sat close to me on my bed, placing his arms on either side of me. On reflex, I sank back into my pillow and stared back with uncertainty.

"What?" I asked, my voice scarcely perceptible. He was silent, pensive, as his eyes rolled over my face. He was so close that I was sure he could hear my jagged breathing. I watched his lips curve into a cheerless smile. "It's not your fault, Dara. It's my own. I let my guard down."

"I don't know what you mean by that."

"I *let* you get under my skin."

"I thought you said that was...a good thing?"

He looked down, crinkling his brow, and then flashed his eyes back at me. "Once you leave, you'll never come back." He said it as a challenge.

"You don't know me."

"No, I guess not," he said, a little too thoughtfully. Somehow, I didn't think I won that round. Though he didn't relax his stare, his voice softened. "So, then tell me, Dara," he brushed my hair to the side and curved his hand around the back of my neck, drawing me closer to him, "what is the key to knowing you?"

I swallowed hard, and hesitated, moistening my lips with my tongue. "Roni," I breathed, "it's not that complicated."

"Oh no? I'm about to make things very complicated." He buried his hands in my hair and lifted my face to his. I took in a quick wisp of air, startled by the feverish glow in his eyes. He inched in closer and I felt the heat of his breath. My eyes rested on his lips and at that moment, all I could think was how they would feel pressed against mine. The tingling sensation that was now all too familiar for me whenever Roni touched me rushed down my spine. His lips just grazed mine, when, without warning, he pulled back, looking to the door of the room that burst open with the next wave of visitors from the kibbutz.

�֍

There was little doubt the staff at the hospital was relieved when the doctor finally discharged me after eleven days. It might have been sooner, but at the end of one week, I had developed a fever, and the doctor wouldn't release me until it was under control. In any case, the flow of visitors from the kibbutz was nonstop, and they were notorious for not adhering to the rules about visiting hours.

One evening, Yaniv brought his guitar and played some cheerful tunes for me. Jenny, Miri, and Rachel came to visit every chance they had as well. Many would stop by on their way back from Haifa after visiting Alana, and the news would always be the same – she was hanging on, but remained in critical condition.

On the day preceding my discharge, Jenny brought me a skirt to wear since I couldn't fit my jeans over the thick bandage around my thigh. She had also brought me all my toiletries soon after my surgery on the very first day. Only a fellow female would think of doing that, I thought. Jenny was very considerate like that. Although grateful to leave the hospital, I could not put all my weight on my leg. Walking was uncomfortable.

Hospital policy required Roni to wheel me to the exit. After having spent practically every waking moment with him during my stay, it was oddly difficult to remember a time when we weren't together. It felt safe and thrilling at the same time. I treasured the wonderful and curious new feeling of opening my eyes to him each morning sitting by my bedside, and each evening, falling asleep under the cover of his warm gaze.

Once outside, Roni stopped and came around to face me. He leaned over me, resting his hands on the armrests of the wheelchair and

I lifted my face to his with a questioning look. "This is where the ride ends, my lady. Now, I know how much you dislike being *manhandled*," he said with a teasing grin, "but it would no doubt be faster if I simply carried you to the car. May I?" I drew in a breath to answer, but his lips suddenly distracted me.

"Dara?"

"Um, sure...okay," I finally managed. I stood up, putting my weight on my one good leg, and wrapped my hands around his neck as he lifted me into his arms. I couldn't help myself from snuggling my head onto his shoulder, feeling the wisps of his silken curls fluttering in the slight breeze.

"Hmm," Roni contemplated. I lifted up my head in curiosity. His lips, pressed together at first, curved into a mischievous smile, a puckish look in his eyes.

"What?" I murmured.

"I just didn't expect you to be this heavy."

My mouth fell wide open, and Roni broke out into hearty laughter. Not a usual occurrence.

Chapter 4

Shortly after returning from the fields the following day, Roni drove me to Haifa to see Alana. At first he thought I should wait another day or two until I became stronger; he was concerned that I would once again develop a fever if I overextended myself. I didn't understand why Roni was being so overly protective. There would be plenty of time for rest. I was off work detail for another full week and expected I would go insane with boredom. But it could have been worse, I considered, as my thoughts drifted back to Alana. I shuddered to imagine that her laughter could be silenced forever and then shook those morbid thoughts out of my head. Sometimes, I had a tendency to get melodramatic. Alana was going to be fine.

Roni was lost in thought during the car ride, as was I. For one thing, I was still trying to make sense of his change in attitude toward me. There was a profound electricity between us that I wasn't sure how to deal with. Everything I was feeling was very new to me. Yet, in spite of Roni's new and welcome demeanor, he continued to confuse me. One moment it seemed that he wanted to get close, with innocent tender touches – caressing my cheek with his hand, or brushing his lips to my hair – and in the next moment, he would pull back. I would catch him staring at me, though tenderly.

And yet, there were times I met his gaze and saw such a deep intensity, which only served to kindle my curiosity. I concluded that the change in his attitude toward me occurred somewhere between the cotton fields and the grapefruit orchard on the day of the terrorist attack. That's how I seemed to measure time now – before the attack and after the attack. Although that didn't offer any sound explanation, all I knew is that I definitely liked him better this way. He smiled more, laughed more and I delighted in his attentiveness.

But it was more than that – there was a heat between us, so strong that I sometimes had to hold myself back from grabbing him and kissing him. It was puzzling why he hadn't tried kissing me since that one "almost kiss" in the hospital. *Could it be that I was reading him wrong?* Perhaps he preferred it this way. If that was the case, then I was in trouble. He was the first thing on my mind when I awoke and the last before falling asleep.

My thoughts were interrupted when Roni shut off the engine. I hadn't realized that we had arrived at the hospital and that Roni had just finished parking. His hands were still on the steering wheel as he turned his head to me, looking very uneasy. He peered at me carefully, and then held out the tips of his fingers beneath my chin, tracing the contour of my lips with his thumb. "You're so innocent," Roni seemed to say more to himself than to me. I wondered if he had any idea at all as to how his small touch affected me.

He placed his hand back on the steering wheel, and it now seemed as if he were using it for support. It was clear he wanted to tell me something and was contemplating just how to say it. After a moment, "Dara, you need to prepare yourself for what you're going to see." He tried to choose his words carefully. "I'm not sure you realize just how critical a condition Alana is in."

"I understand."

"No," he said with a slight shake of his head, "I – don't – think – you – do," emphasizing each word.

"Is there something new about her condition that you didn't tell me?"

"Dara," he paused, furrowing his brows, "Alana hasn't been able to leave the intensive care unit. She's had complications as well as having developed a serious infection. It's not uncommon with wounds such as hers, but…," he trailed off.

"But infections can be treated with antibiotics," I said in a hopeful tone. Roni didn't say anything. He just looked at me with a grave expression, his eyes willing me to understand. I forced myself to look away. "Let's go in now," I quietly said.

We arrived at the intensive care unit and donned the required cloth gown and face mask. Just before entering Alana's room, I saw her through the glass wall. I froze. *That can't be Alana!*

"Dara," Roni put his arm around my shoulder. "Dara, are you all right?"

I nodded in slow motion.

"Are you ready to go in now?"

I nodded again.

Alana was asleep – or in a coma. I couldn't know, and didn't want to ask. Her breathing was labored as she convulsed almost rhythmically. She was attached to a million different things, and the short blips from the machines were constant. Her face was gaunt, her now pale skin taut over her cheekbones. I was staring at a stranger – a ghost of a person who did not resemble her at all. I was so focused on Alana's face that it took me a moment to register that there were two other people in the room, obviously her parents. They stood up to greet us. I quietly said hello and introduced Roni and myself.

"You're Dara?" the mother asked, taking hold of both of my hands in hers. "We heard what you did for my daughter at the time of the attack. We…don't know how to thank you…. God should only bless you." I stood in place, looking dumbfounded. I opened my mouth as if to say something, but nothing came out. What could I say? Thank you? Even if I really didn't do anything, I thought – aside from prolonging Alana's agony, it seemed.

"We're going to grab a coffee in the cafeteria and let you have some time with Alana."

"Thank you," I finally managed to utter hoarsely.

I moved toward Alana's bed and sat on one of the two chairs that was closest to her. Her withered hand peeked out from beneath the blanket and I reached for it, taking it into mine. Roni stood behind me, caressing my shoulders to give me support. I couldn't shake the feeling that I was staring at death's face. But I also couldn't imagine a world without Alana's ringing laughter. In the brief time that I knew her, she had made such an indelible impression on me. In fact, everyone loved Alana. What was not to love about a person who had an uncanny talent for brightening up everything and everyone around her? *No! This was not happening.*

"Alana?" I started, convinced that she must be able to hear me. "Alana…please…pull yourself out of this…. I know that you can…you have to," I said, incredulous that it could be any other way. "Your job in this world isn't done yet…it can't be…we really need you here…," I trailed off, choking back my tears, swallowing the lump that swelled in my throat. Roni squeezed my shoulders, and I took in a deep breath.

"Do you remember how you wanted to learn how to drive a tractor…y'know…so you can race it against the potato combine?" A feeble smile came to my lips at this silly memory…and of how she would race to catch the lizards that would every so often find their way into our room, with Jenny and I cheering her on while not daring to put our feet on the floor until the lizards were gone. She was petite but she was fast. Her funny antics flooded my mind all at once, and I bowed my head, leaning my forehead against her hand, and out of the blue I began laughing, shaking and ultimately plummeting into tears. She was dying and I couldn't face it. My throat tightened and I found it hard to breathe. I let go of her hand and Roni knelt down and held me as I cried on his shoulder. Some minutes passed until my shaking subsided and Roni helped me to my feet.

We walked out of Alana's room and removed our gowns and masks. I looked up at Roni purposefully and said, "I want to go to the synagogue here and pray."

A sphinx-like expression fell across his face. It was impossible to read. Perhaps it was his disbelief that it would do any good. "Come, I'll take you there," he offered flatly, and he took my hand and led the way. He appeared to know the corridors of this hospital very well. I wondered how many of his fellow soldiers he had visited here…and how many died. When we reached the synagogue, he stopped at the door. "I'll wait for you out here."

I stepped out of the hospital synagogue and saw Alana's parents racing through the halls, ostensibly rushing toward the intensive care unit. I shot a quick glance at Roni. He grabbed my hand and we headed back to the ICU, both of us running like wildcats through the hospital corridors. I stubbornly ignored the pain in my leg that protested the rapid pace.

At the ICU, a medical team worked feverishly around Alana. The blip on her monitor was one long monotone. Her parents were inside the room standing to the side, watching with a fright I had never witnessed before, their faces contorted in agony. I don't know how long we stood there. I felt as if in a trance, the entire scene awfully surreal, yet teeming with a furious energy as Alana alternated between fits of seizures and deathly stillness. The team of doctors and nurses made repeated efforts to resuscitate her. I watched as her limbs artificially tensed, momentarily infused with electric currents, followed by her body slumping back lifelessly onto the bed. And then...it all stopped. The medical team stopped, the blipping tones on the machines stopped, Alana's heart stopped. Everything stopped, save for her parents' anguished screams that echoed through the hospital halls.

I turned to Roni and threw my face against his chest. He held my head, his hand clutching my hair, and with his other arm he crushed me against him.

"Come, Dara," he whispered into my hair after some moments. "We should go."

Chapter 5

Alana's parents decided to have her buried the next day in the small kibbutz cemetery. I returned to her grave later, in the evening. Not for any rational reason. I didn't like knowing that she was all alone beneath the ground, and perhaps I just wasn't ready to let go. I didn't let anyone know what I was doing – I preferred to grieve in private. Yet, somehow, Roni knew where to find me. I visited Alana's grave each night during the *shivah*, the traditional week of mourning, and each night Roni would come by to walk me back to my room. The emptiness I felt took over all my senses. I walked around feeling as if a hole burned right through me.

Roni didn't say much, and neither did I. Aside from my occasional tearful sniffles, we walked together in silence. It was comforting to know that he was there for me. I understood that my loss was just a fraction of what he had been through, and I no longer had to wonder what was behind his serious nature. I didn't want to imagine how I would have coped without him and was grateful that I didn't have to. Although, one night – the sixth night, I needed more.

We stood facing each other outside my room, about to say good night. He traced his fingers against my cheek. "I wish I could take your pain away," he whispered.

"Do you?"

"Of course, Dara. Why would you doubt that?"

"Then...would you...hold me?"

He looked at me as if he were unsure about what I just said. "Hold me, Roni," I said again. "Hold me close to you." I wanted him to wrap me in his arms and make me feel safe – to shut out the harshness of the world in which we lived.

He hesitated, but only an instant, and when he enveloped me in his arms it was soothing – as I knew it would be. I felt safe and sound in the cocoon of his embrace. We stood like this for a few moments, and then the familiar heat that was often between us surfaced once again. I could not have been imagining it. He held me tighter, his lips brushing against my hair. His hands glided down my back, pressing me into him. It felt as though he needed me just as much as I needed him. My hands slid up to his shoulders, to his neck, entwining my fingers in his golden mane of curls. I lifted my face to his and met his luminous gaze. His attention drew to my lips and I closed my eyes, feeling his warm breath against my face. "Dara," he breathed.

"Yes?"

"You should go inside now."

My eyes opened to find him staring down at my face, his chiseled features rigid and tense. He freed me from his embrace and lowered my hands from him. "*Laila tov*, Dara. Good night. Try to sleep."

"*Laila tov*, Roni." I turned and went into my room.

On the next night – the seventh and final night of the traditional mourning period – Roni didn't come for me at the cemetery. I supposed

I had no right to expect him to; it's just that he hadn't left my side for several weeks and I had come to depend on him. *What a foolish girl I must be.* No doubt, he thought that as well. My behavior last night must have clinched it. I was obviously mistaken in thinking he had feelings for me beyond friendship.

It was late. I said my good-bye to Alana and parted from her grave. Dear, sweet, giggly Alana was gone, taking with her a piece of my heart. I would never forget her. My eyes to the ground, I followed the dark path out of the cemetery toward the lights of the kibbutz.

"Dara," I heard Roni's voice call out in a muted tone. I looked up to find him sitting on a huge rock by the side of the road. He stood up and walked toward me in a slow yet purposeful gait, and then gently wiped away the few renegade tears that escaped from my eyes. "No more tears for Alana," he said in a resolute tone. "Tears have never helped the Jewish people. Now, we fight back."

He was right, I thought. Roni's words were simple, yet true. There was some solace in knowing that we would fight back. Now that we had an army of our own after nearly two thousand years of horrific persecution since we were exiled from our land, no longer would we turn the other cheek. I met Roni's solemn gaze and nodded in agreement. At the time, I had no way of knowing how his words would come to repeat themselves in my head in the years to come.

I looked toward the kibbutz lights and breathed in the night air. Life goes on. I would pull myself together, and tomorrow, now that my leg was healed, I would go back to work. My thoughts returned to Roni. "What are you doing out here?"

"I was just…thinking."

"Oh. Well, then…I'll…leave you to your –"

"I'm going to miss you."

"Y-you will?" I asked, caught off guard. "Wait…I don't understand. What do you mean?"

"I have to leave in two days for one month of reserve duty." My heart thudded to a standstill. In that instant, I grasped just how much a part of my life Roni had become. In no time at all he had turned into my anchor. He possessed my thoughts. He possessed my heart. I couldn't imagine not seeing him for so long.

"One month?" I whispered to myself. Suddenly, consumed with fear for him, visions of the terrorist attack flooded my head.

"Well, actually it'll be more like five weeks."

"Five weeks," I repeated in disbelief. I was going to go mad during that time wondering if he was safe, worrying for his life.

Seeing my apprehensiveness, Roni assured me, "Don't worry, Dara. Reserve duty is routine. It'll pass quickly." But those words didn't calm me.

"Where will you be stationed?" I asked.

"Up north."

"The Golan?"

"A little further up north."

"Lebanon? You're going into Lebanon? But you were just there! You fought in the war! They can't send you back there again!"

"Dara, that was over a year ago. This is just a matter of routine security patrols – I promise."

But I knew better than that. Ron Arad, a soldier captured during the Lebanon War when his plane went down, was still being held captive. It was a huge coup for the Arabs to capture and kidnap our soldiers. When it came to dealing with our enemies on all fronts, nothing was routine – and nothing could ever be taken for granted. It mattered little to me that the Israel Defense Forces was considered one of the best-trained armies in the world. My fear for Roni's life was so tangible; it was as if the panic were choking me, and a rash impulse took over. "You never kissed me."

"What?" Roni asked, thrown by the direction of the conversation.

"You can't go. You never kissed me." My eyes looked fiercely into his, beckoning him, on some level believing that if I gave him something to return to, he wouldn't get hurt. He said he would miss me – I would show him exactly what he would be missing. Maybe then, he wouldn't play the hero, take risks and carry out daredevil tactics, so that he would return to me in one piece. Maybe then, he wouldn't feel that urge to carry the entire responsibility of protecting his people on his shoulders. And, maybe I was just clutching at straws – desperate to keep him out of danger, yet knowing full well that Roni would never shirk from what he believed he needed to do. God help me, I loved him and was frantic with the knowledge that I was powerless to protect him.

He stared at me for a very long moment with that familiar pensive look in his eyes. It was impossible to tell what he was thinking. "Dara," he finally said in a tone that was gentle while caressing my face with his hands. He glided his fingers back through my hair and tilted my face up to his, searching my eyes – so deeply – as if burrowing to my very soul. "I can't do this anymore."

"What can't you do?"

"It's one thing to fight on the northern front; it's another to fight you off." He bowed his head, brushing his lips to mine. They were soft…warm. He moved slowly at first, as if to taste, lingering as if to savor. Inside of me, the stirrings mounted, hitting me like a tidal wave, and I drowned in his touch. His lips pressed harder against mine, kissing me again with a growing eagerness, his breath hot and jagged. I buried my fingers in his silky curls and melded my body to his. He drew me in tighter, wrapping one arm around my waist, his muscular physique crushing against me. I wanted to get even closer to him, to melt right into his blazing skin. His lips streamed down my neck in a hungry urgency and an electrifying current sped through me as I felt his warm tongue at the top of my chest. Were it not for his firm hold, I would have slithered to the ground. Nothing else existed at that moment. I was completely his, so willing to surrender my entire being in his arms, and then without warning, Roni pulled away. "I should take you back to your room," he breathed heavily, holding me at arm's length.

Surprised, I blurted out, "No, take me to your room."

"Dara…" he shook his head.

"Roni, I know what I'm doing, and I know what I want."

"No, I don't think you do."

"You don't think that I know what I'm doing?"

"Uh…no, you know exactly what you're doing," he swallowed hard. "You just don't know what you want."

"I want you, Roni. And you can't kiss me like that and tell me that you don't want me. Why do you keep pulling away from me?" My eyes burned with the tears that I fought to overcome.

"Dara," he again inched closer and curled his hands in my hair. It was then that I saw the inner conflict etched across his face. "You don't know what you do to me," he murmured, mostly to himself. I leaned into his chest, which was still heaving lightly up and down, in rhythm with mine. He draped his arms around me. "I never said I didn't want you. That's the problem – I want you too much. You consume me." My head snapped up.

"That's not a problem," I said wryly.

As if to accuse me, he continued, "I don't know how I let you affect me this way. From the first moment I saw you…," he trailed off and let go of me. He stood quietly for a moment, deliberating, his eyes staring at me hard. "You don't understand…I'm just going to end up hurting you."

"Why would you say that? Why would you think you'd hurt me?"

He wavered before answering. "My life here in Israel is… unpredictable."

"What does that mean?"

"It means that I don't want to involve you in something that you're not prepared for. Look…I hadn't yet made a final decision – but I'm considering rejoining the army."

"Rejoining? You can do that?"

"I was…asked to come back. And, there's…something else…" he paused.

"What is it?"

He held my eyes with his and slowly emphasized each word, "*I don't want to know what it would be like to lose you.*" *So, that was what this was all about.*

"But Roni –"

"No, Dara," he cut me off, "I let myself become too attached to you as it is. I kept telling myself that I would have to stop whatever it is that's going on between us before we…before I crossed over the line. I just don't know how to stay away from you. I admit it, and I'm sorry because I can see that I've hurt you already and I don't know how to fix it. But I do know one thing," his eyes remained hard and the tone of his voice was severe, "I don't have any more room inside of me for any more losses."

"You're not going to lose me, Roni. I'm here."

"You're here now. But you're planning to return to the States when your year is done."

"That doesn't have to be our end."

"You're putting six thousand miles between us…you have to make a choice."

"It sounds like you already made the choice for both of us. But for the record, my returning to the States to study in no way means that I don't choose you."

"Be realistic, Dara."

"I am. We can both travel back and forth to see each other. I could come back to Israel during the summers, and there are winter breaks, spring breaks, holiday breaks during the school year. And once I get my degree, I intend to return to Israel permanently." I knew my argument sounded ridiculous when I heard the words come out, but I was not going to lose my resolve.

He chuckled almost sadly. "You're talking about four years, Dara. If you would transfer to a university in Israel, then we'd have something to talk about – but you're not ready to commit to that, are you?"

Frustrated with his pessimism and with the finality of his outlook, I felt the tears welling up in my eyes. I hated it when I became so emotional. I tried to fight it off, my response coming out in an angry tirade. "If you want commitment, I'll give you commitment, just please don't tell me what I'm ready to take on or not. I know it won't be easy, but I have more spunk in me than you realize! And if you don't mind, you can stop speaking to me in that condescending manner – accusing me of not being able to handle life in Israel or you rejoining the army. I can handle it just fine! If you need to be the soldier, then I will be the one who waits for you to return home safely. You've gotten under *my* skin, Roni!"

"Dara..."

"No, Roni, I'm not finished. You're so quick to judge! So pessimistic! Do you even know what makes me tick? You don't love Israel any more than I do. You were just one of the lucky ones born into it. Do you have any clue what kind of struggle it is for me to want to be here while having my parents pulling at me to leave? Give me a little more credit, Roni. I'm doing the best I can under the circumstances. Open yourself up to trust me. Just for once, set aside your doomsday approach to life – stop pulling away and grab what life is giving us. For God's sake, Roni, we can't keep denying..." Before I could finish my next sentence, Roni swept me up in his arms and I let out a gasp. "What are you doing?"

"Besides enjoying your little tantrum?" he smirked. "You just said to grab what life is giving us...I'm grabbing."

All at once, I was speechless. He suddenly looked so determined, and I suddenly felt nervous about my own amorous intentions. My heart thumped furiously as he carried me toward his room. I was sure he was able to hear it or at the very least, feel the vibrations. Before long, however, I sank deeper into his powerful hold, calmed by the rhythm of his steady gait. *God, he was strong.* It was then I recalled one particular thing that he said. I looked up to his face and saw his glittering eyes in the darkness staring down at me. "Roni?"

"Yes?"

"You said, from the first moment you saw me?"

His answer was a faint smile.

"But…you… Well…you hated me in the beginning," I finally pushed the words out. He remained quiet.

Before I could press him to respond, we reached the short path to the apartments where the single members of the kibbutz resided. He lowered me down, took my hand, leading me toward a small apartment complex, and guided me inside. We passed through a common room and a kitchen shared by the singles in the building and then down a short hallway, where he unlocked a door on the right. It opened to a vestibule leading to a modest-sized room with just the barest of necessities. On one wall, several shelves of books hung suspended over a three-drawer dresser. Adjacent to it stood a stereo and cassette player on a simple stand, with a collection of records and cassettes neatly piled beneath. His closet door was half open, and I spied a modest wardrobe of clothes, with his army uniform hanging neatly. At the far end of the room stood a desk covered haphazardly with newspapers, with another stack on the floor lined up next to the desk. I noticed that the paper on top was in Arabic. A large wide window that opened above his bed partially filled the adjacent wall, its simple curtain pulled to the side, allowing the moon to cast its glow over the room. He didn't turn on the light.

Roni looked down at my hand he was still holding and lifted it to his lips. "There's even beauty in your fingers," he murmured, tenderly kissing them. It made me shiver, and his eyes flashed knowingly to mine. I felt I was melting at the same time and imagined myself dissolving into a puddle at his feet. I swallowed hard, "You're avoiding my question, aren't you?"

"Not really. I was just sidetracked. Besides, it wasn't a question; it was a statement – entirely inaccurate, however." He stopped then and crinkled his brows as he lingered in thought. "I never hated you, Dara," he softly intoned.

"You didn't?"

"No, of course not. I...," he tapered off.

"You what?"

"I... need a drink. Maybe you'd like a drink? Yeah...that's what we need. Wait right here." My mouth dropped open as Roni zipped out to the kitchen. I turned my attention to the moon, which tonight was three-quarters full, and went to sit on his bed to gaze out his window. Not two minutes later, Roni returned with two glasses filled with some ice and a bottle of liquor. I think it was scotch, but I couldn't be certain. He sat beside me, handed me the glasses, and poured the questionable liquid into them both. After clinking his glass to mine, he downed his drink in one shot, shutting his eyes from the caustic taste. "Ooh, that stuff is bad," he grimaced, setting the glass on the floor. I laughed softly and took a sip from mine, scrunching my face from the bitter tang, and gave the glass back to him. He smiled, brushing the back of his hand tenderly against my face. "Now, where was I?" Roni's voice was more relaxed.

"You were saying that you never hated me."

"Right." He exhaled loudly as his eyes got caught up in a memory. He took my hand while taking a swig from my drink with the other, and then placed the glass on the floor next to the first one.

"Dara," he said in a muted tone, "when I first met you – I remember, it was at Sachna." He looked down as if to study my hand, caressing my fingers, and continued cautiously. "Ever since the war in Lebanon, after…Sultan Yacoub, I was so dead inside for such a long time…and frankly, I was content with that. I didn't want to feel. I didn't want to get close with anyone…ever." He lifted his gaze back to me. "Then…I saw you. It was as if my heart began to beat again. I had no control over what came over me and that stunned me. *You* stunned me. I didn't like losing control over my emotions – and I confess, that made me quite angry. I *wanted* to hate you, but…I couldn't. I didn't want to feel, but you were *making* me feel.

"So…I just stared at you – in your red, polka-dot bikini," he smiled lightly at the memory. "I couldn't pull my eyes away from you. But it was more than that. You were…different. Something about you kept drawing me to you. You weren't like the typical American girls who were seeking adventure and romance – you were…serious and full of purpose. Still, I didn't want to believe that. I tried convincing myself that you were as silly as the rest of them. I wanted to remain dead inside. I wanted to hold on to my anger. But," he cradled his hand around my neck, stroking my cheek with his thumb, "it became harder and harder remaining angry at a world that had you in it."

He was on a verbal roll, and my heart raced with every feeling that floated off his lips. I sat on the bed facing him, transfixed on his every word. It was too powerful; I was going to jump out of my skin. He let his hand fall from my neck, and his fingers slowly trailed down my arm. *Did he not realize what he was doing to me?* He then chuckled under his breath and at first, I was sure it was because of my erratic breathing.

"What?" I asked almost defensively.

"You were actually very oblivious to the advances from some of the guys here. Without meaning to, you broke a good number of hearts. I almost felt sorry for them. *Almost*," he added with a twinkle in his eyes.

"Advances? I don't remember anything like that. They were just being friendly." I realized a second too late that I must have sounded seriously naive.

"Dara," his eyes creased in a smile as he leaned over to whisper in my ear, "have you no clue how beautiful you are?"

"I…um…guess not."

"Trust me; men are never *friendly* to a beautiful woman unless they want something." His eyes trailed over me. "It wasn't easy to ignore you. Even from a distance, you were very…disrupting. So…come to think of it," he pursed his sensuous lips in a devilish curl, "I suppose I did hate you, in a way."

"Then…that day in the cotton fields…and in the jeep…it wasn't my imagination," I put in.

He didn't answer, though his devilish curl turned into a grin.

"You were so…so…"

"Rude?"

"Don't forget offensive, crude and arrogant," I smiled.

"Yeah, I was pretty bad, wasn't I?" he said a little too proudly. "I didn't anticipate we'd be thrown together. My defenses went up," he explained with a shrug. "But I could only take it so far before…I had to admit to myself that I was falling in love with you."

"You…love me?"

"Yes, Dara…I love you," he said solemnly as if he gave me some grave news. He twisted a lock of my hair in his fingers and I trembled reflexively. "Mmm, interesting reaction." His brooding glare turned mischievous. "I knew I was right about that. Seems you go for the arrogant and rude type." He smirked. "I have to admit, it was such a turn-on teasing you and getting you all riled up, I almost took you right in the jeep." And just like that, the amusement in his eyes vanished. A dark cloud fell over him – a flashback that he shook away, and he got up to pour himself another drink. He downed a shot, picked up a pack of cigarettes from his dresser and then thought twice about it and returned to sit with me on the bed.

"What is it, Roni? I can't read your mind. What are you thinking?"

"It's a good thing you can't read my mind. It's a very dark place."

"Are you trying to scare me off?"

"Just giving you fair warning." He stared straight ahead, tensing his jaw. It seemed as if he was watching another scene replay before his eyes, and my heart went out to his tortured soul. His gaze darted back to me. "I should have listened to my instincts and not let you go into the orchard – not let any of you…"

"No, Roni," I cut him off. "Don't even go there. It wasn't your fault. None of it was. Don't do that to yourself."

"Dara, you don't understand," he said, his eyes searing into me. "When I saw you wounded, lying in a pool of blood – I died again. The thought of losing you before I could even tell you…"

"But you didn't lose me, and…you did tell me…and…I get to tell you…I'm in love with you, Roni."

"I know you are," he said grimly. "You don't know what you're getting yourself into."

"What can I say? I like living on the edge."

"Oh, yeah?" his lips arched slightly. "What do you know about living on the edge?"

"I don't have to divulge all my secrets, do I?"

"Secrets," he murmured to himself. The word seemed to trigger something in his mind. He shook his head, as if disappointed in himself. "I shouldn't have brought you here. This was a mistake."

"You said you loved me."

"Forget what I said," he said sternly, getting to his feet. "I don't know what I was thinking. I'm not good for you, Dara."

"You don't scare me, Roni," I threw out with dogged tenacity. A hint of a smile in his eyes alluded to his amusement as they dazzled into mine while he considered that.

"Sweet Dara, trying to be so tough. Fine then." He returned to my side and clutched my arms, pulling me nearer to him. "You don't want to listen to reason? So realize this – you've made a decision here and there's no turning back time. I want you, Dara. I can't hold back anymore – I won't hold back anymore – and I *will* have you." His tone both unnerved me and propelled my desire for him.

"Then take me," my words flowed out in a hushed timbre.

He shot me a foreboding look as if to warn me, to give me one final chance, but I didn't flinch. A menacing smile curled his lips as he moved to close the small gap between us. "There's no escaping me now."

"No escape?"

"None at all." His warm breath touched my mouth, inviting me closer to his.

"Um…Roni?"

"Ready to run?"

"No. But…there is this one thing I want to clarify."

"Clarify?" he raised one eyebrow and unclenched my arms.

"Well…just for the record, I wasn't wearing a red, polka-dot bikini."

"What?"

"At Sachna – I wasn't wearing a red, polka-dot bikini."

"Of course you were. I remember it…vividly," his fingers toyed with the neckline of my blouse.

"Well, actually, I was wearing a red, polka-dot *sundress*."

He looked a tad confused.

"It was a dress…it wasn't a bikini." I watched him rebuild the scene in his head.

"Are you quite sure about that?" he asked almost teasingly as he fiddled open the top bottons of my blouse. "I tend to have a photographic memory about things of that nature." He glided one finger between the space of my breasts. I managed to nod in response.

"Hmm. Fascinating," Roni reflected with a roguish smile. "And I suppose you're going to tell me that you're not lying here in bed, naked in my arms right now?"

"Um...sounds like more of your imagination at work."

"That's something we're going to have to rectify." One by one, he undid the remaining buttons of my blouse, slipped it off and tossed it to the floor. He lowered the straps of my bra and caressed my shoulder with his warm lips. It took a fleeting moment for him to work the back hook, flinging my bra off as if it were a mere annoyance. He coiled his hands around my waist as he allowed his eyes to stream unhurriedly over me. My head clouded up; I was dizzy from the sensations that catapulted through me. I drew in a deep breath, trembling in his grasp, and his eyes flashed up to mine. "I want you to be sure about this, Dara."

"I'm very sure," I whispered. His eyes softened and he swallowed hard, laboring a bit reluctantly to get the next words out, "You know, I was just teasing before...about having you...about no escape...I'll," he swallowed again, "understand...if you..."

"Roni...I want to be with you...now."

"Good – I didn't mean any of that anyway."

"I know."

The silence was absolute, save for our breathing as we stared at each other in the moonlit room.

My heart beat furiously against my chest. I swallowed hard and bit down on my lip. Just then an odd look came over Roni, as if he had unearthed a new discovery. His lips twitched in a faint smile. He leaned in as though he was going to kiss me but instead his lips floated against my cheek, "Dara?"

"Yes?"

"This is your first time, isn't it?"

I nodded. And then I realized, "Oh…I don't have any…"

"Shhh…not to worry, my *motek*, my sweet Dara. I'll take care of it." His lips then met mine, and we fell back onto his bed. I took in his masculine scent – so primal and raw. It was intoxicating. He slid his hand down the length of my body, skillfully and deliberately, slipping off the rest of my clothes, his shimmering eyes taking in every inch of me. I touched my hand to his face, my fingers tracing his finely carved features and then around his lips. "Dara," his throaty voice drawing me over the edge, "damn, you're more beautiful than in my fantasies."

"You've…fantasized…about us?" I could barely speak as his hand trailed up my thigh and slid beneath the small of my back.

"Repeatedly," he breathed.

"What…kind…of…?"

"Trust me…very sordid," his lips attacked mine with a fury. I undid his shirt and he shrugged out of it, adding it to the pile of clothes now draping the floor. My fingers drifted over the lines of his chest. His skin was smooth and hot, his muscles rippling beneath my caress.

I tilted my face back from his. "How sordid?"

His body moved over mine, holding me down in a surrender-like position, my arms spread out to the sides. "You're about to find out." And he devoured me with his lips and with his touch until the moon gave way to the hint of dawn.

⚜

I awoke with a start. Roni stood over me, wearing his uniform with his wine-red beret tucked neatly beneath his epaulet and his M16 slung over his shoulder. There were several insignias attached to the front of his uniform, but the only one I recognized was the wings of a paratrooper. He was impossibly stunning. I smiled lazily at him, and then jolted up to a sitting position with reality hitting hard. "I thought you weren't going up north until tomorrow?"

"I got a call a little while ago. Plans have changed – I have to leave today. And you, my lady," he continued with a smile before I had a chance to pout, "you have to get back to work today."

"What time is it?"

"It's about an hour before dawn. I'm sorry you didn't get much sleep – well, actually," he grinned, "I'm not sorry at all." He brushed my hair back with his hand. "Let me walk you back to your room so you can wash up and change before breakfast. I'll have to catch a ride down the mountain with the work crews."

I knew it was for my benefit that he tried to sound casual about his leaving one day earlier.

Wanting to show Roni that I could be strong, I ignored the baseball-size lump in my throat as I threw my clothes on, very much aware that he was watching me, leaning against the wall with a devastating, sensuous smile on his face. "Okay. I'm ready. Let's go," I said as I headed toward the door. Roni didn't move. He remained in place, leaning against the wall, wearing the same smile, his eyes glittering.

"Why are you just standing there?"

"Oh, I'm just marveling at my brave Dara."

"Are you making fun of me?"

"Never." He eased himself away from the wall, took my hand and started for the door. "But…you might want to button up your blouse," he suggested casually.

I looked down. "Oh."

"Allow me," Roni volunteered, his face growing more serious as he finished with the last button. His eyes caught mine. "I love you, Dara," he murmured.

"I love you, Roni," I whispered back.

We lowered our gaze from each other's eyes and then walked out the door.

After breakfast, we stood with everyone else at the top of the mountain waiting for the rides to the valley below. Yaniv was there, too, clad in his uniform as well, as he belonged to the same unit as Roni. He discreetly stood to the side chatting with Jenny, letting Roni and I have what would be our last moments together for over a month. No one was surprised about us. Ever since the terrorist attack, it was rare to find one of us without the other. So much had transpired in these last few weeks. All of our lives, Israeli and non-Israeli alike, were forever altered.

"Is there any way for you to get in touch with me," I asked, "perhaps through the public phone at the kibbutz office?"

Roni shook his head. "That would only work if I could tell you exactly what time I'd be calling, so you'd know when to be by the phone. But I can never know that. I'll mostly be out in the field, and I can't say when I'll be returning to the base." *Out in the field*, I mulled over the phrase in my mind; it was a euphemism for being out in the war zone. "The best I can do is to leave a message for you from time to time with the secretary at the office," Roni offered. I nodded, fighting back the tears that stubbornly filled my eyes.

"*Chayalim!*" Someone shouted "soldiers"…it was Moti. He would take the reservists down the mountain so they could catch the bus heading north. Roni's head sprang up and then swiftly turned back to me. He held my face in his hands and kissed me and I wrapped my arms around his waist to feel his warmth just one more time, leaning my head against his chest. "Just five weeks and I'll be home," he whispered, brushing his lips to my hair. I lowered my arms and let him go.

Chapter 6

Not a day went by that I didn't scan the newspaper and listen to the radio – praying all the while that there would be no news coming from Lebanon. It was a frustrating undertaking, as the Hebrew in the papers was sophisticated and way above my level of understanding, and the radio newscasters spoke impossibly fast. Jenny would often be at my side helping. It was like the blind leading the blind. Conversational Hebrew was hardly a problem – in fact, my Hebrew was better than most Americans here, which Roni pointed out on occasion – but getting through an Israeli newspaper was a different ball game altogether.

It became a ritual to head straight to the office upon returning from the fields to ask Dassi, the kibbutz secretary, for any word from Roni. For nearly three weeks I heard the same response – "No, Dara, I'm sorry." It was unbearable. I had reached the point where emotional and physical pain converged.

Today was a little different, however. Yaniv had called. There was a message from him for Jenny. I brought the note to her, excited to hear from Yaniv and happy for Jenny as well. I had not realized that their friendship had escalated into something more.

"To tell you the truth, Dara, neither did I. I mean, I like him and I think he likes me, but he's very shy in that way. I'm actually surprised to have received a message from him."

"Well, don't keep me in suspense, Jenny! What does the note say?" She smiled, opened the note, and read it aloud.

> *Dear Jenny,*
> *I finally have a chance to call. They've got me doing kitchen duty for the next few days. Tell Dara that Roni is fine; he's still out in the field but should return to base in the next day or so.*
>
> > *I miss you,*
> > *Yaniv*

"Well, not exactly dripping in romantic drivel, but at least he's safe for a while," Jenny surmised. I nodded in agreement.

Jenny and I had grown closer since Alana had been killed. She was straightforward and considerate to a fault, a friend I could trust and rely on. *Jenny and Yaniv would be great together*, I thought. They complemented each other. He measured his words, while she…well, did not. *I shoot straight from the hip* was her motto. I saw how Jenny brought out Yaniv's personality when they visited me at the hospital. They were warm, caring and genuinely good people. They were also a striking couple – both tall with a pleasant, inviting appearance, he with his wavy, sandy-brown hair, she with long blond hair that fell into natural curls, and both had attention-grabbing green eyes. In the lonely times, I would daydream of the four of us remaining friends throughout our lives.

The next afternoon, the twenty-first day since Roni left for reserve duty, I again went to see Dassi upon returning from the fields. A small crowd of people huddled in front of the modest structure that housed the office. As I neared the group, Doron, one of Roni and Yaniv's friends, noticed me and gave me an unusually animated greeting. "Shalom, Darale!"

I smiled in reflex and returned the greeting, but quickly ascertained the manner of the rest of the group. Their conversation came to an abrupt halt, and their eyes darted from one to another in an awkward attempt to avoid mine. I heard the words slip out of my mouth. "You heard something."

There was silence.

My throat tightened. "What did you hear?" I eyed each one standing there.

Looking very uneasy, Doron answered, "Dara, we really don't know anything."

"Tell me what you don't know." It didn't make sense as I said it, but Doron understood.

"There was some fighting up north."

"In Lebanon," I clarified.

"Yes, in Lebanon. One of our soldiers was killed early this afternoon. They're not releasing his name until his family is notified, so we don't know yet who it is. All we know is what Dassi told us – that Yaniv is safe on the base – apparently he had kitchen duty for the last couple of days."

"There must be a phone number at the base that we can call," I appealed to Doron.

He shook his head. "At this point, they'll only speak with soldiers' immediate family members."

"Well, then, we can call Roni's family." I knew that was a foolish suggestion as soon as I heard my words.

"I don't think that's a good idea," Doron confirmed my thoughts. "Better not to alarm them if they haven't yet heard the news. And…in the worse-case scenario, they shouldn't find out in that way."

I could barely get my next words out. "When will we know?"

"Soon, Dara – soon. Probably within the next hour or so."

I choked back a cry working its way to the surface. "If you hear something, find me, please."

Doron nodded.

It was a struggle to breathe evenly as I stumbled back to my room. I found Jenny there waiting for me. She took one look at my face and said, "I kind of figured you heard."

I nodded, not able to trust my voice.

"It's been a heck of a three months so far, hasn't it? It's a different world out here," Jenny said contemplatively.

"Yeah," was all I could muster.

"Look, Dara, I know this sounds silly for me to say, but I know Roni is okay. I have a very strong feeling about it. You'll see. It wasn't him that was killed today, you have to believe that."

"I'm trying to. But you see, Jenny, if it wasn't my Roni, then it was someone else's. So what am I hoping for…that someone else's Roni was killed? How does one even pray in this situation?"

"You just have to pray that the one you love is safe," she said in a small voice. "That's all anyone can do."

"They're all our boys, Jen, each and every one of them." I exhaled heavily. "Come on; let's get out of this room. It's suffocating here."

We walked to the *mo'adon*, the communal lounge, where there was the only TV on the entire kibbutz. The kibbutz members packed the room, everyone glued to the news program, even though the newscaster kept repeating the same information. The army was withholding the name of the soldier killed in action until his family was properly notified.

Three hours passed and there was no word yet. I was still in my work clothes and decided to take a shower and afterwards head toward the dining hall. It would soon be dinnertime, and surely, someone would have heard something by then.

Doron stood outside in front of the dining hall talking with Ari and Lavi, two other young men from Roni and Yaniv's group of friends. He saw the question in my eyes as I walked toward him and shook his head. "Sorry, Dara, we haven't heard anything yet." *I was going to pieces. I was going to lose my mind.*

"Do you have a cigarette?" I asked him.

"You don't smoke, Dara."

"I do now."

"Here," Lavi offered me one of his and lit it for me. "You might as well take the rest of the pack. You look like you could use it."

"Yeah, thanks, Lavi," I muttered.

"Listen, Dara," Lavi attempted to set my mind at rest, "Roni is a top soldier. He's smart when he's out in the field. He has a mind like a fox. And," he grinned, "he's crazy for you – he'll single-handedly fight the entire country of Lebanon in order to get back to you."

"He might be tempted to first take a detour into Syria though. You know Roni," Ari chimed in with what he thought was a harmless joke. Lavi shot him a dirty look and smacked him on the back of his head. "What? What did I say?" Ari asked dumbfounded.

I tried to smile, but Ari's seemingly harmless joke caused a sickening feeling deep in my gut. *You know Roni.* I flinched at what that meant. It told me something about Roni that was implicit among his friends – that he would never shirk from any dangerous mission, but would likely be the first to volunteer at the risk of his life.

At that moment, Jenny showed up. "Any word?" Everyone shook their heads in unison. "Come on inside," Jenny turned to me. "We might as well have some dinner."

I took a drag on my cigarette. "I can't eat."

"Then watch me eat." She attempted to lighten the mood, wisely choosing not to admonish me about smoking.

I gave her a weak smile. "Okay, Jenny." And to Roni's friends, "You guys coming?"

"Sure. We'll join you in a minute," Doron promised. I put out my cigarette and walked into the dining hall. "I'll grab some chairs, you can grab some food," I said to Jenny.

I spied an empty table at the very end of the hall and went through the usual procedure of tipping the chairs toward the table to save the seats. Several minutes later Jenny joined me, as did Doron, Lavi, Ari and their girlfriends, Shira, Mikki and Adina, respectively. Ari and Adina both grew up on the kibbutz and were engaged to be married. Theirs was a girl-next-door-boy next door kind of romance. Everyone at the table avoided the obvious subject that was on all of our minds, and instead spoke about Ari and Adina's upcoming wedding.

I kept eyeing my watch. It had been close to four hours since we heard any news. *Somebody has to know something by now!* Just then, Dassi burst through the doors of the dining hall and scanned the large room until she met my eyes. My heart stopped dead.

"Dara? What's wrong?" Lavi asked. But no words reached my lips. They followed my gaze to Dassi and watched her as she made her way to our table. I didn't dare breathe. The dining hall seemed longer than usual this evening and it took Dassi forever to reach us. She stretched out her arm to hand me a note. I stared at it, but I couldn't move to take it from her. I was too afraid to get my hopes up. The wildest things swept through my mind. Perhaps it was a note from one of his buddies in his unit breaking the bad news to me. Or else, these were his last words before succumbing to his mortal wounds.

"It's okay, Dara," Dassi said softly. "Read the note," her warm brown eyes prodded me.

He's alive? Roni is alive? A hushed silence fell upon the entire dining hall – all eyes were on our table. I slowly reached for the note. My chest trembled and my hands shook as I opened it. I read it, a gust of air escaped from me and I dropped the note to the table. "He's alive," was all I could manage to say. I bowed my head into my hands and broke into the heaving sobs I could no longer contain. My entire body rebelled and convulsed with the sudden release. Friends stood around to hold me, as well as each other. The entire dining hall erupted into simultaneous tears and laughter.

Tears because Roni was alive, tears because another one of our boys was not, and laughter, because…life goes on, and so must we.

Inside the note, there wasn't any long-winded message. A simple statement:

> *My motek,*
> *Just returned to the base and counting the days till I*
> *return to you.*
>
> > *Roni*

Chapter 7

It was the middle of the night and I had just awakened from a horrific nightmare – again. The backdrop was always the same – the grapefruit orchard. I had just climbed down the ladder that leaned against a tall tree, with my burlap sack loaded down with grapefruit slung over my shoulder. A trail of blood flowed down the dirt path toward my feet. I tracked the red trail to its source; it led to the grapefruit bin. As I was about to unload my burden, I peered into it, and three young, dead bodies stared up at me. Their faces eluded me – unrecognizable – covered in blood.

Disturbing as it was, I refused to give any weight to such a dream. Stress over Roni's safety was taking its toll, I reasoned. That's all it was. Sure, coupled with the fact that I had just lost a dear friend in a terrorist attack where I myself had been wounded, it was only natural for me to have nightmares and some sleepless nights. Still…perhaps Roni was right about me. Perhaps I didn't have what it takes to deal with a loved one in the army. I shook that thought from my mind. I had to be strong. There was no alternative. I loved Roni, and that meant that the army would be a perpetual reality in my life. Until the Arabs were ready to recognize Israel's right to exist as a Jewish State, we would know no peace. We had no choice but to deal with it.

No, I concluded, there would be no peace, at least not in any near future. I had once made it a point to read the Koran as well as the New Testament. Knowing the mind of one's enemies is crucial to survival, I always felt. And even more important was to understand the *endgame*, and in what manner the others believed it would emerge.

In Judaism, the end of days was going to be as in the book of Isaiah: after a final confrontation between the forces of good and evil, peace would prevail among the nations – not just one nation, but among all nations. People would not have any more need for weapons, and nature would be changed – a beautiful end of days and the kingdom of God on earth. Christianity, as is written in the book of Revelation, sees the day when Satan himself would be obliterated. There would be no more powers of evil. It was all about personal salvation through the acceptance of Jesus.

Islam perceives a world that is completely Muslim in the end of days – a world under the rule of Islam. The Koran speaks of an absolute and final victory that necessitates the subjugation of non-Muslims, which will come about through war, an Islamic jihad. Christians will not exist, because according to many Islamic traditions the Muslims who are in hell will have to be replaced by somebody, and they'll be replaced by Christians, and Jesus himself will renounce Christianity. The Jews will no longer exist, because before the coming of the end of days, there will be a war against the Jews where all Jews should be killed – this was the heart of Islamic tradition, found in religious texts read by every child in school. Jews will be running away, hiding behind trees and rocks, and on that day, Allah will give mouths to the rocks and trees and they will say, "Oh, Muslim, come here. There is a Jew behind me. Kill him." Without this, according to the *Haddith*, a collection of the sayings of Muhammad, the end of days cannot come. This was a fundamental of Islam. So how, I pondered, can there be peace with a civilization steeped in such beliefs? Alas, we are doomed to war against the Islamic jihad.

Ugh. Only three hours until dawn and my head was spinning with theological data. I was not going to be worth an old, sick mule out in the fields if I didn't get any sleep.

Weeding the fields was on this week's work schedule for the volunteers – not a pleasant task. The weeds were the size of bushes, with very thick roots requiring a good deal of muscle power to pull them out of the ground. I could just imagine Roni's face had he been here yesterday to watch me struggle with the giant wild growth. One in particular was incredibly stubborn; when I at last succeeded in yanking the bush weed from the earth, the final jerk that wrenched it free threw me back at least two yards, landing me flat on my back. Ari and Lavi, who worked alongside us during the weeding process, enjoyed a good laugh at my expense.

After about another hour of mind calisthenics, jumping from one thing to the next, my thoughts finally rested on Roni. *Roni…in how many days will you be home? Four more days now…with this dawn, four more…* Drowsiness finally began to set in and a merciful, dreamless sleep took over.

I was on automatic for the next several days. Counting the hours, biding my time, doing what I had to do and ignoring the news on the radio, while refraining from reading the papers. I decided that ignorance was bliss. Both Yaniv and Roni had left word with Dassi that they'd be out *in the field* during their final week of reserve duty and wouldn't be able to call again. With Ari and Adina's wedding date getting closer, I volunteered to help Adina with her hair and makeup and busied myself by experimenting on her at the end of the workday. It provided some relief from my incessant worrying.

The nights were lonely though and much too long. I found myself whiling away the time sitting atop the mound of the foxhole outside my room and staring up at the stars. Tonight, however, I was filled with nervous energy, borne out of the excitement of Roni returning tomorrow. Even the proposition of another day of weeding the fields could not destroy my mood.

"There she is," I heard Jenny call out. "I told you she would be here." Ever since the scare over Roni, his friends had rallied around me and taken both Jenny and me under their wings. I felt truly blessed, surrounded by such warm and wonderful people. Roni had a good group of friends.

"Dara, what is it with you and foxholes anyway?" Ari asked.

"Keeping it warm till Roni's return, eh?" Lavi teased.

"Ha! It looks like it would be his idea of a romantic spot," Ari cackled.

"Seems to me you both don't know him as well as you thought you did," I came to Roni's defense. "He happens to be quite the charming romantic."

"Charming? Romantic?" Ari echoed. "Uh…we *are* still talking about Roni, right?"

"I thought the only thing he can get hot and bothered over is his gun," Lavi mused.

"Oh, like you're Mr. Romantic?" chided Mikki.

"I don't know," Doron contemplated while peeking into the foxhole. "Looks kind of cozy in there…Shira? What do you say?"

"Don't even joke about it, Doron!" Shira quipped.

"What's going on, guys?" I smiled at their playful banter.

"We're planning a bonfire at Sachna tomorrow night, when Yaniv and Roni return," Lavi filled me in. "Instead of having dinner on the kibbutz, we figured on having our own private barbeque. You in?"

"Sure. It sounds great."

"Good," Lavi said. "We're going into Beit She'an now to get some supplies. Care to join us?"

"Can't think of anything better I'd like to do!" I jumped down from the mound to join them.

The autumn winds were fierce the next morning on Mount Gilboa, and one could sense that winter was waiting impatiently in the shadows. The day's job entailed pulling out the weeds from the few fields that were located on top of the mountain, as opposed to those in the valley below, yet they were no less daunting.

The soil in general was coarse and more difficult to work with, but miraculously, the kibbutz successfully grew vast fields of carrots, despite our biblical King David's ancient curse on Mount Gilboa. As David grieved over the deaths of King Saul and his sons on the Gilboa, he cursed the area in that there should be no dew, neither rain nor fields of offerings. Even with the efforts of modern Israeli farming, one can still witness huge bald gaps that confirm King David's curse.

I never ceased to be in awe of how much of our history was embedded in the heights of Gilboa. We arrived at the carrot fields just minutes after dawn, and I took a few moments to appreciate the beauty that surrounded me. The top of Mount Gilboa was often above the clouds, and this morning I stood captivated, watching them dissipate in the wind. They resembled a curtain of cotton drawn open to reveal the magical view below. I closed my eyes and tried to envision the paths of our ancestors on this very land, recalling past lessons of Jewish history.

At the foot of the mountain lies Ein Harod's spring – the same waters that quenched the thirst of Gideon's three hundred chosen fighters set to defeat the vast army of the Midianites across the valley, now the modern town of Afula. In the Jezreel Valley, King Ahab was confronted by the prophet Elijah, after he had Navot executed at the advice of his evil Queen Jezebel. And just a few miles in the distance stood the lone, round Mount Tabor across the valley, where Deborah the Judge and Barak led the Israelites to victory over the Canaanite General Siscra and his massive army of nine hundred iron chariots.

"Is she actually sleeping standing up?" Lavi wondered.

"She likes to meditate," I heard Jenny answer. "Leave her alone."

"Uh…I'm not sure she's breathing," Ari feigned concern. I opened one of my eyes and saw his bright smile inches from my face.

"Do you mind if I take a moment to appreciate where I am?" I asked, pretending to be annoyed.

Ari raised his eyebrows. "You're in the middle of a carrot field, Dara. Get a grip. Or better yet, take these work gloves and start yanking weeds."

I grabbed the gloves out of Ari's hands and took my position on the field. "Ari, Lavi, hard as you try, not even the two of you can get to me today!"

"We'll see – the day just started," Lavi kidded.

"Yeah, give us a chance, will you?" Ari threw in.

"One can only wonder if you'd be teasing me if Roni were here."

"Oh, no!" Ari got down on his knees. "You're not going to tell Roni on us, are you? I mean, you can't – you just can't, Dara…. You don't know how he gets when he's really angry."

I shook my head at his silliness and turned to begin working on the weeds. He trailed after me, still on his knees. "I mean it, Dara. He'll… he'll…shout in all these words that no one understands – in dialects no one has ever heard of. It's frightening, I tell you! I can't bear to think about it. God help us, he may as well speak in French!"

Lavi rolled his eyes. "He does, you fool, and you're not funny."

"Oh, yeah. That's right," Ari dropped the drama routine and got up from the ground. Then as an afterthought, "Hey, what do you mean, I'm not funny?"

"Get to work, Ari," Lavi threw his work gloves at him.

"If I could grumble in Arabic, like Roni, I'd have some choice words for you, Lavi."

"Yeah, I'm trembling at the thought."

Ari turned his attention back to me. "You must have heard Roni speak Arabic, no?"

"Yes, I have," I said thoughtfully.

"A word of advice – when he starts rattling off in German – that's when you know to take cover." Ari turned serious. "Gives me the creeps. He even looks like a Nazi."

"Roni speaks German, too?" I asked.

Ari looked at me curiously. "Haven't you two had a lover's quarrel yet?"

"Uh…nooo. We haven't known each other quite that long. What does that have to do with anything?"

"Well, you know, it's just *his thing*. Roni has this way of letting off steam in…foreign languages."

"How many does he know?" I suddenly realized how little I really knew about Roni.

"You don't know?"

"Ari…enough talk – get to work." Lavi's tone had a surprising edge to it.

"Know what?" I pressed further.

"That Roni is fluent in five languages," Ari continued, oblivious to Lavi.

"Five?" I blurted out, taken aback by this new revelation.

"Sure," Ari answered. "That's one of the reasons the army wants him back. Not to mention the fact that he looks like a damn Aryan."

"You forgot the fact that he's *so strong and brave*," Lavi said impatiently. "You're an ass, Ari!"

"What? What did I say?"

"Which languages?" I asked, wondering why Roni hadn't mentioned this. Lavi looked at Ari, blowing out a blast of air and shaking his head in frustration as if the cat was let out of the bag. "Look, it's not a big deal," he finally said. "Aside from Hebrew, of course, he's fluent in English, French, German and Arabic." Lavi shrugged, trying to make light of it. "He has a natural talent for language – self-taught mostly."

"Self-taught?"

"Well, uh, yeah. Of course, it doesn't hurt that his mother is French and that his father is German," Lavi backtracked. "But, hey, don't be upset that he didn't tell you. You know Roni – he's a modest guy; that's the only reason we can stand having him around us," Lavi divulged with a wink.

"Am I the only one who's working out here?" Jenny called out. "Come on, guys, I can't do this entire field all by myself!"

"We're right behind you, Jenny," I responded, donning my work gloves, and with that, Roni's scholarly prowess was placed on the back burner.

We worked for nearly eight hours straight except for the short ten o'clock break where we munched on sandwiches that the kitchen staff brought out to us. During the course of the day, Ari helped me with some of the overgrown weeds in my line of the field – although there was a noticeable toning down on the usual teasing jabs. *Hmm…maybe he really was worried I would tell on him.*

It was nearing the end of the workday – almost two in the afternoon – and everyone was preparing to leave the field. I was stuck, however, with another one of those evil bush weeds. This one had thorns, and I could feel them piercing my hands through the thick work gloves. Leaving it for the next day was an option, but my stubbornness took over and I was determined to conquer this wicked weed. I kicked my heels against the ground, using my leg muscles as we were instructed to do, but the roots were intractable.

Ari once again came to my aid and grabbed onto a part of the bush lowest to the roots, tugging along with me, grunting and cursing under his breath. Lavi, Jenny and several others walked over to watch and with a mocking zest, cheered us on. "Ari, for God's sake, you're a Golani soldier and you can't pull out a little weed?" Lavi called out. A barrage of Arabic curses escaped from Ari's mouth, his face strained in concentrated effort. Foul language, I learned, is limited in Hebrew. I nixed the urge to laugh at Ari's frustration and continued to tug at the weed alongside of him, tensing my stomach muscles, holding my breath in until the obstinate roots finally relented. With the force of our combined effort, Ari and I soared back, his elbow knocking me in the jaw as we plummeted to the ground – the bush landing on top of me. My head banged against the earth and for a moment, I lay there stunned.

"Uh-oh, I think I broke her," Ari said, pushing the mammoth bush weed off me. "Sorry, Dara, are you okay? I didn't fracture your mouth, did I?" Putting his hand to my chin, he instructed me to open and close my mouth in an attempt to assess any damage.

"I think I'm okay, Ari – shaken but not broken."

He grabbed my hand and secured his arm around my waist, lifting me from the ground. All at once, two fists menacingly shot out and grabbed Ari's shirt collar, yanking him away from me.

"That's my woman you're pawing," the tone sounded threatening.

"Roni," I gasped. His stern facade quickly turned into one huge smile as he gave Ari a bear hug, and then jokingly tossed him out of the way. Roni then turned back to face me, but before he could approach any closer, Ari charged back, jumping him from behind, with one arm around Roni's neck and the other mock punching him in the shoulder. In one swift maneuver, Roni had Ari pinned to the ground, and then Lavi rushed over, slapped Roni on the back and gave him a huge bear hug as well. *For tough macho soldiers, they sure hug each other a lot.*

"Forget it guys, we're over," Roni said in jest. "I found a new interest." His eyes glistened in the afternoon sun as he stepped toward me. *Oh, how I missed those eyes.* My heart throbbed so hard I thought I'd explode. All I wanted was to jump into his arms and hold him tight, but I just stood there, immobile as if I had the wind knocked out of me. He drew nearer, grabbing me just above my waist and pulled me into him. His eyes fell to my lips, "God, I missed those lips," he murmured.

"Aw, come on, Roni," Lavi bellowed, "what does Dara have that I don't have?" Roni's mouth curved up into a half smile.

"She kisses better," he said in a soft tone, more to me than to Lavi, and he lowered his head, his lips capturing mine with a burst of longing as if it were our very first time. My arms wrapped around him, meeting his passion with my own.

"Well, at least we know her jaw isn't broken," Lavi thought aloud.

Ari cleared his throat. "Uh, guys, you do know the rest of us are still here, don't you?"

Roni grudgingly peeled his lips from mine and said in a low taunting tone, "Ari, if I were you, I'd keep a low profile. 'For God's sake, you're a Golani soldier and you can't pull out a little weed?'"

My mouth fell into a curious smile, and Ari resorted once again to the few select words he knew in Arabic. "Yeah," Roni shrugged to me with a rascally grin, "Yaniv and I were watching."

My eyes searched for Yaniv and found him several yards away standing with Jenny, looking very content. I turned back to Roni. "Why? What were you watching?" I asked, wondering why he was grinning.

"It was entertaining seeing you battle with that weed." He pursed his lips, finding it difficult to keep from laughing. "You know, you're quite cute when you flex your muscles," Roni added, his hands squeezing my biceps.

"I can hold my own. I'm a lot tougher than you give me credit for."

"Mmm, indeed. That poor little weed didn't stand a chance." He kissed me again, and after a drawn-out moment I reluctantly pulled away. "Roni, we need to go now."

"Hmm," he considered. "I suppose we can continue this elsewhere." He curled his arm around the back of my neck and walked with me toward the jeeps waiting to take us back to the main kibbutz.

"Hey, don't forget about the barbeque tonight!" Lavi called out from behind us.

"I'll fill you in," I whispered to Roni.

"A barbeque?" Roni muttered, raising one eyebrow. "Don't tell me...this was Lavi's brainstorm, right?"

"Uh-huh," I smiled up at him. "You don't like barbeques?" I asked innocently.

"Let me put it this way, Dara...I haven't seen you in over a month. I've been out in the field with a platoon of unwashed, reeking men fighting terrorists in Lebanon.... Fantasizing about hamburgers is not exactly what helped pass the time." He looked me up and down with his mischievous look.

"Roni, stop that...the others are coming," I said, suddenly feeling bashful.

"Okay...I'll behave." Then with a slight shrug, "For now."

The jeeps dropped us all off at the back of the dining hall and everyone went their separate ways for the remainder of the afternoon.

Roni walked with me up the path toward my room. "So, a barbeque, eh?"

I nodded.

"Hmm. I suppose a barbeque with friends is better than having dinner in the communal dining hall."

"It'll be fun, Roni," I said cheerfully. "It actually was meant as a *welcome back* for you and Yaniv."

"If you say so," he smiled. "Afterwards, though, my sweet Dara, I plan to be very selfish. I don't want to share you with anyone else – I missed you like crazy."

"Oh, Roni." I threw my arms around him and leaned my face against his chest. "Thank God you're alive."

"Whoa! Where did that come from? Why wouldn't I be alive?"

"You know why…," I lifted my face to his as the words spilled out. "Two weeks ago when there was fighting in Lebanon and one of our soldiers was killed – I was so frightened it was you. The newscasters couldn't immediately release the name since the army was unable to contact the family of the soldier right away. So we were all walking around for a time not knowing if you were dead or alive. It wasn't until four hours later, when you called the kibbutz office after returning to your base, that we knew you were all right."

"For four hours, you thought…it may have been me that was killed?"

I nodded.

"Dara…I'm so sorry."

I shook my head. "Roni, why are you apologizing? It wasn't your fault. You couldn't have known that they were withholding the name of the soldier for so long. Besides, you were out there, in the fighting and…" I paused, realizing, "you knew him…didn't you? You were there."

He creased his brows, suddenly looking very battle weary. "Yes," he said simply.

I stroked his cheek. "You look tired, Roni."

"I am," he took in a deep breath and blew out heavily as he wrapped his arms around me and tucked my head beneath his chin. "I'm going to get out of my uniform and try to catch a nap. What time is our barbeque?"

"We're all meeting behind the dining hall at six thirty and driving down to Sachna. It's less windy these days down in the valley."

"Would you come by my room around six?" He tightened his hold around me, and added with a smile, "You could be my personal alarm clock and…if I don't wake easily…well, just promise me that you *won't* be gentle."

I lifted my face and smiled back, "I'll see what I can do," and kissed him softly on the lips before turning to enter my room. He caught my hand and pulled me back, embracing me with an air of urgency. "I love you, Dara," he whispered, and then let go and walked away.

As planned, I went to Roni's room at six in the evening to wake him. His door was unlocked and I stepped inside. He was fast asleep, lying on his back, clad only in boxer shorts, with most of his blanket kicked to the floor. He looked so beautiful and peaceful sleeping there in his bed, as if he didn't have a care, his silky golden tresses cradling his face. Resembling very much a bronzed-skin California surfer, one would be hard-pressed to imagine that he walked around with the burden of the world on his shoulders.

I could have watched Roni like this for hours and I regretted the prospect of waking him. *I'll give him a few more minutes.*

I moved toward the wooden chair by his desk, and absentmindedly glanced up at the books on his shelves that lined the wall opposite his bed. I hadn't paid attention to them the first time I was in his room, but now I saw that I had reason to eye them with purpose. I inched toward the shelves to get a better look. Aside from the numerous Hebrew books, there was an assortment of books in English, German, French, as well as in Arabic. Some were instruction manuals, while the others looked like novels. Magazines represented in each of these languages crowded the shelves as well. Piled neatly on the floor to the side of his dresser was a stack of newspapers in the same languages.

I wondered how much more there was to Roni that I didn't know. He obviously didn't treat it as a secret…he just didn't volunteer much about himself. Still, fluency in five languages was exceedingly unusual, and my mind drifted, recalling little bits and pieces of conversation from Roni and Ari: *"My life here is unpredictable." "I'm just going to end up hurting you." "…they asked me to come back." "Sure, that's why the army wants him back." "…not to mention the fact that he looks like a damn Aryan." "I'm considering rejoining the army…they asked me to come back." "…they asked me to come back."*

The ramifications of my recall echoed in my head. I contemplated the type of army unit that would seek out a Nordic or Aryan-looking man fluent in multiple languages. I had heard of a unit where its soldiers would disappear on missions for untold lengths of time. So secret was this unit that it was not known to anyone on the outside by any name. Nor was it something anyone could choose to enlist to. They were chosen. There was evidently some information Roni hadn't told me – or, couldn't tell me. And maybe, I already knew, or at the very least, suspected.

"Not exactly what I had in mind when I asked you to come by and wake me." Startled by Roni's voice, the few books I had skimmed through dropped to the floor. He stood behind me, his hands curved around each of my arms. My head rose up and turned to the side to face him and my eyes widened with guilt, as though he had caught me plodding through a restricted area.

"I was just about to…I just wanted to give you a few more minutes to sleep," I offered a quick explanation. Roni looked thoughtfully up at his bookshelves and then back to me. Without a word, he let go of my arms, bent down to retrieve the fallen books and placed them back on the shelf. He then sauntered over to his desk and grabbed his pack of cigarettes. As he lit one, he sat down in the chair facing me, first twisting it around so that the back of it was against his chest, and his arms casually bent over the top wooden slat. I noticed he was already dressed. *How did I not hear him stir?* It was apparent that Roni had observed me in silence as I probed through his library.

He sat there drawing on his cigarette, looking at me with a poker face, and then shifted his eyes to something else, or more accurately, to nothing else. Though he could be adept at camouflaging his thoughts, the gravity of the moment intensified, with his reticence serving only to lend weight to my fears. I supposed he never expected me to register the meaning behind his array of foreign-language material. Yet, it didn't look like any disclosure or acknowledgment from him was forthcoming. *Wouldn't he trust me? Or, perhaps, there was something more to this picture that I wasn't getting.* His calm, silent facade had me on edge. I stepped past him toward the desk and reached for a cigarette from his pack. His eyes followed me and he raised one brow as I lit it, chuckling softly.

"Did I miss something?" I asked as casually as I could after blowing out a cloud of smoke.

"Dara," he squinted his eyes as if in a smile, but not quite, "you and cigarettes are…incongruous." I shrugged and took another drag, avoiding his stare. "Besides," he added in a tender tone, "it covers up the lilac scent you wear." He drew on his cigarette once more before putting it out, rose from his chair, and edged toward me, lifting my chin to face him. "Your eyes are gray," he said simply. I gathered it was his subtle way of letting me know that my suspicions did not escape him. His own crystalline eyes stared hard into mine as if willing me to see what he would not say. Where no words were voiced, volumes were spoken. A myriad of challenges confronted us.

I forced myself to look away, moved from him to put out the cigarette, and went to wash the smell from my hands in the bathroom. Then, with a sigh, I squeezed some toothpaste onto my finger and rinsed my teeth. Roni came up next to me and handed me a clean towel. "It's time to meet the others," he murmured, taking my hand in his and attempting a smile. He glanced fleetingly at his books on the way out.

We ran into Lavi in the common kitchen. "Hey, Roni, help me with this." He handed Roni two bottles of liquor to carry while he grabbed two more from the cabinet. "Dara, you and Mikki can be the two designated drivers on the way back." Lavi winked. "I have very serious plans to get sloshed tonight."

"Okay, but just keep your face out the window."

"You know this stuff is like drinking rusted metal," Roni sneered.

"Yeah, well, the grocery store was all out of single malt scotch," Lavi quipped. "At least I was able to get us two jeeps. No piling into a pickup truck tonight!"

"How did you manage that?" Roni asked suspiciously. "Moti reserves them for use out in the fields and for guard duty."

Lavi grinned, "He finally caved in when I told him you would give them each a full tune-up in the morning."

Roni shot a disapproving look at Lavi.

"Hey, what could I do? He treats those damn cars like his babies."

"Actually, better," Roni said thoughtfully.

❈

Each grabbing an arm, Yaniv and Roni hoisted Lavi from the jeep and carried him to his room. "You would think he might have made it at least past ten," Yaniv chuckled as he and Roni dropped Lavi onto his bed.

"Yes, you would think," Roni agreed as he threw off Lavi's shoes.

"While you're tucking him in, I'm going to walk Jenny to her room. She's waiting for me outside. See you in the morning," Yaniv patted Roni on the back.

"No problem, I got it covered here," Roni answered.

"Mikki!" Lavi cried out. "Where's Mikki?"

"She said she'll see you at breakfast. Just sleep it off, Lavi." Roni turned to leave.

"Hey, Roni," Lavi called out again. "What's your rush? Let'sav anudder one for de road," he slurred, his eyes half closed.

"Don't take this the wrong way, Lavi, but I prefer to get back to Dara – she smells better."

"Hey, Roni," Lavi called out once more.

"What?" Roni looked back over his shoulder.

"You got to tell'er."

"What are you talking about?"

"Dara...," the rest was muffled.

"What the hell did you tell her?" Roni asked, aware that there was more to his friend's mumbling.

"*Gute Nacht mein freund*," Lavi mumbled before slipping into a drunken sleep.

"Good night, Lavi," Roni answered, hitting the light switch as he walked out.

⚘

When Roni came through the door, I was on his bed, propped up on my elbows, glancing through one of his French magazines. "Well, that didn't take long," I looked up. There was something that I wanted to tell him all night long, but chose to wait until we were alone. Not sure how to broach the subject, I instead asked, "How is Lavi doing?"

"He'll live." He then glimpsed at what I was reading. "Into French, are we?"

"No, but some of the pictures here are quite interesting." The page was open to an advertisement showing a male model with a scantily clad woman in a more than evocative pose.

He smirked, "Maybe so…but they lack the mystique."

"Mystique?"

"The magic. There's no air of mystery. Little is left to the imagination. It takes all the fun out of the pursuit," he winked.

"Well, if it's the pursuit you crave, then, perhaps I should play hard to get?"

Roni's eyes crinkled with his wide smile. "I think it's a little too late for that. The lion has found his prey." He sat down beside me and toyed with my hair, knowing all too well how it made me feel.

"I could always escape, you know."

"Not from my lair, my sweet, delicate flower," he leaned down to kiss the back of my neck. "Besides," his lips brushed against my ear, "I've had five long weeks without you, and…" he didn't finish his sentence.

"And what?" I asked.

"And…I'm in the mood for some music." He got up and casually walked over to his stereo system. "Do you like the Moody Blues?" he asked, as he slipped in a cassette.

"I love them." I bounced off the bed to check out his music with him. "Which of their cassettes do you have?"

"Just two, *Seventh Sojourn* and *Long Distance Voyager* – there's one particular song that makes me think of you. He pressed a button and it started to play softly.

> *My boat sails stormy seas,*
> *Battles oceans filled with tears.*
> *At last my port's in view*
> *Now that I've discovered you.*

"'For My Lady,'" I said under my breath, immediately recognizing the song. "It's one of my favorites."

His lips arched seductively. "Let's get the right ambience then, shall we?" He went to switch off the light and, similar to that one time five long weeks ago, the moon shone through the window – this time full – its soft, luminous glow casting a silvery hue, my eyes drawn to it. "I love the moonlight," I said wistfully. "Don't you?"

"You sound almost sad," Roni remarked as he moved toward me.

"Not at all," I said, turning to Roni. "I just like to take a step back every now and again and appreciate beauty."

"I know what you mean," he said in a mellow voice, taking me in with his eyes. "I would have preferred not sharing you with anyone else tonight. My friends are great, but...," he trailed off, drawing nearer, caressing my waist beneath my sweater. At that moment, the light of the moon danced off the blue brilliance of Roni's eyes, making them nothing less than spellbinding.

"Well," I said, taking a breath, "we did need to eat dinner."

"Yes, but it wasn't exactly what I had in mind for this evening's menu."

The chorus began to play in the background, and in a voice that was as a whisper carried on a breeze, Roni recited the lyrics together with the music. *I'd give my life so lightly*, and with that he kissed my hair; *For my gentle lady*, he then kissed my cheek; *Give it freely*, his lips drifted just below my ear; *and completely*, sliding, unhurried down the side of my face; *To my lady*, finishing with a tender brush of his tongue to my lips. "Mmm. Delicious," he moaned, gliding his tongue beneath my chin. My heartbeat went wild.

"Roni?" I managed to find my voice.

"Yes?" His lips traced the curve of my neck.

"I need you...to know something." My voice quivered as my ability to speak now was highly compromised.

"Tell me...I'm listening," he murmured, and slowly, his tongue once more circled the contour of my lips, and I forgot what I wanted to say. *This is going to be challenging.* I was heady taking in his scent, while his lips glided up the side of my jaw and then back down again to meet mine in a faint touch. "Well...it's something I wanted to tell you all night, but," I paused, needing to take in some air, "I wanted to wait till we'd be alone."

"We're alone now," he whispered with a light release of his warm breath into my opened lips. He gripped me tighter around my waist and I could feel the heat of his body through his clothes.

"Um...Roni...you're making it very hard for me to speak."

"Am I?" One corner of his mouth turned up in a sly smile as he lifted my arms, resting them on his shoulders, and nimbly tossed off my sweater in one quick, smooth swoop, leaving me...amazed, not to mention impressed. "I'm so very sorry," his eyes twinkled deviously at my surprise. Before I could catch my breath, Roni edged a few steps back, toward his bed; he sat down taking me onto his lap, and nibbled amorously, bit by bit, down the length of my neck.

"Roni," I attempted once more, though barely audible.

"Mmm. Did you say something?" his tongue now finding its way from my shoulder along my collarbone.

"I...I understand...what you have to do," I somehow managed to get the words out.

"I was counting on that." His lips continued to float down my skin.

"...and I want you to know how I feel."

"Trust me, Dara, that's exactly what I'm working on." His breath brushed against my décolleté as his hands glided up my back, caressing my skin. I moistened my lips with my tongue and swallowed hard, straining to continue. "Look...I know that you can't talk about it."

"Mmm, words are superfluous at times, don't you think?" He lifted his lips back to mine, teasing again with a feathery touch, and then slipping down my neck to my shoulder. In an unexpected move, he bit down with force, squeezing me harder into him. I heard myself moan as I trembled in his firm hold. He was driving me mad. But I needed him to know.

I lifted his face in my hands and looked into his eyes, as the words I wanted him to hear finally streamed out in shallow gusts of air. "Roni, I need to tell you…I'll stand by you, no matter what…I'll wait for you, no matter how long…. You don't have to worry about hurting me or losing me because…I believe in you, and in what you need to do. Your life is my life, Roni…your mission…is my mission."

Roni's expression was all at once serious. He lowered my hands from his face and looked down at them as he held them in his. It was a very long moment before he spoke. "Dara," he raised his head and narrowed his eyes, "do you understand what you're saying?" His tone was muted and cautious.

"I understand more than you realize."

He stroked my cheek with the back of his fingers, and then it was as if a shadow fell over him – he looked conflicted about something, almost pained.

"Roni?"

"Shhh," he touched his finger to my lips, skimming my face with his eyes. "My *motek*," his voice was low and husky as he gently weaved his fingers in my hair, "I cannot fathom how I ever lived before you came into my life." He swallowed hard, his face tensing, and his eyes were on fire. He drew my face in closer to his, and his lips ghosted to mine, kissing me, at first gently, as in a tender caress, and then more deeply, building in its fierceness. He let go of my hair, gripping my shoulders with force as he glided down my neck and kissed the softness of my chest. Everything about him – his skin, his breath, his coconut-scented hair – saturated my senses, and an electrifying hot sensation jetted through my entire body. I sank into him as his hands floated sinuously down my back to my waist.

"Mmm. Your skin is like velvet," he moaned in a sultry tenor that entirely did me in. In a sudden move, he took hold of my arms, firmly grasping them as he curved me around him, sliding me off his lap to cast me on my back, my head falling against his pillow. His lips arched to one side in a devilish smile as he leaned over me.

"Now," his voice hard and determined, "time for dessert."

I reached up, entwining my fingers in his mane of curls and pulled him down to me.

Chapter 8

There was one public telephone booth located near the post office boxes, just outside the kibbutz office. Privacy was nonexistent unless one made a phone call in the wee hours of the night. More often than not, it was crowded before dinner so I opted to try my luck upon returning from the fields. A seven-hour time difference existed between Israel and the United States, and at two thirty in the afternoon, it would mean that I would reach my mother shortly before she would leave for work.

As soon as I returned to the top of the mountain, I raced to the office and found several people retrieving their mail, but incredibly, the phone was free. My hands shook as I dug the coins out of the pocket of my jeans, and I felt my heart beat hard against my chest as I reached for the receiver. It dawned on me that I was not even sure what I was going to say. *Why didn't I rehearse?* This was going to be a long and torturous conversation. It would also have to be a collect call, I realized.

I waited for the generic-voiced operator to go through the customary script. "I have an international collect call from Israel for Lillian Harow from Dara. Will you accept the charges?"

"Yes. Of course," the voice on the other end responded.

"Hi, Mom."

"Dara, why are you calling?"

Nice to hear your voice, too. "I needed to talk to you about something important. But first of all, how are you and Dad?"

"We're fine, Dara. Please, what is this all about?"

Okay, Dara, you can do this – just sound resolved. "Mom, I understand that you and Dad have your own set of priorities, and I've always respected them. But I need you both to consider that I have my own priorities as well."

"Dara, would you just get to the point?"

"My life is here…in Israel, not in the United States. I've decided that I want to transfer out of Columbia after one year to a university in Israel."

The silence from the other end was suffocating. After several nerve-wracking moments, my mother started, "Dara, you're talking nonsense. Someone on that kibbutz filled your head with silly ideas. You're not even there for a full four months, and already you're changing your worldview. I warned you about this before you left. You will finish your education in the United States at Columbia University. End of discussion."

"Please, Mom, don't just discount what I say as a silly idea. Try to see it from my perspective. It's what I want. It's how I've *always* felt… you know that. I've never shared your worldview. My convictions are anything but new – I don't belong in the United States."

"You're only eighteen, Dara! How could you know where you belong? Wait just a second…it's that Roni person we met at the hospital, isn't it? Oh, my God, Dara! I thought you were smarter than that. Are you actually falling for his lines? He's a soldier! Don't you know how Israeli soldiers take advantage of naive female American tourists?"

"It's not like that, Mom."

"Of course it is." I heard the laughter in her tone and felt my confidence ebb.

"And...I'm not a tourist," I went on the defense. "I'm here as a volunteer on a national service visa."

If it was at all possible, I would have heard her impatience rumbling beneath her breath. "Dara, I will not stand by and let you ruin your life, *or ours*. As for where you belong, you belong with your family. You will get the best education at an Ivy League university. Doors will be open to you with a degree from Columbia. This is what your father and I worked for all our lives. And now, you want to abandon us?"

"But Mom..."

"We had an agreement, Dara. Or does your word to your parents mean nothing to you? Have you even considered what your actions would mean to your father's career? This will ruin him. How can you be so selfish? How can you even think of betraying us like this?"

Great. Lay on the guilt. "I know I gave you my word. But you can't hold Dad's career over my head. That's not fair. Besides, your fears about that are merely conjecture. And as for the agreement, well...life isn't always so black and white. Things change, circumstances change..."

My mother would not allow me to finish. "I've heard enough! Your father and I will not stand for it. We will cut you off without a penny. I promise you, Dara, it is not just an idle threat."

"What? Y-you would do that?"

"Trust me, daughter of mine – you don't want to test me. The only reason we agreed to let you volunteer on a kibbutz for one year was so that you can finally get those absurd Israel dreams out of your system. You let Pops' stories influence you beyond all logic. Just remember though, in the end, Pops returned to the States."

"And he's regretted it ever since," I quickly responded. "Mom, this is important to m –"

"I have to go to work, Dara. I don't have time for this now. You will do what we expect of you. By the time the year is over, you will be thinking more clearly – you'll see. Do not disappoint us. Good-bye now and…stay away from that Roni. You may consider this a final warning."

"Mom, wait. Please don't hang…up." I stood there, not moving, staring at the receiver in my hand with the dial tone humming.

"Are you finished with your call?" I heard someone ask impatiently. I looked up and saw that it was Orli, the feared mistress of the kitchen. I hung up the phone and walked away as she muttered "Americans" under her breath, shaking her head at me.

I headed toward my room to shower, but stopped first to sit at *my* foxhole to think, allowing the time to flow by. I watched the sun drop in the sky, casting shadows on the valley below, signaling the onset of twilight – my favorite time of day. For me, it usually generated an overall feeling of peacefulness – a calmness that blanketed the world with the setting of the sun. But today it was different. A dagger-sharp dread pierced my insides. I felt trapped.

There was no talking to my mother. Not about this – not about anything, for that matter. We never had a close mother-daughter relationship. She had always been too self-absorbed with her art career, her networking and her social climbing. We resided in the same house, but we lived in two separate worlds. I didn't know what possessed me to think that I could reason with her now. Nor was there any point in speaking to my father, as they were in total agreement about this. Neither was there any purpose in telling my mother about my relationship with Roni. It was beyond her comprehension. I never really felt my parents had a marriage – more like a polite arrangement. If not for Pops, I would have known no warmth in my life. He taught me about passion, about following one's dreams, about living a life without regret. He helped me discover my soul. *Oh, I wish he were here for me to speak with.* I missed him dearly.

But Pops had not been himself for quite a while now. He had become very ill – heart problems, in addition to his progressing dementia. My mother wanted to place him in a nursing home, which horrified me. I knew she resented my attachment to him. I pleaded with my father not to let that happen. Thankfully, my father agreed that he remain with us at home and arranged for a full-time health aide to care for him.

I hadn't told Roni that I planned to call home, which was good since now I didn't have to immediately tell him how my mother *welcomed* my new plans. There had to be a way for me to work this out. I couldn't allow myself to be imprisoned. My life was in Israel, and with Roni. But I felt guilty about disappointing my parents, not to mention, abandoning them. As a child, I always sensed that, at least on an emotional level, they needed me more than I needed them. Often, I felt sorry for them. From a young age, I recognized that my small family was dysfunctional – *emotionally handicapped.* In spite of everything, however, they were the only family I had, and I didn't want to lose them.

I wondered if perhaps there was something wrong with me – something that prevented me from cutting the cord – something that goaded me into blindly accepting the plans they mapped out for me. I was sure a psychoanalyst would have a field day with me. Nevertheless, from a practical standpoint, with no serious money of my own, I had no viable recourse. Pops once told me he set up a trust fund for me, but it was under the custodianship of my parents until I would reach the age of twenty-one. I was at a loss as to what to do.

"Hey, Dara," Jenny called out from the window of our room. "Why don't you come down from that mound? I think I might have left you some hot water for your shower."

"Thanks, Jen," I smiled faintly. "I'll be right there." I took in a deep breath and blew out wearily. A hot shower sounded very good.

꙰

With Ari and Adina's wedding just two weeks away, dinner conversation this evening centered on the institution of marriage, and the guys were as animated as usual. I was grateful for the distraction from my own angst, finding the group's rowdiness entertaining. Doron and Lavi were true to form in their boisterous ribbing of Ari.

"Just you wait," Ari warned. "I may be the first among us to bite the dust, but you're all not far behind," he avowed, winking pointedly at Roni, who was sitting across from him. All at once, everyone's eyes darted to Roni and me, and I noticed that Roni shot Ari a look that could kill.

"What? What did I say?" Ari asked innocently. "I was just razzing you over taking Dara to meet your family…this…Shabbat…" Ari broke off when he saw my confusion and Roni's face garnering more steam. "Uhh, I gather you didn't tell her yet?"

"*Sie sind eine klassische Moron,*" Roni fumed under his breath. Although said in a hushed undertone, the German caught me by surprise. When I glanced at Roni's face, it was like seeing a different person altogether. He suddenly looked so…*Aryan*, and so out of place in this kibbutz setting.

"Oooh, things might start to get ugly," Lavi alerted the table only half in jest.

"What did he say anyway?" Doron asked.

"It's my guess he's intimating that Ari's mental acumen is well below par," Yaniv offered.

"Hey, Roni, how was I to know that you didn't tell her? I mean, what were you waiting for anyway?" Ari squealed in his own defense. Roni continued to stare at Ari in disbelief.

"Ari, I'm going to take a long shot here and recommend you not say anything more on the matter," Yaniv advised good-naturedly.

"But…"

Adina interrupted him, "Ari…shhh."

"Uhh, just out of curiosity," Lavi said, facing Roni, "you know Ari has a big mouth. Why would you tell him your business?"

"I didn't," he answered tersely.

"I guess I sort of overheard him talking to his mother on the phone when I picked up my mail," Ari explained sheepishly. "Look, Roni, Dara, I'm really sorry."

"Forget it. You can't help being an idiot," Roni sneered.

Roni turned to me and apologized. "I'm sorry, Dara; I meant to discuss this with you after dinner," he shot another glaring look at Ari, "*privately*," he accentuated. He shook his head in frustration. Jenny and the other girls gave me a sympathetic look, and I just sat there stunned and wide-eyed, and even a tinge embarrassed. I was almost relieved when Lavi interjected, "*Nu*, so you're going to meet your boyfriend's *maman*," he used the French pronunciation for mother. "What in God's name will you wear?"

As if I didn't have enough to worry about.

✹

Later that evening, Roni and I strolled to the playground located behind the kibbutz synagogue. Hours after sundown, the place was empty, as children had long been tucked away in bed. A sharp chill was in the air and we cuddled together on one of the park benches, with the glow of a nearby lamppost washing the area in a soft yellow light.

"Dara, you've hardly said a word since dinner. I can't imagine that the news Ari spilled would be that upsetting to you."

"Of course not. I'm thrilled that you want me to meet your family. I suppose it's just a lot for me to process right now."

"That's a curious statement. What do you mean by 'a lot to process *right now*'?"

"Well, I...I don't know what I mean," I said, frustrated with myself for sounding confused. Roni placed his fingers beneath my chin, lifting my face to look into my eyes. "Just as I thought," he smiled. "You know your eyes always give you away, Dara, so why not just tell me what's wrong. Whatever it is, I'll understand – I promise."

"Nothing is wrong, Roni. Really." I tried to shake the dread from my voice but I knew he could tell I was hiding something. When it came to the age-old adage that eyes are the mirror to one's soul, mine were the classic example. Still, I just wasn't ready to talk about the conversation I had with my mother earlier today. Roni wanting me to meet his family was supposed to be a happy moment in my life, and I didn't want anything to taint it.

He considered my evasive response for a moment and then started, "Look, Dara, I have a very close-knit family, and with you being the most important thing in my life, it's only natural for me to share that with them. I want them to meet you – to meet the woman who has managed to wipe the scowl off my face." His eyes sparkled with enthusiasm. "I want them to love you as I love you. And...you don't have to be nervous, if that's what's troubling you. My parents are great – very easygoing. I know they'll love you. How could they not? On the other hand," he added introspectively, "my sister, Dalya, has been known to frighten off many a visitor." He bared his brilliant smile.

"Roni, I'm not nervous about meeting your parents or the rest of your family. I'm actually looking forward to it. But," I said, trying to lead him off track, "won't they mind that I'm American? I mean, wouldn't they have preferred that you be with someone born in Israel?"

Roni chuckled. "My home is like the UN as it is; we're like a poster family for the ingathering of the exiles. What's one more nationality? Now, what's *really* worrying you?"

"Nothing," I lied, leaning my head against him to avoid him looking at my eyes.

He didn't pursue it.

After a few moments, "Roni?"

"Yes?"

"Promise me one thing."

"Anything."

"If you should ever get angry with me, please get angry with me in Hebrew. German is so…well…you know, German. Very creepy," I shuddered.

Laughing heartily now, Roni said, "I guess I picked up that habit from my father. I only do it to Ari though, because I know it especially makes his skin crawl. His parents' family was wiped out in the Holocaust – he hates anything that's German."

"I thought he was a good friend of yours."

"He is," Roni shrugged with an impish grin. "I like to see him squirm. It's funny."

"You are so evil," I giggled.

"Oh, just every now and then – I find it's good for the soul," he said with a wicked smile. "Anyway, Dara, I could never get angry with you. You're my life. I'm sure we'll have our share of disagreements, but anger isn't part of the equation."

"That sounds fine to me," I murmured, content to continue snuggling in his arms.

"Mmm," Roni tightened his arms around me. "*Je t'aime*, Dara. *Vous êtes l'amour de ma vie*," he said softly and kissed me tenderly over and over. *Wow. What was it about French? Or was it just the way the words flowed with effortless beauty from Roni?* Even so, it was a struggle to keep my mother's stern voice out of my head. Instead of enjoying what should have been a romantic moment, I clung to Roni, trying to shut out her words that echoed in my mind. *How was I going to tell him? What was I going to do?* I wanted nothing more than to commit to Roni. I made him a promise the other night – one that I meant with all my heart – and now…I felt as if I were being ripped in two. *God, what was I going to do?*

He studied my face, crinkling his brows. "What's worrying you, *motek*?"

"Roni, really…nothing is worrying me." He narrowed his eyes knowingly. "Like I once told you, Dara…never play poker." And he let the matter drop…for now.

⚜

Roni's family lived in Migdal, a community in the northern part of Israel, which hugs the shores of the Kinneret. Just north of Tiberias, the drive up to Migdal was not too far from Gilboa, but it encompassed beautiful and contrasting scenery – mountains and valleys, fertile plateaus and stark cliffs.

The modern community of Migdal was established in 1910, whereas the ancient city of Migdal was one of the fortified cities under siege by Vespasian, the Roman commander against the Jewish revolt in 67 CE. I loved how our history filled every crevice of this land. Roni from time to time pointed out prominent spots as we drove along, and in my excitement, I told him everything I knew about the sites. Amused, he said I was like a kid in a candy store when it came to exploring our country.

Upon entering the community, we drove through charming streets lined with sycamore trees and red-roofed stucco homes, set against a backdrop of magnificent green hills. The house that Roni's parents lived in was the last one in a cul-de-sac surrounded by aged olive trees that had sturdy trunks and thick, twisted branches. The scent of eucalyptus hung heavily in the air. Once Roni parked the car, he leaned over to grab a *kippah* out of the dashboard glove compartment and clipped it to his hair. I looked at him questioningly. He simply shrugged in his characteristic boyish style, "It's out of respect for my parents."

I didn't think he could have me fall in love with him any more than I already had. I was wrong. "What?" he asked in response to what must have been a strange admiring look on my face.

"I love you, that's what."

"Good, hold on to that thought," he grinned.

Then, turning his attention to the house in front of us, "Well this is it. You're not nervous, are you?" Roni asked as we got out of the car.

"Should I be?" I posed as we walked up the path to his parents' house. He considered that question for a moment, his face exploding into a radiant smile.

"Roni?" I supposed I started to look apprehensive, which just made him laugh.

Before I could give it further thought, three adorable, cherubic children, one girl and two boys, rushed headlong out the front door, jumping on Roni, cheering exuberantly that Uncle Roni was home. He fell to the ground, pretending they overpowered him, and the giggles that ensued were positively manic. The girl, about three years old I estimated, had inquisitive, round, hazel eyes and raven black hair that fell to her shoulders in lustrous curls, and the two boys, twins, not too much older, looked as though they could have been Roni's sons, each with stunning, light-blue eyes and a full head of golden curls. They were incredibly lovable; it was difficult to tear my eyes away from them.

"Hey kids, don't you want to know who this beautiful lady is?" Roni's face pointed in my direction. All the children nodded shyly, and Roni carefully lifted each one off him, got up on one knee and said, "Yoni, Yair and Yardena, I want you to meet Dara," and then he whispered something in their ears, to which the boys giggled some more and Yardena shrugged her shoulder, jutting out her lower lip in a frown.

"Don't worry, Yardena," Roni comforted her, giving her a small peck on the cheek. "You'll always be my favorite." Her face beamed at that and her attention then turned to the front door of the house. She and her brothers ran toward an attractive woman, petite in stature, as she gracefully stepped out to the front path. She had the same raven-black hair as Yardena and the light-blue eyes of the twin boys. Although the coloring was all off, she shared a striking resemblance to Roni. While her features were softer, there was an edge to her appearance, and I thought I detected a sadness in her eyes.

"Well, it's about time you decided to come home and visit. It's been months!"

"Ahh, Dara, meet my annoying, opinionated, nagging older sister, Dalya." Roni grinned.

"Shalom, Dalya. I'm very glad to meet you, and Roni actually speaks very highly of you." I shot a teasing look at Roni.

"I'm glad to meet you, too, Dara. And yes, I know," she flashed a warm smile while giving Roni a squeeze around his waist. "Despite everything, my little brother adores me." It was comical to hear her refer to Roni as her "little brother" when he towered over her. "Please come in," she offered. "Our parents are dying to meet you."

In that instant, the front door burst open to the outside, and a loud voice roared, "Roni, you bum, where the hell have you been?" A very tall, burly and rugged version of Roni stormed out the front of the house and was about to rush Roni when he noticed me and stopped in his tracks. "*Ooowah!* Don't tell me you're Dara," he said as he openly appraised me up and down.

I guess it runs in the family.

"Hey, knock that off, Gilad," Roni said, shoving him lightly. "Where were you raised…in a barn?"

Smiling broadly, Gilad turned to me, and with a familiar-looking twinkle in his blue eyes, he said, "My baby brother is right. Please accept my apologies, Dara."

"Well, now I know where *he* gets it from," I said.

"Aha, so you *did* learn some of my sophisticated moves after all!" He jokingly shoved Roni back. That naturally followed with each giving the other a huge bear hug. I wouldn't have expected anything less.

"Roni! You're home! Come out, Shimshon, Roni is home!" A bubbly, older woman floated down the short path toward us. She had olive-toned skin adorning her prominent Mediterranean-looking features, crowned with shoulder-length, shining, wavy, black hair. She was almost regal in the delicate way she moved. I imagined she must have been a ballet dancer in her youth. Roni enveloped her in a bear hug, though in a gentler manner.

"Imma," he said with a huge smile, "this is Dara. Dara, this is my mother, Evaleen."

"So, you're the special lady who put the smile back in my son's eyes," she said in a Hebrew that had a French twang to it. "I love you already." Her hazel eyes glistened in the afternoon sun, and she gave me a kiss on each of my cheeks, followed by a warm hug. "Come Shimshon, *je vous en prie*, come meet Roni's Dara."

"Why is everyone congregating in the street? What do you think a home is for?" Roni's father called out in a commanding tone from the front door. Everyone bustled into the house all at once. Shimshon, Roni's father, stood at the door in a stately manner. Though his golden hair had grayed with age, his eyes were still a striking blue. He was terribly handsome and dignified in appearance. He seemed a little out of place in the overexcited tumult of his family.

"Abba," Roni hugged his father, and then turned to me. "This is Dara."

"Hmm. I can tell already, she's too good for you." Then directing his words to me, "Is he treating you nicely? Because, you know, if he doesn't, you come to me...and I will immediately set him straight."

"He's been a perfect gentleman," I smiled.

"Ha! We always are...in the beginning," Gilad blurted out. Roni elbowed him, shaking his head and rolling his eyes.

"Say, where's Margalit?" Roni asked cuttingly. "She finally got wise and left you?" Sure enough, that statement escalated into an all-out wrestling match, yet, somehow Evaleen's delicate body managed to get between the two of them and break it up.

"Boys, be useful and get some drinks out for everyone. Dara, first something to eat and drink, yes? And then, Dalya, be a dear and show Dara to her room. Dara, do you bake? I'm sure you bake. Who doesn't bake? You can help me make some last-minute sweets for Shabbat. But please first get comfortable and then I'd love you to join me in the kitchen so we can have our girl talk, yes? Margalit is Gilad's wife, by the way. She's out picking up some spices at the market for me. Everyone is staying over for Shabbat, and in all the excitement, I ran out of cinnamon! And Roni loves cinnamon on his croissants."

"Imma, take a breath," Dalya laughed. "I think Dara is in shock."

I imagined that's what it must have looked like to everyone as I stood there in a trancelike awe, basking in every wonderful moment of this glorious and enchanting family. *What a comical scene*, I thought – but so full of love, warmth and good-hearted humor that continued through the Shabbat evening meal. Everything I never had growing up in my home. The emptiness I was raised on, save for the love of my grandfather, suddenly felt profoundly severe. I immediately fell in love with each colorful character that made up the Ben-Ari clan.

On Shabbat morning, I walked to the neighborhood synagogue with Evaleen and Margalit. The men had gone earlier and Dalya stayed back with her children. After the prayer services, when everyone piled out and congregated on the front lawn, Evaleen made sure to introduce me as Roni's girlfriend to all her friends. It was a little overwhelming for me, but it was flattering to have Roni's mother show me off so proudly.

I couldn't recall a time when my own mother showered me with such affection – with any affection, for that matter. Evaleen was an enigma to me, and being with her was a surreal experience. It was impossible not to adore her.

As we waited for Roni, Gilad and Shimshon to exit the synagogue, Evaleen said softly yet pointedly to me, "You know, Dara, this is the first Shabbat that Roni went to synagogue since the Lebanon War." She squeezed my hand and I noticed that she had tears in her eyes. I had an urge to hug this loving and lovable woman.

Before long, Shimshon met us on the front lawn with Roni and Gilad at his side. "Evaleen," he approached her and stroked her cheek with the back of his fingers, *reminding me of Roni*, "you cry too much."

"These are happy tears, Shimshon. How often do we get to have our two sons home for Shabbat?"

He smiled and put his arm around her. "Not often enough."

Shabbat lunch at the Ben-Ari home proved to be as animated as I expected. What made it both noteworthy and altogether wild was Gilad's surprise announcement that Margalit was expecting a baby. All at once, everyone around the dining room table roared with merriment at the great news. Evaleen could hardly contain herself as she bubbled over with excitement. Shimshon brought out the good liquor. Dalya was already giving parenting tips to Margalit. Roni was slapping Gilad on the back and Gilad reciprocated in kind – inevitably leading to another *playful* wrestling match, which Evaleen broke apart. Yoni, Yair and Yardena contributed to the hubbub – jumping and cheering about having a new playmate, and of course, Ben-Ari bear hugs to go all around. It was loud, it was rowdy and it was wonderful. Eventually things did quiet down as everyone settled into the rich rituals of the Shabbat meal, culminating with songs of praise and blessings to God.

I noticed that Roni didn't partake in the singing, but rather sat quietly and respectfully, pretending to glance through the pages of a prayer book so as not to bring any attention to himself. He did not make his conflict with God blatant, and would never disrespect his parents' home with any display of contempt – it was a private matter.

After everyone helped clear the table and clean up, the day progressed into a peaceful Shabbat afternoon. "Come, Dara," Roni took my hand, "let's go outside." The weather was pleasant even though the winter season was upon us. There was a slight chill in the air, though tamed by the sun; it had an invigorating, crisp feel to it rather than cold.

"So…how are you at climbing trees?" Roni led me to the huge oak tree that overshadowed the front lawn of the Ben-Ari home; its leaves stubbornly clinging to the branches still bore the autumn shades of red, orange and yellow.

"Actually, I'm quite good at it," the tone in my voice challenged him to dare me.

"In that case, ladies first."

Only then realizing the drawback of my attire, I expressed my reluctance, "But I'm wearing a skirt." Roni pursed his lips, his eyes gleaming in the sun, "I know."

"You are impossible," I pretended to admonish him.

"Mmm. It's part of my charm. Now don't try to get out of this… climb, woman."

"Well, okay…but only if you promise to behave. I mean, most of your family is sitting in the living room, and they can see right through the window."

"Sorry, Dara, but I don't make promises I don't intend to keep. As for my family," he considered, "…they'd probably cheer me on." I thought about that for a moment and realized that he'd be right. Rather than bow out, I decided to climb the tree. Besides, it was as if the branches of this magnificent old oak were reaching out to me. It had been a while since my tomboy days and I suddenly felt a craving for it.

Grabbing a solid foothold, I hoisted myself up and darted up the web of branches with Roni right behind me. At one point, a large gap presented itself between the branches, but I grabbed a hold and stubbornly pulled myself up to the higher limb. "Hey, monkey," Roni called out from behind me, "not that I'm not enjoying the view from here, but are you planning to stop anytime soon?"

"What's the matter, soldier boy?" I called from over my shoulder. "Too high for you?"

"Actually, I was thinking that it may be too high for *you*."

With a slight turn of my head, I glanced back at Roni on the branch below me, and gasped as my eyes gazed further downward. I hadn't realized how tall this tree was and how far up I had climbed. I froze, forgetting how to climb back down.

"It's okay, Dara. Just don't look down. I got your…uh…back."

"Um, this is no time to joke…I'm kind of panicking right now."

"Trust me; I take your backside very seriously. Just hug the tree Dara; crouch down a bit and…"

"I don't think I can do this."

"Sure you can. Don't worry – I'm right behind you, I won't let you fall…" Short of calling a rescue squad, I had no other choice but to follow Roni's instructions. "…that's it," he continued in a soothing voice, "just drop one leg from the branch that you're on toward me – I got you. Now, ease your other leg off the branch, and glide down." I did what Roni suggested, and he wrapped one arm around my legs and let me slide down into him. His arm moved to my waist in a tight hold until I could get a foothold on his branch. "Okay, Dara," he whispered into my hair, "we're good. You just move with me now."

When we reached the last tree limb before the short jump down to the ground, he stopped and twisted me around to face him. "Are you okay?" *There was too much amusement in his eyes*, I thought.

I nodded…a little embarrassed.

"Ha ha, God I love you!" He pulled me in tight and kissed me.

I drew slightly away, "You're never going to let me live this down, are you?"

He chuckled, "My sweet, delicate Dara...always trying to prove how tough you are...just like that first day in the cotton fields." He jumped down from the tree and I followed straight into his outstretched arms. "By the way, the lace underwear – nice touch." He leaned his head down to kiss me.

"No, Roni," I inched back, "someone from your family might see."

"I have a feeling they suspect we kiss."

"Yes, but..."

"But what?" He seemed entertained by my sudden shyness.

"Well, I would just feel more comfortable if we were more discreet here."

"Mmm. Then you should have thought twice before you put on the lace."

"You weren't supposed to see that."

"But I did. So it's too late – the damage has been done." Before I could raise any further objections, his lips hungrily found mine – it was impossible not to melt when he held me close. Thoroughly immersed in each other, it was all the more surprising that we heard several determined knocks from the window facing the front lawn. Our lips parted as we turned our heads toward the distraction. It was Gilad, his face plastered against the living room window with a broad smile, giving Roni the thumbs up sign. Mortified, I hid my face in Roni's chest. "If anyone can kill the mood, it's my brother," Roni huffed. Lifting my head from his chest, he smiled, "You don't have to be embarrassed, Dara. If Gilad wasn't such an oversized bear, I might have a chance at teaching him a lesson or two. C'mon...let's go inside."

"How purple am I?"

"Hmm," Roni studied my face. "As purple as the Gilboa Iris, yet far more beautiful."

✿

In the later hours of the afternoon, I sat in the kitchen with Evaleen, Dalya and Margalit, drinking tea and munching on croissants while combing through photograph albums of the family. Roni strolled in to steal a croissant and munched contentedly while looking over our shoulders. "Imma, I hope you're not giving away all the family secrets. I don't want to scare Dara off."

"Oh, shoo, we're having some girl talk here," Evaleen waved him away. He was quick to grab another croissant before being chased out. Just then, Dalya excused herself from the room, and moments later I noticed her and Roni through the kitchen window walking together. I enjoyed seeing the closeness between Roni and his siblings. It was a very new experience for me. The one member of the family I had yet to meet was Dalya's husband, Natanel. He was away on business, and from what I understood, his job required him to travel frequently. I imagined it was difficult for Dalya, taking care of three young children with her husband away so often, and when I asked her what he did, I detected a vagueness in her response. Whatever the story was, it was no doubt the source of the sadness in her eyes. Not wanting to pry, I dropped the subject.

✿

"Come, Roni, let's walk to the rocks." Dalya took hold of his arm, leading him behind the house where there stood a small forest of trees. They followed a winding path laden with fallen pinecone needles, which led to a formation of huge stones that jutted out from the hill. "It's been a while since we spent some time together," Dalya said wistfully. "It's taken you a long time to get back to yourself."

"Back to myself?" Roni contemplated. "I'm not sure I remember what that is."

"Well, at least you're talking now instead of grunting. And I never thought I'd ever see you smile again."

Roni sat down on one of the large rocks and narrowed his eyes at his sister. He knew her too well. "Why do I get the feeling that all this is leading somewhere?"

"She's a lovely girl, Roni."

"Thanks, Dalya. I know," Roni said, still wary.

"She's clearly very good for you. I can see that."

"She gave me my life back."

"And now…you're going to take hers away."

Roni shot his sister a hard look. "Stop right there, Dalya."

"I know you, Roni. I know what's in your head. You don't have to spell it out."

"Dalya, I told you to stop. I can't talk about this with you."

"Then don't. But I can talk."

"I won't listen. You're bitter."

"I wasn't always like this, Roni. You know that."

Shaking his head, he said in a low voice, "She's not like you."

"I doubt that Dara truly understands what she's getting herself into."

"You don't know her."

"But does she understand?"

Roni's eyes blazed at his sister. "She understands that this is our land; she understands that we must safeguard it for the generations to come; she understands the burden that God has entrusted us with. Yes, she understands and she accepts it!"

"Ahh, now you're a man of God again. I thought you two had parted ways."

"This conversation is over." He rose from the rock and started for the path heading back to the house.

"Look, Roni," Dalya hurled herself in his way, clutching his arms before he could leave, "it's easy to see how much you love her and why. She's warm and she's kindhearted; at first glance one can tell how truly special she is. The whole family is taken by her…"

"So, Dalya? What's your point?"

"So don't curse her with the kind of life I have. My children don't know their father – is that what you want for yourself? And for Dara to constantly be alone, never knowing when she'll see you next, or for how long, and never knowing what God-forsaken part of the world you're in – it's a miserable existence, Roni."

"I'm not like your husband," he lowered her hands from him.

"But you're planning to be."

"I'm not planning anything. You're talking nonsense."

"I'm married to a Mossad agent! Do you really think I'm clueless?"

"Your imagination is running wild. I have nothing to do with the Mossad."

"You're not regular army!"

"And I suppose you get your information straight from the chief of staff."

"Joke all you want, but I know you probably better than you know yourself."

"Dalya, you know pathetically little. Don't ever bring this up again." There was an implicit warning in his tone, and he stared her down with a burning glare before walking away.

"This is not something you can walk away from. It's not just about you," she called out after him. He stopped short and turned slowly and deliberately around to face her.

"No, it's not about me." His voice was acid. "It never was. I've always looked at the bigger picture, Dalya. It's time you did that instead of wallowing in self-pity."

"Don't you dare judge me."

"In this land of ours, until there is peace, we all have a price to pay.

What Natanel is doing, he's doing for your children – for all our future children. Don't ever forget that Dalya, and don't ever forget all that *he* is sacrificing."

"Forget it? I live with it every day of my life. Years of waiting take a toll on a woman, and Dara will be no different."

"You've said enough. It ends now."

"Just one last thing, Roni, and then I'll leave you to your thoughts. If you need to follow this course, then follow it. If anyone was born to it, you were. But if you really love Dara, then you'll set her free." With that, Dalya ran past Roni and headed back to the house.

"So soon?" Evaleen asked Roni when he announced that we were leaving. "It is just one hour past sundown. What is the hurry?"

"Imma," Roni explained, "you know Dara and I have to get up well before dawn for work."

I was surprised myself at Roni's rush to leave but saw that there was something bothering him. In fact, since his little excursion with Dalya, he was noticeably agitated.

Nor did it escape his mother's notice. "All right, Roni," she said, not wanting to press him. "But please, don't wait too long to come home again." Then turning toward me, she put her hands on my arms. "Dara, you will make sure the two of you come back soon, yes?"

"Of course," I answered as we hugged each other.

She turned back to Roni, hugging him as well, and then said in a soft voice but with hardened eyes, giving her loving words an even deeper meaning, "You *deserve* happiness, Roni, and you found it in Dara. God has given you a gift." For a second her eyes darted sharply to Dalya, who stood next to me. I had no time to ponder this, however, because at that instant Gilad grabbed me in a bear hug, "Don't be a stranger, Dara," his robust enthusiasm practically choking the air out of me.

After I exchanged hugs with Margalit, Dalya and the children, Shimshon approached me. "It was such a delight to meet you, Dara," he said, taking my hands in his, his tattooed number from the Nazi death camp visible from beneath his rolled-up sleeve. He then gazed at me with eyes that conveyed a great deal – eyes that had once seen much affliction, yet now brimmed with a deep love for his family. When he spoke again it was in a hushed tone. "You know, Dara, the Torah says that one who saves a life, it is as if he has saved an entire world." I looked at him, puzzled. He leaned down to whisper in my ear, "There is more than one way to save a life, dear Dara. You have saved my son."

That was it. That did me in, and I burst into tears. All control was lost as I stood there bawling in the middle of the Ben-Ari living room. "Dara? Abba – what did you do?" Roni asked, rushing to my side. Shimshon, wide-eyed and looking innocent, shrugged in the same boyish way I've seen Roni do so many times before, which all at once turned my tears into spirited laughter.

"I knew it," Gilad cracked. "Leave it to us to take a perfectly normal person and drive her insane in just twenty-four hours."

"Do you realize just how blessed you are?" I asked Roni as we drove back to Gilboa.

He glanced at me thoughtfully. "They adored you, you know. But, of course," he said, brushing the back of his fingers against my cheek, "I knew they would." His eyes returned to the road. "Hmm, the skies are unusually cloudy tonight," Roni remarked. "It even smells like rain. Well, we can only hope. We never seem to have enough. Of course, if it does rain tonight, working in the fields tomorrow will be a muddy mess. Which work detail are you assigned to for tomorrow?"

"I don't know," I answered faintly, my response detached as I stared out my side window watching the black clouds ominously sweep over the sky. It seemed to mimic the sense of foreboding building inside of me. What I had tried to suppress suddenly fell over me like a tidal wave. It came on swiftly, ruthlessly and with a vengeance. It took on a life of its own. I couldn't rein it in. A sensation of dread and panic flooded my veins, my heart pounding furiously with the fear of losing the one person in my life who meant more to me than anything.

"Dara?" Roni saw the change in my mood.

I couldn't answer. I could no longer find my voice. The sinking feeling in the pit of my stomach that I worked so hard to contain these past several days slithered its way up and grabbed ahold of my throat. It was burning. My breathing, labored, made every breath I took painful. I turned my body to face away from Roni. I didn't want him to see me like this, and I could no longer find the strength to pretend that nothing was wrong. Because everything was wrong. My time with Roni's family forced me into a temporary state of denial. But their easiness and open affection underscored how altogether opposite my upbringing was from Roni's – how different my parents were from his. I longed for the unconditional love and support that enveloped him and his siblings, and I knew that I would never have it.

It was as if I could feel my parents physically ripping me away from Roni, shredding the life right out of me. He was a major threat to their plans for me. My mother's words hammered away in my head. *Stay away from that Roni.*

I knew Roni would never understand what I had to deal with – not coming from his type of home. Yet, despite it all, I found it too difficult to turn my back on my parents. For better or for worse, they were the only family I had. More to the point, I was the only family they had. It was a burden, but one that I couldn't dismiss. And as my mother pointed out, I *did* make a promise to them.

Nor could I abandon my grandfather. On some level, I knew I protected him from my mother. Who could know when she would again try to cast him off to a nursing home? She already blamed him for my pull to Israel. Her incessant arguments with Pops over me, played out in my mind. Now that he was so vulnerable, would she take her anger toward me out on him? In my heart, I knew the answer. I felt so alone with my unabated gloom and saw no way out of the darkness. I curled up in my seat, recoiling from the weight of my thoughts.

"Dara? What is it? Are you feeling ill?" Roni asked. All I could manage was to shake my head no. "I'm pulling over."

"No!" I burst out in a desperate tone. "Just take me home. Take me back to Gilboa."

"Dara, what's wrong? Please…you're scaring me!" But I couldn't even conceive of talking about it. I didn't want my own ears to hear the words. "Just take me home, just take me home," I cried.

In that instant, the skies exploded in a downpour and the unexpected blast of rumbling thunder gave me a jolt that made me scream. The rain came down alarmingly hard; it was frightening as it was impossible to see anything out the window even with the windshield wipers going at full speed. Just then, Roni slammed down on the gas pedal, defying the storm that raged around us, screeching around the bends of the highway, careening through the spontaneous pools of water, and raced the car on the winding road that led back to Gilboa.

I only knew we arrived safely at the kibbutz when Roni slowed down to stop at the security gate. The storm was relentless, and with the car now idling, the thrashing of the raindrops against it was deafening as the wind howled threateningly in the background. The electric gate opened and he coasted toward the parking lot behind the dining hall until he brought the car to a standstill and turned off the engine. I remained curled up in the corner of my seat.

"Dara," Roni's voice called to me softly. "Don't you know by now that you can tell me anything?" He leaned in nearer, trying to turn me toward him. "Dara?" I wouldn't budge, silence remaining my only answer. I couldn't handle this tonight, not with the stranglehold I felt twisting around my neck – maybe tomorrow, but not tonight. I couldn't bring myself to look at him, knowing what I would be forced to tell him. As irrational as I knew it was, I had to escape from the moment. It didn't help that his father's words kept playing in my head. *There is more than one way to save a life, dear Dara. You have saved my son.* Only now, I was going to destroy him just when he opened his heart to me. What was it that Roni once told me? *I have no more room inside of me for any more losses.*

"Dara…look at me. *Talk* to me," he pressed me again.

"I'm sorry, Roni. I can't… I have to go." I choked out the words, bolted out of the car and sprinted into the storm.

"Dara, no!"

The combined force of the wind and the rain caught me by surprise. Never having experienced the rainy season in Israel, much less on the heights of Mount Gilboa, I was unprepared, and the brutal power of the violent tempest nearly thrust me to the ground. The light jacket I wore offered no protection. In mere moments I was soaked to the skin – my teeth rattled in rhythm with my shivering body while battling against the wind, struggling just to stand upright. My body weight was no match against the powerful gusts. The imposing blackness of the night contributed to the existing chaos in my head. Completely disoriented, I couldn't discern the path leading to my room, nor could I any longer make out where the car was parked.

"Dara, what are you doing?" Roni chased after me, shouting over the din of the storm.

I turned in the direction of his voice and detected his approaching silhouette. "No, Roni, don't come after me," I cried out and ran from him in a desperate thrust of energy. A stray branch swept wildly across my path and I stumbled over it, losing my footing, falling to the sodden ground and scraping my head against the pebbles.

"Dara!" I heard Roni call out to me again, but I couldn't see him as I fought to get to my feet. There was a rumble of thunder followed by a shaft of lightning that sliced through the night. In that split second of light, I saw Roni dash toward me, and then once more he was gone in the darkness. I felt his outstretched arms wrap around me. Every instinct of mine begged to resist, but my efforts proved futile against the pounding downpour and the thrashing winds that sapped my strength. I was beaten, powerless against the elements, and fell to my knees, surrendering to Roni's arms as he gathered me up and hurried me to his place, out of the twisting wind.

Once inside, Roni removed all my wet clothes while I clung to him, still shivering, my head leaning into his chest. I couldn't look him in the eye. He hastily grabbed a sweatshirt out of his dresser drawer, slipping it over me with one arm, while holding on to me with his other arm, and then laid me down on his bed, wrapping me in his blanket. "Hmm, that'll leave a bruise," he said as he tended to the cut on my forehead, "but it's nothing serious." At that moment, I forced myself to steal a look at him. His drenched mane formed into ringlets around his face, was moist from the storm. Droplets of water fell from his hair to his cheeks as he dabbed my brow with a towel. Worry colored his countenance, which made me feel all the more guilty.

"You should get out of your wet clothes, too," I said in a small voice.

"My *motek*," he whispered as he kissed me tenderly on the forehead. "Don't worry about me. Are you warm enough? Should I get you another blanket?" I shook my head and inched my way up into a sitting position. "I'm fine now."

"Are you?" He looked intently at my face, trying to read me, attempting to understand my irrational behavior. Once again, I felt the panic take hold of my throat, not allowing me to answer. He crinkled his brows and turned away to gather up my wet clothes that he had thrown to the floor. He hung them over the shower in his bathroom.

I watched Roni as he slipped out of his own wet clothes and felt a longing for him to wrap me in his muscular arms. I wanted him to make me feel safe from the hopelessness that washed over me. To tell me that everything will work out. But…I knew it was pointless. It was just too…complicated.

He donned a pair of sweatpants and sat on the bed, facing me.

"You're not cold without a shirt?" I asked him. His mouth curled up in a half smile. "No. But if my bare chest makes you nervous, I could always throw something on."

I looked down, shaking my head.

"You know, Dara, you didn't have to go through the trouble of running into the storm just to get me to carry you off to my room and take your clothes off. I'm quite happy to accommodate you without all the theatrics." He tried again to lighten the mood.

"You must think I'm crazy," I whimpered, still not able to look him in the eye.

"Not at all, Dara. I just wonder what could be so terrible that would cause you to run from me into a raging storm."

I didn't answer.

"Dara," he cupped my cheek in his hand and lifted my face to meet his soft gaze. "Please…don't hold anything back from me. Whatever it is, whatever is troubling you, I'm sure it can't be as bad as you think. We'll handle it…together."

"You can't help me with this," I looked away from his eyes.

He cradled my face in both of his hands, forcing me to look at him. "Try me."

It struck me how his eyes could be so staggering and so soothing at the same time. I lowered his hands from my face and held them in mine while considering what to say. After a couple of false starts, I began, "I called my mother a few days ago. I told her…that I no longer wanted to go to Columbia University for four years…that I would transfer to a school in Israel after the first year."

"And she was against that idea," he stated, not at all surprised. I nodded.

"That's not such a shocker, you know," Roni said with an encouraging smile. "It will take more than just one phone conversation to persuade your parents."

"You don't understand, Roni. My parents are very different from yours. They're…I suppose one might say, harsh. Don't get me wrong, I mean…they do love me…but, in their way. In the only way they're capable of, I guess. Anyway, they have plans for me…plans that are very important to them. And…if I don't adhere to these…*plans*, if I don't keep the promise I made to them – to attend college in the States – they'll…cut me off."

Roni stared at me as if he didn't hear right. "They'll *cut you off?*" he questioned, clearly not comprehending my reality. "They couldn't have meant it. They're just upset, that's all."

"Trust me. They don't make idle threats."

"You're telling me that they were serious?"

I nodded.

"I can't believe they would do that to you," Roni said in quiet surprise.

"You come from a different world, Roni. You have parents who love you unconditionally. They're warm and loving and supportive. They're…amazing. Let's face it – they're unique. I don't think most parents are like yours. At least mine aren't." I paused and then blurted out, "My mother warned me to stay away from you."

"Dara, forget about what they think of me for the moment. The bottom line is that you don't deserve to be treated like that. It's one thing to disagree with you, but it's another to threaten to cut you off. For God's sake, it's not like you're doing anything irresponsible…you simply told them you want to study in Israel."

"It's not that simple to them."

"You're eighteen; you have a right to make decisions about your own future. Your parents should respect what you want, and what's in your heart."

"Yes," I sighed, "yes they should, but they don't. They're not going to change...it's who they are."

"It's who they are?" he repeated incredulously. "They threatened to cut you out of their lives." His eyes widened in disbelief. "Who does that? Dara, that's unacceptable!"

Just as I expected, Roni was having a difficult time grasping the situation. "I knew you wouldn't be able to understand."

"There's nothing here to understand. Just for the record, Dara, you need to realize that most parents *are* like mine and *not* like yours. Your parents are wrong. And that's putting it mildly."

"Deep down they believe they're doing what's best for me."

"No, Dara, they're doing what's best for *them*. Your parents are putting you in a position of choosing them over your own dreams. The way they're treating you, threatening you, is incredibly inappropriate. No, scratch that...it's obscene. You do see that, don't you?" He looked down, shaking his head, and then his eyes flashed back to mine. "Don't go back there, Dara. Stay here."

"Don't you think I've thought of that? But, right or wrong, they're my parents...and...if they are treating me inappropriately, it's... because they need me. And then, there's my grandfather...I can't just abandon him, too. This is more than just a matter of standing up to them."

"From what you told me about your grandfather, he'd want you to remain in Israel."

"Maybe so. But I would never be able to live with myself if I never went back to see him. He's not well. I need to spend some time with him while he can still recognize who I am. And I'm worried my mother may send him to a nursing home. She tried to once before. I can't let that happen. If I'm not there…" I trailed off in frustration. "It's complicated, Roni – there are also…other factors involved." I didn't know what else to say…how to explain it. I myself didn't quite understand the unhealthy hold my parents had over me. Nevertheless, I was torn. I had a strong sense of responsibility toward them, or rather, a need to protect them. From what, however, I wasn't entirely sure. But one thing I was sure of was that Roni would not understand the promise I made to my parents.

Roni was silent. He was thinking, mulling over everything I told him and everything I did not tell him. He shook his head again, looking puzzled. "I'm having trouble figuring you out right now. I mean, you took a death leap to save Alana's life. And yet, you're hesitant to save your own. Or…is that it?" He now spoke as if thinking aloud. "Is that the real problem? You're so accustomed to doing things for others, putting your own wants and needs as secondary…you'll sacrifice yourself…." His eyes then fixed on mine, "I gather you didn't tell your mother that we love each other."

"No…I didn't. I wanted to, but she didn't give me a chance. Anyway, it's useless. She just sees you as an obstacle. Love is simply not in my parents' vernacular. It wouldn't help my case at all."

"There's…something else though, isn't there? This whole thing just doesn't make sense. There's a piece to this puzzle that I'm missing, Dara. What is it? What would make your parents threaten to go to such lengths as to cut you off?"

I looked at him uneasily. "Wait a minute," he said with a scrutinizing stare, and I could almost hear the click as he put the entire picture together. "Your father holds a sensitive position in America's Department of Defense. That's what this is all about, isn't it? It's precisely because he's a Jew in a high-level security job that he is dead set against you living in Israel…and having anything to do with me. Isn't that right, Dara?"

"Yes," I admitted in a subdued voice. "He said that if I were to live in Israel, even though, on the surface, Israel was considered an ally, it would undermine his high-level security status. He didn't want to attract any suspicions of dual loyalty. And now, with you in my life, it complicates matters for him even more."

"So they're trying to force you to remain in America. They're... using...you." Roni's expression was a mixture of shock and disgust.

"Look, Roni," I tried to explain, "my parents know that they can't keep me prisoner in the United States forever, but because of my father's position, they want to buy more time – to keep me in the States for as long as possible."

This just made Roni more furious. "If he's worried they would suspect his loyalty, then perhaps he should consider that he's working for the wrong government!"

"You and I understand that, but they don't quite see things that way. So...I made an agreement with them; if they would let me take one year off before college to volunteer on a kibbutz in Israel, then I would return to attend Columbia University for the full four years. Only after I'd get my degree, would I be free to move to Israel. But...they were betting on me giving up on my dream, and that was why they allowed me to go to Israel this year – *to get it out of my system*. Of course, I knew that wouldn't happen.

"I also knew they counted on me meeting someone while at Columbia, marrying and settling down there. But all that doesn't matter. The bottom line, Roni, is that I did promise them that I would return to the States for four more years. I was just hoping that with the circumstances as they are between you and me, they wouldn't hold me to it. But they will. So, you see, Roni, if I go back on my word, it would be as if I'm betraying them, and I wouldn't be an innocent victim in this whole scenario."

"Dara, you *are* an innocent victim. You're excusing their behavior." The fury was prominent on Roni's face, though he attempted to restrain his voice. "That was an unfair burden to put on you."

"I didn't think so at the time. It was before I met you, obviously... so I didn't mind going to college in the States before moving to Israel. But now...I feel...trapped."

He wiped away the silent tears that escaped from my eyes. "You can only be trapped if you let yourself be trapped."

"I don't see a way out. I don't want to be cut off, and they *will* do it. My parents would do anything to preserve their social standing."

"My God, Dara. If that's how they are, what are you holding on to?"

I lowered my head, pressing my lips together to keep from bursting into a deluge of tears. The truth about the type of parents I had was too painful to accept. I took in a deep breath. "We don't get to choose our parents, and they're the only ones I've got. And...I don't have any other family. No sisters or brothers. No aunts, uncles, cousins...nothing."

We sat in silence for a few moments, and I watched Roni wrestle with his thoughts as he looked right past me, his jaw clenched. He was seething. He then set his eyes on mine in a determined stance, underscoring his tone, which was hard and resolute. "Dara, sometimes there is such a thing as being too forgiving. Your parents using you is despicable; their threat to cut you off if you don't play according to their erroneous rules is unconscionable. You cannot allow yourself to be kept as a virtual prisoner in a country in which you do not wish to be. They have no right to threaten you. They have no right to keep you from Israel or from me."

"But Roni..." I tried to cut in.

"Dara, no buts – please, listen to me. You should return to the States to spend some time with your grandfather, but then, you need to follow your heart. And if your heart is with me, as I know it is...then it's with me that you belong." His eyes were like smoldering ice and his mood, adamant. "I will *not* lose you."

"Roni," I wrapped my arms around him, leaning my head against his shoulder, "I don't want to lose you. I don't want to leave, but...how do I keep from losing my parents?"

"They don't deserve your loyalty." His voice was stone cold as he pulled my arms off him, his hands gripping them firmly. "Dara," his eyes burned into mine, "I will not make things easier for you. Hard as it is, you're going to have to face certain unpleasant truths about your parents. *I am your family now*, and I will fight for you – relentlessly and unremittingly – and I promise you this...I *will* win."

He threw the blanket to the floor and grabbed me again, his lips meeting mine in a frantic rush as if to seal his oath to me. He kissed me forcefully, wildly, his surging strength dissolving my fears – at least for the moment. Suddenly, Roni stopped. "One more thing," he said. "I don't plan to fight fairly." And with that, he ravaged me in a feverish passion.

Chapter 9

 *The Wedding*

Adina looked strikingly beautiful in her flowing white gown, and Ari was glowing from ear to ear. As was customary, he wore a simple white shirt with dark pants – no suits at a kibbutz wedding. The weather cooperated with the occasion, as the Beit She'an valley even in the winter tended not to get too cold like the rest of the country, and the wind was nothing more than a subtle breeze.

It was a twilight wedding set in the fields, with the backdrop of the Jordanian mountains to the east. Adina sat in a tall-backed, wicker chair decorated with swags of flowers, surrounded by friends and family – her father and Ari's father taking turns to bless her. In the distance a tractor, driven by Roni, carried Ari. As it came nearer it was encircled by relatives and friends enthusiastically singing traditional wedding songs. The tractor came to a stop several yards before Adina, and Ari jumped off and stepped toward his bride. Upon reaching her, he drew the veil that fell over her hair, slipping it to the front to cover her face, according to an age-old Jewish tradition stemming from our matriarch Rebecca, who veiled herself when she first met her husband-to-be, Isaac. Ari was then ushered away from Adina under a stream of song and dance, until they were brought together shortly after under a simple canopy consisting of a prayer shawl tied to four poles, where they were wed under the stars. In the final moment of the ceremony, Ari shattered a glass cup beneath his feet to commemorate the destruction of our Temple in Jerusalem – even at the height of our joy – and a euphoric shout of *mazal tov* rang out from the crowd, leading to wild dancing of the hora, the national dance of Israel.

Spent from the first round of celebrating, guests sat down for a festive meal with a generous buffet set up in a huge tent. Midway through the meal, Roni whisked me away from the table and led me out of the tent.

"Roni, what's going on?"

"This is the part of the wedding with too much small talk. It gives me a headache. Let's go for a drive."

"A drive? To where? And with what? We all came down to the fields in a bus, remember?"

"Well, it just so happens that I have an *in* with the guy at the *radrah* who maintains all the vehicles."

"And that would be you, I presume?"

"That would be correct, my *motek.*"

"But we can't just leave the wedding."

"We'll be back for the next round of dancing, I promise. I estimate that there's at least an hour of small talk left."

I smiled. "Okay. Where do you want to go?"

"To where it all began."

I looked at him, completely mystified. "Trust me," he said simply.

He took my hand and trotted with me toward the *radrah*, where he led me to a pickup truck. It looked very much like the one Roni drove taking me for the first time to the cotton fields. I raised my eyebrow at him, questioning his choice. "Trust me," he repeated with a sly look looming across his face.

"You know, the more you say that, the less I do." Roni's only answer was a soft chuckle. We drove not more than ten minutes before coming to a stop. Although the moon shone bright, with the sky layered in stars, it was still difficult to tell where we were. Roni grabbed a flashlight out of the dashboard glove compartment, and as I moved to open my door, I was not surprised to find that it stuck. He leaned over and grinned as he jerked it open. "Oh, about this door…it's a little tricky…it will open only if you push the lever down and then inward – pretty much the opposite of what you'd be naturally inclined to do."

"Uh-huh. I thought it was the same truck. So, did you rig it that way on purpose?"

"You would think so, right? But, no, I didn't." Roni laughed. Once out of the car, he switched on the flashlight and I could see the tall cotton plants surrounding us. "I hope you're not planning for me to fall flat on my face again."

"Heavens no, not in that dress," he feigned alarm. "By the way," he said, putting his arms around my waist, "did I tell you how beautiful you look tonight?" I looked down and nodded. He lifted my chin to face him. His eyes crinkled in a smile. "It's cute how you turn bashful whenever I compliment you. You *do* believe me when I say you look beautiful, don't you?" I nodded again. He pulled me into him and whispered in my hair, "You stun me, Dara."

I stun you?

"…and, this dress," he glided his hands down my sides, "great dress – smartly done."

"Smartly done?" *That was an odd comment*, I thought.

"No buttons, just one zipper, easy access." He began nibbling at my neck.

"You are horrible." I pulled away from him.

"Am I?"

"Yes, you are." I fought back a smile.

"But I really do like the dress on you. It is a shame though..."

"Why?"

"You won't be wearing it for much longer."

"I should have seen that one coming."

"Come with me," he snickered as he took my hand.

"Um, where exactly are we going?"

"Not far…trust me." He led me several more feet toward the back of the truck, and then he stopped. "We're here."

I looked at him inquisitively. "Roni…what's going on with you tonight?"

He lowered the back latch of the pickup, flashing the light on its contents. A thick layer of hay filled the tub of the truck, and a large fluffy blanket was spread across the top. My eyes widened in surprise. "When did you do this?"

"After you," he gestured.

"What else do you have up your sleeve tonight?" I asked as he lifted me up to the blanket and then jumped on afterwards.

"Savor the moment, my *motek*. I bet you never stared up at the stars from the back of a hay-filled pickup truck in the middle of some cotton fields."

"That's a pretty safe bet."

"Is it so bad?"

I lay down on the blanket and stared up at the sky. "Actually…it's… amazing." I turned my head to face Roni but he was busy searching for something beneath the hay.

"Ahh, here it is."

He unwrapped what looked like a small, white linen tablecloth, and from it he uncovered a bottle of wine with two wineglasses. "Did you take that from the wedding?" I asked, sitting back up.

"Don't worry…they won't miss it."

"What are we drinking to?"

"To us, of course. But…more specifically, my *motek*, to our future." I was quiet. In my heart, there was nothing more on earth I wanted than sharing a future with Roni. But, in my mind, my dilemma with my parents was still unresolved.

"Actually, I drink to you, Dara," he continued in a soft tone. "To the woman who gave me my life back. To the one I want to grow old with. To my one and only love."

"Roni," I started, but then he stopped me, touching his finger to my lips. "Dara, this is where we drink. That's usually how it works after one gives a toast." I resigned with a smile and drank my wine with him.

"You know," he said in a wily tone, "there's an ancient civilization that would consider us married after toasting our future over wine."

"Oh really…and which civilization is that?"

"Trust me," he murmured, gently kissing my forehead. "But… there's just one more thing about the ritual that I need to take care of." He reached into the hay and pulled out a small jewelry box.

I took in a short breath. "Roni, what did you do?"

"I'm giving you my heart to hold." He opened the box and inside was a heart-shaped ruby encircled with narrow slivers of brilliant diamonds set in a band of white gold. It was exquisite. "Marry me, Dara."

I stared at him in shock and his sparkling eyes radiated straight back into mine. "You know, there are some civilizations that consider silence as acceptance."

"Do they?" I finally choked out.

"Mmm," he smiled. "Trust me." He pulled the ring from the box and slipped it on my finger. "Perfect."

Chapter 10

 *Spring 1984*

"Make the call, *motek*."

"I'm not sure that *now* is the right time."

"You can't keep putting it off and it's already been a few months. I'm right here with you, Dara – you're not alone. Go ahead, make the call."

"I already know how the conversation will go."

"Nevertheless, you still have to let your parents know."

"I thought I might tell them face-to-face…when I go back for the year."

"Uh…I don't think so. We've been over this – not if I can't be there with you. I would like to speak with your parents, too. I want to get it all settled so that we can finally break the news in a joyful manner to my parents. I don't want any cloud hanging over us."

"And you think if you speak to my parents that it will change their minds?"

"It's not up to them. Whom you want to marry is up to you. But perhaps I can encourage them to fly out here and meet my family."

"You know that's not what it's about."

"I know."

"Then why bother?"

"Because we have to exhaust all avenues. You should know by now that I won't accept defeat. Now, Dara, I've been very patient, but we're not going to put this off any longer, so…please…make the call."

I reluctantly took the phone receiver from Roni and dialed the overseas operator to place the collect call to my parents.

"Hello, Mom?"

"Yes, Dara, what is it? Is everything all right?"

"Yes, Mom. In fact, everything is perfect," I said with a forced resolve.

"Then, why are you calling?"

"I have some very good news to tell you. Now…I know this may come as a surprise to you but…"

"Dara, I have an art show to get to. Please just get to the point."

"Roni asked me to marry him and I said yes," I blurted out.

Silence.

Finally my mother spoke. "Is he planning to live in the States?"

"No, Mom. He's an officer in the Israeli army. He…took a temporary leave, but will be returning to service in a few months. I plan to come back to the States for a year and then return to Israel to marry him."

"Dara, how could you? An officer in the Israeli army, no less! Don't you know what this means for your father? This is incredibly selfish of you. And what about your education?"

"Mom, you can't tie my life to Dad's job. And…I'm not altogether going back on my word. I said I would go to Columbia for the first year. Please, can't you just try to be happy for me?"

At that point, Roni took the phone. "Hello, Mrs. Harow, this is Roni Ben-Ari, Dara's…well there's really no reason to raise your voice – I understand your misgivings, but Dara and I love each other and we intend on building a life together *in* Israel, and…yes, I…Mrs. Harow… this can be discussed calmly…." Roni looked at me in astonishment and, switching back to Hebrew, muttered, "How does she do that without taking a breath?" Then back to the receiver, "Mrs. Harow, perhaps you and Dr. Harow would like to fly out here and meet with me and my fami…on the contrary, I believe we have much to discuss…

"Oh, Dr. Harow? I'm glad you're on the phone, too. As you may recall we met when…yes, that's right, I just…No, I am not after your family's money and I take offense that you would insult your own daughter…no, she is not pregnant…What?…Well, I'm sorry you see it that way, but I'm not trying to ruin your life and I fail to see…hello?" Roni covered the mouthpiece and mumbled to me in Hebrew, "I could be wrong, but your father didn't seem happy about our engagement," he winked at me before getting back to the phone. "Hello? Mrs. Harow, are you still there? I realize this is a surprise to you but I love your daughter very much and…yes I…well, apparently your daughter does not agree. You know her heart is in Israel and…"

He looked at me incredulously. "This is ridiculous." After apparently being cut off again in midsentence, Roni quietly set the receiver down on the table. My mother's shrill voice was still going nonstop. We both just stood there staring down at the phone. Roni stroked my hair and reassured me. "Don't worry, Dara. It will be all right. I have a feeling their bark is worse than their bite."

I picked up the phone and interrupted my mother's tirade. "Mom, it's Dara again. I…I will not speak to you until you can discuss this in a calm manner. Good-bye." I hung up the phone, not at all certain if she heard me or not. I looked up at Roni completely dejected. "So, do you really think her bark is worse than her bite?"

"You don't want to know what I really think," he tried albeit unsuccessfully to hide the fury in his voice. "But I will say this. You can't go to the States for the year…just go to visit your grandfather, for a few months at most, and then return here quickly. I'll get you the money for your ticket back to Israel – you don't have to worry about that."

"I don't know, Roni…I just don't know. I've let them down."

"Dara, you've done nothing wrong – they're letting *you* down. The way they treat you makes my blood boil. What I can't understand is why it doesn't make *your* blood boil?"

"You know what, Roni…I don't want to think about them anymore for now. It's been a long, hot day in the fields, and I want to take a shower before dinner. I'll see you later."

I started to walk away, and he grabbed my arm, turning me back to him. "Dara, you can't keep avoiding the situation. We've held off telling my parents about our plans long enough."

"I know," I said, hearing the discontent in his voice. "You're right and I'm sorry. I haven't been fair to you. But this is killing me inside."

"You wouldn't be you if it didn't," he sighed and then tenderly stroked my cheek. "But you have to stop torturing yourself." His tone was once again resolute.

"This hasn't been easy on you either. Sometimes I wonder why you put up with me."

"Hmm. Good question. I suppose I must be insanely in love with you."

"I'm so glad you're insane." I closed my eyes and leaned into his comforting arms. "Thank you for being so patient with me."

"You're welcome." I heard the smile in his voice. He held me tight and brushed his lips against my hair. "Perhaps I shouldn't leave you right now when you're this upset. You know…I can always help you with that shower…"

"I'm sure you can," I smiled. "But I think I've got this one under control. I'll be fine, Roni. Really. I just need to clear my head from that horrible phone conversation."

"Okay, Dara. But just remember, you're not alone in this."

"Promise me one thing, Roni?"

"Anything."

"Don't bring it up anymore tonight."

"You mean at your birthday party?"

"It's not a party; we're just having a night out with friends."

"And you just happen to be nineteen today," he smiled.

"It's just another day in the year. No need to make a big deal over it."

"I gather that's how your parents look at it." He right away regretted saying that. "I'm sorry, Dara. That was insensitive." *But he was right.*

"Please, Roni, let's just forget about it all tonight, okay?"

"I promise. Not a word, for tonight that is. But I need you to promise me something in return."

"What?" I asked hesitantly.

"Promise me you won't feel guilty over any of this. You've done nothing wrong."

"I promise…I'll try."

"Uh-uh, not good enough."

"Okay…no guilt…I promise."

He kissed me tenderly. "I'll come by for you later."

We spent the evening at Sachna. Rather than have Roni make a whole production over my birthday, I suggested we just go out with our friends and simply enjoy a relaxed and carefree evening. Now that spring was in full bloom, the place was lively with youth from all the surrounding villages and kibbutzim. Families as well were having late-night picnics. The easygoing company of all my friends comforted me, and I found the rushing water of the springs a soothing tonic to my inner turmoil. Not too many people were swimming though, as the water was still quite cold. This didn't stop the guys from jumping in, however. Everything always boiled down to who was more macho. And, as expected, they emerged from the water and raced to cradle us in their cold wet arms amid our protesting screams, finding our unreceptive responses enormously amusing.

Lavi passed the beers around, and Roni, Ari and Doron busied themselves with building the "perfect" campfire. Yaniv brought his guitar, and soon our small circle of friends attracted others who joined us in song. It was a perfect night in its sheer simplicity.

Jenny was the first to notice. "What's going on there?" She looked beyond our circle, past Roni and me. An Arab family was standing several yards behind us at the water's edge, yelling frantically. Someone was in trouble.

Roni hurried over there and, in fluid Arabic, asked one of the family members what was wrong. There were two teenage boys diving repeatedly into the water, springing up for air and then diving in again. The next thing I saw, Roni jumped in and searched the waters with the other two boys. After a minute or two, he resurfaced dragging a young boy's body behind him and lifted him to his waiting family, who pulled him to the surface.

The boy looked no more than eight years old. His lips were blue – his young, thin body, lifeless.

Hoisting himself from the water, Roni didn't waste time and began CPR, while the mother tearfully prayed in the background for her son, whom she called Ibrahim. Finally, a cough, and a spurt of water gushed from the boy's mouth and his eyes slowly opened.

"Lavi!" Roni ordered. "Get one of the jeeps; drive him with one of his older brothers to the hospital." Roni then turned to the family and explained that Lavi was taking Ibrahim to the hospital in Afula, and that they should follow him in their car. Little Ibrahim's older brothers hugged Roni, as the mother and two girls, whom I assumed were Ibrahim's sisters, thanked him profusely, repeating over and over to him a phrase I couldn't understand.

"Nice work." Ari patted Roni on the back and handed him a beer.

"What did they say to you?" Yaniv inquired. "They kept calling you something – what was it?" Roni shrugged it off, "I don't know…I wasn't paying attention."

"Oh, Roni," I snuggled into his chest, no longer minding the cold wetness. "You are truly a golden angel." He stepped back, staring at me questioningly. "What? What is it?" I asked, puzzled at his reaction.

"You know Arabic?"

"No. Why?"

Like clockwork, Yaniv and Ari spit out a mouthful of beer and burst out laughing.

"And so it begins…" Roni grimaced.

"What am I missing here?" I asked.

"So that's what they called you! A golden angel!" Yaniv revealed, after catching his breath. "Imagine that! All this time in our very midst and we never had a clue. You're a regular wonder boy – truly a marvel – no, a deity." He raised his beer bottle up high in a mock salute to Roni.

"Legends will be told about you," Ari jumped in with his usual dramatic flair, his eyes raised to the distance, as if seeing the future. "Just think – stories of wonderment whispered to children in the stillness of the night about the great golden angel. I dare say, it will become Arab folklore."

"As if he doesn't have enough feathers in his cap," Doron groaned from his reclined position on the ground, "now we've got to deal with him having a halo."

"Pardon my French, guys, but go piss off!"

"Sorry, Roni…didn't realize what I'd be starting," I said, and then bit down on my lip to try to keep from laughing.

"You, too? Well, my little traitorous one, I'm afraid 'sorry' just doesn't cut it. I'll have to suffer from their lousy jokes for weeks."

"You can't be upset with me. It's my birthday."

He raised one eyebrow.

"I suppose you're going to make me pay dearly for it?"

Roni considered that for a moment, rolling his eyes over me, his mischievous grin back in full form. "Count on it."

Chapter 11

"Mind if I intrude on your solitude?"

"Of course not, Jen." Jenny hopped up on the mound above the foxhole and sat beside me. I found myself taking refuge atop my foxhole more often now. It was just a couple of months away from our planned departure from Israel. Fighting off the melancholy of leaving Roni, the kibbutz and all the friends that I'd made throughout the year was becoming more challenging with each passing day. And my parent's horrific reaction to my engagement to Roni was wearing me thin.

Roni wanted to set a date for our wedding before I returned to the States and before he returned to the army, but I kept putting him off. He became more insistent about me cutting short the length of my stay in America. I stubbornly clung to the notion that I could somehow resolve things with my parents, and I made that a priority. He was trying to be patient, but time was running out for both of us, and it was unreasonable for me to keep him dangling on a string; surely, his patience had a limit. He was already displeased that we hadn't yet gone to break the news of our engagement to his parents.

"It really is a magnificent sight," Jenny said, breaking into my thoughts. "Nothing like having an aerial view right beneath our feet."

I sighed heavily. "I'm sure going to miss this. What are your plans, Jenny? Did you decide on a college yet?"

"Yes, that's part of what I wanted to talk to you about. I've decided to stay on in Israel. I'm applying to a university here, either Bar-Ilan or Tel Aviv U. Yaniv is going to check out the schools with me. We're both interested in computer science."

"That's great news, Jen."

"Um...maybe you'd like to come with us? You know...to check out the schools for yourself."

"I suppose it couldn't hurt to get information on transferring here from the States."

"Or...applying as a freshman..." Jenny slipped in.

"*Et tu, Brute?*"

"Dara, Roni is right about your parents. You can't let them come between the two of you. I know you didn't ask for my opinion, but I'm going to give it anyway."

"I know what you're going to say."

"Well, I think you have to hear it. I'm siding with Roni. You shouldn't go back for a full year. Your parents have this unhealthy hold on you. I've got to say that it surprises me how you let them take advantage of you."

"I guess I don't have to ask if your parents took kindly to your new plans."

"Of course they did, Dara. A – it's my life. And B – Israel is our country, it's where we belong. They get it."

Yeah, well, life isn't so black and white for others.

"Look, Dara, you're a strong person, and you're smart, but… well…this is a no-brainer…it's time you started to think about yourself. And…you can't keep putting Roni off. You're hurting him."

"Oh, Jenny," I buried my face in my hands. "That's the worst part of it. It's killing me, and I don't know what to do. I just can't entirely disregard my parents."

"Seems to me they're ready to do that to you."

"I don't know what's right or wrong anymore…I feel like I'm hurting everyone involved. I can't help but think…well…I hate what this is doing to Roni…I hate putting my burdens on him. The other night he was ready to give up his army career and take on a mechanic job somewhere in Jerusalem just to pay for my college tuition! I'm totally messing him up. I was thinking, that maybe…it would just be best for him if…I broke things off. He doesn't deserve what I'm putting him through."

"Are you crazy?" Jenny's eyes bulged out in shock. "You can't do that, Dara! *I* won't let you. What would even make you consider something like that?"

I took out a folded yellow paper from my pocket and handed it to Jenny.

"What's this?"

"It's a telegram from my mother. Dassi caught me on my way back to the room and gave it to me."

Jenny unfolded the telegram and read it.

There are consequences to your plans *stop* You are destroying your father *stop* Your marriage to Roni will not be accepted or supported *stop* We will be forced to cut you off *stop*

"Wow, they fight dirty, don't they," Jenny quipped. "They don't sound like parents – they sound so cold. The way they treat you is downright cruel. It's no wonder you can't see things clearly." Jenny shook her head in astonishment. "How did you end up being so sweet?"

"I don't feel so sweet. I feel that I'm just causing aggravation for everyone. And…they're not cruel…they're just…misguided, I suppose. They're…acting out of desperation. They fear my actions will destroy their perfect world. Anyway, we can't choose our parents, Jenny."

"True, but you can choose to do what you want with your own life."

"It's not that simple."

"It should be."

I sighed heavily and stared up at the sky.

"Look, Dara, I don't know what it's like to be in your shoes, and it pains me to see how much you're hurting when this should be the most joyous time of your life. But…and I don't say this lightly…it seems to me that you need to accept some hard facts or you'll never be able to find happiness. The bottom line is that your parents are willing to write you off. It's an ugly truth, but it's one you have to finally face and just move on. You can't give in to emotional blackmail. And you can't break it off with Roni. You two belong together. Don't do something that you'll regret for the rest of your life. Forget about this horrible telegram." She scrunched it up and threw it to the ground several yards away.

"Jenny, you know better than to litter on our holy land." Roni bent down and picked up the crumpled paper.

"Oh, hi, Roni," Jenny said, flustered.

"No need to look so guilty. I'm not going to turn you in." Roni looked at Jenny warily and then at me. "Actually, you both look kind of guilty. What's going on, ladies?"

"Um, nothing, Roni. Can I have my paper back?" Jenny asked hastily.

"But you threw it away. And I found it, so now it's mine," he teased.

"Well, yeah, but now I want it back."

He wrinkled his brows in mock suspicion. "Dara, what do you think?" Roni's eyes fixed on mine as he uncrumpled the telegram. "Is this paper mine now or," he gave the yellow page a fleeting look and all at once turned serious. "Western Union Telegram, attention, Dara Harow?"

"Roni, you don't have to read that," I heard myself practically plead. "Don't I?"

"Um, I'll uh…see you later, Dara." Jenny gave me a quick hug and whispered in my ear, "Don't do anything stupid."

I climbed down from the mound. "Please, Roni, give me the telegram."

"No, Dara. I've been very tolerant. But I'm tired of you avoiding the issue. It stops today. I thought we would go to my parents this weekend and finally tell them about our plans. Or, is there something about this telegram that will once again put a damper on things?"

I parted my lips to speak, but no words came out. Roni clearly had run out of patience and I was at a loss as to how to deal with it.

"What's the bottom line, Dara? Are you committed to us, or not?"

"Roni…please…" I didn't finish my sentence. Just those two first words were enough to see the stabbing pain in Roni's eyes. I saw my reflection in their gaze and despised what I saw. A look of disbelief swept over his face. He looked down at the telegram and read it, crumpled it up and threw it to the ground, and then…just walked away.

I didn't go to dinner that night. I just sat on my bed in the room that I shared with Jenny and stared at the heart-shaped ruby stone, set in a sea of diamond shards that adorned my finger. It was his heart, Roni said. His heart that he gave me to hold. And now, I crushed it. What was wrong with me? What was I doing? Of all people, how could I hurt Roni? *My Roni.* I wouldn't blame him if he didn't forgive me, although it would kill me. I couldn't live without him. I didn't want to live without him. He meant everything to me. He was the reason I got up in the morning. He was the smile on my face, the glow in my eyes. He was the vibrant rhythm in the beat of my heart. He was the very breath I breathed. *My Roni.* He was my life. *He was my life. Oh my God. What was I doing? He was my life.*

I jumped off the bed, bolting for the door, and collided with Jenny and Yaniv as they both entered the room. "Whoa! Take it easy, girl. Where are you rushing to?" Jenny asked.

"Where is Roni? I have to find him."

"He left."

"He left? What do you mean?"

"He wasn't at dinner. Lavi said he saw him drive down the mountain."

"Where was he going?"

"Don't worry, Dara," Yaniv tried to calm me. "He's just blowing off some steam. He'll drive around for an hour or two and then he'll be back."

"You don't know that, Yaniv. I really hurt him."

"He'll forgive you."

"I don't know about that."

"I do," Yaniv said pointedly. "He was dead till he met you. He'd forgive you anything."

"You don't understand, Yaniv. I just killed him, again."

I decided to take a walk. It was a warm June night with a slight hint of a cool breeze – just enough to remind me that I was on top of a mountain and not in the valley. My stomach twisted at the thought of soon returning to New York City, so far away from the fragrant mountain breezes that now filled my senses. So far away from Roni.

But it would only be temporary, I told myself. A short pause in the scheme of life. For the first time in months, I suddenly saw things clearly, owing to the reflection I caught of myself in Roni's pained eyes. It was haunting. Nevertheless, I was grateful for it. It jarred me into seeing things about myself that until now had eluded me.

Until now, I was *allowing* myself to be trapped, to be taken advantage of. *Well, that ends today.* I would not give in to my parents' emotional blackmail. They had no right to keep me from living in Israel and they had no right to keep me from Roni. Yes, I would return to the States – if only to see my grandfather once more. I would not permit my parents to suppress what I believed in or to rip the life from me. Should they choose to cut me off, that would be their decision and I would live with it, as would they.

I passed by the *mo'adon* and the kibbutz office, and found myself walking over the lawn past the dining hall toward Roni's apartment. It was still light outside – sunset wasn't for another half hour or so. I hoped his door would be open. He often neglected to lock it, as most people on kibbutz rarely locked their doors. I entered the apartment complex and ran into Lavi and Mikki in the kitchen. "Is he back yet?" I asked.

"No, not yet. What did you do to him? I haven't seen him like that since his return from the Lebanon War."

"Thanks, Lavi, I needed that." I stepped toward Roni's apartment and tried the door. It was locked. *Not a good sign.* Mikki came up behind me with a tiny screwdriver and picked the lock for me in seconds. "We women have to watch out for each other," she winked and sauntered back to Lavi, who was watching from the kitchen with a frivolous smile.

"And who's going to watch out for us poor, helpless guys?" he asked as she led him away.

I entered Roni's room not really knowing what I was going to do next. All I knew is that I needed to be near him somehow, near his things, his books, his scent. I fished out the Moody Blues cassette from his collection and played it on his stereo and, after slipping my sandals off, crawled into his bed and snuggled in his blanket.

The warm hues of sunset washed over the room, enveloping me in the dark shadows of dusk. I cuddled into his pillow, comforted by his scent. *Roni had been so patient with me*, I thought, and more understanding than I deserved, no matter how enraged he was at my parents. Yet, I acted irrationally, not to mention stupidly, as Jenny would put it. And Roni was perfectly correct. My parents *were* treating me in an unconscionable manner. Deep down, I never doubted it, though I had trouble accepting it. Jenny was right on the mark about that. I suppose I would have done anything to try to please them, to gain their approval or simple acknowledgment.

I couldn't blame Roni if he decided he had had enough. Even so, I was going to fight for him to trust in me again. I resolved that I wouldn't go back to the States for a year. I couldn't be away from Roni for that long. But I did need to see my grandfather.

Tears filled my eyes and a terrible fear pervaded the pit of my stomach. *What if Roni would not forgive me?* I closed my eyes and tortured myself further with dreaded thoughts until finally a merciful sleep swept me away into nocturnal oblivion.

🌿

My eyes opened to Roni watching over me. He held an almost empty beer bottle in his hand, and sat in his desk chair, facing the bed. I inched my way into a sitting position. I would pour my heart out to him – beg him if I had to – but the cool expression he wore made me think that I might be too late.

"Hi," I whispered. He didn't respond. His ice-blue eyes bore indifference as they glistened in the starlight that stole through the window. They were like camouflage – obscuring his thoughts. "I hope you don't mind," I continued. "I wanted to wait for you here. Mikki let me in."

"I know." He lit a cigarette. He always did that when he wanted to mask some emotion.

"What time is it?" I asked.

"It's late, Dara. Too late."

"Roni, please forgive me," I blurted out. "I've been so foolish and self-involved."

"It doesn't matter anymore."

"No, don't say that."

"You've been under much pressure. I understand that," he said flatly. "Regardless, you made your choice."

"No, Roni. There won't be any more pressure, because I won't accept it anymore."

He took a drag from his cigarette and gazed out the window right past me, avoiding my eyes.

"Roni, I love you. You're my life. I promise you, my parents won't come between us. I won't allow it."

"Even if it means being cut off from them?" he asked skeptically, dismissing my declaration, his eyes now cutting into mine with distrust.

"Yes."

"But you're still going back to the States," he continued in an interrogating tone.

"For five months only – to spend time with my grandfather, and while there, I'll attend one semester at Columbia. That's it. Not a year, just five months. The thought of being away from you for even that long is too much – but then I'm returning to Israel, to you. I'll get a job and work my way through school here. I'll make it work. I promise you this," I then added, evoking his words, "*I am committed to us.*"

I was hoping for some reaction, some kind of response –

frustration, even anger – but he just sat there with his stony facade, staring at me poker-faced.

"I know you love me, Roni."

Silence. He drew on his cigarette. I went on. "So…if you…still want to go to your parents…and tell them our good news, well…it just so happens, I'm free this weekend…" I tapered off, my heart sinking at his aloof manner, certain now that he wouldn't forgive me for putting him through an emotional roller coaster. He took another drag of his cigarette and casually blew out a cloud of smoke before he spoke.

"And you no longer have a problem betraying your parents." It wasn't a question. I could have sworn he was mocking me.

"I no longer believe that I'd be betraying them."

"Just like that."

"Yes, just like that."

"You'll have to forgive me if I'm not entirely convinced." His tone was frighteningly dispassionate.

Damn you, Roni. I'm not giving up on you. "I came here to tell you that I was going to start living my own life. I once told you that I would be the one waiting for you to come home, and I meant it."

"Did you? I would say that's debatable."

"Roni," I breathed. "I *did* mean it."

"Possibly." He shrugged and took a swig of his beer before continuing. "It makes little difference; once you're back in your parents' house, they'll pressure you to stay."

"I won't let them manipulate me again. Why won't you believe me? My life with you is more important to me than anything else. I may very well lose them, but I will *not* lose you."

He put out his cigarette in his beer bottle and nonchalantly tossed it into the garbage can beneath his desk. "You don't exactly have a great track record in standing up to your parents, Dara."

"Perhaps you didn't hear me," I said, determined to penetrate his impassive front. The next few words I uttered were measured and resolute. "I will not lose you." I rose from the bed and moved closer to him, caressing his face in my hands. "Don't give up on me, Roni. I will do whatever it takes to get you to believe in me." I leaned down, my lips just a hair's breath away from his. "Oh…by the way, I don't plan to fight fairly." And with that, I kissed him – passionately, raking my fingers through his thick mane of curls, and he surprised me – rising from his chair and pulling me closer to him, kissing me back even harder. We tumbled onto the bed, still clinging to each other. I moved to kiss him again, but this time, Roni stayed my advance, eyeing me with a serious glare.

"It's not that easy, Dara. It's going to take a hell of a lot more than that to persuade me. In fact, I should warn you, it will take a lot of extensive…how shall I put this," his lips twisted into a devious grin and the warmth returned to his eyes, "widespread effort on your part."

Relief washed over me. I shot him a wicked smile as I maneuvered myself to sit playfully on top of him. "I think I'm up to the challenge."

"Well," he said, sliding his hands up my legs, "I know I am. Oh, and by the way, Dara – you actually won me over as soon as you opened your eyes."

"What? But…then…why…why did you keep questioning me – testing my resolve – have me go on and on? You…you…gave me such a hard time."

He shrugged boyishly, "I couldn't help myself."

"That was nothing less than torture!"

"Torture? Really? Hmm…I found it rather entertaining."

"How could you!"

"Quite easily, actually."

"You are so arrogant!"

"You're exasperating!"

"It was…uncalled for."

"You had it coming."

"It was evil."

"It was hot."

"*That* made you hot?"

"Don't you know by now, Dara? Everything about you makes me hot." His hands trailed further up my legs, giving me the shivers. "Hmm. Nice skirt – smartly done," he pursed his lips in that sensual way of his. "Now, if I'm not mistaken, and I rarely am, I believe you have some serious persuading to do."

"You are incorrigible, Mr. Ben-Ari."

"Mmm. Like I once told you, it's part of my charm."

"Roni, you have no clue," I answered softly, and threw myself into the art of persuasion.

Chapter 12

"I think a couple of my ribs are broken."

Roni chuckled as he kept his eyes on the road.

"It's not funny. I love your brother, but he doesn't realize his own strength."

"I'm sorry, Dara. Gilad was just demonstrating how happy he was for us."

"I know. I'm just surprised that Margalit is still alive…she's so tiny and Gilad is, well, Gilad."

"It was a great weekend though, wasn't it?"

"It was the best, Roni. I love your family."

"And they love you."

"I'm not sure Dalya does."

"Ignore Dalya."

"So…she *doesn't* like me?"

"Actually, she likes you very much."

"But she didn't exactly seem thrilled about our engagement."

"Pay no mind to her. She's a bit self-absorbed these days." His voice suddenly took on an edge.

"It's because Natanel is never around, isn't it?"

Roni shrugged. "Probably."

I saw that Roni did not want to get into it, but I pursued the subject anyway. "Why is it that Natanel is never home? What does he do?"

"Some sort of international business, import-export, that sort of thing. He needs to travel a lot."

"When does he come home? Am I ever going to meet him?"

"What's with all these questions, Dara?"

"Well, if I'm going to be part of your family, I would just like to understand the dynamics."

"There's nothing to understand. Natanel is building up a business and it takes time. He needs to travel a lot for it – that's all."

"It must be so hard on Dalya."

"She knew what she was getting into." He answered in a tone that decidedly ended the conversation. Still, something about Dalya gnawed away at me. I could understand her unhappiness about rarely having her husband around, but what didn't make sense was the stern look she gave Roni when he announced our engagement, and then…the way he stared her down. They held an entire conversation with their eyes.

The next several weeks passed too quickly. The week before my departure, Roni and I took three days off to go hiking up north in the Golan. He knew the terrain like the back of his hand and turned out to be an excellent tour guide. We hiked in Jilabun, where we came across two of the most beautiful waterfalls, as well as a village uncovered from the time of the Second Temple, and pools of clean, fresh water. We canoed down the Jordan River and toured Gamla, the capital of the Jewish Golan from 87 BCE to 68 CE, when it was ultimately destroyed by the Romans.

On the last night, we headed back south to the beach at Lake Kinneret. Roni surprised me by inviting the gang to meet us there for an impromptu *l'chaim* – what they call an engagement party in Israel. *L'chaim* means "to life," and what can be more appropriate than toasting to life when planning a new life together? Our friends came up from Gilboa with wine and plenty of food for a barbeque on the beach. And, of course, there was no outing worth mentioning without Yaniv's guitar and his melodic voice. It was a wonderful celebration under the stars, set against a backdrop of rolling waves.

As the night wound down, everyone settled in to sleep on the beach. Roni and I walked down to the water's edge. I stared out at the sweeping water of the broad lake and began thinking about the too-near future. "Five months," I said sadly.

"It will pass quickly, Dara."

"Are you trying to convince me, or yourself?"

"The way I see it is that for the next several months, I'll be so heavily into training with my new unit that I would rarely get a chance to be with you even if you were in the country."

"Hmm, the next time I see you, you'll no longer have your long blond curls."

Roni laughed softly, "You may just walk past me without even realizing who I am."

"Not a chance." I nestled against his chest, my back to him, as he wrapped his arms around me.

"There's one more thing, *motek*. You know I'll try to write as often as I can, but…there will be times when…"

"I understand, Roni." I didn't need him to finish his thought.

"I know you do."

We were both quiet then, deep in our own thoughts as we gazed out at the blackened water of the night, serenaded by the rhythm of the crashing waves. "Dara?" Roni broke the silence. "I've been meaning to ask you something." He sounded very serious.

"What?"

"How many children would you want?"

I smiled broadly. "Oh, that's an easy one – five strapping boys just like their father. What about you?"

"Five delightful girls, just like their mother," he nuzzled his lips against my neck.

I laughed lightly, "That's ten kids…I don't know about that…"

"Mmm," he bit down softly on my shoulder, and nibbled his way back up my neck. "I suppose we could whittle it down." I delighted in the caress of his lips and drew his arms tighter about me. "How about two of each, then?" I offered.

"Perfect," he whispered into my hair. I turned around to face him, his prism-like eyes glistening into mine.

"Roni, I want our home to be noisy. Loud, noisy and full of energy. And I want music. Lots of music. I want our children to play the drums, guitar, the violin and the flute."

"Sounds to me like you want to give birth to an orchestra," his eyes creased in amusement.

"Oh, Roni, I wish this night wouldn't have to end." I leaned my head against his chest and stared out at the water, so content in the moment.

"Don't worry, *motek*. We'll have a lifetime of nights together. Look at the beach's edge. Even the thrashing roll of the waves lands in a soft splash of tranquillity. We'll have ours."

Chapter 13

The drive to Ben Gurion Airport was quiet. Strange how it felt to embark on a journey that would lead me backward in time, to an old world in which I no longer belonged, to which I no longer related. The only part I looked forward to was seeing Pops.

Roni held onto my hand throughout the drive, clasping it, caressing it as if to make the touch endure through the next several months. Words were unnecessary. No doubt, the next half year would be emotional agony for the both of us. Roni, scheduled to join his new unit in just days, said virtually nothing about his forthcoming tour of duty, and I knew better than to ask any questions. Army secrecy in this case was a blessing. I was sure that I would not want to know more than I already did. He had to do what he had to do, and I had to face the looming wrath awaiting me in New York City. In that respect, emotional agony would be putting it lightly. I wasn't sure what was more daunting...

dealing in counterterrorism or dealing with my parents. I was resolute, however. I would not have my life shackled to my father's career with the United States government. If they wouldn't trust his loyalty once I moved to Israel, then, as Roni said, my father should consider that he is working for the wrong government.

My parents made their choices; it was time for me to make mine. Should they cut me off for it – then, so be it. I knew I was making the right choice – not only for myself, but also, for my people.

Roni parked the car and helped me with my suitcases. We arrived at the entrance to the airport and didn't venture another step. Instead, we faced each other under the sweltering heat of the Tel Aviv sun, staring silently into each other's eyes, studying each other's faces, permanently etching them into our memories. The blur of travelers, luggage and taxicabs whizzed around us, all melding together into a moving canvas of the indistinct. He wrapped his arms around me, and I clung to him, relishing his solid strength. It was unthinkable that I would not feel his arms around me for five long months.

The time of my flight was fast approaching and I had yet to go through all the routine airport security checks – it was impossible to suspend the inevitable. Roni held my face in his hands and tenderly kissed the tears that ran down my cheeks. His lips then repeatedly kissed mine, neither one of us wanting to pull away. "I have something for you," Roni murmured between kisses. "I put it in your carry-on bag. Don't open it until you're on the plane."

I nodded, silently kissing him back.

"You have to go now, *motek*."

"I know."

"We're not going to say good-bye."

"Never."

"Take care of my heart."

"I will. And you, take care of mine."

"I will."

"Roni?"

"Yes, Dara."

"May God watch over you."

"Over us both." He curled his hands in my hair, his eyes boring into mine, never failing to stun me, and we kissed one last time until our lips slowly and grudgingly parted.

Once seated on the plane, I looked in my bag and found the box that Roni had placed into it. I lifted the lid and found wrapped in tissue paper a Gilboa Iris, its vibrant shade dancing in a symphony of deep amethyst. There was a small note.

> *My Sweet Dara,*
> *As is the Gilboa Iris,*
> *You are light, you are perfection, you are life.*
> *My life.*
>
> *Roni*

Chapter 14

"Mace! What a surprise."

"Hi, Dara. You look wonderful. I guess farm life agrees with you."

"I was on a kibbutz, Mace, not a farm."

"Whatever. You look great. Your parents are going to be thrilled to see you, finally."

"I thought they would be here."

"Well, turns out, your mother had an art show, and your father is still in Maryland at RDECOM. You know the drill, Dara, he'll be back tomorrow for the weekend."

"Yeah, I know the drill. How did *you* get out?"

"Your father sent me. I took the early morning shuttle from Washington. He didn't want you landing at JFK Airport without anyone to greet you."

"How thoughtful."

"Hey, if anyone should gripe, it's me. Apparently I'm pretty dispensable in the research lab."

"You know my father thinks the world of you, Mace."

"I know. It's just a matter of paying my dues. So, anyway, Columbia in the fall, huh? You must be excited." I nodded to be polite. We made our way to the airport parking lot and Mace threw my luggage in the back of his trunk, which was a chaotic jumble of disheveled clothes, research papers and empty beer cans.

"Still living out of your car, I see."

"You know me," he said with a wink, "I'm a man of perpetual habit." He opened the passenger door for me and then walked around to the driver's side. "Okay, I think we're good to go." He backed out of the parking space, burning rubber as he did so, and flew onto the Van Wyck Expressway toward the city.

"So, Mace…did you ever think of finding someone and settling down? Maybe even getting a *permanent* residence?"

"Well, I've been waiting for *you* to grow up, Dara."

"Mace, you're like a generation ahead of me," I teased.

"Hey, I'm only twenty-eight, and you're what, nineteen? That's only a nine-year difference – I think there's potential," he said, flashing an ample smile.

"Ever the optimist! I guess you never bothered checking out the singles scene in Maryland. Do you still spend weekends in New York?"

"Yeah, I don't like mixing work with play," he threw me a playful fiendish look. "Anyway, there's nothing like New York City."

"So I hear. Where do you stay these days when you're in the city and not in Maryland?"

"Oh, here and there. That's never a problem."

No, I wouldn't think it would be, I thought. Mace Devlin, graduate of engineering from MIT, was charming to a fault. He boasted a clean-cut, Midwest American look about him, Nebraska to be more precise, and was a real ladies' man. His chocolate-brown hair was close-cropped, and he had smoldering dark eyes, almost black, that were smooth and penetrating at the same time. His nose was broad and looked like it had been broken more than once, but he had a ready smile that displayed deep dimples on his cheeks as his redeeming feature. I never thought he was particularly handsome, not in the classic sense, although he had a quality about him that was extremely alluring. And he knew it.

We drove up the road to my parents' house, a brownstone on Seventieth Street, off Central Park on the Upper West Side of Manhattan. It was a quiet, tree-lined street with diverse-colored brownstone buildings and their grand, sandstone-raised entrances lining the way. Ornate carvings and ornamentation characterized the nineteenth-century architecture. My parents' house was in the center of the block. They owned the entire building, consisting of four floors, the bottom of which hosted my mother's art gallery.

Mace double-parked the car on the street and walked me to the door, carrying my suitcases with casual ease. He looked more like a marine than someone cooped up in a lab doing research. "Well, this is it, Dara. Welcome home, again."

"Thanks for picking me up from the airport."

"Hey, anytime. You know where to reach me if you need me. I have all my calls forwarded."

"To where? Your car?"

"Go out with me one night, babe, and you might just find out."

I rolled my eyes at him. "Bye, Mace."

"Take care now, Dara."

I pressed in the security code numbers to the house alarm and let myself in. Nothing had changed. The deep-red walls of the gallery greeted me with the theatrical drama to which I was accustomed. My mother loved vivid colors. She shunned muted shades, such as mauve, beige or teal, claiming they were non-colors used by uninspiring people who were too fainthearted to be bold or who were just mind-numbingly boring. I didn't agree with my mother on most things, but I did appreciate her style. She decorated the house in a myriad of Old World motifs sprinkled with a combination of Victorian touches and with what I referred to as dungeon flair. At the foot of the staircase stood a larger-than-life knight in shining armor, that I affectionately called "Charlie."

I left my luggage in the front vestibule and, not bothering to take the elevator, sprinted up two flights of stairs to Pops' room. Looking almost wistful, he was sitting in a plush, winged-back chair by the window staring listlessly to the outside. In addition to his heart problems, he was suffering from Alzheimer's, and his lucid moments, even a year ago, were becoming less frequent. I stepped nearer to him, kneeled by his chair and gently took his hand into mine. "Pops. It's Dara. I'm back."

"Dara?"

"Yes, Pops."

"Stand up. Let me look at you." I did what he asked. "Israel agrees with you, my dear Dara. Did your parents see you yet?"

"No. They're not home. I just arrived this minute."

"You need to go back…to Israel," he said in a hushed tone. "Do not make my mistake. Go back, before it's too late."

"I will, Pops. I promise. I'm only here for a few months. I came back because I wanted to see you. I missed you so much."

"So, now you've seen me. You can go back now." He turned his face back to the window.

"Pops, I want to spend time with you. I'm taking a semester at Columbia, but I'm not dorming. I wanted to be with you as much as possible before I return to Israel."

"Fine, Dara. Perhaps we'll take a walk in the park after you finish your dinner and do your homework."

"Oh, but Pops, classes don't start until —"

"And if you're a good little girl, I'll buy you an ice cream from Mr. Softee. Run along now."

"Sure, Pops, sure. That'll be great."

I scurried downstairs and rummaged through supplies that my mother stored in a back room behind the gallery until I found the frame I was looking for. I then dragged my luggage into the elevator and brought it to my bedroom on the top floor. Before unpacking, I took out the box that Roni had slipped into my carry-on bag and pressed the purple flower into an antiqued silver picture frame, his note tucked and hidden in the back. I took down the Monet that hung on the wall over my desk and replaced it with the Gilboa Iris.

Chapter 15

My reunion with my parents was as expected – impassive. Neither one of them spoke about my future plans. Nor did they venture any questions about Roni. It was as if he didn't exist. Knowing how they tended to think, they assumed that I had succumbed to their pressure – or would eventually *come to my senses*. They even ignored the ruby and diamond ring I wore. While not a traditional engagement ring, it could not have gone unnoticed. Whatever strategy they thought they were pursuing, I was relieved at not having any confrontation and likewise opted to remain silent on the matter. I would simply inform them that I would be leaving when the time for my departure neared. In the meantime, Roni, true to his word, had already reserved a return ticket for me five months from now.

I registered for all my courses, consisting of journalism, writing and communications classes, including an elective in beginners' Arabic.

The Upper West Side of Manhattan was a hot spot in the city, and I lost no time in building up my Israel college fund by obtaining a waitressing job in a neighborhood restaurant. Having the endgame in sight and keeping insanely busy, I told myself, would make the time go faster.

Every now and then, I would receive a call from Roni. They were few and far between as he was only able to make international calls from home when he received time off from training, which was not very often. I wrote to him every night. It was the only way I could fall asleep, and with six thousand miles separating us, it was the closest thing to being with him – a cathartic coping mechanism. I would write to Shimshon and Evaleen, as well. Jenny and I kept in contact, too, and I looked forward to hearing how her relationship with Yaniv progressed.

Other distractions helped the time pass. Three of my friends from high school remained in New York for college. The rest left for universities out of state. I wasn't one to cultivate many friends, but the few I had were pleasant enough. Still, I never had much in common with them. My head was always in Israel, and theirs was not. While I did try to get together with them from time to time, now, more than ever, with all that transpired during my year in Israel, I felt far removed from them.

Two months into the semester, my beloved Pops' heart gave out, and he passed away. The night of his passing, I had just finished reading to him the last pages of his favorite book, *O Jerusalem!* by Larry Collins and Dominique Lapierre. It encompassed the reestablishment of the State of Israel in 1948 and brought alive the memories of my grandfather, who fought in Israel's War of Independence in the wake of the Arabs refusing the United Nations' partition plan. He never forgave himself for returning to the United States, but I had promised him that I would fulfill his dream – the journey back to our homeland. Pops died that night peacefully in his sleep.

At the end of the *shivah*, my father peeked into my room. "May I come in?"

"Of course, Dad."

"I know how much you loved him, Dara."

I nodded.

"You know, when you left to work on the kibbutz, he was very proud of you. But I'm glad you're home."

"Dad."

"Yes?"

"I plan to continue making Pops proud of me."

He lowered his eyes, wrinkling his forehead in thought. "Dara," he finally said, "your intentions will make my position at RDECOM very difficult. They already are. I cannot allow you to move to Israel and marry an IDF officer. That will just complicate my situation."

"What do you mean by 'they already are'?" I asked, disregarding his last comment. I refused to get into an argument over it.

"They're watching me – checking up on me." His voice was strangely agitated.

"Dad, you've been with RDECOM for years. Why on earth would they be watching you now?"

"I haven't figured that out yet," he answered, distracted, and walked out of the room.

✺

After grandfather's passing, my life in the States turned into one huge blur – the weeks all running into each other, void of significance. Even seeing my mother was a rarity, as she occupied herself with her art shows and her cultural pursuits – that is, when she wasn't teaching. Just as well. For when she was around, our relationship was strained, and I didn't care for the pretentious company that she kept. On weekends, when my father would be home, he would spend most of his time working in his library. Without Pops, each day was more inconsequential than the preceding one.

I toyed with the idea of leaving the States sooner than I had planned, but I decided it made sense to finish the semester. Roni had called the previous day and told me that he would be in a training exercise outside of Israel for the next several weeks and I wouldn't be hearing from him for quite some time. He could not tell me where. There was little to look forward to outside of crossing off the days on my calendar, marking the time until my semester was over and I would return to Israel, and to Roni.

Soon, however, I would be longing for the repetitive, lackluster life.

It was a Saturday night at the end of November when I returned home from a late-night shift at the restaurant. I saw from the street that my parents had the lights turned on at each floor level. I glanced at my watch. It was three in the morning. *That's odd at this late hour.* I punched in the security code and entered.

Random papers strewn all over the floor greeted me. Paintings were thrown off the walls. Those that weren't, hung askew, and the wind from the opened door blew white fuzzy stuff around like leaves in an autumn dance, the stray papers rustling around my feet. I took several cautious steps into the gallery and noticed that someone had repeatedly slashed my mother's English Victorian couches, their white fillers bleeding out. *Oh my God. We've been robbed.*

But where were the police? Why hadn't my parents called the restaurant to tell me – to warn me about the robbery? They had gone out with friends to a Broadway play, but surely they should have been home...hours ago. I studied the gallery more carefully. The expensive artwork was not taken. In fact, nothing of any obvious value was taken. Someone had ransacked the place…looking for something specific. After fumbling through the mess, I found the phone in the disarray and called the police. The smart thing would have been to leave the house and wait outside until the police arrived; only I wasn't too smart that night.

I don't know what prodded me, but I started up the flight of stairs leading toward the main floor of our home. The creaks in the wooden staircase seemed louder than usual and I stepped lightly, as if walking on broken glass. Upon reaching the first landing, shockwaves flooded my veins, my knees buckled and I screamed in horror. There, on the steps before me, just past the landing, my father's body, riddled with bullets, lay facedown, his blood splattered on the adjacent wall. I pulled myself up by grabbing onto the stair rail for support and stared in disbelief, transfixed, frozen in terror, my heart pounding ferociously against my rib cage.

Gradually, I struggled out of my semicatatonic state and tried to think coherently. "Mom," I uttered under my breath. "Oh, my God, Mom!" I yelled out and staggered up the rest of the steps to the upper floor. The living room was identical to the gallery – in total disarray. I spun around in every direction, confused, tripping over the tangled mayhem. From the corner of my eye, I spotted red splotches on the white-tiled floor of the kitchen and forced myself to follow the trail around the large rectangular island. I found my mother sprawled out on the floor in a pool of blood, her eyes wide open, revealing her final look of surprise, and her body, like my father's, sprayed with bullets.

A bloodcurdling scream escaped from my throat. In my hysteria, I hadn't noticed that I was no longer alone and jumped when two hands gripped my shoulders from behind me. I went wild. The hands held me more firmly. "Easy, Miss. You're safe now, we're the police!" The floor beneath my feet began to sway like the ocean. The kitchen cabinets swirled around me, black patches clouded my vision and I crumpled into unconsciousness.

When I came to, I was on the living-room sofa. The tumult throughout the house buzzed in my head, and I realized that I had not awoken from a nightmare; I was living it. Strange men traipsed throughout the house, combing every room, dusting for fingerprints and taking what seemed like hundreds of pictures. It was all true. Someone had murdered my parents, yet my mind couldn't fully accept it. I rolled my head to the side to find a man dressed in blue jeans, tan Frye boots and a worn-in brown leather bomber jacket. He introduced himself as Detective Tanzy. Although he was right next to me, his voice seemed thousands of miles away. I sat up and stared at him as though in a haze. He had the look of a jaded warrior. Another officer brought me a glass of water.

"Miss Harow, is there anything I can get you?" Detective Tanzy asked in a compassionate tone.

"No...thank you," I murmured, zombie-like. From where I sat, I saw a man carry a body bag into the kitchen. I gasped loudly. It hit me with a sickening jolt that my mother would be placed in that body bag. I jumped up, wide-eyed, and yelled, "That's my mother in the kitchen! W-where are they taking my mother?"

"Miss Harow, we're taking your parents to the medical examiner for autopsies. It's routine in a homicide. We require a forensic report."

"No...that can't happen." Something mechanical inside me took over, snapping me out of my dazed state.

"Pardon?" He eyed me with suspicion. The absurdity of it struck me. "Detective Tanzy," I began in a tone that was comparable to reprimanding a child, rather than addressing a forty-something detective. "Jewish law is very sensitive to the way we treat our dead." My entire world now was out of my control, and a natural instinct kicked in to regain some. Even in my state of shock, I was cognizant enough to remember that autopsies were forbidden in Jewish law. I couldn't let that happen to my parents. I didn't know if there were exceptions in cases of homicide, but I had to find out. I started to move toward the kitchen when Detective Tanzy grabbed my arm to stop me. "Miss Harow, please…don't go in there now. I don't advise it."

"The phone book is in there."

"Whose number do you need?"

"My rabbi."

"What's his name?"

"Rabbi Joseph Sanders. His number is in the phone book on the kitchen counter."

The detective delegated one of the uniformed police officers to the task before turning his attention back to me. "Please, Detective, you can't let them perform an autopsy…not until I speak with Rabbi Sanders. It may be allowed in this case, but I need to make sure." It was strange for me to hear my voice sound oddly in control as I spoke. All the while, inside my head, an inner voice was screeching, *No! No! No! This can't be happening!*

"Miss, this is a double homicide. Your rabbi is not going to be able to prevent a forensic investigation." He must have thought it bizarre that I was harping on the autopsies. I suppose it was. But who can say what a *normal* reaction should be when one stumbles across murdered parents? I certainly didn't feel normal. Nothing was normal. Normal had died this night.

Detective Tanzy led me back to the couch. It was jarring to hear him categorize my parents as *a double homicide*. I felt as if I had tumbled into a television set, Alice in Wonderland–style, but wound up in a horrifying crime drama. "I know this is a devastating shock for you," he continued in a gentle tone, "but I have to ask you a few questions." I nodded and then rose from the couch. There was one thing I needed to do before facing any questions. "Uh, Miss Harow, where are you going?"

"I must find a phone."

Detective Tanzy tilted his head to one side, rose from his chair and followed me with curiosity to my father's library, which doubled as his home office. It resembled a war zone. After adjusting my eyes to the bedlam, I found the phone on the floor, buried beneath some of my father's documents. The number I needed was on speed dial.

"Hello?"

"Mace...it's Dara."

Chapter 16

"Do you have any idea of who would want to kill your parents?"

"No, of course not," I shook my head, taken aback at the thought, while clutching nervously on a couch pillow.

"Miss Harow, there was no sign of a break-in. Whoever did this knew the security code. Can you tell me who besides you and your parents had access to the code?"

"The cleaning woman."

"What's her name?"

"Maryann. Maryann Chezkow." Detective Tanzy jotted down the information in a small notepad.

"Do you know her number?" he continued.

"No. But...it's on the message board in the kitchen."

"And do you know anyone by the name of Charles, or Charlie or Charlotte?"

"No...why?"

"Your father managed to write in his own blood the letters C-h-a-r-l on the stairs before he died."

"I...I didn't see that."

"You were in shock. That's understandable."

"I'm sorry...I...I don't know any Charles or Charlotte."

"Who else knows the code?"

"Um...Mace."

"Who exactly is this Mace?"

"Mace Devlin. He's worked with my father for the past few years at RDECOM."

"What's RDECOM?"

"It's the US Army Research, Development and Engineering Command. It's based in Maryland."

Detective Tanzy looked up from his notepad. His eyes narrowed in interest. "What kind of work did your father do there?"

"I don't know much detail. It had to do with missile development and missile defense systems."

"And you say that Mace Devlin worked with him?"

"Yes...as his assistant. Mace had become like family. He'll be here any minute."

"Miss Harow, how long have you known Mace Devlin?"

"About two years, maybe a little more...ever since he began working at RDECOM."

"Two years, huh? It might be best for you if you weren't so trusting. It just might save your life." He then turned to one of the other detectives who was sitting in on the questioning. "Nick, get the captain on the phone. The FBI is going to want to be in on this. And... let's get a workup on Mace Devlin."

"The FBI?" I murmured.

"I suggest you try to get some sleep, Miss Harow. You'll need to come into the station tomorrow for more questioning. Do you have anyone you can stay with?"

"No. I…I want to stay here. This is still my home."

"This is a crime scene now."

"Well, you and your men should do whatever it is you have to do, but I want to stay in my home."

"She can stay with me." Mace suddenly appeared in my living room.

"Who are you?" Detective Tanzy asked.

"Mace Devlin. I'm a friend of the family." He sat down beside me and put a comforting arm around me.

Detective Tanzy's face took on a cynical glare as he sized him up. "So I hear. I take it you won't mind then if I ask you a few questions."

"Not at all."

"The name's Detective Tanzy."

"Well, Detective, I'll try to help in any way I can."

"I'm counting on that. Here's my card. I'd like to see you at the station tomorrow with Miss Harow, or I should say later today, since it's already almost six o'clock. Be at the precinct at one o'clock."

"Certainly. We'll be there. Come, Dara."

"Where are we going?"

"You can't stay here. Not now. We'll get a room at the Mayflower Hotel. It's just a few blocks from here. You need to get some sleep."

What I really needed was Roni. I didn't know if I would be able to hold it together without him. But he was unreachable, and I had no idea when he'd be back from his training exercise – whatever that meant.

"Don't worry, Dara," Mace said as he led me to his car. After the police finish their business, I'll have a team come in and clean the place for you. In the meantime, you'll stay with me. I'm not going to take my eyes off of you."

I suppose I should have felt some relief in that, but all I felt was numb. *They were gone. They were really gone. Forever. Just like that. I was an orphan.* I couldn't grasp that my parents were dead, murdered. "Mace...why would anyone want to kill my parents? What could they have been searching for?"

"I have no idea," he shook his head. "I'm so sorry, Dara. You know I thought the world of your parents."

"I'm so scared."

"Hey, sweetness," he turned to me and held my face in his hands, "I won't let any harm come to you. Like I said, I won't let you out of my sight."

"You can't be with me all the time, Mace. You have to return to RDECOM Monday morning."

"You let me worry about the details. Now, let's get into the car and find a room at the Mayflower. You've got to try to get some sleep. You'll need your strength."

I awoke with a start. "Charlie." It suddenly dawned on me who Charlie was. I looked around at the unfamiliar trappings of the hotel room. Mace had gotten a room with two single beds, but he wasn't in his. I heard the shower from behind the bathroom door, and took advantage of the situation. Still in my clothes, I jumped out of bed, slipped my boots on and grabbed my bag and jacket. It was just a few blocks to my house.

There was no one in sight when I arrived at the front door. I ducked under the police crime-scene tape and then punched in the security code to gain entrance. There he was, Charlie, the larger-than-life knight that stood vigil at the foot of the staircase. Standing on the tips of my toes, I lifted the visor on the closed helmet. My hunch was right, for when I reached inside, I yanked out a thick file of papers wedged within. Without looking at it, I stuffed it into my bag. When I opened the front door to leave, Mace had just walked up to the entrance. "My God, Dara!

You scared the hell out of me! What were you doing in there?"

"I needed to get something."

"So you had to sneak out of the hotel without telling me? What was so urgent?"

"I had to get…money. I realized that my wallet was empty."

"And that couldn't wait?"

"I'm sorry, Mace. I didn't mean to worry you. I guess I'm not thinking straight."

He blew out a gust of air and put his arm around me. "Well, I suppose I can't blame you for that. C'mon, we've got a date with a detective."

"H…how did you know I was here?"

"Where the hell else would you go?"

Chapter 17

 Police Precinct, West Eighty-Second Street

"You're a very interesting person, Mr. Devlin."

"How so, Detective?"

"We've done a little homework on you. It's not every day that a kid from the back roads of Nebraska gets to travel to exotic places like Lebanon."

"Last I checked it wasn't against the law to travel."

"Did you hear me accuse you of anything, Mr. Devlin?"

"No, sir," Mace whipped out his dimpled smile.

"Why Lebanon of all places?"

"Why not?"

"Oh, I don't know," Tanzy's tone dripped with sarcasm. "Maybe because there's a civil war there? Maybe because it has become dangerous for Americans to travel there without getting kidnapped."

"Maybe I like living on the edge," Mace quipped.

"What were you doing there for six months?"

"Lebanon is a fascinating place, Detective Tanzy. I wanted to travel after getting my degree from MIT before settling down in a job."

"Where did you travel besides Lebanon?"

"It appears to me that you already have that information."

"Just answer the question, Mr. Devlin."

"Germany. I traveled to Germany for several months and then to Lebanon."

"What did you do in Germany?"

"Drank beer and hung with the *fraulein*."

"Do you know a Gerhard Kestel?"

"No."

"Are you sure about that?" Detective Tanzy asked with a skeptical frown that seemed to be a permanent fixture on his face.

"Yes. I'm sure."

With a contemptuous smirk, the detective excused himself from the room. A few minutes later, he returned to the interrogation room with a man in a dark-gray suit. His forehead bore a deep-set widow's peak and his black-rimmed glasses hung low on the bridge of his nose, imparting an appearance of an IRS auditor. "Mr. Devlin, this is FBI Special Investigator Harris Taylor."

Traces of his smile vanished. Mace was visibly annoyed. "Should I be calling my lawyer?"

"Do you think you'll need one, Mr. Devlin?" Agent Harris was expressionless as he seated himself across from Mace, placing a file on the table between them.

"Why am I being questioned by the FBI?"

"That's a simple question to answer," he said, almost bored. "It probably has something to do with your affiliation with Gerhard Kestel, your denying that you know him, your work at RDECOM and the double homicide of Dr. and Mrs. Gabriel Harow." The FBI agent opened his file and took out a photo, placing it on the table in front of Mace. "That person that you're standing next to in this photo is Gerhard Kestel. This picture was taken two years ago in Lebanon, in 1982, and two years after Gerhard Kestel moved his paramilitary training camp to Lebanon with PLO assistance. Mr. Kestel is a neo-Nazi leader with close ties to Yasser Arafat, the Hezbollah and the Muslim Brotherhood…but you already knew that, Mr. Devlin, didn't you?"

Mace stared hard at the photo, furrowing his brows in confusion. "I don't know any Gerhard. This guy introduced himself to me as Wilhelm Hess. We met at a bar in Berlin, and I didn't ask him about his politics. We got friendly and he invited me to a party at his apartment – so I went. I figured what could be so bad…women, beer…why not?"

The investigator coolly conveyed his disappointment. "Surely you can come up with something more creative."

Mace eyed both Detective Tanzy and Special Investigator Harris Taylor with a condescending grin. "You're both picking at straws here. You've got nothing to go on, so you're wasting your time questioning me about some bum I hung out with at a bar in my travels. Well, let me save you some time, gentlemen. I'm a man who enjoys a good beer or two – or three," he added, as an afterthought. "I meet plenty of questionable characters in the lairs I hang out in. It makes life interesting. But I don't give a damn about their politics and they don't give a damn about mine. We get drunk and we get laid. End of story."

Taylor stared at Mace as if looking straight through him, disregarding what he considered a poor attempt at a cover-up, and then continued with his questioning as if Mace had not uttered a word. "Before traveling to Germany, Mr. Devlin, you spent some time in Elohim City in Oklahoma."

"Yes. My sister lives there with her husband. What of it?"

"So your sister is a neo-Nazi, too?"

"Now wait just a minute!" Mace stood up from his chair.

"Sit down, Devlin!" Detective Tanzy ordered, shoving him back into the chair, startling him.

"We know what kind of place Elohim City is," Taylor continued in a monotone voice. "You're a Nazi, Mace Devlin – a home-grown, white Aryan supremacist, scum-of-the-earth Nazi."

"I don't have to take this crap! Are you arresting me, or what? Because if that's all you've got, you have no right to hold me here."

"With what kind of work were you and Dr. Harow involved at RDECOM?" Taylor asked, ignoring Mace's outburst.

"That's classified," he spit out.

"But you don't have the same security clearance as Dr. Harow did. Do you?"

"No."

"Still, you had two years to ingratiate yourself with Dr. Harow and gain his trust. So much so, that you were often a houseguest in his home."

"I had a tremendous amount of respect for Dr. Harow. And yes, he and his wife were very gracious to me."

"Did they know you were a neo-Nazi?"

"I'm not a neo-Nazi."

"Mr. Devlin, you run from one neo-Nazi stronghold to another, from here to Germany to the Middle East. You met with Gerhard Kestel in Berlin and then met up with him again in Lebanon. This picture of you and Kestel was taken at his paramilitary base in Lebanon."

Mace shifted uneasily in his chair, his Midwestern charm cracking under the strain. "This is all pure conjecture on your part," he insisted. "While in Berlin, I mentioned to him that I was planning to travel to Lebanon and since he was planning to be there as well, he told me to look him up when I got there."

"Your explanations are ridiculously flimsy. Who do you think you're talking to?"

"I'm telling you the truth."

"Mr. Devlin, we can place you at the headquarters of the National Socialist German Workers Party in Lincoln, Nebraska. Here's a copy of your membership ID card." Taylor pulled out another sheet from his file and placed it in front of Mace.

Mace's expression turned cocky. "That's not illegal."

"It is if you're involved in the coordination of neo-Nazi and Muslim terrorist activities."

"I don't know what you're talking about."

"Of course not," Taylor said dryly. "Let's get back to you and Dr. Harow: You took the shuttle together to New York on Friday. Isn't that correct?"

"Yes. We traveled together every Friday to New York."

"So, he must have mentioned his weekend plans to you."

"He may have said something about a Broadway show."

"For that reason you didn't expect him to come home early Saturday night."

"What the Harows did on their weekends did not affect me one way or another."

"What were you searching for last night in the Harows' home?"

"I wasn't there."

"You were after some classified material that Dr. Harow had in his possession. Material that you didn't have security clearance for – material that you wished to pass on to Arab terrorists."

"That's pretty far-fetched, even for the FBI. But anyway, I told you, I was nowhere near the Harows' home on Saturday night."

"Where were you?"

"With a lady friend."

"All night?"

"Pretty much. That is, until I got the call from Dara, which was about, I don't know, maybe four in the morning. The detective can back me up on that." He nodded his chin toward Detective Tanzy.

"And, needless to say, your lady friend will back you up on your alibi."

"She has no reason not to."

"What is your interest in Dara Harow? I understand you shared a room with her at the Mayflower after the double murder."

"*She* called me. She doesn't have anyone else here that she can trust. And I think it's understandable that I'd try to be a comfort to her at this time. She needed a place to stay – I wasn't going to leave her high and dry. The poor kid is in a state of shock."

Detective Tanzy, until now, remained quiet while observing Taylor and Mace. He had a look of disgust on his face. "That's touching. Quite a balancing act, Devlin – being a neo-Nazi and comforting a Jew at the same time." Tanzy started for the door. "I've heard enough."

"I told you, I'm not a Nazi." Mace glared at him.

"Then how is it that you are a member of a neo-Nazi organization?" Taylor broke in. Mace rolled his eyes and sighed loudly. "I joined when I was eighteen. It was a social thing – I never took it seriously."

"Now I've heard everything." Detective Tanzy left the room. Taylor showed no emotion on his face. He simply took out another photo from his file and placed it on the table. Mace's face turned ashen, his lips twitched involuntarily.

"I think we can stop dancing around the truth now…don't you, Mr. Devlin?"

"I'm very sorry to have kept you waiting, Miss Harow."

"That's all right."

"How are you holding up?"

"I don't even know how to answer that," I said numbly to Detective Tanzy.

"Miss Harow…"

"Please, Detective…can you call me Dara? I'm just not comfortable with this Miss Harow stuff."

"Sure. Sure, Dara…. Look, there are some things I need to clarify with you. I spoke with your parents' friends, the Neilsons, the ones that they had gone out with last night. According to them, none of them cared for the Broadway show they attended and so they walked out and had a bite to eat. Your parents then returned home early. We don't believe the murder of your parents was premeditated. In fact, we think the people who killed them knew of their plans to go out and didn't expect them to be home. We don't know what they were searching for, but our guess is that it was tied in to your father's work at RDECOM. Mace Devlin is a suspect and is being questioned right now by Special Investigator Harris Taylor of the FBI. The double homicide of your parents is from here on in an FBI case."

"I don't understand. When Mr. Taylor questioned me earlier he didn't mention his suspicions about Mace. Why would Mace be implicated in any of this?"

"We think he was involved in the murder of your parents. He had the capacity and the motive. I'm not saying that he pulled the trigger, but he was the only other person outside of your housekeeper who knew the code to your home security system. We believe he was involved in the entire operation. As I said, the fact that your parents were home was a surprise – Devlin expected them to be out for the night.

"We're sure that the purpose of the break-in was to acquire classified information from RDECOM, which Devlin suspected was in your house. He didn't have the security clearance to get hold of it at RDECOM, but he could steal it from your father's home office, if he had reason to believe that your father brought his work home with him."

"Detective Tanzy, I think you're wrong about Mace. He would never harm my parents."

"Think again, Dara. We have proof that he's a neo-Nazi with ties to Arab terrorists."

That couldn't be true. Impossible. Mace? A neo-Nazi? Arab terrorists? This was too big to wrap my head around. *Roni, where are you now? I need you.* No. It couldn't be true. Mace was a character, but he was no neo-Nazi. Detective Tanzy *had* to be wrong. I trusted Mace. "Is Mace under arrest?"

"Not yet. The FBI doesn't have enough hard evidence to make anything stick. But they'll get it."

"In other words, you *don't* have any proof. Mace has always been kind and considerate to both my parents and me. You're making a mistake. You must be. Did…did he admit to being a neo-Nazi?"

"He doesn't have to. We know he has a membership with a neo-Nazi organization based in Nebraska. He claims he joined just as a social thing when he was eighteen – that he didn't really buy into any of it, but," Detective Tanzy scoffed, "that's a hard sell.

"Look, it seems like it's a family thing – his sister lives in a neo-Nazi community called Elohim City in Oklahoma. His friends – his affiliates – are neo-Nazis. Believe me, Dara, he's not to be trusted. He's dangerous and I don't have a doubt in my mind that he was involved. But be smart about it…until he's arrested, don't let him think you suspect him of anything. Just keep a distance. It'll be healthier for you."

My head was spinning, not to mention pounding from a massive headache. "Detective Tanzy," I said wearily, "at this point, I trust no one. Not even you."

"You can't afford to have misplaced loyalties. You don't owe anything to Devlin. Listen to me, Dara –"

"No…I've had enough!" The words thundered out of me, and the tears, for the first time since last night, came streaming out. I could no longer discuss my parents' murder. I could no longer stand hearing the words. I couldn't process what the detective was saying about Mace. It didn't make sense to me. None of it did. I hadn't even had a chance to absorb that my mother and father were dead…that I would never see them again…that I would never have the chance to make peace with them…that they were gone…forever. I didn't even know when I would be able to bury them, for God's sake. I was losing it. No. I had already lost it. I wanted to run. Run far away from all of this. I rushed out of Detective Tanzy's office just as Mace walked out of the interrogation room. He grabbed me, seeing the tears run down my face. "Hey, Dara! What happened?"

"I have to get out of here," I blubbered.

"You and me both, babe. Let's go."

Chapter 18

 IDF-Aman Special Operations – Field Training Base

"At ease, Lieutenant. Have a seat."

Roni sat down in the chair in front of the desk opposite Colonel Dani Yamit.

"Roni, I summoned you in from the field to see me because you'll be going out on a special mission. Initially, you'll be doing it solo, joined up later by an operations team when it becomes necessary. You'll be leaving four days from tomorrow."

"What about the rest of the training exercise?"

"There's no need for you to finish the current exercise. You've more than proven yourself in your training; you came back from your previous ops with flying colors, and your talents meet the criteria. You're ready."

"What is the mission?"

"The Islamic population in Europe is growing rapidly, especially in England, France, Germany and Belgium. Their influence is prominent in public opinion all over the continent, through the press, universities, funding and in the surge of underground anti-Jewish groups. Global terrorism is about to explode and influence foreign policies. We have every reason to believe that the Jews of Europe are targets, as well as our embassies. Neo-Nazis are well into the picture. That's where you come in, Roni. Coordination between the Arabs and Nazis is as old as World War II, but it's growing and gaining momentum. In addition, arms trafficking between neo-Nazis and Arab terrorists like the Muslim Brotherhood have grown to significant proportions. For years, neo Nazis have funded Islamic terror, and white supremacists have likewise received funding and training from Pan-Arab Socialists like Arafat and Colonel Gaddafi of Libya – also from Wahabi Islamists and Shiite revolutionaries."

As Roni listened, his gut drew taut at what Dani was about to ask of him. Dani read the suspicion in Roni's eyes, but continued undaunted. "Your goals, Roni, will be multiple, at times overlapping. We need you to infiltrate the neo-Nazis' operation in Europe. You're going to be German and you're going to become one of them. You will gain access to the top brass and gather information on the covert operations between them and the PLO and Hezbollah, for starters."

"Wait a minute, Dani. I don't like the direction this is going."

"Let me finish, Roni. I promise all will be clear to you. We also need to get a handle on the connections between the neo-Nazis and Iraq and Iran. By taking out the Osirak nuclear reactor, we've contained that particular Iraqi threat for now, but Iraq and Iran are actively looking to enhance their missile capabilities. They're in the market for technologically advanced intercontinental ballistic missiles. Now we know Iran purchased short-range Scud missiles from North Korea, but they're shopping around for missiles with advanced solid-fuel and multistage missile systems, which would enhance survivability and range in flight. We know what that means for Israel. And we know the neo-Nazis are offering themselves up as suppliers, both in technology and resources – not to mention 'terror for hire' squads. We need to recognize who is who in these radical movements and prevent them from becoming the hired guns and suppliers of missile technology, forged documents, weapons and explosives to be used against our government and governments at war with Jihadi Islam."

"Just as I thought, Dani – you're talking about a mission that will span years."

"That's right, Roni."

Roni shot him a stern look "That's not what I signed up for. That's more the Mossad's line of work."

Dani had dreaded this moment. But he also knew there was no choice. "This is actually a joint effort between the IDF's Aman Special Operations Unit and the Mossad. And…the Mossad wants you to head this mission."

Wary now, Roni narrowed his eyes at the colonel.

"Fine, Roni…*I* recommended you to them, but they had already singled you out."

"Hold on there, Dani. This isn't a mission. It's a life sentence! I joined Special Ops to take on short-range missions, at the most two, three weeks at a time."

"Look, Roni, you're top rate and this is right up your alley of expertise. The threats are multifold, and I just gave it to you in the abridged version. This is too important to settle for second best. And… the wheels are already in motion for this op."

"What? Why throw this in my lap? What about Kobi?"

"He has a wife, two kids and one on the way. And…he's good, but he's not you."

"You're going to tell me that the Mossad doesn't have anyone else in their ranks?"

"Look, Roni, there are no two ways about it. You're the best for this job. Your German is flawless. You're a natural, not to mention a perfect-looking Aryan, and you are by far the sharpest, most well-oiled counterterrorist elite soldier, both physically and mentally. Once the Mossad has its sights on someone they don't give up easily. You were made for this mission. I know it, the Mossad knows it and, more importantly, you know it."

"The hell I do! You had no right!" Roni stood up in a fury.

The colonel rose to his feet as well and roared back. "I did what I knew was best. There's too much at stake here! The mission comes first, Roni!"

The two men stared at each other in silence. There was a knock at the door, and Aliza, Dani's secretary, tiptoed in, placed a fax on the colonel's desk and left as silently as she came in. Dani skimmed over the fax and then looked up at Roni, his manner more composed. "Your handler is Dov Regev. You're to meet him at his Herzliya office tomorrow at 1400 hours. He'll brief you on all the logistics."

Barely containing his rage, Roni plodded past Dani's desk to stare out the window, shaking his head from side to side. "This is bullshit. I have a life."

"And you'll get it back, Roni. You're young. You can be out of this by the time you're…thirty…max, thirty-five."

"You know damn well that's not the case," he spit out from the gut. Every muscle in his body tensed under the weight of the somber choice set before him.

"Roni, it's always the outstanding ones who make the greatest sacrifices."

Roni glared at him from over his shoulder. He turned his face back to the window. He was burning, his chest heaving in anger with his every breath. Without looking back at the colonel, he shot out, "And what if I refuse?"

The colonel moved from his desk and stepped slowly and thoughtfully toward Roni. He put his hand firmly on his shoulder. "I know you. There's a lot riding on this mission. You won't walk away from this one," and then added, "Look, Roni…just…think it over."

Roni closed his eyes and bowed his head. "Screw you, Dani," he hissed through clenched teeth.

Without another word, Roni turned to leave. He threw open the office door, banging it into the adjacent wall, shaking the room to its foundations. He walked out, the door tottering closed behind him.

Colonel Yamit sat back down in his chair by his desk and rested his chin wearily on his clasped hands. He took in a deep breath and blew out loudly before reaching for the phone to dial a number in Herzliya. "Dov? We've got him. He'll report to you tomorrow."

⚜

Roni hovered around the secretary's station. It took several long minutes for him to get his seething under control, as he paced back and forth, deep in thought. Aliza found it difficult to concentrate on her work. It wasn't so much the pacing, as Roni himself being the main distraction. He was clearly the most strikingly handsome man at the base, or rather the most strikingly handsome man she had ever met. It was an effort to remember that she was engaged to be married. In any case, she knew Roni Ben-Ari was all business and never fraternized with any of the female personnel at the base, a rarity among the soldiers. So when he finally looked straight at her and spoke to her, she was more than just a bit flustered.

"Aliza?"

"Y-yes, Lieutenant?" She looked up, startled, his luminous eyes making her feel unhinged. "I'll need an empty office and a phone for a little while."

"Yes, sir. Right this way, please." She ushered him to an office down the short corridor. "In here, sir. No one is using this office for now."

"Would you see to it that I'm not disturbed?"

"Certainly, Lieutenant."

"Thank you."

Aliza closed the office door behind her and returned to her desk, quite flushed. Behind the closed door, Roni proceeded to make a call. At the other end a woman's voice answered, "Hello?"

"It's Roni. We have to talk."

Next Day, Mossad Headquarters, Herzliya

"Glad to have you on board, Roni."

"Thanks, Dov."

"Let's get down to business. You'll only have a few days to learn all the information."

"I'm ready."

"Dani told me you're a no-nonsense kind of guy," Dov said with a warm smile. "Okay then, what do you know about Gerhard Kestel?"

Chapter 19

 Lincoln Center Coffee House, Columbus Avenue, New York

"Feeling better now?"

"Yes, Mace, thank you. I didn't even realize that I hadn't eaten in twenty-four hours."

"Hey, that's what I'm here for. Don't worry about a thing, Dara. I'll look out for you. Which reminds me...you should call Rabbi Sanders and find out about funeral arrangements."

I nodded, my despair resurfacing.

"On second thought, I'll call him. You just concentrate on getting your strength back. I'll also find out when you can get back into your house. In the meantime, you can stay with me at my friend's apartment uptown. Just leave everything to me, sweetness."

"Your friend won't mind?"

"Not at all. Besides, he's out of town for a couple of days and by the time he returns, you'll have your house back."

"You seem to have friends all over the place."

Mace chuckled over his coffee. "Hey, you know me, Dara. I guess I'm well connected."

"Mace...thanks...for everything. I don't know how I would manage without you being here."

"Don't even think about it. Look, your parents were always kind to me. It's the least I can do. And besides, it never hurts to be seen with a pretty woman," he winked. I attempted to smile. "Now, that's what I want to see. Don't worry about a thing, Dara. No one will harm you under my watch. Speaking of which, what did Detective Tanzy do that upset you so much?"

"I...I just couldn't handle all the homicide talk anymore. I felt choked from all his...conspiracy theories and...I just had to get out of there."

"You were upset over what they were saying about me, too, right? It scared you?"

"Yes," I confessed.

"Are you afraid of me?" He leaned over the table to brush away a tear that escaped down my cheek.

"I don't want to be." My voice cracked.

"Look, Dara, they have nothing on me. Back in Nebraska, when I was just a teenager, I did some stupid things, and they're making all sorts of assumptions about it. I didn't even understand what I was doing back then. Hell, I was just a typical kid getting stoned all the time and sometimes hanging with the wrong kind of people." He let out a wisp of breath while shaking his head at a distant memory. "I even joined a local neo-Nazi organization. I'm embarrassed to say so, but I'm telling you this because it really didn't mean anything to me. It's not as if I believed any of their propaganda, or even had half a mind to listen to it. Like I said, I was frying my brain in a perpetual buzz during those years. It's a wonder how I ever made it into MIT," he added with a crooked grin.

"Anyway...I'm not that stupid kid anymore. That was a long time ago. I've grown up; I know better. Unfortunately," he leaned back in his chair and sighed heavily, "my past has come back now to haunt me. But...it'll all get straightened out. I'm not worried." He leaned in and reached for my hand across the table, "You can trust me, Dara."

Mace certainly had a way about him. He was smooth and very convincing. I wanted to be convinced. He studied my face as he held my hand. "I suppose Tanzy also mentioned my sister."

I nodded. "Well...I'm not my sister. And I'm not her keeper," he explained. "She knows I don't approve of her...lifestyle choices. I tried talking some sense into her years ago, but..." he trailed off and simply shrugged his shoulders. Then, looking down at my plate, "Are you finished with your sandwich?"

"Yes."

"Good, let's blow this joint." He stood up and tossed a few bills onto the table. "I'm going through beer withdrawal. I might just have a stray can in my trunk," his face opened in a broad smile.

❃

Across the street, Harris Taylor sat with a younger FBI agent in a nondescript four-door sedan watching Mace and Dara leave the coffee shop.

"How did he weasel himself out of the last photo you showed him?"

"The one with him and Saddam Hussein?"

"Yeah, that one," the younger agent answered as he turned the ignition.

"Well, Parker, it did put a wrinkle in his face, but he insisted the photo proves nothing. Unfortunately, he's right. We don't have any hard evidence on this guy, except that he keeps poor company. He said we may as well take down the entire US government since it stocked up Saddam's arsenal for years in their war against Iran."

"He's got a point," Parker said after considering that.

"Yeah," Taylor agreed. "Devlin is very smooth. I'll give him that much."

"You think it's still wise not to show all the photos to Dara Harow?"

"Absolutely. It was bad enough Detective Tanzy put doubts in her head about Mace before I could put a gag on him. I want to see why Mace is sticking so close to the girl. I have a feeling it'll be his undoing."

Chapter 20

We went inside the empty house, so eerie upon our return from the funeral. Mace and I walked up the staircase to the main floor, his arm around me for support. I stopped at the spot where I had found my father a few days ago, shot to death – the splattered blood now bleached away. "Hey, sweetness," Mace said softly, squeezing my arm, "don't torture yourself. Let's get you settled in the living room and I'll make you some tea."

"Thank you, Mace," I said through my tears. "I think I'd like to go to my room and freshen up first. I won't be long."

"Take your time, Dara. I'll be here."

I climbed up the next set of stairs to the bedroom level, feeling some solace that Mace was around. Just as he had promised, Mace took care of everything. Over the course of two days, he made the funeral arrangements with Rabbi Sanders, obtained clearance for me to move back into my home, hired a cleaning crew and prepared the house for the week of mourning. He helped me survive the unbearable and I was deeply grateful to him. Detective Tanzy and Harris Taylor had to be wrong about him. Whatever mistakes he made in his youth, were just that – mistakes. I believed Mace.

Upon entering my bedroom, I noticed the red light blinking on my answering machine. Most certainly a condolence call, I thought. I pressed the play button and started for my bathroom. "Dara, it's me." My heart stopped when I heard Roni's voice, and I whirled around and sprinted back toward the answering machine. "I've been trying to reach you for the past couple of days...I...needed to hear your voice. I wanted to try one last time before I had to leave again...for a few weeks. This time, well...it was unexpected. I just wanted to tell you, I love you. I'll always love you...for eternity – remember that. You hold my heart. Shalom, my sweet Dara, my *motek*."

"Roni," I whispered. "I love you, Roni."

There was something extremely discomforting about Roni's tone, the way he phrased his words. It was clear that he was going on a dangerous mission. But then, what mission wasn't dangerous? Still, this time it must be different. It was good, I decided, that I was unable to contact him and tell him about my parents. It was important for him to have a clear head. The last thing he needed was to worry about me while he was out *in the field*. I would get through my nightmare on my own. I played the message over, just so that I could hear his voice again – and then, played it over once more. I missed him so much. I ached for him. "Roni, stay safe for me. Oh God, please...please watch over him."

I calmed myself and was about to leave my room when I spotted the bag I had thrown my father's file into – the file I found hidden in Charlie, our armored statue, the morning after the murder. Mace kept his word by not letting me out of his sight, and I never had an opportunity to look at the file. I wanted to do it alone. Now that I was back in my house, I would be able to look at it in the privacy of my own bedroom. I would do that tonight, I decided, and closed the door behind me as I left my room.

Mace stood at the foot of the stairs ready with my cup of tea in hand. "I just wanted to warn you that several people have already arrived to make a condolence call," he said in a muted voice.

"Thank you," I said, peeking through the archway. I saw some of my old school friends as well as several of my parents' friends. Before entering the living room, I spied the platter of finger sandwiches set up on the coffee table and shot Mace a surprised look. "When did you become so domesticated?" I whispered.

"Shhh. I'll just deny it if you ever tell anyone."

"You're something else, Mace."

"Listen, Dara, before you go in there, I need to tell you that I'll be leaving tomorrow on the early shuttle. I have to get to RDECOM and handle a few matters. I should be back by Friday evening. Will you be okay on your own?"

"Oh, Mace." Prompted by his kindness, I instinctively embraced him. "You've helped me so much already. Please, don't give it a thought. I'll be fine." As I let go, he clasped my hand in his and looked at me with worried eyes. "I don't like leaving you alone in this house."

"I promise, I'll be okay. Besides, by the time I blink, it'll be Friday. And...anyway, sooner or later, I'm going to have to deal with reality on my own."

"No one should have to deal with this kind of reality by themselves." He had me promise that I would not hesitate to call him if I needed him.

Shortly before ten o'clock that evening, a man I had never seen before came to pay a condolence call. He carried himself with a remarkable air of confidence, and I assumed he was another official from the Defense Department. He shook hands with Mace, walked over to where I was sitting in the living room and then surprised me when he introduced himself as David Lev in a distinct Israeli accent.

He looked about my father's age, perhaps a few years his junior, since his coffee-brown hair showed just a small hint of gray. "I was very sorry to hear about your mother and father," he offered in a soft-spoken tone. "I can only imagine how dreadful this must be for you."

"Thank you and...yes...it's been a nightmare."

"I never had the pleasure of meeting your mother, but I knew your father well. I had the greatest respect for him – he was a brilliant man. Your father spoke about you often, especially about your feelings regarding Israel. I feel like I know you."

"How did you know my father?"

"I met him years ago at a science technology conference in Tel Aviv. We conferred much over the years with one another, as we were both in the same line of work."

"Are you still living in Israel?"

"Yes, I'm only in the States briefly for business reasons." For a moment, his eyes darted to the other end of the room toward Mace, who was talking casually with one of the last few visitors. It was then that I realized that Mace's attention was focused on us as well. Turning his eyes back to me, David continued in a muted tone, "Dara, it is important that I meet with you privately as soon as possible. I recognize that it is highly irregular during the week of mourning, and I apologize for that, but can you possibly meet me tomorrow? I wouldn't ask if it wasn't essential and...it must remain just between the two of us."

David Lev piqued my curiosity. I had a gut feeling that somehow he held the key to my parents' murder. With Mace leaving tomorrow morning for Maryland, I saw no impediments. I agreed to meet him at noon at the Mayflower Hotel coffee shop. It was customary that people did not pay condolence calls during the lunch and dinner hours. No one would even have to know that I had left the house.

❦

Later that evening, I retired to my bedroom exhausted and emotionally spent. Mace was staying in the guest bedroom on the main level. It was comforting that I didn't have to stay all alone in this big house, at least not for the first night.

I was still unable to wrap my head around the violent circumstances surrounding my parents' death. Rather than break down, I went about my days mechanically, going through the motions and simply doing what I had to do. After washing up and changing into my usual tank top and shorts for bed, I pulled out my father's file from my bag and crawled under the covers to read it. But before I could get to the first page, there was a knock at my bedroom door. Instinctively, I shoved the papers under my blanket and went to open it.

"Mace?" The change was instantly perceptible. His eyes were cold and vacant, his expression, emotionless. "Just wanted to check and see how you are. I know that today was difficult for you." He entered my room, his gait purposeful. The air about him was disconcerting, and all at once an uncomfortable feeling fell over me. "I'm fine, Mace. I was just getting ready for bed."

"I can see that." His eyes leered over my body as he stepped closer to me. Too close. There was no smile on his face and no friendly teasing in his approach. "I was just thinking," he continued, as he began to toy with the silver chain around my neck, "it might feel strange for you to stay all alone up here on the bedroom level. I mean…it being the first night in the house since the murders."

"Um…no…I'm fine, Mace. I'm too exhausted anyway to think about anything besides getting to sleep."

"Of course." He let my necklace fall from his fingers but didn't make any move to leave my room. I took a step back. "So, you'll probably be leaving very early in the morning to catch the first shuttle out of LaGuardia Airport. I guess I'll see you on Friday, then," I said in an attempt to end this uneasy visit.

"Are you trying to get rid of me, Dara?"

"No, Mace. I mean, well, it is late, and…you're right, it was a difficult day for me and I am exhausted. I…really need to get some sleep."

"I'm just looking out for you, sweetness. I feel responsible for your safety." The words were familiar, but the tone was all off. His manner was deliberate as he again moved closer to me, sweeping the back of his fingers down my arm. "Don't you feel comfortable with me? After all, if you can't trust me, who can you trust?" His touch, though subtle, felt threatening, and a surge of adrenalin raced through me. *This was Mace. Why was I feeling this way?* Maybe I wasn't reading things clearly – I just buried both my mother and father today. It would be no surprise if I had a distorted sense of judgment.

"Speaking of trust, Dara, that last visitor of yours, David Lev, what did he want?"

"Want? He…didn't want anything. He was just paying a condolence call. Why? What don't you trust about him?"

"Let's just say I didn't like the way he looked at you. I know David Lev. He has a reputation for being a ladies' man." Mace's eyes roamed over my body once more. "You know, Dara," his face drew close to mine, brushing against my cheek, "you're quite beautiful. Someone like you needs to be very careful."

"I…I can take care of myself." I took another step back. *What was Mace doing?*

"I'm sure you can. I just feel better about being close by…just in case. Did David by any chance say where he was staying?"

"No, I didn't ask. He did say, though, that he was returning to Israel tomorrow," my gut feeling told me to lie.

"What did he talk to you about?"

"Mostly about Israel – my experience on the kibbutz – stuff like that." I heard my voice shake as I lied once more.

"You seem a bit nervous, Dara." He wrapped his hands around

each of my arms. "You wouldn't be holding back anything from me, would you?"

"Of course not, Mace. I…I trust you, you know that."

"And yet, you seem so…tense? Maybe you shouldn't be alone. Maybe I should stay here in your room with you for the night. I promise I'll be the perfect gentleman, although you do look like you could use some strong arms around you." His hands moved down to my waist in a rigid hold and he jerked my body closer to his.

Don't let him think you suspect him of anything. He's dangerous. Detective Tanzy's words leaped into my head. "Oh, Mace," I gave out a nervous laugh, "always the flirt. But I'll be fine, really."

His lips curled into a scowl and he had a menacing look in his dark eyes. He squeezed me tighter to him; it was beginning to feel painful. "Mace, you're hurting me," I finally choked out. But he didn't let go. His black eyes narrowed as he stared into mine. He leaned in to kiss me on the forehead and I literally felt my hair stand on end.

"Good night, Dara. I'll see you on Friday. Make sure to behave while I'm gone." He flashed a cold smile, finally let go of me, and then turned and sauntered out the door.

I stood frozen in the middle of my room. Where did this Mace come from? It was like night and day. Mace meant to threaten me and I had no clue why. While I was able to depend on him like a brother since the night of the murder, now, he frightened me. He *wanted* me to be frightened of him. Something about David Lev triggered a change in his manner. Whatever it was, I would find out tomorrow.

I grabbed the file from under my blanket and shoved it between my schoolbooks piled on my desk. It was too great a risk to look at it while Mace was still in the house. I couldn't be sure that he wouldn't try to steal into my room again tonight. It would have to wait until morning.

Chapter 21

 Thursday, 7:00 a.m.

Only after making certain Macc had left for the airport, I began to read over my father's file. It was beyond my comprehension – all about a hypersonic missile cruise system, containing specifications on mach speeds, shock waves, three-dimension gas-flow systems, along with formulas, diagrams and technological words I couldn't pronounce. It included a section on its devastating effects, which I did understand. The most relevant bit of information for me was the title page, where it listed Dr. Gabriel Harow and Dr. David Lev as coauthors. I closed the file and hid it well this time, back inside Charlie's helmet, and then readied myself to face all those who would pay condolence calls this morning.

Mayflower Hotel, Thursday, 12:10 p.m.

"We've been sitting here for ten minutes, David, and so far you haven't given me any reason to believe in the urgency of this meeting."

"I apologize. I just wanted you to feel comfortable with me before delving into some serious matters."

"You're gauging me," I accused him. His lips curved into a slight smile and he placed a few bills down on the table for our coffee. "Let's take a walk," he said simply.

"It's cold outside."

"It's necessary." His confident tone reminded me somewhat of Roni.

He led me across the wide street toward Central Park. We followed a path that ran parallel to a huge green lawn, and once we crossed over the bike path, he began to speak. "Your father and I had been working together privately on technology for a new missile prototype meant as a joint effort between Israel and the United States. He had mentioned it in passing, in general terms, to Devlin because he had no reason not to trust him. But, while Devlin knew of our research, he had no access to it. Our missile project was in the developmental stages. The technology was all worked out – aside from a few minor kinks that we needed to resolve before proposing it to our respective governments. I was supposed to meet with your father this week, which is precisely why I'm in the States. But then I heard the tragic news, and knew that it was critical that I speak with you."

"You believe then that he was murdered over this project?"

"Yes – without a doubt. Prior to your father and I arranging to meet this week, he was very tense. He presumed RDECOM no longer trusted him."

"Yes, he told me that, too, although I didn't take it seriously. But what did this project have to do with his suspicions?"

"Nothing, actually."

"You lost me."

"Dara, I hope this doesn't come out the wrong way, but...your father was brilliant – truly a genius. And sometimes, geniuses can be... eccentric. I knew your father for a long time, and was accustomed to his occasional bouts of paranoia. In fact, I'm aware of the reason why he didn't want you moving to Israel."

I looked at David in surprise. "My father told you about that?"

He nodded. "I tried to reason with him, but I couldn't convince him otherwise. His fears became an obsession – they plagued him. In any case, I didn't believe for one minute that RDECOM had him under surveillance – not over this project or any other that he was working on. However, just about two weeks ago, he told me of a curious incident that occurred one evening after he had left the office for the day. Before leaving the building he realized he forgot some mail on his desk, and when he went back to retrieve it, he saw that his office door was partially open and witnessed Mace searching through his desk. He left before Mace noticed him, but in his mind, it confirmed that RDECOM had hired Mace to keep an eye on him.

"I didn't see it that way, though, and I said as much to your father. But I did suspect something about Mace. I couldn't put my finger on it, having only met him once. Yet, there was something about him that just didn't sit right with me. So I took the liberty of having some of my contacts do a background check on Mace. Turns out, he has ties to the neo-Nazis, the PLO and Hezbollah for starters – offshoots of the Muslim Brotherhood, and I was quite surprised that he had passed scrutiny to work at RDECOM. I could only surmise that Mace was very well connected. I believe that RDECOM is in dire need of a serious housecleaning. Mace isn't necessarily working alone."

"The PLO and Hezbollah," I repeated to myself.

David eyed me attentively. "This isn't the first time you're hearing this about Mace, is it?"

"No. The FBI had the same opinion."

"Then…why on earth do you have Mace staying in your house?"

"I didn't want to believe it. Mace had a very good relationship with my parents…they trusted him…he was a frequent houseguest…and… well – frankly, he's been so good to me. It all seemed too implausible to believe until…" I trailed off.

"Until what, Dara?"

"Ever since the murders, Mace has gone out of his way for me, to take care of things – the funeral, and…making sure I felt safe – but… last night, something changed."

David's eyes narrowed with concern. "What happened last night? Was he violent? Did he hurt you?"

"It was more like a threat of violence…. It's hard to explain. At first, I thought…well, I didn't trust my own judgment. I thought perhaps I was just reading him wrong…but…"

"But you weren't," David finished.

"No."

"And last night was the first time you felt in danger?"

"Yes. He asked many questions about you…and what we spoke about."

"My visit to you riled him – it got his guard up."

I stopped in my tracks and turned to him. "Why didn't you tell my father about your findings on Mace?"

"Because I just received the information on Sunday…the morning after the murders." He grasped my arm, prodding me to move with him. "Keep walking, Dara."

"So, why are you still in the States?"

"I had convinced your father to hand over all the research papers to me for safekeeping. One positive outcome of your father's paranoia was that he didn't want to enter the data into the computer. He was wary of hackers. In retrospect, I'm glad I indulged your father on that account. We couldn't risk having this missile technology fall into Mace's hands. That was the reason he and I planned to meet. Your father finally agreed that it wasn't safe to keep this research at RDECOM where Mace could get his hands on it. Of course, I have a copy of the project's data, but not any of your father's most recent entries." David then looked me square in the eyes. "Dara, I can't return to Israel without that file."

"David," I asked cautiously, "if Mace wanted the file, and if he had any reason to believe that I know where this file is, then why hasn't he made any attempt to ask me? He hasn't even so much as hinted anything about it."

"He's biding his time. Mace is in no rush as long as he thinks his acquisition is imminent. He'll first gain your trust, have you feel that you can rely on him, even make you dependent on him, and if he felt it necessary...intimidate you and even terrorize you into compliance."

"Which would explain last night," I confirmed.

"Yes, Dara, I'm afraid so. He was threatened by my appearance and felt he needed to assert more control over you."

"And the reason you wanted to meet with me...?"

"...Was to ask you if you do indeed know where this file is. Your father brought it home with him the weekend of his murder. I'm convinced that whoever ransacked your house didn't find it."

"How can you be so sure?"

"Had it been found, I doubt that Mace Devlin would be hanging around at the house with you. He's involved in this mess, Dara. I realize you're confused about him, but you must believe me. You cannot trust him. He's treacherous. He thinks that the file is still hidden somewhere in the house or that you might know of its whereabouts."

"Why would Mace be so interested in this particular missile project?"

"We're talking about advanced hypersonic cruise missile technology, Dara. It does not yet exist in any country's arsenal. That alone makes it very valuable, not to mention its payload. For instance, an ultra-high-speed weapons system would enable targets virtually anywhere on earth to be hit within two hours of launch from the continental United States. It can strike targets up to 16,700 kilometers, which is just over 10,000 miles. Imagine what that means for Israel if such technology fell into the hands of our enemies who sit right on our borders, or if Iraq, Iran or Libya got hold of this. Imagine if a nuclear warhead was attached to this missile. We're not far away from a nuclear arms race in the Middle East. What's more, the fate of the United States and Europe would be no different from Israel's."

"And Mace's role in this…?" I asked with naïveté.

"Dara, please understand. If Mace got hold of this file, he would sell the technology, and it would most certainly fall into the wrong hands: the Hezbollah or the PLO, or some rogue Muslim country that wants to destroy Israel just as much, along with all its Western allies. It would be a devastating strategic gain for global jihad."

"And why should I believe you, David? Why should I even believe you are who you say you are?"

"I could answer that the security of Israel depends on you believing me, and I could tell you that your life depends on you believing me, but…you're right, Dara, why should you trust a total stranger? So, let me ask you this. Would you trust someone in Israeli intelligence?" Once again, I stopped in my tracks and my eyes widened in awareness.

"Are you Mossad?" I whispered the question.

"Keep walking, Dara." He reached under his winter coat, removed a small notepad from his inner jacket pocket, scrawled out some information and passed it to me. "If you have the file in your possession and if you don't want to hand it over to me, then you must fly to Israel and see this person," he motioned to the note. "His name is Dov. Dov

Regev. You and that file will only be safe in Israel. Even if you did decide to hand it to me, I would insist that you get out of the United States and straight to Israel for your own safety. My contact number is on there, too. Call me, or call Dov directly. The less time you walk around with that file on your person the better. It is much too dangerous."

David Lev continued to speak, but I no longer heard what he was saying. I was on overload and tuned out. Every instinct implored me to delude myself, to close my eyes to the surrealistic plot of conspiracy, deception and trickery into which my life had plunged – though the way to escape this reality eluded me. As much as I craved denial, the fear that enveloped me was a constant affirmation that I was facing anything but an illusion. It was real – terribly real. I was embroiled in something too big and too frightening for me to handle. The only thing I was sure of was that I wasn't cut out for this world of intrigue.

"Do you, Dara?"

"Um…do I what?" I snapped back to attention upon hearing my name.

"Dara, bottom line – do you have the file?"

"I…might."

"I'll take that as a yes. Where is Mace now?"

"At RDECOM."

"When is he returning to New York?"

"Friday."

"That's tomorrow," David said, contemplating the next move. "And no doubt he'll continue to stay with you at the house."

I nodded. "He said he doesn't want to let me out of his sight."

"Hmm. That doesn't give you much space to maneuver. What does the next week look like for you?"

"Um…I have finals."

"Perfect. Listen to me, Dara. You don't have the luxury to dawdle in confusion. You must keep your wits about you and play this out very carefully. Do not raise Mace's suspicions. Avoid asking him any probing questions. Go about your daily routine as usual. Take your finals, tie up any loose ends, and arrange to leave by the end of the week. As long as Mace does not get hold of the file, and as long as he does not suspect you have it, your life is not in any immediate danger. I will not call the house, in case Mace answers the phone, so call me from a pay phone at school and I'll give you further instructions. Make sure no one around you is listening. Oh, and you will have to travel light. No luggage. Mace, of course, shouldn't know you're planning to leave. You'll buy whatever you need in Israel. And I suggest you remain there; it will be too dangerous for you to return to the States."

"I don't want to be here anyway, but you already knew that from my father."

"Right. Does Mace know about your plans to live in Israel?"

"No."

"Good. It's important that you don't give him any reason to have you followed or you won't make it to the airport alive. Spend the next few days gaining his trust." David gave me a hard look and added, "Dara, please…don't take too long to decide whether you can trust me or not."

I nodded. "What do I do if Mace asks me if I know anything about the file?"

"Lie."

Chapter 22

The temptation to avoid Mace and run to a friend's house for the weekend was more than compelling. But I knew it was crucial not to raise his suspicions. David Lev was right; I had to play his game and pretend that I was under his control. If Mace was indeed after my father's file, my life would be in no danger as long as he didn't uncover its hidden location.

There were still many unanswered questions, though. I called Detective Tanzy to ask him why, if they had information that tied Mace to a neo-Nazi organization, was he allowed to remain at RDECOM? He explained that it was the best way the FBI could keep an eye on him, and the higher-ups at RDECOM were well aware of the situation. But Mace was no fool. Wouldn't he wonder why his job seemed secure in light of the FBI investigation? There were flaws in the stories on both sides. Still, if there was one thing I was sure of, it was David Lev's warning – I didn't have the luxury to dawdle in confusion. And I was sure that Roni, as well, would direct me to hand over the file to Israeli intelligence. It was a no-brainer. I could only trust the Mossad.

When Mace returned Friday evening, his manner didn't suggest any chilliness. Rather, a look of satisfaction washed over his face when he walked into the kitchen and saw that I had prepared dinner.

"Did you miss me, Dara?" He put his arm around my shoulders and gave me a small peck on the cheek.

His touch set off an internal alarm, making me shudder inside, but I continued to play my role. "Yes, Mace. I'm glad you're back." I handed him a beer.

"Of course you are, sweetness. Who else is going to look out for you?"

"I know you look out for me, Mace, and I wanted to show you how grateful I am. Are you hungry? I fixed some dinner for you."

"It smells great. You'll join me, I hope."

"Sure," I said, relieved that Mace was in an affable mood. I went to get two plates out of the cabinet, and proceeded to set the table in a nook at the other end of the kitchen.

Mace edged toward me, hovering, taking an occasional swig from his beer. I glanced at him, and he gave no outward sign of any threat.

"Did David Lev come over to the house while I was gone?"

"No. I thought I told you – I think he flew back to Israel yesterday."

"Right. You did say something like that. So, what shall we do this weekend?"

"Well, although I have no head for it, I'm going to try to get some studying done. I have finals this coming week."

"Hmm. Doesn't sound like much fun. I think you could use a night of enjoyment. Let me take you out tonight."

"I appreciate the thought, but I'm not really in the mood these days for amusement. It's too soon, Mace."

"But...you *could* go out in broad daylight with David Lev?"

My heart thudded to a stop. Mace had me watched! I felt a wave of panic creep up my spine. I tried to come up with some kind of sound explanation, but I couldn't think fast enough. "We just had a friendly coffee. That's all."

"And a stroll through Central Park, don't forget."

"Why are you having me watched?"

"For your own safety, Dara." His tone was deceptively soft. He stood over me, looming, staring down at me, a silent threat in his hostile dark eyes. "Do you think I would leave you alone here in this house, unprotected? You lied to me, after everything I've done for you. Now, Dara, why would you do that?"

"I-I just didn't want to upset you. I knew you didn't like him. But David Lev was a friend of my father's and it was comforting to speak with him. That was the only reason I saw him again. You can understand that, can't you?"

Mace seemed to relax with my explanation and broke into a warm smile as he assured me, "Of course I can understand that." I was relieved to hear him answer in a kindly tone. "Let's not give it any more thought, sweetness," he added, the compassion in his voice once again discernable. I began to breathe easy again. Perhaps I was hasty in thinking that he meant me any harm. It must have been my own overexerted imagination that caused me to feel intimidated. My meeting with David Lev had just exacerbated my irrational fears. *What did I know of David Lev, anyway?*

I smiled back at him appreciatively. This was the Mace that I knew, and I felt guilty for misjudging him just as everyone else had. He took another swig from his beer and started to turn from me, but just then, with lightning speed, he slammed my face with the back of his hand, the force of it sending me flying onto the kitchen table – the plates and glasses taking to the air and smashing to the floor. In the next second, he was over me, pinning me down on the table with my hands over my head – his powerful body between my legs that were dangling off the table's edge, and his face just an inch away from mine. "You're lying to me, Dara, and I don't like being lied to."

"No, Mace. Stop this. I'm not lying. I swear it!" The shock and panic hit me all at once.

"What did David Lev want from you?"

"I don't know what you mean!" I wailed.

"He came here to ask you for something, Dara. What did he ask for?"

"Nothing!"

"You bitch, I'll take you right here and now if you don't tell me the truth!" He shifted both my wrists into one of his hands. He was incredibly strong, and with his free hand, he reached under my skirt and ripped my panties off, cutting into my skin.

"No, Mace! Don't!" I tried wriggling myself free, but he pressed hard against me, trapping me on the table, and I felt like a crushed insect beneath him. He forced his mouth on top of mine and shoved his tongue inside. It was so rough I couldn't breathe. I thought he would smother me. Yanking one of my legs farther to one side, he withdrew his mouth from mine, and through his gritted teeth, he threatened, "One last chance, Dara. What did Lev want?"

I gasped for air. "A file!" I cried out. "He wanted a file."

"Go on!"

"I didn't know what he was talking about. I didn't know anything about my father's work. I couldn't help him."

"You're a lying bitch!"

"No! You know that I don't know any details about my father's work."

"Then why did you hide the fact that Lev wanted a file?"

"He told me not to tell you."

"And you listened to him over me?"

"You scared me the night before you left. I didn't know whom to trust anymore."

"What reason did he give you to keep it from me?"

"He said you wanted the file for yourself."

"Why, Dara?" He pushed more of his body weight against me. I thought quickly. "He said that you wanted to pass it off as your own research, so you could take all the credit."

"And you believed him?"

"I don't care anymore who's telling the truth. I don't care about this file. I just want this nightmare over with!"

Mace relaxed his grip on me and lifted me from the table, holding my trembling body in his arms, leaning my head against his shoulder and caressing my hair. "There, there, Dara, I promise you, the nightmare will soon be over." *It was like being with a schizophrenic.* "Though I'm afraid it won't be over until this file is found."

"W-what do you mean?"

"David Lev is an underworld character. He sells technology to the highest bidder. He's not going to give up trying to get that file. I have to get it back to RDECOM where it will be secure. If it's not anywhere in the house, Dara, then your father hid it somewhere else – perhaps in a safety deposit box. You'll meet with your parents' lawyer this week and arrange to get access to it. You're the only heir – you have to meet with the lawyer, anyway. Do you understand, Dara?"

"Yes, Mace. I'll do that."

"Good. That's what I like to hear, sweetness. Now, clean up this mess and let's have some dinner."

Chapter 23

Living with Mace in the same house was unbearable. I never knew when his mood would change or when he would find a reason to blow up at me. He took sadistic pleasure in intimidating me and in keeping me guessing with his mood swings. I hated the way he leered at me – the way he touched me with the threat of violence hanging in the air. I held on to the hope that the act of scaring me with the threat of rape excited him more than actually carrying it out. What's more, he wasn't planning to return to Maryland until I met with the lawyer and gained access to my father's safety deposit box. He claimed that RDECOM considered getting the file back top priority – that it was a matter of national security.

On Sunday, I told Mace that I needed to study at the school library. As soon as I arrived at Columbia's campus, I called David Lev from a phone booth at the student lounge and told him what had transpired between Mace and me. "I want to leave for Israel tonight. I'm scared. I have to get away from Mace."

"Dara, where are you now?"

"In the student lounge at Columbia."

"Is anyone standing within earshot of you?"

I looked around me. "No."

"Listen to me carefully. Mace isn't stupid. I'm sure he has someone watching you right now. You cannot act out of panic and you cannot just run off to the airport on your own. His goons will take you out before you get through the revolving door. And even if you get past them, the last thing you need is for him to send someone after you to Israel. This has to be well planned out. When you finally do leave, he mustn't know that you left the country. It must be done without a clue, without a trace. If you want this nightmare to end, Dara, you must follow my instructions. Continue playing along with him. Use the next several days to wipe away all of Mace's doubts about your loyalty to him."

"I can't do this." My voice shook as I tried to contain the terror I felt.

"You can, Dara. You must. Get hold of yourself. Take your finals this week, meet with the lawyer, and just do what you have to do. Do everything Mace expects you to do. In the meantime, I'll have someone by the name of Iddo pick you up Thursday at two in the afternoon. from the student lounge to take you to JFK airport. Don't worry, he'll find you. If anyone is following you, he'll lose him. When you get to the airport, go straight to the first-class line of El Al and show security your passport. They'll be expecting you and will have your ticket waiting for you there. You'll have people at the airport and on the plane looking out for you. You won't know who they are, but they'll know you. You'll be arriving at nine in the morning on Friday at Ben Gurion Airport. Someone will meet you at customs to take you straight to Dov Regev. Iddo will give you his name. Did you get all that, Dara?"

"Yes, I got it."

"It's all going to be okay. Just follow my instructions. Once you're in Iddo's hands, you'll be safe. You can do this Dara. Tell me you can do this."

"I-I can do this."

"Good. Now, before you hang up, I want you to act as if you're laughing with a friend over the phone. Pretend to make a date to meet this friend at the school library to study together. Do you understand?"

"Yes, I understand."

"Okay. I'm going to hang up now. Put on a good performance."

I did exactly what David instructed me to do. I went about taking my finals, going through the motions really, since serious studying was impossible. I met with my parents' lawyer. Their will was clear-cut with no complications. Aside from a few charitable endowments, I was the sole beneficiary of the balance of their estate and arranged for its assignment to my name, as well as transferring the cash assets into my Bank Leumi account that I had opened during my year in Israel. I also arranged to forward all the mail to the lawyer's office as of Thursday. I told him that I would get in touch with him shortly with my new address and contact information. I did not let him know yet that I was moving to Israel. While I was at it, I hired a real estate management company to handle the sale of the house, and gave my lawyer power of attorney to push it through.

I told Mace I would meet him Thursday afternoon at three thirty, after my last final, at the Chase Manhattan Bank on Columbus Avenue and Sixty-Sixth Street. By then, the locksmith sent by the management company would change the security code of the house and I'd be on board an El Al flight to Israel. I was cutting off all ties and tying up all loose ends.

I woke up before dawn on Wednesday to retrieve my father's file from Charlie without any chance of Mace detecting me. He was not an early riser. I didn't want to leave anything for the last day, and I wanted the file with me. I had two finals scheduled for the day. Actually three – the third being a bit unorthodox. It was for my Arabic language class and it entailed going out for dinner with our professor and spending the entire time conversing only in Arabic in an Arab restaurant located in a Brooklyn neighborhood that over the years had been dubbed "Little Palestine." The professor was a bit unconventional. I didn't mind, though, as it meant that I would be spending less time with Mace at the house today.

I was feeling heady about returning to Israel and finally making it my permanent home, a home I planned on building with Roni. I didn't want to think of anything but once again being in his arms – the only thing that was getting me through this atrocity.

Saving my sanity required that I put this horrific episode in my life behind me. The pain of losing my parents weighed heavily on my heart, and it was odd to think of myself as an orphan. My regret was that I never had the ability to break through my parents' fears and encourage them to share in the happiness I had with Roni. And now, there would never be a chance for them to have any part in it. They may not have been the greatest parents, but they were mine. And...what a horrible way for them to die. While I was sure at this point that Mace wanted to get his hands on my father's file, some part of me harbored the hope that he was not directly responsible for their murders. It was more palatable for me to believe that his hired guns pulled the trigger rather than he. I supposed I didn't want to think of Mace as entirely evil. Perhaps naive on my part, it was too painful to accept that one can be so treacherous.

I left a note for Mace on the kitchen table informing him that I left early to study at the school library before my morning final and reminded him that my last final of the day, scheduled at a later hour, meant I would be returning at night. I was in no mood to come home to one of his crazed tantrums. Being so close to freeing myself from his control, I didn't want anything to hamper my escape plan.

Al Mansaf Middle Eastern Cuisine, Brooklyn, New York

There was something eerie about my last dinner in the United States taking place in an Arab restaurant. I hoped it was not symbolic of anything to come. Considering my current state of affairs, who would blame me for my propensity toward melodrama?

I shouldn't have been surprised when Mace entered the restaurant, but seeing him there jolted the calm composure I had tried to generate. I assumed he had followed me to make certain I'd return straight home afterwards. But he didn't glance at any of the tables and took no notice of me. He sauntered past the hostess station and strode up a side staircase, looking like he knew precisely where he was going, looking like a man with a mission.

When the waiter came over to our table to take our dessert order, I inquired with an innocent curiosity whether there was another dining area upstairs, pointing to the side staircase. He politely informed me that it led to the office of the proprietor of the restaurant. *Interesting.* I complimented the waiter on the excellent food and the fine service and asked what country the owner came from. His answer: Syria. *Of course, the patron of Hezbollah.* That clinched it. The final proof. That bastard Mace was a neo-Nazi.

I arrived home later in the evening, relieved to have the house to myself, at least until Mace returned from his "meeting." If I were lucky, he would make an extra stop at one of the many girlfriends he always seemed to have, and not return until the wee hours of the morning. I flipped through the mail as usual and found a letter from Dalya. I noticed that she had sent it express. Excited, I raced up the stairs to my room to read it.

> *Dear Dara,*
>
> *It is with a broken heart that I write these words to you. They are words that do not want to escape my lips, yet, I am left with the task of breaking your heart and shattering your world. There is no easy way to say this — to cushion the shock or diminish the disaster that has befallen our family.*
>
> *Dear Dara, Roni is dead — killed in the line of duty. We do not know any details, as the army has explained that his mission was a covert operation. All we know is that he fell in enemy territory. To further the pain, we do not even have a grave over which to grieve. His commander informed us that retrieving Roni's body at this time would be nearly impossible.*
>
> *I know that Roni was your sunshine, Dara, as he was ours. Roni was the central force of our family. He radiated light, and his strength of spirit had a unique way of tying the family together. It is hard to imagine that the sun will ever shine again for the Ben-Ari family. As you can imagine, the news of Roni destroyed my parents. From this, they will not recover. And so, I ask you not to contact them, as it would only serve as a painful reminder of what could have been, what should*

have been, and it would be too much for them to bear.
If it would bring some comfort to you to speak with me
when you return to Israel, please do call me.

In spite of everything, Dara, I ask you to find
the strength to go on. For Roni's sake. Yes, grieve for
your lost love, but then, you must move on — find a new
happiness. Do not give up on your dream to build a life
in Israel. You know that is what Roni would want for
you. He loved you with all his heart and soul.

Dalya

"No no no no no no nooo! Roni! Roni! RONI! NOOOO!" I ran to
the bathroom and vomited my guts out. I slumped to the floor and
remained there. *Roni. My Roni. My Roni. My Roni.*

Chapter 24

I wasn't sure what made me get up from the floor the following morning. An unsolicited survival instinct kicked in, though I was sure that I wanted to die. How dare the sun rise? How dare the world continue?

Roni was my world. And now, that world was gone forever. I knew that he wouldn't want me to give up on life. But what was life worth without Roni? What was it he once said to me? Oh yes. "No more tears, Dara. Now, we fight back." Except, I didn't know where I would get the strength or the will to go on. And yet, I did get up – and went straight to the toilet to vomit again, though this time I was empty. Even the tears would no longer flow. I exhausted all that I had throughout the long hours of the night, until none remained. And now, I was a walking corpse, void of spirit. Void of my heart. He took it with him. I was done.

Zombielike, I grabbed my passport, the letter from Dalya, my bag that contained my father's file and a modest-sized backpack that I usually used for my books, but today instead it carried a few essentials, a family photo album and a change of clothing. If Mace were up at this hour, which was unlikely, it would not have raised his suspicions. Before leaving my room for the last time, I took down the framed Gilboa Iris from the wall above my desk and placed it into my backpack as well. I lifted the cassette from my answering machine, the one with Roni's last message to me, and slipped it in my bag. My engagement ring from Roni would remain on my finger. I walked down the staircase, out the front door and didn't look back.

Dov Regev's Office, Herzliya, Friday, 10:00 a.m.

"*Boker tov*, Dara. Good morning. I regret that we had to meet under such circumstances. I'm truly very sorry about the loss of your parents."

I could only nod an acknowledgment.

"I trust your flight went smoothly?"

"Yes, it did."

"Would you like some coffee?"

"No, thank you. I would just like to get on with the purpose of this meeting, if you don't mind." I opened my bag and pulled out the cursed file, placing it on the desk between us. "Here is my father's file."

"Thank you, Dara."

I watched him as he leafed through it. Dov Regev was younger than I imagined he would be. He could not have been much older than Roni. He, too, exhibited a confidence and quiet strength so rare in men his age – or rather, so rare in men I met in the United States, for example. I recognized it right away. It was the solemn strength of one who was battle worn.

Dov proceeded to question me about Mace Devlin, and I told him everything I knew, including the meeting he had with the owner of Al Mansaf restaurant in Brooklyn.

"Dara, I would like to thank you for all your help in this matter, as well as for your courage. David Lev filled me in on all that transpired in New York. I know how terrifying this entire experience has been for you." He looked at me, conveying a genuine warmth.

"Well…now, I would just like to put the whole thing behind me."

"Of course. I understand. Do you have family in Israel?"

"No."

"Friends?"

"A few."

He crinkled his brow in concern. "So…you're nineteen and alone in the world?"

"Yes, I suppose I am." I felt my face fall into a cynical smirk, the kind that Roni had sported when we first met.

"Do you at least have plans to stay at a friend's over Shabbat?"

"Actually, I made no plans. If you can direct me to the nearest hotel, I'll get a room before I figure out what to do next."

Dov picked up the phone and instructed his secretary to reserve a room in my name at the Tel Aviv Hilton. "You have the room for a week; the expense is taken care of."

"Thank you, but that's not necessary."

"Please, don't give it a thought. You put your life at great risk by providing us with your father's file. It's the least we can do for you. Oh, and if there is anything I can help you with in getting yourself settled in Israel, don't hesitate to call me." He handed me his card.

"Thank you, Dov."

We shook hands, and I walked out of his office just as another man walked in.

"Whoa! Who was that?" the man exclaimed once he closed the office door behind him.

"Did you notice her eyes?" Dov asked.

"Let's just say I noticed the whole package…why?"

"Well, they looked…battle worn."

"I guess you would know, Dov."

✳

Two days after I met with Dov Regev at his office, I received a call from him. With the additional information that I had provided Dov – information that his office subsequently passed along to the FBI – the FBI arrested Mace for double homicide and conspiracy to commit treason. They raided the apartment where Mace was staying – the same place he had taken me after my parents' murder. There, they found the murder weapon, although there were no fingerprints on it. It had been wiped clean. "The apartment," Dov explained, "was actually used as a safe house for Mace and his neo-Nazi cronies."

I felt no relief at this news. I felt nothing. I questioned if I still had a pulse. "I suppose I have to go back and testify, right?" The lack of emotion in my voice sounded odd to me. Dov hesitated before he answered. "Dara, there may not be a trial."

"What?" I suddenly found my pulse.

"Mace may be able to make a deal."

"He murdered my parents! What deal?"

"He can provide the FBI with valuable information. He'll do time, but it won't be life."

"No! I won't allow it."

"I'm very sorry, Dara; I know how painful this is for you. But… as I understand it, it's…not up to you. It's up to the state prosecutor and the FBI. You see, Mace Devlin is small-fry compared to what's out there. To avoid the risk of a life sentence, Mace may decide to turn over significant information on the neo-Nazi network."

"But he committed a double murder…" I trailed off.

"Yes, he probably did. But the evidence is at best…circumstantial. They can't categorically pin him as the triggerman. Plus, Mace seems to have an alibi. Still, Devlin doesn't want to run the risk of a trial, and the FBI feels it has much more to gain in making a deal with him."

I didn't answer. I was wondering what other bombshell awaited me. "Dara? Are you still there?"

"How many years will he get?" I found my voice again.

"I don't know that yet."

"Well…I appreciate you calling and apprising me of the situation."

"Are you going to be all right?"

"I won't fall apart and cry over this, Dov, if that's what you mean. Tears have never helped us," recalling Roni's words. "One way or another, the Jews will fight back."

"Yes, Dara. That is one thing that I *can* promise you."

Chapter 25

 Five years later – Jerusalem, 1990

"Dara! Finally! I was beginning to think you threw away your phone."

"Sorry, Jen. I forgot my cell phone at home and I just got in. What's up?"

"What's up is that Yaniv and I are not taking no for an answer this time. You're coming for Shabbat, end of discussion!"

"Jenny, I –"

"No, Dara," she cut me off. "You've run out of excuses. You're coming!"

"You and Yaniv just want to set me up with someone."

"So what if we do?"

"I'm not interested."

"Dara, you wouldn't be betraying Roni if you went out with another man. Roni would want you to get on with your life."

"I *have* gotten on with my life. I have my degree and I'm working. I'm satisfied."

"Are you really, Dara? What about having a family, and...finding love? You should have some kind of life plan. It's as if you just exist for the moment."

"I don't exist for the moment – the moments simply mark my existence," I said wryly. "Look, Jen, you'll just be wasting your time."

"Let me worry about my time. Just come...please, please, please?"

Sigh. "All right, all right. I'll come for Shabbat."

Jenny was a good friend, truly the best. She was my support system. And Yaniv was like a big brother, always watching out for me. I was happy for them when they married. In fact, it was the only time I could remember being genuinely happy since the day I found out Roni was killed in action.

"Great! Yaniv can pick you up in Jerusalem and drive you over."

"Thanks, Jen, but there's no need for that. I can take a bus. It's not a long ride to Gush Etzion. Don't worry, I'll be there – I won't stand you up."

"Okay, Dara. Can't wait to have you here! You haven't seen our new home yet – you'll love it!"

"Looking forward to it, Jen. You know I love spending time with you and Yaniv."

"Then I want to see a happy face when you get here."

"So you can try to auction me off to the highest bidder?" I cracked.

"Something like that," Jen laughed.

❈

Sde Dovid, Friday

I took in a deep breath. "Mmm. It smells wonderful out here."

"Those are the *za'atar* plants," Jenny informed me. "They're deliciously fragrant, aren't they?"

"I love your home, Jen. The view is…breathtaking." I stood on her terrace looking out on the Judean Hills.

"I wish you would join us here." Jenny sounded wistful. "Yaniv and I are very happy in Sde Dovid."

I shook my head at the thought. "Sde Dovid is for family living – not for singles. Jerusalem suits me better. Besides, it's just a short drive down the road."

"Dara, you're not going to be single forever."

"Starting on me already? I just got here ten minutes ago."

"Just prepping you," she retorted.

"Prepping me? Why dillydally? Why not just bring out the beef right now?"

"The beef's coming a little later with Yaniv. They went running."

"Running, huh? That's something I can get into."

"As long as you would be running *to* something, instead of *away* from it," Jenny quipped.

"Is that what you think I'm doing? Running away?"

"Dara…I…well…yes, I do think you're running away."

"From what?"

"From reality! You're still pining away for Roni, and he's gone, Dara. You refuse to accept that. It's been five years and you're still wearing your engagement ring on a chain around your neck! You've got to let go!"

But I couldn't let go. I wouldn't. Logically, I knew Jenny was right – but I couldn't accept Roni's death. Maybe it was because there was no grave over which to cry. Maybe it was because the circumstances of his death were so murky. And maybe it was because I was slowly but surely losing my grip on reality by thinking he might still be alive somewhere, somehow. "Dara," Jenny put her arm around me, rousing me out of my self-reflection. "You're my best friend and I love you. I just want you to be happy."

"I know you do, Jen."

"Then, please, give this guy a chance."

"Okay. Okay. So...tell me about this *great catch*," I slipped into sarcasm.

"As a matter of fact, he *is* a great catch."

"Then why hasn't anyone caught him?"

"He just hasn't found that special someone...yet," she looked at me pointedly. I rolled my eyes. "Okay, Dara, here are some specs: first of all, he's a good friend of Yaniv's."

I nodded in agreement, "That does certainly work in his favor."

"Secondly, next to Yaniv, he just happens to be the sweetest guy I know." I rolled my eyes again. "Thirdly," Jenny continued, "he's gorgeous."

I couldn't help but smirk. "You do know that you're beginning to bore me, don't you?"

"There's more to the list."

"How about his name, Jenny...does he have one of those?"

"His name is Uri. Uri Amrani. And he lives here in Sde Dovid."

"Uri Amrani? The real estate mogul?"

"Well, he's the son. Not bad, huh?"

"Jen, I think you know me better than that."

"Perhaps you'd be impressed that in addition to dabbling in the family business, he's also a professor at Hebrew University."

"Hmm. Finally, we're getting to some substance. What does he teach?"

Jenny hesitated. "Mathematics. He's a math professor. Math is... well...okay, so it's kind of his first love."

I flashed a derisive smile. "Fascinating. I'm sure we'll have lots to talk about."

"I promise you, Dara, there's a lot more to him. You'll see soon enough. You'll have plenty of opportunity to get to know him; I invited him over for both Shabbat meals – tonight's dinner and tomorrow's lunch."

"You never do anything halfway, do you?"

"Nope," she laughed. "C'mon friend, let's go back inside the house now. You could help me in the kitchen. I was hoping you would make that strawberry salad of yours."

"Sure, Jen. My pleasure."

"...And while you're chopping away at the strawberries maybe I can convince you to join Yaniv and me next weekend when we go up to Gilboa to visit the old gang?"

I pressed my eyes closed and shook my head. "No. I can't. Please don't push that one...it would be too painful for me."

Jenny couldn't help showing disappointment. "So let's talk about something painless...how's work at the *Jerusalem Post*?"

I shrugged. "Fine, I guess. I enjoy writing human interest stories."

"Did you ever consider writing a book?" She moved to the kitchen sink and busied herself with washing some dishes.

"A book? What on earth would I write about?"

"Your life. You have to admit, it hasn't exactly been run of the mill. And I think it might be cathartic for you. It may help you to move on."

"Personally, I like books with happy endings."

"Hmm," Jenny looked up from the sink and out the window. "I have a feeling your happy ending will be upon you in no time." There was a sly lilt to her voice.

"Ever the optimist," I smiled, and moved toward her to see what she was looking at. The window faced a winding path to her house that led up to a side entrance just off the kitchen. My mouth dropped open and Jenny's face exploded in a hearty grin as I watched Yaniv and his friend Uri walk up the path to the house. "Oh, I neglected to mention that Uri is also a physical trainer *slash* bodybuilder," she said matter-of-factly, flaunting her satisfaction at my reaction.

"Talk about bringing out the beef," I murmured, as I continued to stare. "So let me get this straight, Jen. He dabbles in real estate, is a professor of mathematics at Hebrew U, he's a physical trainer *slash* bodybuilder – what does he do in his spare time, advise the prime minister on foreign policy?"

"No, but he does volunteer twice a week at Tel Hashomer Hospital with wounded soldiers."

I shot her a look of disbelief. "No one can be that perfect." My eyes darted back to Uri. "There's got to be something wrong with him. I bet he's secretly a serial ax murderer."

"Ha! Ever the pessimist, Dara! Shh! They're at the door." She glared at me, "Behave!"

"Dara!" Yaniv said brightly as he entered the kitchen. "You're here! I was afraid you'd cancel out on us!"

"Couldn't. Jenny threatened to get the Border Police after me." He flashed his dimpled smile and leaned over to give me a peck on the cheek. "I'd hug you hello, but I'm all sweaty at the moment."

"Not smelling too good, either," I joked.

"Hey, don't drip, I just washed the floors." Jenny grabbed a couple of dish towels and tossed them to Yaniv and Uri to wipe themselves off.

"Uri," Yaniv put his hand on his friend's shoulder, "I'd like you to meet a very dear friend of ours, Dara Harow."

Uri's lips curved into a pleasant smile as his eyes gave me the male-reflex swift head-to-toe once-over. "It's a pleasure to meet you."

I decided to do the same – looking him up and down, perhaps in a less subtle manner, to make a point. "Likewise," I tossed back. Jenny shot me a reproachful look. Yaniv held in a laugh, clearing his throat.

"Okaaay…I think I'm going to head to the shower. See you later, Uri."
Jenny followed Yaniv out of the kitchen, leaving me alone with the
brainiac hunk who seemed to find something about me amusing.

"Is there a joke I missed?" I asked, keeping my voice casual and
trying to "behave," as Jenny requested.

He opened the refrigerator door and pulled out a pitcher of orange
juice, his amused eyes still on me. They were an interesting shade, warm
mocha brown with a splash of yellow circling the iris, giving an effect of
gold topaz. It was difficult to envision him as a professor. His tousled,
fawn-colored hair framed a face that was more pretty than intellectual.

"You're a spirited one," Uri finally commented. He took out two
glasses from the cupboard and placed them on the counter. "Care for
some juice?"

"Okay, thanks," I answered with a shrug of the shoulder. He
poured the drinks and handed me one glass. Before I took one sip,
he gulped his juice down and poured himself another. "I guess I was
thirstier than I thought," he confessed. I didn't say anything. I wasn't
any good at small talk, *just like Roni*, and I decided I was not in the
mood to socialize. *This was ridiculous.* I would never be interested in any
other man after Roni. *Never.* While I attempted to think of an excuse
to exit from the kitchen, he posed a question that was more akin to an
accusation. "So Dara," Uri seemed to be studying my face, analyzing
me, "how is it that a woman so young can be so…guarded?"

"Guarded? I'm not guarded," I insisted, taken aback by his
forwardness.

"Sure you are. It's written all over your face, and it's in your body
language as well."

"You know me for thirty seconds, and you think you're an expert
on me?"

"No, Dara, I don't know you at all. But maybe if you remove your
protective shield, I *would* get to know you." His brazen familiarity

stunned me. I had no comeback and just stared at him flabbergasted. Uri smiled, pleased at my reaction. He put his glass in the sink and walked toward the door. "I guess I'll see you later?" He turned to face me, waiting for an answer. I stood there like an idiot and nodded yes.

For the remainder of the afternoon I helped Jenny in the kitchen prepare the Shabbat meals. I was uncomfortable about the prospect of Uri coming over that night for dinner as well as for Shabbat lunch the next day, after the morning prayer services. He was right on the mark. I *had* spent the last few years building a protective shield around me, and I wasn't prepared to meet someone like him who could peel through the layers in seconds. "Guarded!" It was one thing to think it – it was another to throw it in my face like that. And to be so smug about it, too. In our brief encounter, he had made me feel completely transparent. I wanted to remain a closed book, and his boldness disturbed me.

"You seem to be deep in thought, Dara. Is it the zucchini that's so interesting, or…by any chance, are you thinking of Uri?" Jen's eyes brightened in hope. "You have to admit," she prodded, "he does make quite a first impression."

"I guess – if you go for the sweaty, overbearing, brazen type."

"And I suppose you didn't find him attractive at all?" she teased. "If you ask me, I thought there was instant chemistry."

"Jen, you're a hopeless romantic."

Chapter 26

Dinner conversation consisted of the usual topics one would find in any Israeli household. World politics, national politics, and then winding its way back to world politics. Ultimately, we all conceded that it was us against the world and moved merrily right along to dessert. "This was a delicious dinner, Jenny. Thank you," Uri graciously offered. "You're very welcome. But it was actually a joint effort with Dara."

"Well then, my compliments to both chefs." He lifted his wineglass for emphasis.

"It just dawned on me," Jenny turned to me all chipper-like. "This was the first time since our kibbutz days that we worked together in the kitchen."

"You're right," I succinctly acknowledged, hoping the conversation would not progress further on our time spent at Gilboa. I automatically tensed up whenever Jenny or Yaniv brought up the kibbutz. It only inflamed the ache in my heart for Roni.

"Do you remember how you always had to bail me out of one thing or another with Orli?" she continued. I nodded, smiled lightly and took a sip of my wine. *Let's just move on, Jen.* In that instant, I caught Uri staring at me with interest. *Damn. Was I that obvious? Or, was he that good at reading people?* Clearly, he noticed my discomfort with the topic.

"Who was Orli?" Uri asked deliberately, without relaxing his scrutinizing gaze from me. *Was he intentionally trying to make me feel ill at ease?*

"She was the formidable head of the kibbutz kitchen that no one dared to cross," Yaniv jumped in. "That is, except for my Jenny."

"Yes, and she absolutely detested me!" Jenny added with a proud smile.

"Well, maybe if you hadn't kept sticking lit cigarettes into the mouths of the fish, she might have detested you less," I playfully chided Jenny, pretending to enjoy this unwelcome excursion down memory lane under Uri's analyzing gaze.

"I just wanted to see if they could smoke," she defended herself, feigning innocence. "Their mouths were still moving! They were even jumping in the crates when she asked us to cook them! I was traumatized! To this day I can't bring myself to cook fish."

"I suspect the fish were more traumatized than you, Jen," I quipped, eager to end the subject.

"Well, I was just relieved when Orli finally banned me from working in the kitchen," Jenny continued. "That was sheer torture! You know, that also reminds me –"

"Is there any more wine?" I broke in – my attempt to get Jenny off the kibbutz track.

"Allow me," Uri offered, refilling my glass. "So, Dara," Uri's tone was casual, but his eyes were probing, "when you were on the kibbutz, did you work in the kitchen the entire time?"

He was not going to let the subject drop. "No, kitchen duty lasted

246 The Gilboa Iris

for four weeks only," I answered as indifferently as I could. "Most of the time I worked in the fields."

"*B'emet?* Really?"

His astonishment was a tad too excessive, I thought. "Yes, really. Why so surprised?"

"You just look too…delicate for field work."

Yaniv and Jenny shot each other a look. "Um, more dessert, Dara?" Jenny quickly tried to change the subject.

"I held my own just fine, thank you," I responded firmly to Uri.

"I didn't mean anything negative by it. There's really no need to get defensive."

"I'm not defensive."

"Sure you are."

"Would you kindly not tell me what I am?"

"More wine anyone?" Yaniv interjected.

"I'm just telling it as I see it."

"Well, your vision is evidently impaired."

"But you *are* delicate. What's wrong with that?"

I didn't know what to answer and simply looked at him. I wasn't sure why it bothered me so much. He was just so…opinionated.

"It's not a sign of weakness, if that's your concern," Uri continued.

"Don't presume to know my concerns."

"It's obviously important to you to present a strong facade."

"Jenny, you didn't tell me that he also moonlights as a psychoanalyst," I said, glaring at him.

"Actually, I just read people well," his lips curved into a smug grin.

"More cake anyone?" Jenny pleaded. "It's chocolate rum!"

"And you think you have me all figured out." It wasn't a question – it was an accusation. If not for seeing Jenny's pleading expression out of the corner of my eye, I would have smacked that smug look right off his face.

"Uh...Uri, how about you leading us in the after-the-meal blessing?" Yaniv urged. Uri complied, and after the blessing he picked up right where he left off.

"You know," he leaned in toward me across the table, "most women would consider it a compliment to be called delicate."

"You were not complimenting me; you were implying that I couldn't handle field work."

"Well, you just look more like the planting flowers type than the driving the tractor type."

"It seems you have a bad habit of judging a book by its cover."

"Maybe if you weren't such a closed book, I'd be able to see past your cover."

All I could do was stare at him, speechless, taken aback by his gall but most of all, shocked by his intuitiveness. Jenny and Yaniv rose to clear the dining room table. I stood up from my chair to help, anxious to get away from Uri, but he followed me, carrying a few things back to the kitchen as well. Not sure why I just didn't let the subject rest, I turned to him and insisted, "I'm not hiding anything."

"Aren't you?" The gold in his eyes seemed to laugh at my displeasure.

"Well, since you claim to be an expert on me, why don't you tell me what I'm hiding," I challenged, as Jenny, without losing a beat, grabbed the crystal wineglasses that I held and carefully put them on the counter. Yaniv took Jenny's good porcelain dishes from Uri's hands and did the same. "We'll take it from here, guys," Yaniv said as he and Jenny nudged us to the living room, both of us barely noticing that we were just ousted from the kitchen.

"Look, Dara, I don't see what you're getting so riled up about. I happen to like delicate women."

"Oh, praise the Lord! Now that I know that, I think I'll sleep better tonight." *What was Jenny thinking?* I turned away from him, and went to sit on the couch by the bay window. With my back to him, I stared outside, trying to ignore the chuckling under his breath, but he followed me to the couch and sat down beside me, allowing only a mere few inches of space between us. "And just for the record," I turned back to him in a huff, "I am not riled up. Being riled up would indicate that I care what you think. And I don't."

"All evidence to the contrary," he shot back with a huge smile.

"Excuse me?"

"I think you care very much what I think, Dara. In fact, I think you like me."

"Somehow, I'm not surprised that you would think that."

"I like you, too."

"Well, don't." For some reason, that sent a feeling of alarm through me.

"Why not?"

"Because…," I trailed off, not able to finish the sentence. I looked back out the window with a sigh.

"Because…you're afraid I might break through your *tough* exterior?" he asked in a soft tone.

"Look," I said, facing him again, suddenly noticing that his topaz eyes were…were…beautiful. "Jenny shouldn't have…I'm just not…," I shook my head, frustrated with my inability to finish a coherent sentence. "Look," I tried again, "I don't mean to be rude, but…you're wasting your time with me. I don't go out with men."

"You prefer women?"

"That's not what I meant." I rolled my eyes.

"What *did* you mean?"

"I can't explain."

"You mean, you won't explain."

"I really wish you would stop that."

"Stop what?"

"Telling me what I mean."

"I wouldn't have to if you would just explain yourself."

"You seem to be deriving some strange pleasure in trying to figure me out."

"Let's just say you intrigue me."

"Well, let's just say that I don't want to be figured out."

"Too late."

"Oh? Have you cracked the code where I'm concerned?"

"Not yet. But I do believe that you *do* like me."

"I suppose you see *that* in my body language as well?"

"It's more like a combination of things."

"And what if I told you that you couldn't be more wrong?"

"Let's go out dancing."

"What?"

"Dancing. Tomorrow night, after Shabbat. You and I should go dancing."

"I don't dance. And stop changing the subject. You're confusing me."

"That's impossible."

"That you're confusing me?"

"No, that you don't dance."

"Well it's not. I don't dance."

"Why not?"

"I don't know how."

"I don't believe that."

"Why is that so hard to believe?"

"Because you have the body of a dancer."

"Don't look at my body." *Could this guy be more annoying?*

"You've got to be kidding." His eyes creased in a roguish smile. *Apparently, he can.* "Excuse me?"

"Do you genuinely think any man would not notice your body the minute you walk into a room?"

"Are you always so bold with women you've just met?"

"Actually, no."

"So, why am I so lucky?"

"Okay. So I won't talk about your body anymore. But that doesn't mean I can't appreciate what I see." His eyes rolled over me.

"Please stop that. It's rude."

"Can I talk about your eyes, then?"

"I think it would be best if you simply didn't talk."

"They're incredible."

"What?"

"Your eyes. They're incredible."

"Thank you."

"So, then it doesn't bother you if I talk about your eyes."

"You complimented them. I thanked you. There's nothing more to say about it."

"I disagree."

"Of course you do."

"I could have sworn when I met you earlier this afternoon they were a deep blue – like the ocean. But now, they're silver…like silver ice."

I let out a frustrated sigh. "If you must know, my eyes turn gray when I'm upset."

"Silver."

"Whatever."

"How unusual."

I shrugged.

"So…that would mean I *do* have an effect on you, which of course discounts what you said earlier."

I looked at him, utterly confounded.

"You said before that you don't care about what I think."

"I don't."

"Then why are you upset?"

I sighed again. "I'm tired. I'm going to turn in."

"Now who's rude?"

"It's late. I'm not being rude."

"But I'm a guest."

"So am I."

"Hmm. Seems we've reached an impasse. You know what that means, don't you?"

"I'm afraid to ask."

"It means that it's time for tea. Herbal or regular?"

Tea sounded good, actually. "Herbal."

He got up and sauntered to the kitchen, and a minute later, he called out, "They have lemon, cranberry and apple cinnamon – which do you prefer?"

"Surprise me."

"Ah, *sababa*! A woman of adventure. I like that."

I rolled my eyes. *Ili, I'm Uri, I'm in love with myself, you're so lucky to be in my presence!*

Uri returned with a tray of tea and set it down on the coffee table before us. "Looks like Jenny and Yaniv went to bed. I guess they sensed we wanted to be alone."

My eyes widened at his audacity. "Please tell me you really don't believe that."

"I'm not afraid to admit that there's a definite chemistry between us, Dara. Why fight it?" He handed me my cup of tea.

"You're delusional. And…," I resigned grudgingly, "thank you for the tea."

"You're welcome." His lips arched in a playful grin.

We sat there drinking our tea, and I was grateful for the blissful silence. The hour was late and I felt the fatigue setting in. *One glass of wine too many at dinner.* I set down my cup on the tray and leaned my head back against the chenille throw draped over the rear of the couch, closing my eyes. After we finish the tea, I decided, would be the perfect time to call it a night without being discourteous.

"You know what I find interesting, Dara?"

"Mmm. No." My eyes remained closed. I thought I felt a headache coming on.

"Your writing is very open and unguarded...almost vulnerable. Refreshing really."

I rolled my head slightly in Uri's direction – my eyes now half open. "You've read my column?"

"Yes. For fluff pieces they're really quite good."

"Fluff?" I breathed, too tired to register my outrage in my voice.

"You know – soft-core news as opposed to hard-core news."

"Human interest stories are not fluff." I crinkled my brows, my eyelids feeling heavier. He laughed under his breath.

"Relax, Dara. I was just teasing. You write very well, in fact. Your articles are not only entertaining, but also insightful. You never fail to reach the heart and tickle the brain at the same time."

"Tickle the brain," I repeated in a whisper, chagrined at the imagery, but too weary to differ. Humph. As if my writing could do no more than *tickle the brain.*

"Yes. *And* reaches the heart. It takes an open heart to reach another. It's fascinating how you set yourself free in your writing."

"I have no heart," I thought I heard myself mumble. So...tired. *Did I say that aloud?*

"You're wrong, Dara. You're *all* heart. I told you, I read people very well."

Was that Uri's voice? It sounded...far away. He must have gone home and I must be dreaming. Did he say something about...my heart? Mmm...unlikely. I have no heart. Roni took it with him....

I sensed the early sun breaking through and splashing the room with its soft rays as I stirred, hovering between sleep and semiconsciousness. It felt wonderful to lie once again in Roni's strong embrace. So warm. So secure. *Roni, my Roni, you've come back to me.* I purred in contentment, edging toward wakefulness. The powerful arms that held me responded tenderly with my movement.

I traced my hand over the muscular arm clasped around me, and over the sturdy chest that my head rested upon. Something was...off. It felt more than muscular...it was...brawny. *This...is...not...Roni.* My eyes flashed open to see myself enveloped in arms I didn't recognize. I gasped aloud and lifted my head to see that I had fallen asleep on the living room couch in...Uri's arms.

His eyes opened to see mine staring bewildered into his. I wriggled out of his embrace and sprang off the couch. Disoriented and alarmed at the same time, I checked to see that my clothes were still on and backed away toward the staircase at the edge of the room, my eyes burning into him in a gradual fury with each second of awareness.

"Dara, wait...nothing happened. It was all innocent."

I didn't know whether to pounce at him or to run from him. The staircase behind me creaked under the weight of someone's step. I whirled around and darted up the stairs, not stopping to look at Yaniv as I passed him, and flew to the guest bedroom.

"Dara?" Yaniv called out, and then noticed Uri standing in the living room, folding the chenille throw. He glanced back up the staircase, and then back again to Uri. "Why...why are you still...you didn't go home last night?"

Uri blew out a gust of air. "No."

"Did you lose your way?" Irritation marked Yaniv's words.

"It's not what you think, Yaniv."

"All I know is that I saw Dara running upstairs in a very distressed state. What the hell happened?"

"We fell asleep on the couch."

Yaniv narrowed his eyes. "Uri, you just met her yesterday. What were you thinking?"

"I guess I wasn't," Uri muttered as he placed the folded throw on the couch.

"Dara isn't like one of your casual one-nighters. She's different. I thought you understood that."

"I'm sorry, Yaniv...I didn't mean for..." He broke off and raked his hand through his hair in frustration.

"Sometimes I just don't get you, Uri. Hell, she's my wife's best friend! Dara is family to us."

"Yaniv, I promise, nothing happened."

"Then why was she so distraught?"

"Look, we were sitting on the couch and talking. It was late and she fell asleep. I tried to wake her, but she was out cold. So I covered her with the throw and she... kind of tumbled into me, and...damn, she was so...beautiful...I just wanted to look at her, and then," Uri shrugged, "I suppose I dozed off myself."

Yaniv's face grew into a wide dimpled smile.

"Yeah, you can wipe that smile off your face. You and Jenny knew I would go for her. Wasn't that why you wanted me to meet her?"

"We had a hunch. We actually wanted to get the two of you together sooner, but it took a long time to get her to agree to meet you – to meet anyone for that matter."

"So I understand. What's her story?"

"It's not mine to tell."

"Ah, always the gentleman, Yaniv."

"And so had you better be – that is, if Dara ever speaks to you again. I told you she was different from the kind of women you're used to, so don't screw with her."

"Then what's the point?"

"You know damn well what I mean. Besides, didn't you say yourself that you've grown tired of all the nameless women in your life?"

"I did say that, didn't I?" he said thoughtfully, sitting himself on the couch.

"Look Uri, had you not told me that, I wouldn't have let a letch like you within an inch of Dara. Bottom line, you should have tried harder to wake her and let her sleep upstairs in her bedroom, *alone...without you.*"

"Yaniv, I told you the truth. I intended on waking her. I didn't plan to fall asleep myself. I guess we both had a little too much wine last night."

Yaniv glanced up the staircase, shaking his head, "The poor kid must have been shocked when she woke up to see you right next to her."

Uri blew out heavily. "She was shocked all right – didn't help that my arms were sort of around her."

Yaniv's eyes darted back to Uri. "Sort of around her?"

"Uh...yeah. We were a bit...intertwined. It's not exactly a spacious couch."

"Uri," Yaniv said with a snicker, standing over him, "for a smart guy, you're a real dumb ass. You know, you're going to have to make this right."

"How the hell am I going to do that? She thinks I'm a lech."

"You are, but that's beside the point. *You're* the genius professor. By the time lunch rolls around, I'm sure you'll figure something out."

"She's not going to make it easy. The woman's a spitfire."

"Yes, I know," Yaniv chuckled. "I have one of my own. C'mon Uri, *yalla*, go home, change and I'll see you at the synagogue."

"Right. Synagogue. Shabbat prayers. I'm on it."

Chapter 27

"So what if you fell asleep on the couch together?" Jenny exclaimed as she poured me a second cup of coffee.

I shot her a look. "He should have woken me up."

"Dara, you know how you are after just one glass of wine. A bulldozer would be hard-pressed to wake you. I'm sure he tried." She set down a platter of pastries on the kitchen table.

"Why are you so determined to match Uri and me up? It's not going to work, Jenny. He's not my type."

"Right," she said, unconvinced. "So how did it feel?"

"How did what feel?"

"How did it feel to wake up in Uri's arms?"

I grabbed a cinnamon bun and took a bite out of it. "Why are we eating this right before lunch? Yaniv and Uri will be back any minute."

"Not *too* obvious there, Dara. Why are you avoiding my question?"

"It's not worth answering."

"You're forgetting how well I know you."

"So, you answer the question."

"Okay, I will. I think you liked it and I think you like him, but you won't let yourself admit it because you feel you're being unfaithful."

I clutched the engagement ring around my neck and stared into my coffee.

"Oh, Dara," Jenny's shoulders slumped and her eyes all at once filled with sadness for me. "What am I going to do with you?"

"I don't want your pity, Jen. I'm perfectly fine."

"You've suffered so much in your life; I just want you to find some happiness. You deserve it. But...don't you see? Happiness won't come to you on a silver platter. You have to grasp it when you have the chance. You have to open your heart to it and be ready to accept it."

"I can't, Jenny. I will never love anyone the way I loved Roni."

"You don't have to. Roni was your first love, and no one can ever take that away from you. But that doesn't mean you can't love someone else on a different level, and have it be something special, too." She sat down after filling her own cup with more coffee and broke off a small piece of one cinnamon bun from the platter. "Look, Dara, you just met Uri. You don't have to make any life-changing decisions about him...but you *can* give him a chance. Go out with him...have some fun."

"You don't even know if he's interested in me."

Jenny broke into laughter. "Wow, Dara. For a smart woman, you can really be a dumb ass." I flashed a look of surprise at her, and she just shook her head in frustration and continued to laugh.

After finishing our coffee, I stood up from the table to rinse our mugs in the sink and Jenny left the room to put a clean tablecloth on the dining room table. I glanced out the kitchen window and spotted Yaniv and Uri on their way back from the synagogue. Jenny had woken up late this morning, and I wasn't in the mood to venture out. Praying wasn't my thing lately. I continued to stare at Uri through the window. *He certainly is easy on the eyes*, I thought as I watched him walk in a fluid and sinuous stride – his light, sandy-toned hair, almost chin length, billowing casually in the breeze. For all his brawn, he had a gentle face and kind smile, and yet, he had a bad-boy quality in his features that was awfully enticing. It wouldn't have surprised me if he trekked around the country on a dirt bike. Had my brain been working right, perhaps I *would have* been attracted to him. Then again – he was also pompous, obnoxious and smug, I quickly remembered – not to mention offensively provocative. I turned away from the window and went to help Jenny set the dining room table for lunch.

"*Shabbat shalom*," Yaniv said as he and Uri came through the door. He walked over to Jenny and kissed her tenderly on the cheek. I enjoyed watching the two of them together. I couldn't think of a more perfect couple. Well, except for…*sigh, Dara, stop torturing yourself.* I finished placing the cutlery at each setting and noticed Uri hovering near me. Jenny and Yaniv were suddenly and conspicuously absent from the room. "*Shabbat shalom*, Dara." His tone sounded uncertain. *Hmm. And I thought he would be parading around in self-satisfaction.*

"*Shabbat shalom*," I answered, making an attempt at civility. He stepped closer to me. It was hard not to notice how well he filled out his button-down white shirt, his sleeves rolled up revealing his strong forearms. *No doubt, he stares at himself in a mirror longer than I do.*

"I'm very sorry about last night, Dara," he sounded almost sheepish, but I wasn't about to let him off easy.

"Which part?"

"The part where you fell all over me pretending to be asleep," he pitched back without skipping a beat.

"Nice try," I smirked. "But I'm not going to let you get to me today. In any case, we should be courteous to one another until the end of

Shabbat, just for the sake of Jenny and Yaniv, and then we can forget we ever met."

With a slight tilt of his head, Uri just looked at me in silence. I didn't realize how harsh my last words were until it was too late. "I'm sorry," I quickly apologized. "I didn't mean to be so rude."

"Don't give it a thought, Dara," he said in a muted tone and walked out of the room. I felt terrible.

❄

"So, how did it go?" Yaniv asked, pulling Uri to the side. "Is everything all right between the two of you?"

Chuckling under his breath, Uri answered, "Oh, it will be." He walked casually out to the terrace with Yaniv following.

"What game are you playing?" Yaniv raised an inquisitive brow.

"No games, Yaniv," Uri shrugged. "Just like army training – never go into an operation without having a clear-cut strategy, always keeping an eye on the objective."

"I have a feeling this is going to be too painful to watch."

"Relax. I'm going to be very *courteous*," Uri smiled to himself, enjoying a private joke. He'd do exactly as Dara suggested. A serious look then fell across Uri's face and he glanced questioningly at Yaniv. "Are you really not going to tell me what the mystery is about her? She's like…a wounded bird…a tortured soul."

Yaniv raised his brows in admiration. "I still get a kick out of how you pick up on things so quickly. One might think you're even sensitive."

"Yeah, I'm a teddy bear. So tell me, Yaniv, what's her story?"

"Sorry, Uri, it's not my place to say. She's going to have to tell you herself. I will give you one thing, though. She *does* have a tortured soul, but it's a gentle soul and she has a heart of gold…just like you, actually, when you're not being a jerk."

"Thanks, pal. I love you, too."

"You know, she once took a bullet trying to save a friend in a terrorist attack back on the kibbutz." Yaniv shook his head in awe as he remembered. "It was crazy – the bullets were flying and she ran out into the open to drag her wounded friend to a safer position. When things quieted down, we found Dara under a tree with...Alana, was her name. Dara was covered with blood from head to toe – took off her clothes, using them to apply pressure on Alana's wounds to stop the bleeding. Dara was shot in the leg but ignored it while she tried to save Alana's life."

"That's quite a story. What about her friend...did she make it?"

"No."

"But something else happened to Dara on that kibbutz, didn't it?"

"Like I said Uri, that's for her to tell. Anyway, with your knack for reading people, I know you can break through Dara's...*tough* exterior. Besides, admit it, you love a challenge."

"A woman that's a challenge...hmm...can't say I know what that is."

"Then get your brain out of your pants for a change and use your head. This one's a *keeper* – not a conquest. Dara is the kind of woman you can finally appreciate."

"I take it you mean, *aside* from her being hot as hell?" he kidded Yaniv.

"Yeah," Yaniv smiled, shaking his head at his friend. "C'mon, let's get back inside and see if Jenny has lunch ready. I'm starved."

The afternoon meal was strange. Polite, restrained and annoying to the hilt. Uri took pains to be unmistakably courteous. Irritatingly so. He had made it a point not to speak to me or even look in my direction, unless it was necessary. It never went further than polite *pass the salt* conversation. He was so...cold.

What a big baby. Okay, granted, I suggested we be courteous to each other, and yes, I did insult him, but I apologized immediately. Why wouldn't he just let it go? Even Yaniv was rolling his eyes at Uri, and Jenny looked entirely confused.

Certainly, what I had said to him could not have been worse than what he did to me. The nerve of him falling asleep on the couch with me – and how was it that I ended up with his arms around me? Accident? Oh, right! And *he* was giving the cold treatment *to me*? It took every ounce of restraint I had to keep myself from pouring the wine right over his head and his crisp white shirt that he sported like a damn model. I had no patience for his infantile behavior. I could not suffer sitting across from him for another minute, and as soon as it was socially acceptable, I stood up to clear the table before dessert and avoided any more of the dining room scene by dallying in the kitchen. The entire drama with Uri was so *high school*. I didn't need this, not any of it.

I busied myself with rinsing the dishes and stacking them in the dishwasher, and attempted to divert my attention by leaving a spic-and-span kitchen for Jenny. Only then, out of nowhere, I burst out crying – sobbing would be a more accurate description. I couldn't stop. The sadness I felt was razor sharp – the wretched loneliness, the hopeless longing for Roni, all at once hit me like a rockslide, and I couldn't climb out from under it. The tears flowed relentlessly. They were tears that I never indulged in, that I never allowed myself to yield to. *Why now?* I had always been able to control my emotions – bury them deep inside me – careful never to allow any outward show of the pain that had become my constant companion. My pain was the one thing I could depend on. It was familiar and reliable. So why was this happening? *Damn!* I was frantic at the betrayal. Was everything now beyond my control? I wanted to sink to the floor and not get up. But I couldn't. I wouldn't have my vulnerability on display. The others were bound to come into the kitchen at any moment.

My eyes darted around the room in search of a box of tissues. There was none. I grabbed some napkins out of a cabinet and proceeded to wipe away the evidence – but the tears were persistent, rolling down my cheeks. My sadness was too deep, the sounds of my sobbing were too audible – my body shaking from it, and then…they came in.

I held my breath as I stood with my back to them. "Wow, Dara," Jenny exclaimed, "you really cleaned up fast. You didn't leave anything for the rest of us. Thanks!" I didn't dare turn to face them. I nodded my head and hoped that would suffice. Only, at that moment, a muffled sob broke free, my hand jumped to cover my mouth, but my sniffing and the involuntary emotional trembling that seized my body was a dead giveaway and I lowered my head, mortified.

Not a peep came from Jenny, Yaniv or Uri, and the silence was excruciating. I didn't turn around to them, yet sensed that they stood just steps behind me, dumbfounded. I prayed they would have the good judgment to retrace their steps and head back into the dining room. They did. *Terrific. Now what was I going to do?*

※

"Great strategy, Uri," Yaniv said in a dry, muted voice.

Jenny looked at Yaniv questioningly and then glared at Uri. "What strategy?" she whispered so Dara would not overhear her from the kitchen. "You mean your weird behavior toward Dara was a *strategy?* I'd never seen you act so stone cold. Uri, what's going on?"

Uri dropped down in the dining room chair without a word. "Uri, say something," Jenny urged. He glanced up to Yaniv and Jenny standing over him. "I didn't mean to be cold to her," he finally said, his tone subdued. "I think I did enough damage here. I'm going home." He stood up. "Thanks for lunch, Jen."

They watched as Uri, dejected, walked out the front door. "I don't understand," Jenny said, turning to her husband. "I thought they would be perfect for each other." Yaniv placed his arm around Jenny's shoulder and gave her a comforting squeeze. "They are perfect for each other –

they just don't know it yet. And," Yaniv let out a sigh, "it seems that Uri still has some growing up to do."

"Well, you're his good pal, can't you tell him to get on the ball? I mean, isn't he like…thirty-something?"

"He is *something*," Yaniv chuckled. "Come, we should check on Dara." They stepped into the kitchen, but the room was empty. Their eyes automatically flitted to the door that led out to the side of the house. Jenny turned to Yaniv. "She's gone."

※

It was a quick walk to his house – down a hill, taking a shortcut through an open field that hugged the outskirts of the southern edge of the town. Uri trudged along with his hands in his pockets and his shoulders bent, with the image of Dara crying lodged in his mind. *Yaniv was right. I am an ass.*

Something in the remote landscape caught his eye. He glanced up to the knoll that stood beyond his home and spotted the rush of raven hair fluttering in the distance. "Dara?" *Where is she running?* He dashed into his house, grabbed his gun and raced up the knoll toward Dara.

She must have a death wish, he thought. *Thank God she runs like a girl.* "Dara!" Uri shouted out as he closed in on her. *Crap! She doesn't hear me.* "Dara!" He sprinted up the steep incline in an urgent rush as he kept his eye on her, now scurrying down a ravine, her pace accelerating. When he reached the crest, he called out to her again, darting after her. "Dara!" Finally she stopped and spun around, surprised to see Uri chasing after her. She stood in place watching him, her head tilted slightly in curious regard.

Heaving heavily, he hastened toward her and grabbed her arm. "What are you doing?"

"What are *you* doing?" I stepped back from him and he let go of my arm easily.

"Don't you know how dangerous it is to be in this area by yourself? *Ein lach neshek*, you're not armed!" he responded firmly. It was then that I noticed the Arab village less than a quarter of a mile to the east from where we stood. "Dara, just the other week, two hikers were attacked here and they barely made it back to safety. That village is not exactly known for its hospitality toward Jews. This region is teeming with terrorists. You should know better."

Of course, he was right, I thought. I *should have* known better. I wasn't thinking sensibly. I hadn't paid attention to where I was going. All I wanted to do was to run. It didn't matter to where. Just as long as it was...away. I felt so stupid. This day was just getting worse and worse. I had nothing to say. "C'mon, Dara," Uri's tone softened. "Walk back with me."

Neither one of us spoke as we headed back to Sde Dovid. The afternoon sun was strong yet soothing, and I allowed my head not to engage in any thoughts except for concentrating on the path through the hilly terrain. The last thing I wanted was to think of how I repeatedly humiliated myself.

A short time later, we reached the edge of Sde Dovid and neared a house that stood at the southern edge, as if on guard. "This is where I live," Uri said simply. "Jenny and Yaniv are just up this road, through the field and around the hill." I glanced up the road and nodded.

"Uh...would you like to come in for a cold drink...before you head back to them?"

I looked down and shook my head no. *I already overstayed my welcome in this town. I knew I shouldn't have come. I didn't belong here. I didn't belong anywhere.* I glanced up at Uri, his topaz eyes intent on me, and spoke the first words to him since he caught up to me near the Arab village. "Thank you...for...coming after me."

"You're welcome, Dara."

I felt his stare as I continued up the road.

Chapter 28

I found Jenny and Yaniv sitting in their living room. "Hi," I murmured, taking a seat in an easy chair across from them. "I'm sorry for my disappearing act, I just…"

"No, Dara," Jenny cut in. "I'm so sorry about how this day turned out. I don't understand it – Uri is usually such a sweet guy."

"Don't blame him, Jen. It's not his fault. It's mine."

"That's very gracious of you," Yaniv interjected. "I feel I especially have to apologize for my friend."

"Please, Yaniv, Jen. Uri didn't do anything wrong. It was all me. I was rude to him and…it doesn't really matter anymore…just please, don't blame him."

"He made you cry, Dara. I've never seen you cry since…well…not for a long time."

"Uri wasn't the reason I had…an emotional moment. Look, I couldn't even say what made me cry…it just happened." I shrugged. "I guess it had to come out sooner or later."

"If it means anything to you, Dara," Yaniv offered, "Uri was very upset about everything. He genuinely liked you…he just…actually, I really can't explain what he was doing. Maybe," Yaniv smiled warmly, "he had finally met his match. Perhaps you and Uri –"

"No, Yaniv." I wouldn't let Yaniv finish his thought. "I know you and Jenny are just looking out for me, and I appreciate it. I love you…you're my family, and I don't *want* you to give up on me. One day, maybe…I'll be normal again. But…right now, I just can't meet other men."

"Dara, Roni was my best friend. Believe me – he would want you to get on with your life." He paused for a moment. "You know, before he left on his last mission, he called me…to speak about you, specifically."

"What did he say?" My voice was barely a whisper.

"He said that if anything should happen to him, I should make sure that you would move on, meet someone else, build a family and be… happy. He didn't want you to waste the best years of your life mourning over him. He made me promise him that I wouldn't let you do that."

"It's as if he knew he was going to die," I thought aloud. "Somehow, *he knew*. You see, he had also called me right before he left on his last mission, only I wasn't home. It was the day of my parents' funeral, and when I returned to the house I found a message from him. I remember thinking how strange it sounded, as if he were saying good-bye to me forever."

Jenny turned to Yaniv. "Do you think he knew? Do you think Roni had a premonition that he would be killed in action?" Yaniv didn't answer. He glanced at Jenny and then at me and appeared very uncomfortable with the question. His eyes seemed to reflect the pain I felt, and he looked away. Yaniv and Roni were close like brothers. There was no doubt that Yaniv sorely missed him.

For the rest of the day, conversation was lighthearted. We caught up on each other's lives and shared in a few good laughs. I was also happy to hear the latest news about some of our old friends. Lavi and Mikki as well as Doron and Shira were all married and living on the kibbutz, along with Ari and Adina. I missed them, and I missed the good old days. I would have liked to join Jenny and Yaniv on the following weekend to visit them, but I couldn't bring myself to return to Gilboa.

After sundown, once Shabbat was over, Jenny and Yaniv walked with me to the bus stop where I would catch the bus back to Jerusalem. I said my good-byes to them and promised to get together with them again soon.

I loved my Jerusalem home. It was in Katamon, on a tree-lined street with overflowing blossoms from the neighboring homes draping the walkway. A wrought-iron gate opened up to a stone pathway leading to my house. It was set back in a quaint garden surrounded by aged, towering trees, whose twisted branches dangled and arched as if to embrace the structure within. Its location suited me well and afforded the privacy I craved. Though it was not a very large house, by Israeli standards it was quite comfortable, and I cherished its ambience.

I remember thinking when I had purchased the house, how much my mother would have appreciated its old-world flair. It was unusual that a single woman my age would own a home of this type, but with the money that I inherited from my parents and from Pops, not to mention the proceeds from the sale of the house in Manhattan, financial concerns were no hindrance.

Once inside, I turned on the light and dropped my bag on the floor in the entry hall that opened up to a comfortable living room. I had decorated it sparsely with a distinct Mediterranean flair that boasted dark wood accents, muted washed walls and my favorite, an antique white overstuffed couch with a myriad of colorful pillows strewn about.

I frowned to myself. Another night, alone. After spending time with Jenny and Yaniv, it was difficult returning to an empty home. I went to the kitchen, fixed myself an iced coffee, and then plopped myself on the couch in my living room. Television didn't interest me and I was not in the mood to curl up with a good book...*again*. The night was young, and I was bored. Hmm, maybe I'd throw in an old video in the VCR. Just as I was leafing through my pitiable collection of movies, the doorbell rang. *Who could that be?* I rose from the couch and went to look through the peephole. *No!* I hesitated, taking in a deep breath before opening the door.

"You're not ready yet?" Uri asked, his tone feigning surprise. He stood leaning against the doorpost – self-assured – wearing blue jeans that were a model fit, with an aviator jacket opened over a fitted, deep-brown T-shirt. In one hand, he held a motorcycle helmet.

"Ready, for what?" I asked, baffled at his presence.

"We had a date to go dancing, don't you remember?"

"I-I guess I recall some kind of conversation about dancing, but..."

"Aren't you going to invite me in?"

Still puzzled, I mumbled, "Um, sure...come in."

Uri stepped inside and edged toward the living room. He gazed around the room and turned to me with a warm smile. "You have a beautiful home."

"Thank you." I wasn't sure what to do next. "Um, can I get you something to drink, coffee or something cold?"

"I suppose I could drink a coffee while I wait for you to change."

"Change?"

"It's not that you don't look very pretty, but you're still in your Shabbat clothes and where we're going tonight, I think you'd be more comfortable if you dressed casually."

"Uri, I...I can't go dancing with you."

"Why not?"

"I told you, I don't know how to dance."

He looked pleased that I gave no other reason. "I'll teach you," he suggested in a warm and inviting tone. "And I promise you, Dara…I'll go slowly." His golden eyes held mine as I absorbed the double meaning of his words. I lowered my eyes, uncertain, and then slowly turned my face back up to his. "Do you take your coffee with sugar?"

"Just milk, thanks."

I wasn't sure what to put on. I'd never been to any nightclub in Israel. Taking my cue from Uri, I opted for casual. I slipped into my black jeans, tucked them into a pair of high-heeled ankle boots and eased into a fitted, pale-blue knitted top. After doing a superquick job at refreshing my makeup, I brushed through my hair and then added the right touch of jewelry. Taking one last glance in the full-length mirror in my bedroom, I was satisfied – casual, but with flair. It dawned on me that I was excited to go out.

When I returned to the living room, I pretended not to notice Uri giving me a quick once-over with his eyes. *I just wish men would attempt to be more subtle about it.* He stood up from the couch and stepped toward me. "You look…amazing."

"Thank you." I answered in a muted tone, surprised at feeling shy.

"You might want to take a jacket."

"But it's warm out."

"The ride may be a bit…breezy," he smiled impishly.

It was then I recalled that he had a motorcycle helmet with him when he came to the door and caught a glimpse of it on the floor next to the couch. *I had him pegged right from the start.* "Um…where exactly are we going?"

"To Tel Aviv."

My eyes widened in alarm. "You want me to ride on the back of a motorcycle all the way to Tel Aviv?"

"It's not that far – less than an hour," he tried to reassure me.

"Less than an hour? That's a long ride on a motorcycle." I was terrified.

"Trust me, Dara. You'll be safe with me."

Trust you? I barely know you! I took in a big breath of air and grabbed a jacket out of the coat closet. It happened to be a black leather motorcycle jacket that I had bought on a whim. *Little did I know.* Uri eyed my ensemble with a huge grin. "Don't even start," I warned him.

"I wouldn't dream of it." He pursed his lips in a feeble attempt to hide his amusement.

We walked out to the street and I eyed his motorcycle with trepidation. It was a Harley-Davidson, a frightening piece of machinery. "What do you do when it rains?" *What made me ask that?* He must have wondered the same thing as he found my question humorous. He had a warm laugh that had a way of almost relieving my fear. Almost. "I drive a car when it rains," he answered, his lips arched in a smile. *Oh, that's right. I forgot he wasn't cash poor like most Israelis I knew.* "But tonight," he continued, "was such a beautiful night, I thought you might enjoy riding on a motorcycle."

"I thought you knew how to read people well," I said, my sarcasm dripping.

"Here," he chuckled as he took out an extra helmet from the back compartment and fitted it on my head. "Hmm," he studied me.

"I must look ridiculous," I said, feeling self-conscious under his gaze.

Uri cleared his throat as his eyes trailed over me. "That's uh, not exactly what I was thinking."

I stood there, still in disbelief at the thought of what I was about to do when he mounted his bike and asked me to do the same. "C'mon, Dara, hop on."

"Why am I doing this?" I asked myself aloud.

"Because you find me irresistible and you can no longer fight it."

"You are so pompous!"

"I know," he said casually. "It's part of my charm."

I froze. *What did he say?* He looked at me curiously. "What's wrong?"

"Nothing." I could barely whisper as I was having a Roni flashback. "Don't be frightened, Dara. Just hold on tight, and you'll be fine." Uri's voice penetrated my momentary plunge into the past. I blinked the memory of Roni out of my head. Scared stiff, I climbed onto the seat behind him, placing my arms around his waist. He turned his head to speak to me over his shoulder, "Now, Dara, whatever you do, don't let go."

"I won't let go," I practically whimpered. He revved up the engine, and on reflex, I squeezed tighter into him. I couldn't hear him over the motor, but I felt his body vibrate in laughter. The ride through the streets of Jerusalem was choppy, but once we reached the highway to Tel Aviv, Uri sped up, weaving his way through the other cars. Everything was a blur and the night lights glared dizzily as we dashed through the air. I tried closing my eyes, but that made the ride more frightening, and I clung onto Uri for dear life. It took him an impossible thirty minutes to reach our destination, which was a nightclub called Avant-Garde on Lilienblum Street.

"Dara? We're here. You can…let go now." I couldn't move. I was concentrating on getting my heart rate down. "Or not," Uri offered in good humor when he saw that I was frozen in place.

"I need a minute here, Uri," I breathed.

"No problem, Dara. Whenever you're ready – I won't move until your feet are safely planted on the ground."

I finally let go of Uri and maneuvered myself off the seat. The ground felt strange beneath my feet, as if it were moving. Or, maybe it was my body moving although I thought I was standing still. It was hard to tell. Uri stood before me and lifted the helmet off my head. "Hey there," he said with a mixture of concern and amusement, "are you all right?"

"I think so." I heard the uncertainty in my voice.

"I think you could use a drink." He offered his hand to me.

"I think you're right." I grasped his outstretched hand, still not feeling too steady and not sure at all that I could walk in my high heels without falling on my face.

We found a small cocktail table in the corner of the club, away from the spirited crowd that lounged around the bar. The place had a warm, candle-lit ambience and the music was good – a lot of classic American rock. I had a rum and Coke and Uri ordered a beer. "*L'chaim*," he clinked his glass to mine. Without thinking, I polished off more than half my drink straightaway. He raised his brow in surprise. "Someone's thirsty this evening," Uri said with a smile. I looked down at my nearly empty glass, wondering where my drink had disappeared to, suddenly feeling more relaxed and able to enjoy the atmosphere. I shrugged out of my jacket and hung it over the back of my chair. Uri inched closer to me and fiddled with the ring I wore on a chain around my neck. "I noticed you wearing this on Friday and earlier today. Do you always wear this?"

"Yes."

He examined it, a crease between his brows, and then looked at me, attentive to my expression. "It's quite lovely," he remarked, letting the ring fall free.

"Thank you."

"You know, Dara, I know very little about you. Yaniv was very vague."

"He obviously told you where I live."

"Not without first giving me a hard time," he smiled. "He's very protective of you. Why is that?"

"Both Jenny and Yaniv are like family to me. We all developed a strong bond back on kibbutz, and it has remained strong over the years."

"What about your real family? Do you have any in Israel, or are they all still in the United States?"

"I have no family," I blurted out. *Why did I do that?*

"None at all?" He crinkled his forehead, hoping for an explanation.

"I have no siblings, and my parents are dead," I clarified matter-of-factly. "My mother was also an only child and my father had one brother who married a non-Jew and moved south, I think to North Carolina. They were never particularly close, as I understand it. My father's father, Pops, lived with us in New York until he passed away."

"When did your parents pass away?"

"Five years ago."

"Both of them – at the same time?"

"They were murdered," I explained with a deadpan face. Uri stared at me, stunned by what he had just heard. He was studying me, reading me, and I knew he would very likely be accurate with his assessment. Somehow, I didn't care anymore. I didn't feel like hiding the truth tonight.

My family, or lack thereof, was not something that I ever talked about with anyone. I was always elusive whenever people would ask me any pointed questions. All I knew is I didn't want to lie tonight. I wanted to feel unhampered. Sometimes it felt exhausting trying to cover up the truth. In a way, I was also curious as to how this devil-may-care man would react to the morbid reality that shaped my life.

He didn't immediately probe further, but waited to see if I would offer more information on my own. I decided to answer his unasked questions with as little emotion as possible and regaled him with the entire episode surrounding my parents' murder.

"So Mace is still in jail?"

"For now."

"Does he know where you're living?"

"I don't know. I tried leaving no traces behind, but…I suppose, in this day and age, if someone wants to find someone badly enough, he will."

"Does that frighten you?"

"No," I said it more out of stubbornness than out of truth and noticed Uri's lips arch into a subtle smile.

"Is that…your mother's ring that you wear around your neck?"

"No."

"A different story then?"

I averted my eyes from his gaze, and stared into my now empty glass. Uri flagged down the waiter and ordered another rum and Coke for me. "You don't have to talk about it if you don't want to, Dara."

I clutched the ring in my fingers. The chain around my neck all of a sudden felt heavy. It was either the rum or the compassion I heard in Uri's voice that made me feel that I wanted to tell him. I had already told him so much, I thought, there was no sense in not telling him the rest. *Yeah, it was probably the rum.* Besides, he already ascertained within seconds of meeting me that I was *guarded* – he may as well know why. I started slowly. "It's…from someone I once knew – someone I met on the kibbutz."

"Someone you loved?"

"Yes."

"What happened?"

"He was killed in action."

Uri was wordless but his eyes spoke volumes as he tried to absorb everything I had just told him. After a few lingering moments, he asked softly, "When?"

"Five years ago."

"Five years ago? You mean…"

"Yes, about a week after my parents were killed." I felt the familiar lump swelling in my throat. He reached out across the table and held my hand, his eyes penetrating deeply into mine, the golden hue shimmering in the flickering candlelight. He was not sympathizing – he was feeling it. I could see he was making sense of what he referred to as my *guarded* demeanor – now recognizing the source that initially generated a feeling of hostility toward him. I didn't notice the waiter bring over my second drink, but when I took hold of my glass, it was once again full.

I realized I had just exposed myself – made myself thoroughly transparent to Uri. Until this night, only Jenny and Yaniv knew everything about my life. But, from the first moments of meeting, unlike anyone else, Uri had astutely detected that I enveloped myself in a protective shield, and for some reason I wasn't entirely aware of, I decided to let my guard down.

"You don't want another beer?" I asked, changing the subject, more out of a desire to lighten the moment as I casually slipped my hand out of his. Uri shook his head no. "I'm driving," he shot me a slight smile, courteously letting me change the tone of the conversation. "But perhaps we should order something to eat. That's your second drink, and I don't want you to…"

"I can handle my liquor." I cut him off.

"Like you handle your wine?" His smile grew into a grin.

"As I recall, you didn't handle your wine too well either last night. I'm assuming you were just as much knocked out from it as I was."

"It wasn't the wine, Dara. It was you."

"Pardon?"

"You hypnotized me."

"I *what?*"

"You never did let me explain what happened. You see, I tried waking you, but you fell into a very deep sleep. I reached behind you to get the quilt from the back of the couch so that I could cover you, and that was when you tumbled into my arms. I sat there…holding you, listening to the soft rhythm of your breath – you looked so tranquil, so serene. I didn't want to take that away from you. And…your gentle breathing was so…soothing, spellbinding actually, that it lulled me to sleep. So you see, Dara, you hypnotized me."

Wow. That was good. I took a huge sip of my drink and swallowed hard. "I see…so in other words…it was all *my* fault."

"Entirely your fault," he teased.

"I'm sorry I put you through such a harrowing experience."

"Mmm. Yes, falling asleep with a beautiful woman in my arms…I can't think of a worse torture."

I took another huge gulp of my rum and Coke. It didn't escape Uri's notice. He once again caught the attention of the waiter and ordered some food. "Whether you're hungry or not, Dara, I'm going to have to insist that you eat something. I can't have you taking advantage of me again," he said with a devilish charm.

In no time at all – *was it even two days?* – Uri had utterly broken through my defenses. I didn't see it coming and I wasn't sure at all how I felt about it. *Why was I allowing it?* I decided to change the focus of the conversation to him. "It's your turn now."

"My turn?"

"Yes. I don't know much about you either."

"What is it that you *do* know about me?"

"Well, Jenny told me that you work in your family's real estate business, you're a physical trainer, you volunteer at Tel Hashomer rehabilitating wounded soldiers, and that you are also a…professor of mathematics at Hebrew University." I couldn't help but break into a wide smile at the last one.

"It amuses you that I'm a professor?"

"Yes." I couldn't hold in my laughter. The rum had definitely taken effect.

"Why?" he asked, a jovial crease framing his eyes.

"You don't seem the professor type, especially of mathematics."

"Hmm, what type do I seem to you?"

"The bad-boy type," I let slip out.

"The bad-boy type? What does that mean exactly?"

"Let's put it this way. I wasn't shocked that you rode a Harley-Davidson," I broke into another bout of laughter. "I mean, the thought of you giving lectures on...math..." I trailed off, continuing to laugh. *Wow, better not drink anymore!*

"So, you think motorcycles and mathematics don't mix?"

"You're a dichotomy, Uri. But I suppose that lends to your sex appeal." *Did I just say that?* At that moment, the waiter brought over a large pizza and a huge salad.

"Uri, I'm sorry."

"For what?"

"I...wasn't...I mean...I didn't mean to laugh at you...I mean...it's just that... Oh, I don't know what I mean." I gave up.

"You're adorable, Dara." He inched the food toward me.

"Would that be your professional assessment, Professor Amrani?"

"It's more than an assessment, it's a mathematical certainty." He lifted a slice of pizza from the plate and fed me a bite. I swallowed it and reached for my drink, which I noticed he had watered down with the pitcher of water that came with the meal. "I'm not drunk, you know."

"I know." He didn't sound too convinced.

"So you don't have to feed me."

"I know that, too – you're perfectly capable of feeding yourself."

"I am."

"I'm afraid you'll have to prove it to me."

"You're actually insulting my intelligence by using reverse psychology on me."

"I apologize." He tried not to smile. "I didn't mean to insult you."

"I'm really not hungry."

"I'll make a deal with you. Have five more bites of the pizza and then I'll share the salad with you."

"Two bites."

He shook his head no. "Four," he said firmly.

"Deal," I gave in reluctantly. He sat at the table watching me eat, an amused look fixed on his face.

"So tell me, Professor, how do you find the time to do everything you do?"

He shrugged. "I like making the most out of life, and I have many interests. I've also been given a lot of blessings, and I don't take them for granted."

Is he that perfect, or is it the rum that's affecting my senses?

"I believe it would be a sin if I didn't utilize everything at my disposal to the best of my ability – to live life to the fullest."

God, he's cute. Yeah, must be the rum – nobody can be that perfect.

"Dara, you still have two bites to go."

I realized I was staring at him, my chin resting in my palm. I snapped out of my trance and took another bite of the pizza, ignoring his chuckling under his breath. I swallowed my last bite and quizzed him further. "Tell me about your family. Are your parents native Israeli?"

"Well, I can trace my family in Israel back to the Middle Ages. They came from Spain in the late 1200s and settled in various places in the land throughout the centuries until they finally wound up in Jerusalem. I'm an eighth-generation Jerusalemite." He moved the salad bowl closer to me.

"Do you have any sisters or brothers?"

"I have three brothers."

"That must be wonderful! Are you all close?" I realized I sounded ridiculously animated. But hearing about large families tended to excite me.

"Yes, and yes." He looked at me thoughtfully.

"It must have been difficult on your mother to watch each of her four sons go through the army."

"It was."

"What unit were you in?"

"I was an air force pilot."

I smiled. I should have guessed that. "And your brothers are likewise all finished with their army service?"

"Except when we have to report for reserve duty."

"Right...reserve duty." I repeated the words in a whisper. My mind wandered, caught up in another flashback, my fingers finding their way to my ring, clutching onto it.

"Dara? Dara, come back to me."

My eyes flashed back to his. "I'm sorry."

"Where were you?"

"Nowhere," I said in a hushed voice.

Uri reached for my hand that held onto the ring. "Come with me."

I gave him my hand. "Where are you taking me?"

"I promised you that we'd go dancing." It was then that I noticed the music in the background had changed to swing. "Oh...no...I can't."

"Of course you can."

"No, really Uri. I can't dance, especially not to swing."

"I'll teach you." He stood up and took hold of my other hand as well, lifting me from my chair.

"Uri, you're going to regret this.... I-I'll just end up embarrassing you...don't make me do this," I pleaded with him.

"It's too late, Dara. You can't say no."

"Too late?"

"Mmm. You can't resist my...*sex appeal*, I believe was the term you used."

"That was the rum talking."

"Rum is like a truth serum, my dear. And this 'bad boy' won't take no for an answer."

"Must you hang on to every silly thing that comes out of my mouth?"

"I'm afraid I must," he feigned somberness.

"Well, just because I said you had sex appeal doesn't mean that I'm attracted to you. In fact, I'm not. Not at all. Now let go of my hands, I don't want to dance."

"Trust me, Dara. I'll guide you all the way through it." He inched us bit by bit to the dance floor, with me protesting the entire way. "Ready?"

"No."

"Just let the music guide you."

"I thought *you* were going to guide me."

He wrapped one arm around my waist. "Do you trust me?"

"No."

His lips curled into his bad-boy smile. Then, in a burst of energy, he twirled me away at arms' length and spun me back to him in a tight embrace. I gasped, not expecting that move. He whirled me around the dance floor, his movements astonishingly fluid as we glided together in rhythm to the vigorous beat. He lifted me as if I were weightless, twirling me again and swinging me back into his arms. It was…fantastic. It was exciting. And it was…hot.

The dance ended with Uri spinning me one final time and then back into his strong hold, leaving me breathless. Maybe it was the liquor, but I didn't want to let go. Or, maybe it was me. Neither was Uri quick to let go. I closed my eyes, wrapping my arms around his back. I didn't stop to think what kind of message I was giving him. I didn't care. It felt nice in his embrace, pinned against his strong chest, feeling him breathing against me. It felt safe and it felt…familiar. The next song began, but we remained in place. His hands traced up my back, squeezing me closer to him as he whispered my name. He lifted my chin to face him; his eyes were on fire, like liquid gold burning into mine, and my heart pounded with both excitement and fear. I took in a quick wisp of air, surprised at the stirrings I felt inside of me. It was something I hadn't felt in a long time. Something I hadn't allowed myself to feel. And I was scared. Scared about what I was suddenly feeling for Uri, and scared that it was not with Roni. "Dara," Uri spoke with a throaty voice, "I think I had better take you home."

He ushered me off the dance floor and grabbed our jackets from the back of our chairs, tossing some bills down on the table before leading me outside where a gentle, refreshing breeze met us. I took in the fresh air, still a little buzzed from the rum but feeling a slight relief. Uri stepped away from me. He breathed in deeply, raked his hand through his hair and shook his head slightly as if to rid himself of an unwanted thought. *Did I do something wrong?* "What's the matter, Uri?" I asked unwittingly.

"Nothing. It was getting a little...warm in there, that's all."

"I thought you liked going to these clubs."

"Sometimes."

"Was I that bad on the dance floor?"

"Is *that* what you think?"

I shrugged. "I don't know. One moment we were on the dance floor and in the next moment, you rushed us out of there. I'm not sure what to think right now."

"Let's just say that *I* should do the thinking for us tonight." His eyes roamed over me as he muttered, "You sure as hell don't make it easy." With what I thought was a pained expression, he grabbed my hand and led me to his motorcycle. He helped me with my jacket and the helmet and then hopped on his bike, waiting for me to sit securely behind him, my arms wrapping tightly around his waist. "Ready, Dara?"

"Yes."

"You're not scared anymore?"

"More like petrified."

He turned his head, looking at me over his shoulder through his helmet visor. "No need to be petrified, Dara. You're with me now. Hold on tight."

We zoomed out of Lilienblum Street, onto the highway, leaving the Tel Aviv night lights behind us. In what must have been record time, we arrived at my house. The ride, as I expected, made me feel wobbly, and I slid off the bike not too sure of my footing. I took off the helmet, handed it to Uri and shook out my hair. *Bad idea.* The jerky motion made me woozier than I already was, and I grabbed onto the iron gate behind me to keep from falling. It didn't help. After placing the helmet in the back compartment of his motorcycle, Uri turned around to find me on the ground. "I turn away for a second and look what happens," he laughed and sat on the ground next to me.

"It wasn't my fault," I protested. "Your motorcycle made me dizzy."

"Shhh, Dara. My Harley is very sensitive. Be careful with what you say around him."

"*Him?*"

"Yeah, he's my buddy. We've been through a lot together, he and I."

Smug as he was, Uri made me laugh. We remained sitting on the sidewalk leaning against the gate, staring up at the stars. I felt an unexpected calm wash over me. It wasn't long before I sensed his eyes on me, and I turned my head to meet his gaze. He reached over and swept his fingers through my hair, "It's like silk." I lowered my eyes in evident unease. "Hey," his voice was as soft as a whisper, "why do compliments make you uncomfortable?"

My eyes darted back to his in surprise. "I-I don't know."

He studied my face. "Your parents…they never complimented you?"

At first, I was taken aback by such a question, but I stopped and took a moment to give it thought. I realized, *My father was always too engrossed in his work to notice me — and my mother...well, that was a whole other talk show.* I shook my head as if to keep from remembering anymore. "No...I guess they never did." It was more of a revelation for me than for Uri.

"Well, I'm happy to make up for lost compliments," he offered. "Now let's see, I already covered your writing, your eyes, and just now, your hair, and..."

"And I believe you already touched upon my entire body."

He ran his eyes over me, whipping out his bad-boy smile. "You can't blame me for that. There *is* much to compliment. You'll just have to get used to it from me."

"I will?" I asked, not quite certain what he was trying to tell me.

"Is that a problem?"

"I'm not sure. I'll...have to let you know."

"Mmm. I love a mystery."

There was no use fighting it — I was unquestionably and undeniably drawn to him.

"Dara?"

"Yes?"

"Do you play basketball?"

That was an odd question. "Well, I used to. It's been years since I've played, but I suppose I have a few good moves left in me."

"I bet you do," he murmured, more to himself. "What's your schedule like tomorrow?"

"I have interviews set up early in the day for a story I'm working on. Why?"

"I get out of Hebrew U at three and then I'm off to Tel Hashomer. I promised the guys at Sheba Hospital I'd give them a couple of hours of basketball practice. They're training for the Paralympics. Would you like to come?"

"You want me to play basketball with them?"

"Sure, it'll be fun. You'll love the guys and…they'll definitely love you. You may even want to write an article about them."

"Well, okay."

"And afterwards, perhaps you and I could go out for dinner?"

"Um…that sounds…nice," I all but stuttered, grimacing inside at my schoolgirl-like manner.

He looked entertained by my discomfiture. "Great. Then I'll pick you up sometime after three. Oh, and by the way, Dara," his expression turned devilish, "the teams are divided up between shirts and skins. I'm shirts."

"You had better be kidding," I got back to myself.

He shrugged, "Look at it this way. It'll save you time on deciding what to wear."

"How thoughtful of you."

"You sound surprised. You mean Jenny didn't tell you I was thoughtful?"

"She left that one out," I retorted.

"Well, I can be." His tone turned tender and he cupped his hand to my cheek. His eyes swept over my face and then stopped at the ring that dangled from my neck. "We should probably get off the sidewalk now." He stood up and offered me his hand, lifting me off the ground. "I'll walk you to your door."

I unlocked the front door and turned back to Uri. "Would you like to come in for a cup of coffee?"

"Yes, I would – very much, but…" At that moment, his cell phone rang. He gave a quick look to see who was calling, and smirked before turning his attention back to me. "I'd better not."

"Well…then…thank you for tonight. It was…nice." *Nice? That's all I can keep coming up with?*

He leaned in, giving me a gentle kiss on the cheek. "Good night, Dara. I'll see you tomorrow.

Uri stood for a moment outside Dara's door, taking in her scent that drifted on the breeze. *Mmm, lilac – nice.* He walked with a contented gait down the path, back to his motorcycle. Before putting his helmet on, he dialed a number on his cell phone. "You rang a moment ago, Yaniv?"

"Just wanted to check up on things, Uri."

"You have impeccable timing, my friend. If you must know, I just dropped Dara off and I'm on my way home – straight to a cold shower."

"Ha ha! Glad to hear it. This must be a first for you."

Uri took in a deep breath. "Yeah."

"So tell me, how was your evening with Dara?"

"It was…nice."

"Nice? That's it? That's all you're going to say?"

Uri grinned to himself. "Yeah."

Chapter 29

I was running late and grabbing a coffee in the kitchen when my cell phone rang. "I can't believe you didn't call me!" the shriek came from the other end.

"Jenny, it's only Sunday morning and I've got an appointment. Can this wait?"

"No, it most certainly cannot wait! I have to find out from Yaniv that you and Uri went out last night? What happened? Where did you go? How was it?"

"He showed up at my door, we went to Tel Aviv and it was nice."

"Nice? That's all you're going to give me? Nice!"

"Jen, I have a bus to catch."

"You can talk to me on the way to the bus stop."

"Okay, okay. Give me a minute." I put down the cell phone and gulped down half my coffee, grabbed my bag and the cell phone and hustled out the door. "Okay, Jen, what do you want to know?"

"Are you kidding me? Everything!"

I laughed. "I enjoyed myself. He was good company...fun."

"Fun? That's it?"

"Okay...he was more than just fun. He was...charming, and thoughtful."

"And?"

"And sweet – just as you said." I could actually hear Jenny's satisfied smile over the phone.

"So, what did you do?"

"We went to a club in Tel Aviv, talked, drank, ate and even danced."

"You know, Dara, for a writer you're very bad with the details."

"I'm sorry, Jen. It's just difficult to get into it while running through the streets of Jerusalem." *I have to get myself a car.*

"Well, answer this one thing: How did the evening end?"

"He was an absolute gentleman. He kissed me on the cheek and said he'd see me tomorrow."

"Tomorrow? That's today! He asked you out again for today? And you said yes?"

"Yes, Jenny," I chuckled at her exuberance. "I just hope he picks me up today in his car rather than his motorcycle. Oh, there's my bus, got to go, we'll talk later!"

"Hold on! You rode to Tel Aviv on his motorcycle? Dara? Dara, are you still there? You can't leave me dangling with that."

"Got to go, Jen!" I cackled into the phone and hung up.

The entire day was such a mad rush that I hadn't had any time to analyze all that happened the previous evening with Uri. *Perhaps it was better that way*, I thought. I wasn't ready to face anything serious like *feelings*. In any case, I had to deal with a problem that was more urgent. It was a quarter to three in the afternoon – Uri would be here shortly and I had nothing appropriate to wear to play basketball. The only shorts I owned were…way too short. I scrutinized my reflection in the mirror. *Not good.* I tried to think of alternative wear as I packed an outfit for after the game. It was no use. I didn't even have a T-shirt long enough to cover the shorts – it simply was not part of my wardrobe. *Maybe it won't make such a difference,* I thought. *Shorts are shorts.* I threw a towel, hairbrush and makeup into a bag along with my extra outfit, and then the front doorbell rang. *Is it after three already?* I grabbed any skirt out of the closet, threw it on over my shorts and went to answer the door.

"Hi." I sounded breathless.

"Hi. You sound excited to see me. I like that." He leaned down to kiss me on the cheek.

"You are so… "

"Pompous?" He cut me off with a grin.

"How did you guess?"

His eyes cruised over me. "You're not planning to wear a skirt to play basketball, are you?"

"I'm wearing shorts underneath my skirt, but I don't have basketball shorts."

"Any shorts will do. Don't even think twice about it. Are you ready to go?"

I nodded. No use in harping over something that couldn't be helped.

This time Uri came with his car. It was a sports car, of course – a sleek, silver Mazda Miata. I gave him a look. "I like fast cars," he confessed with a glint in his eye.

"Hmm. And fast women, too, I suppose?" I asked playfully.

"No, Dara," he said, tenderly sliding his palm along my hair. "Don't you remember? I like my woman to be…delicate." He winked at me and then placed my bag in the trunk with his and opened the passenger-side door for me. I took a deep breath and slid into the car. *What was I doing?* Was I ready to become involved in a relationship? I didn't feel ready. I was scared to move ahead, scared to let go of my past.

I turned to look at Uri as he pulled out of the parking space and careened down the road. Sure, he was pompous, but in an engaging sort of way, and...in his own unique style, he was very sweet...and... funny...and...warm...and...*damn,* there was no mistake about it...I was attracted to him. Very attracted to him. He stirred up feelings in me that I hadn't felt since...Roni. But Roni was dead, I reminded myself. It's been five long, lonely years. Five long years of foolishly hoping that somehow Roni would reappear, that somehow he wasn't *really* dead. It was time I faced reality. And right now, my reality was that Uri was here, next to me – attentive, caring, fun-loving and...devilishly attractive.

Uri glanced away from the highway to me. "You do realize that you're staring at me, Dara, don't you?"

"Am I?" I quickly turned to face the front window. He smiled, turning his eyes back to the road. "Does this mean you're ready to admit that you're crazy about me?"

"Not even under torture."

"Hmm. If you'd like."

I glared at him and then couldn't help but break into a smile.

"But you do like me a little."

"Yes, Uri, I like you...a little."

I noticed how his smile reached his eyes and I found myself staring at him again. His sandy-colored hair fluttered with casual indifference in the wind from his open window. He had a carefree look about him – to go with his carefree personality, I suppose. So different from Roni, who burned with intensity – who carried the burden of the world on his shoulders. I felt the familiar ache inside of me whenever I thought about Roni. *Stop, Dara, not now.* Yet, Uri was deep-thinking as well, but...in a different way. Not better, just different.

"I would love to know what's going on in that pretty head of yours," Uri said, still focused on the road ahead of him. I remained silent. He turned off the highway, passed through security and headed for the parking area for the Sheba Medical Center. "Perhaps you'll tell me later?"

"Let's go play basketball," I said with a bright smile, conspicuously changing the subject.

"Let's," he graciously gave in.

When we arrived at the gym, the soldiers were waiting for Uri, clad in their gym attire and ready for action. Uri introduced me to everyone. They were all very welcoming and very flirtatious, and Uri had to remind a number of them that they were married, and several others, that they had girlfriends. Nevertheless, a candid discussion ensued, each team vying for me to play on their side. "Uh, guys, once and for all, stop drooling. Let's not forget who Dara came with." He flashed a jaunty glance to me. "Dara, are you ready?"

"Oh, just a sec." I went to the side of the gym where Uri placed our bags and slipped out of my skirt, folding it into my bag. When I turned around, I met about twenty sets of eyes plastered on me. *Knew it. Wrong kind of shorts.* Oh well, once the game started, they'd get over it. *I hoped.* I walked toward Uri, feeling self-conscious, but tried my best to be nonchalant. "Okay, I'm ready." He was just as frozen in place as the rest of the guys, his mouth agape. "Uri? I'm ready," I repeated. He swallowed hard. "Okay then," he said in a husky voice, "let's uh, start with…layups."

It was a fun game. I was in awe at how well they played, despite the fact they were in wheelchairs. I actually scored a few points, though I suspected that they let me, and each time, both teams ended up cheering wildly for me, until Uri had to quiet them down by repeatedly blowing his whistle. At one point, he called a foul on a player who gave me the once-over once too many times. "What's the matter, Uri?" I posed casually. "Can't handle a little competition?"

"Oh, I can handle the competition," he countered. "I just think you're enjoying all of this a little too much."

"Am I?" I asked with wide-eyed innocence. He laughed good-naturedly. Just then, the buzzer went off signaling the end of the game. "Who won?" I glanced up at the scoreboard.

"I win," Uri beamed. "I get to leave with you." He snapped his head back to the soldiers. "Okay, that's it for today. Hit the showers. And before you ask, *no*, Dara will not help you in the showers!"

I said my good-byes to all the guys, and they kindly invited me back to play basketball with them again. Several joked that next time I should leave Uri behind in Jerusalem. I promised them that I would return and that I'd write an article about them. After a number of attempts, Uri finally succeeded in prying me away from their attention and they all exited the gym, leaving Uri and me alone. "Well, I never figured you for a flirt," he teased.

"I never figured you for the jealous type," I shot back.

"Me? Jealous?"

"Yes, you."

"I was just…being…"

"What?"

"Protective."

"Protective?"

"Did you not notice the way they all ogled you?"

"You mean the same way *you* ogled me?"

"That's different."

"You're right, they were all just doing it in exaggerated fun, but when you look at me, you…" I trailed off, not wanting to finish my thought.

"I what, Dara?"

"Well…it's just…different."

"Good different or bad different?" he asked suggestively.

"Is there a place here where a girl can take a shower?" I refused to answer his question.

"You didn't answer my question."

"I'm not going to."

"Ah, so it's good different."

"I never said that."

"You implied it."

"I most certainly did not. And what are you grinning about?"

"Come with me, Dara, I'll show you where you can shower. Seems like I got you all heated up – again. And this time I didn't even have to dance with you."

I glared at him. "You are so…"

"Pompous, I know." He laughed heartily.

⚜

I found Uri waiting for me at the farther end of the hallway, leaning against a wall. His fawn-colored hair fell across his forehead, just flanking his brow. He looked so at ease – so suave in his simple, white-linen, button-down shirt, his sleeves rolled up casually, alluding to his strong arms, the definition of his muscular legs evident beneath his khaki pants. Uri watched me with thoroughness, his eyes meticulously taking me in from top to bottom as I walked toward him. *I wished he wouldn't do that.* I feared I would trip over my feet.

He was both annoying and alluring at the same time. I couldn't deny that I was excited to spend time with him – something about his effortless sophistication coupled with his Bohemian unconventionality. He was worldly, established and responsible, and yet he gave off the impression of an unorthodox adventurer. He was a real estate investor, a university professor and a bodybuilder who sported a pretty-boy look and rode a Harley.

As I came closer, he stepped away from the wall and sauntered over to me. "You know, Dara, you're killing me."

"What do you mean?"

"I'm trying very hard to be a gentleman where you're concerned, but you're making it exceedingly difficult."

"I don't understand. What am I doing?"

"First you show up in microscopic shorts, showing off a set of legs that should be outlawed, and now," he toyed with the straps of my sundress, "in this little number." He bent forward, brushing his lips against my ear. "I'm not made out of stone, you know." His subtle touch against my skin sent an unexpected rousing sensation down my spine. I held my breath for a moment so he wouldn't notice and avoided his gaze.

"I don't know what you're talking about," I shrugged. "It's just a simple dress."

"There's nothing about you that's simple."

"Really? I thought you can *easily* read me?"

"I can," he said smugly. "But that's beside the point, and for another time. For now, I have other plans," he said with an air of mystery. "Let's get to the car." We headed out of the hospital center toward the parking lot.

"Where do you want to go?" I asked as we neared his car.

"How do you feel about boats?"

My eyes flashed up to his in an incredulous smile. "It's as if you can't have your feet planted on the ground for any length of time. I bet if you could fly, you would." Uri raised one eyebrow at me, as if I missed the obvious. "Right," I recalled. "Silly me. You're an air force pilot."

"At least I now know you were paying attention," he said as he opened the passenger-side door for me.

"You mean you had doubts about that? I thought you assumed I hang on to your every word," I tossed back as I took my seat in the car.

He crouched down beside me, looking me straight in the eye, "Clearly, you do." I looked back at him…having no answer. He rose, and closed my door.

Uri slipped into his side, started the engine – his eyes crinkled in a winning smile, no doubt pleased by his own wit. "Now, on to Herzliya."

As we neared the marina, we noticed an unusually large crowd on the beach nearby – a festival of some sort. We decided to check it out. There was spirited music playing in the background and all sorts of booths selling an assortment of goods and food. We munched on falafel, and Uri picked up a kite in the shape of an eagle. There were also carnival-like booths – ring toss, basketball toss and water pistols targeting clown heads. Uri tried winning a prize for me at the ring toss, but after a multitude of failed attempts, he finally gave up. "Damn thing is rigged!"

I tested my luck at the basketball toss, and on my second try I won a cuddly brown teddy bear. "Beginner's luck," Uri grumbled.

"Aw, Uri, I don't want you to feel bad," I said with big sympathetic eyes. "Here, you can have my bear."

"Don't think I won't take it," he sneered, grabbing the bear. "C'mon, let's hit the boat."

"Ay, ay captain."

We arrived at the marina and Uri led me to a sleek speedboat that sat six comfortably. He hopped on board and gave me his hand as I stepped off the dock. "Do you go boating a lot?" I asked.

"Not as often as I'd like. What about you – have you ever been on a speedboat?"

"No."

"Have you ever been on any boat?"

"I once canoed down the Delaware River. Does that count?"

"White water?"

"Some."

"Only some? Then, no."

"Hmm. Tough words coming from a guy holding onto a teddy bear."

"I just wanted to make sure that he's properly secured." He placed the bear on a seat and belted him in. "There, that ought to do it."

"You're funny, Uri," I smiled widely.

"Good. I like making you laugh. Now, come up front with me, Dara. I saved you a seat near me."

"Nice to know that I come before the teddy bear." He looked at me thoughtfully at that moment, his eyes sailing over my dress, and then he moved to the rear of the boat, flipping up the cushion of the backseat. "Good. I thought I remembered there being a blanket back here."

"Blanket? Why would we need a *blanket*?" I asked pointedly.

"You're a suspicious one."

"Considering our dubious beginning, I think I have reason to be, don't you?"

He peered at me with a self-righteous gleam in his eyes. "Dara, I was simply worried that once we'd get going you'd be cold in that little dress of yours. I wanted to be certain I had a blanket on board, in case you needed it."

"Oh."

He strolled past me, hardly attempting to hold back a victorious grin, and turned the key in the ignition, starting the motor. I sat down and secured myself in the seat, and Uri eased out of the dock. "Ready, Dara?" I nodded yes. "Hang on!"

Uri literally flew the boat over the Mediterranean, crashing down over the waves, repeatedly soaring into the air and landing on the water with a powerful thud. The exhilaration was all over his face. He was wide-eyed, excited, energized and without question...insane! I found myself wishing we were back on his motorcycle. I held on tight; my knuckles, white, gripped the edge of my seat. I tried to hold out for as long as I could, but my body took a merciless beating with each crash-landing thump on the sea. When I couldn't take a moment more of it, I called out his name, but he didn't hear me over the motor and the whipping wind. In desperation, I reached out and grabbed Uri's arm. He turned to me and, seeing the terror in my eyes, immediately slowed the boat down and turned off the motor – the boat now rocking in harmony with the mild waves. "Sorry, Dara, I guess I got carried away."

"Y-you *guess*?"

He stood up to unbuckle my seat belt. "Come here," he said, lifting me from my seat and drawing me closer to him. "I'm really sorry. I wasn't thinking." He rubbed my arms to warm me up.

"You weren't *thinking*? Perhaps you were just confused – you were piloting the boat as if it were a plane."

"Well, since you insist you're not as delicate as you look, I assumed you could handle a bit of the rough seas," he cracked. "But I should have known better and trusted my first impression. I won't make that mistake again." The smugness was in high gear.

"This has nothing to do with being *delicate*, which I'm not. You're simply a maniac." I heard the weakness in my voice. It was more like a whimper than a rebuke. I supposed that was the reason behind his pretty-boy smile.

"The wind is picking up. Would you like the blanket?" he offered.

Hell yes. I'm freezing! "No, I don't mind a little wind as long as we're not flying through it. I'm…fine now."

"Are you sure?" He sounded skeptical; his manner was more protective as he caressed my arms. "I promise you, Dara, I won't think you're, *God forbid, delicate* if you change your mind."

I couldn't stay angry with him. I could only think about his warm hands around my arms. He had such a tender touch, so at odds with his powerful build. I was keenly aware that I preferred him to a blanket. This time, however, I couldn't blame my attraction to him on any rum, and I suddenly couldn't look him in the eye.

The boat jerked without warning and jostled me; my hands reached out for Uri as I fell against his chest – his arms instinctively wrapped around me. His warm, golden-brown eyes caught mine, and I suddenly had to swallow a huge lump in my throat. I wondered if he could feel my heart beating against my chest.

"Um, how about trying to fly that kite now?" I thought I heard my voice shake.

"We could do that," he said with a gleam in his eyes, enjoying my unease a little too much. He let go of me, and took the eagle-shaped kite out of the bag and started to unravel the string, bit by bit, as I looked on. The eagle took to the sky as the wind lifted it. "Come, Dara, you hold it."

I grasped the handle of the control line and at once felt the force of the wind. "Whoa, this thing has a mind of its own."

Uri moved to stand behind me, his arms enveloping me as he draped his hands over mine to help me control the kite. "Find your center, Dara."

I tried to put the feeling of his chest close against my back out of my mind. "My center?"

"That's right. You see, there are three forces at work here – the weight, the aerodynamic force and...the tension. You need to find a balance between them. "

"Sounds...complicated for a simple kite."

"Not really. There's a natural flow, a mathematical rhythm guiding the different forces all working together in sync." It struck me how his voice was so hypnotically smooth. *I bet all his classes were overflowing with female students.* "Everything in life has its own rhythm," he continued as if reciting poetry, "and every force is a small part of a greater equation." He lifted his hands from mine, caressing my arms as he inched his way toward my shoulders. I held my breath, and bit down on my lip. "Close your eyes, Dara," he murmured into my ear. "Try to feel one with the wind." I closed my eyes. "Envision yourself as an extension of the kite – feel the rhythm of the forces surrounding you." I sensed the pulse of the wind, its force meeting the eagle's wings. "You feel it, Dara, don't you?" I nodded. "That's good," he continued – calming, tranquil. "Now…the weight acts from the center of gravity – the aerodynamic force acts through the center of pressure. And the tension, Dara…has two components, each having its own rhythm."

"Two?" I breathed.

"Mmm. The vertical pull and the horizontal pull," he explained as he rested his hands at my waist. "Can you feel the tension, Dara?" I swallowed hard and nodded yes. "You control the tension," he whispered into my hair.

"I do?"

"Yes, you do – but not with your eyes – with your mind and body. Don't think of anything else but the wind…the pull…and the tension. Let yourself flow with the forces of nature. Can you do that, Dara?"

"Yes."

"Good. Now, let your eyes remain closed, and imagine…you're that eagle in the sky." I allowed my mind to imagine, his soothing voice guiding me. "You're flying now, Dara…carefree – fluidly – rising on the wind…leaving everything else behind in the distance…freeing yourself from the weight of the past and seeing nothing else but the horizon ahead as you're carried atop the rush of the wind."

Several minutes passed in silence, hearing only the gentle rock of the boat.

"It's beautiful, isn't it, Dara?"

I nodded.

"Open your eyes now."

I opened my eyes and gazed above at the eagle in flight. Its rising ascent was even and rhythmic – harmonious with the force of the wind. I gasped at its gracefulness. "You did that, Dara. You made it happen," he whispered into my hair from behind me. "Now there's only one thing left to do."

"What's that?" I asked, whispering back, my eyes still on the eagle.

Uri's hands drifted back to mine, then to the string, ripping it free from my grasp. "You set it free." I watched as the eagle flew above the clouds, rising higher, touching the sun, until lost from view – bound for a new and untried horizon.

Uri turned me around, locking my eyes to his. He held my face in his hands and wiped away the tears that until then I was unaware of, running down my cheeks. "Dara…take off the necklace."

"What?" My voice, a shallow breath.

"The necklace – with *his* ring on it. Take it off."

I stared into his eyes, stunned.

"I won't share you with a ghost from the past. Don't be afraid, Dara…take off the necklace…be free."

But I was afraid – extremely afraid. I edged back from Uri and turned away from him, facing the now setting sun. My breathing was unsteady and I stood there, trembling. "A new and untried horizon," I whispered to myself. I took a deep breath, reached for the chain and undid the clasp – removing it from around my neck, letting it drop into my bag that rested on the floor of the boat.

I turned back to Uri and met his eyes once more, now honey-yellow with the reflection of the setting sun. He drew nearer to me and cupped my face in his hand. I knew this was the point of no return. I was caught up in a whirlwind, but could still stop it now and insist Uri take me back to shore, or, I could let come what may. His hand felt hot against my skin and I could no longer deny how I felt by his touch. He grabbed on to my waist with his other hand and pulled me close. I was unprepared for my reaction – consenting, surrendering. It was reckless. *It had to be.* It didn't appear to take Uri by surprise, however. He looked distinctly haughty as he gazed at me with the now familiar *I can see right through you* look. He knew me better than I knew myself. Damn him. It had been so long since Roni – so lonely – such a long time since I had felt any stirrings inside of me…until now. Uri's lips hovered close to mine, as if doing a sultry dance about them. I could feel his breath. I could sense him breathing in my scent as I breathed in his. It was welcoming, inviting and dizzyingly enticing. Just as I thought I would jump out of my skin, his lips met mine – warm, sweet and eager – and I fell readily into his embrace, kissing him back unfettered and unchained.

Chapter 30

Who was I trying to kid? Concentrating on work the following day was impossible. Uri had taken over my thoughts. It was difficult to come to terms with the cyclone of events that shaped our relationship – one I never expected to be involved in. I didn't quite understand how Uri managed to usurp my heart in such a short span of time. Yet, he did. Oddly enough, when he called me at the office asking what time I'd get out of work, it felt *normal*. He asked me to keep my evening free for him, and I didn't hesitate to say yes. Time did not go fast enough, knowing that I would see Uri later. The hours dragged and the minutes seemed to run past their term, until the workday had finally ended.

Just as I stepped out of the *Jerusalem Post* building, my cell phone rang. Fumbling with the stack of manuscripts in my arms, I rummaged through my bag for my phone. It was Jenny.

"Must I beg for morsels of information from you?"

"Sorry, Jen, I didn't have a moment today. I promised the editor that I'd help him out with book reviews, and we were swamped. I'm even taking work home with me," I explained, as I crouched down to retrieve several manuscripts that had fallen from my grasp.

"You're boring me, Dara. You know what I want to hear."

"Yes. Yes. I know…you want to hear about my day with Ur –" I didn't finish my sentence, for just as I stood up straight, my eyes met Uri's. Parked not two feet away at the edge of the sidewalk, Uri sat on his motorcycle, holding a spare helmet in his hand.

"Dara? You still there?"

"Um…yes, Jen."

"Well?"

"I-I can't talk now."

"Oh, no you don't! You can't do this to me, Dara. I'm sitting here on pins and needles. You've got to give me something! Are you going to see him again? Did you guys kiss yet? C'mon, Dara, give me the lowdown." Jenny's voice came through the phone in a loud screech that I was sure Uri heard when he pursed his lips to restrain a smile. He then motioned to me to hand him my cell phone. I gave it to him apprehensively, yet curious at the same time as to what he would say to Jenny. He put it on loudspeaker.

"Jenny, shalom!"

"Uri?"

"Dara can't talk to you now as I'm about to whisk her away. But, to answer your questions, yes, we did kiss, and, if you must know, it was mind-blowing amazing, and yes, she will see me again as she is just as crazy about me as I am about her. Now, do you think you can be satisfied with that until Dara can regale you with more details at a later date?"

"Uh, yeah." Jenny was uncharacteristically embarrassed.

"Ah, you're a good sport, Jenny," he said, with a smile, into the phone. "*L'hitraot.*"

"Uh, yeah... *l'hitraot* – see ya."

I shook my head as Uri returned my phone. "You are positively wicked."

"But you *will* join me for a ride anyway, won't you?"

"I must be insane."

"No, Dara. Not insane...just crazy – about me, that is." He handed me the spare helmet, taking my bag and manuscripts and placing them in the back compartment of his motorcycle.

"Don't you think you're getting a little ahead of yourself?" I asked as I climbed onto the back of his seat. "I never said I was crazy about you."

He looked back over his shoulder with a smug grin. "You didn't have to; it's in your eyes." With that, he revved up the motor and raced through the streets. He was infuriating, and God help me, he was right.

We rode to the center of Jerusalem until we reached Shimon Ben Shetah Street. "We're here, Dara," Uri turned his head, speaking over his shoulder. "You can let go now...unless, of course, you don't want to."

"I think you do this to me on purpose," I whimpered, still clinging to him.

"I don't understand what the problem is – you're a strong, tough woman. Unless you're finally conceding that you're as delicate as I thought you were?"

"Never. You're simply a menace on the road, *and* on the sea for that matter."

"Or, maybe you just feel the need for an excuse to hold on to me longer."

"Unh! You are so..."

"Pompous?"

"I was actually going for overbearing and conceited." I pushed myself off his motorcycle – a little too quickly. The familiar unsteadiness after one of his wild rides hit me and I would have tumbled backward to the ground had Uri not grabbed me by the waist.

"You're adorable, Dara." He slid off the motorcycle, keeping one arm around me.

"Thanks, I think," I said, frowning. "Do I want to be adorable?"

"May I tell you that you're also dangerously sexy? Or will you bite my head off for that as well?" He removed my helmet and his.

"You think I'm sexy?"

"Dangerously."

"I suppose that's nice to know," I shrugged my shoulder, "in a general sense, that is."

"Come here," he smirked, pulling me closer to him.

"Uri, we're in public."

"I don't see anyone but you." He leaned down to kiss me.

This was not a fleeting fancy. In a matter of mere days, he had broken down the self-imposed wall that imprisoned me. He had severed the incessant flow of pain that accompanied my life and propelled me to a new sense of light out of the darkness. Uri did what no other person could do in the five years since Roni's death. He salvaged a piece of my heart, something that till now I thought was beyond the bounds of possibility – the barriers were down and he conquered me. I didn't want him to let go, or for his lips to leave mine. I found myself wanting him more, though I was not prepared to admit it to him, at least not in words. It was too soon, too fast and too outrageous to come to grips with. Yet I became different in his arms. I couldn't stop myself from drinking in his warmth, and I kissed him with an aggressive longing.

Taken aback by my spirited response, he parted his lips from mine, his hands clutching my arms – holding me back. He stared at me –

intently – and I watched his lips gradually arch into his bad-boy smile, a look of gratification in his eyes. "Hmm, my delicate blossom is really a wildflower – seems like you need to be tamed," he said, satisfied with himself at uncovering another layer.

"You can wipe that smug look off your face now."

"So you admit it."

"Admit what?"

"That you're crazy about me. Or rather – that you're *wild* about me."

"I admit nothing."

"Ha! Come on," he wrapped his arm around my waist. "Let's go have dinner. There's a great steak place on this block."

After dinner, we strolled carefree through the center of town, mainly on the popular promenade on Ben Yehuda Street. It was bustling with tourists, students, soldiers on leave and animated shopkeepers displaying their colorful wares. A tourist trap, where people bartered over clothing, Judaica and jewelry. A peephole into the soul of the country, where Jews of various denominations snatched a corner of the broad walkway to sing and play their instruments to the passersby. Occasionally, one would come across a modern-day Christian soothsayer predicting the "second coming."

As the hour was getting late, we strolled back to Shimon Ben Shetah Street and cruised around for a while on Uri's motorcycle, before we reached my house. This time Uri was careful to go slower, and for the first time, I enjoyed the ride. Once we were at my door, I expected him to come inside for a nightcap. "Won't you come in – have a drink?"

He seemed to be having a conflict with himself. His usual relaxed and casual demeanor vanished. "Uri…it wasn't such a complicated question."

"That's what you think," he appeared to mumble more to himself. "Look, Dara, I…can't. I shouldn't."

"Why not? Wouldn't you like a cup of coffee before heading back to Gush Etzion?"

"I think you know it's not about the coffee."

"Maybe I need things spelled out for me."

"Let's just say…I'm trying to protect your virtue."

"Don't," I blurted out without thinking.

Uri raised his brows, swallowing hard as he struggled to remain resolute. "Then let's just say…I'm trying to protect mine." He grimaced, as if he couldn't believe the words that just came out of his mouth. "Look," he labored with the next words, "I just…want to do things right with you. But…" he swallowed again, wavering, his breathing uneven as his topaz eyes melted into mine and then drifted to my lips, "damn," he took in a deep breath and sighed, "you're killing me, Dara."

"I'm sorry."

He laughed lightly. "You don't have to apologize. Don't ever apologize for being you." He buried his fingers in my hair and lifted my face to his. "I better go," he muttered and brushed my lips with a light kiss before turning away. I watched him as he walked briskly down the path. *I'm out of control. He must have me under a spell. Yeah, that must be it.*

The ensuing days grew into weeks, and Uri and I were constantly together. He was careful, however, only to enter my home when picking me up, and never came in at the end of our night out. Early one evening, with what had become a regular routine, Uri came over to my house after work. I noticed there was something different as soon as he walked through the door. An energy I was unfamiliar with hovered over him. His boyish features looked strained.

"What's wrong, Uri?"

"Nothing. Why?"

"You aren't your usual laid-back self."

"Just a busy day, nothing more."

"Can I get you a drink?"

"That's all right. I'll get it. You still have work to finish. I'll stay out of your way till you're done." He fixed himself a drink while I returned to my computer in a small room off the kitchen that I used as my office. I had a deadline for an article, which I had to fax to the *Jerusalem Post*.

Some minutes later, drink in hand, Uri sauntered into my office. "How long will it take?" he asked, looking over my shoulder as I was typing. Or, at least I *thought* he was looking over my shoulder.

"I'll need another hour or so." I turned to him. That was when I saw him staring at the pressed flower preserved beneath the glass of a silver frame hanging on the wall above my computer desk. I realized this was the first time he had ever stepped into my little home office.

"Another hour," he repeated, sounding distracted, his tone subdued. "What kind of flower is that?" he asked, nodding at the frame.

"It's the...Gilboa Iris." I hoped he wouldn't put two and two together. He didn't comment, yet there was a long moment of uneasy silence. He tore his eyes away from the frame, getting back to himself, and glanced at his watch. "It's good that you have some work to finish, since I have a last-minute meeting to go to in about twenty minutes."

"Oh," was all I could muster. I was afraid my Gilboa Iris had something to do with his "last-minute meeting."

"Hey," Uri lifted my chin, seeing my disappointment. "I'm hoping it won't take too long. I don't intend on going a day without you."

"For a moment there...I thought..." I trailed off.

"You thought what, Dara?" That smug look of his told me he knew what I was thinking.

"Nothing."

"Mmm hmm. When are you going to realize that your silver eyes tell all, my dear?"

How could someone be so good at reading people? It was uncanny. "Well, maybe you should stop looking at my eyes." I couldn't help being annoyed.

"Trust me, Dara, that's not *all* I look at."

"Like I don't already know that. You don't even try to hide it when you give me the once-over."

"I take offense to that. I'm sure I do it more than just once."

"Uri, sometimes you make me feel totally naked!"

His eyes widened in surprise, and he grinned as if I said something comical. "And that *bothers* you?" There was a sly lilt to his tone.

Shrugging my shoulder, I confessed in a small voice, "Not anymore."

He smirked, the gold in his eyes dancing. "Shocking."

I frowned, but was inwardly relieved that Uri seemed to forget about the framed flower. "So, where is your meeting?"

"In the city center, on King George. I'm meeting a prospective investor at his office. But we have plenty of specifications to go over. It may run for a couple hours."

"Well, coincidentally, Jenny called me just before you arrived. She's working late today and wanted to pop over before she drives home. Why don't I just ride back with her to Sde Dovid and wait for you there. It'll give Jen and me a chance to catch up."

"Sounds like a plan." He bent down to give me a light kiss on the lips, but I grabbed onto him, kissing him harder. His restraint was driving me crazy. "Mmm, Dara," he pulled away, "you're a very bad influence on me."

"Oh? Am I compromising your virtue?"

"You're trying to."

"Still playing the gentleman role?"

"Yes, and you're not making it easy on me."

"Hmm, well *I* think you're just not that attracted to me."

"You can't be serious."

"Why not?" I answered playfully.

"Dara, I could be in the *Guinness Book of World Records* for taking the most cold showers in the span of three weeks."

"I don't know what you're talking about," I shrugged.

"My little temptress, it's almost cute how you play the chaste one. *Almost.*"

"I've been on my best behavior."

"Right. And I suppose it's mere coincidence that you're wearing *those* shorts. Did you really think I wouldn't notice?"

"Oh, these?" I stood up from my desk, posing a tad too provocatively. "I just find them comfortable to lounge around in when working at home," I said innocently, tracing my fingers over one leg that I lifted up on the chair.

Uri stood in silence and I watched his eyes travel over me bit by bit. He took a deep breath and raked his hand through his hair in frustration. A sense of guilt crept over me and I gave up the pose. But before I could do any backtracking, he grabbed me by my arms, looking at me with eyes that were glassy like molten gold. "Come here," he said in a gritty whisper, pulling me into him. His lips met mine with an intensity that took me by surprise. The strength of his ardor had thrust me backward, pinning me against a wall, his body grinding against mine. He pulled at my blouse, its delicate fabric no match for his frenzied advance as he found his way to my skin. He slid his lips down my neck, his tongue caressing me in his steady descent, my blouse no longer a hindrance – and then back up again, finding my lips once more, kissing me hard, and kissing me madly. I was on fire.

This was the first time Uri was so forceful. He had made it a point to take things slow with me, behaving with maddening self-discipline, always kissing me in a gentle…tender way, never allowing himself to lose control. Not that that wasn't nice…it was. In fact, it was very nice… and very sweet. But I craved the heat – like the way he was kissing me now – I desired his eager touch, his sensual hunger, and I didn't want him to stop.

Much too soon, he pulled his lips from mine and wrenched himself free from me. He stretched his arms out above my shoulders, leaning his hands against the wall behind me for support while gazing down at me. "I have to go," he breathed heavily.

"I know." I looked up at him, out of breath myself.

"Sorry about your blouse."

"I didn't like it much, anyway." I managed to answer.

His eyes trailed over me, looking as if he were in agony in his effort to regain control. "Dara…"

"Yes?"

"Change out of those shorts before I see you again tonight. If not, I'll go mad."

I glanced up at him demurely, trying to hide a smile.

"One more thing, Dara…," his eyes burned into mine.

"Yes, Uri?"

"The Gilboa Iris – get rid of it. Or at least put the damn thing away where I can't see it." He shook his head and walked out of the room and out the front door.

Closing the outer iron gate behind him, Uri took out his cell phone and dialed. "Hi, Jenny."

"Uri, you sound out of breath. Are you okay?"

"Yeah, yeah…. Listen…she'll be working at her desk for the next hour or so."

"Good. I'll take care of everything on my end. Don't worry about a thing."

"Thanks." He closed his phone, mounted his motorcycle, fastened his helmet and zipped south, out of Jerusalem.

※

Would I ever be normal? I wondered as I placed my Gilboa Iris on the bottom of my desk drawer. All logic and every sense inside me knew that Uri's request was reasonable. At the very least, whatever memorabilia I had from Roni should be concealed in a memory box, not hanging on my wall.

Uri was the man in my life—not Roni, I told myself. I shook my head to clear all thoughts of Roni and resumed my typing. I managed to wrap it all up and fax my article before the deadline, despite it being nearly impossible to concentrate after the passionate interlude with Uri.

I took a quick shower and slipped on a dress that I hoped Uri would find more "suitable." *It was charming how he wanted to take things slow with me,* I thought while sitting at my vanity table applying my makeup. It was as if he understood what was best for me more than I did. Ours was a whirlwind romance; he must have taken into account how it took years to open myself to a new man in my life, and it would be wise not to rush things. At least, I assumed, that was his reason. It couldn't have been easy for him. Jenny had hinted to me about the kind of social life he had before meeting me, and I appreciated the special way he treated me. Then again, I didn't exactly regret his lapse earlier this evening, I smiled into the mirror. In truth, it was reassuring to know that he wanted me in that way. Reassuring and...important for me to know – important for me to know because...because...my God – because I loved him. My image in the mirror stared back at me, reflecting the truth that I was too fearful to admit aloud. Just then, the front doorbell rang, jarring me from my thoughts. It was Jenny.

We lounged around a bit in my garden drinking iced coffee; hers, however, had to be decaffeinated. She was four months pregnant. She broke the news by informing me that I was going to have a niece. It was so exciting. Family – new beginnings – so much to look forward to.

Later, when we arrived at Jenny's house, Yaniv was already home from work and in the midst of preparing dinner. It was so sweet to see how Yaniv worried about Jen's every move and was attentive to a fault. Theirs was a relationship of deep and selfless caring for one another.

It wasn't long before Uri came by to get me. "How was your meeting?" I asked him as we drove down the road to his house.

"It went well. Did you finish your article?"

"Yes. It was a little difficult to concentrate though," I teased.

He leered at me. "Dara, don't even start."

"Well, if I remember correctly, it was *you* who started."

"I refuse to be held responsible," he narrowed his eyes at me. "You're a temptress."

"What?"

"You heard me. You bewitched me."

"Why can't you just admit that you want me?"

Uri stopped the car in front of his house, and turned to me. "Dara, *I* have no problem admitting my feelings for you." The challenge in his simple statement was not hard to detect.

We walked toward his front door and he let me in. I was met with a soft glow emanating from numerous lit candles lining his front hallway. "What's all this?" I turned to Uri. He didn't answer, but took my hand and led me further into the house. The path of lit candles continued into the dining room, where the table was strikingly set, with white orchids adorning its center. "It's…beautiful," I whispered.

"I thought I'd cook dinner for you tonight," he said simply.

"But…when did you…you had a meeting…" I said, confused.

"You…didn't have a meeting?" He shook his head no, his golden eyes gazing warmly into mine.

"Uri, this was so sweet of you…and so…" I trailed off, speechless.

"Romantic?"

"Uh-huh."

He flaunted a furtive smile, pulling back the dining room chair so that I could sit. "Don't go anywhere, I'll be right back."

I couldn't believe all the trouble that Uri had gone to. I wondered if Jenny knew what he had been planning. It occurred to me at that moment that it was too coincidental that she had to work late, and too convenient that she would while away the time with me at my house before driving me to Sde Dovid – giving Uri enough time to surprise me with this dinner. But…why go through all this effort just…for… *Oh my God!* Before I could think further about it, Uri returned with the salad. "Can I pour you some wine?" he asked.

Make it a liter. "Thanks," I answered in a quiet voice. He filled two wineglasses and handed me one. "A toast," he lifted his glass. "To wine."

"A toast to…wine?"

"Mmm. For it was the wine…that made you mine."

I broke into a wide smile. "You're crazy, Uri."

"Yeah…crazy for you."

We drank our wine and we ate what was a sumptuous meal of roast sirloin, glazed sweet potatoes and marinated hearts of palm. I was beyond impressed. "Where did you learn to cook like this?"

"Oh, it's just something I picked up along the way," he sported that bad-boy look of his. "More wine, Dara?"

"Sure. Thank you…tell me, Uri," I looked at him in wonder, "is there anything you can't do?"

"I don't know…you tell me."

I slanted my head, puzzled.

"Have I captured your heart, Dara?"

I stared at him, not certain if I should answer, suddenly fearful. Terrified, really. Terrified of being vulnerable once again…to loss. But then, as if taking a leap of faith, I did answer. "Yes," I whispered.

"You captured mine, Dara…from the first moment we met." He then laughed softly, remembering that initial meeting several weeks ago. "The way you challenged me by giving me the once-over after I did it to you – that was priceless. Before dinner was over, I was hopelessly in love with you."

"Really?" I was truly surprised.

"Yes, really, and…" he vacillated, his eyes squinting in an impish smile, "I have a confession to make."

"What is it?"

"Well…to be honest…I *didn't* try too hard to wake you up."

I gazed across the table at this crazy, wild urban cowboy-professor, the candlelight dancing between us, the tears all at once welling up in my eyes. Ignoring the fear that threatened to take hold, I finally confessed, "I love you, Uri."

"I know."

Sigh. "You're so…"

"Pompous?"

I nodded.

He stood up from his chair and stepped over to me, taking my hands. "Come here," he said. I stood up and he kissed the lone tear that escaped down my cheek. "I think it's time for dessert."

"Dessert? You made dessert, too?"

"I have to admit, I sort of cheated with the dessert."

"Don't tell me…store bought?"

"Afraid so."

"Chocolate?"

"Is there anything else?" He led me out of the dining room, following the trail of candles to the living room. On the surface of the coffee table, he had spread out an array of assorted chocolate truffles, some wrapped in bright, decorative foil. Except that wasn't what caught my eye. In the center of all the chocolates, surrounded by a circle of tea lights, sat a small, white velvet box. I looked from the box to Uri, and then back to the box. I knelt down on the rug and lifted it from the coffee table but hesitated to open it. Uri sat down on the rug beside me. He cupped his hand to my cheek and said in a soft voice, "Dara, I love you – I'm crazy in love with you and I want to spend all my life loving you. Say you'll marry me."

I knew that I should be happy. I knew that I should have said yes right away. There was no reason not to. I loved him, he loved me – it wasn't complicated. But I also knew that marrying Uri would be unquestionably a final good-bye to Roni. *What was wrong with me? Roni was dead.* Why did he have to pop into my head just now? I loved Uri. He was incredible. He was the best thing that ever happened to me since…since Roni. I suddenly felt sick, queasy sick – undeniably sick. I dropped the box and I bolted away from Uri, escaping to the bathroom, locking the door behind me.

Uri's eyes followed Dara running from the room – running from him. He picked up the white velvet box from where Dara had dropped it and removed the ring. "Damn ghost," he muttered as he shoved the ring in his pants pocket. He remained sitting there on the living room floor, pondering his next step, while listening to Dara's muffled cries in the distance. *Oh God, Dara, I wish I could be the one to take away all your pain. But...* he chuckled to himself, shaking his head. "Who the hell can compete against a ghost?"

I was in the middle of rinsing out my mouth when I heard Uri tapping on the door. "Dara, are you all right?"

"Yes," I answered through my tears. I didn't know anymore why I was crying. Whether it was over Roni, or whether it was because I just hurt the most amazing man in my life…a man who just professed how much he loved me – a man I loved as well. *This must be a first*, I thought. How many women run to vomit in the bathroom in the wake of a marriage proposal? I was certain that I was the only one.

I searched through Uri's mirrored cabinet, desperate to find some mouthwash, or at the very least, toothpaste. This was the guest bathroom, so I wasn't too hopeful. Relieved, I found a small tube of travel-sized toothpaste and smeared a huge glob of it over my teeth and my tongue before rinsing my mouth out another dozen times. I took one last look in the mirror before walking out, and…*oh no*. My gray eyes stared back at me. There was no way Uri would not notice. He noticed everything. *Why now?*

The man I loved just asked me to marry him! My eyes should be blue!

Uri stood right outside the door as I exited the bathroom. "Are you feeling better?"

I nodded yes. *Except for ruining the perfect romantic moment. Sure – I'm great.*

He led me to the living room couch where he snuggled with me, cradling me in his arms. "I'm sorry, Uri. I don't know what came over me. I…guess it was all the wine…and the excitement of…"

"Dara," Uri cut in, "I understand. Evidently…I didn't capture your heart."

"What?" I gasped.

"*He* still holds your heart." I had never told him Roni's name, and he never asked.

"No, Uri. That's not true. I love you."

"*I* know you love me, Dara. The question is, do *you* know it? I mean, deep down, in your soul, do you know it? And are you ready to accept it – are you ready to give me your whole heart, or will part of it still belong to him?"

How could I have hurt him like this? I'm insane. "Uri…" I began to sob again. "You have my heart."

"You have an interesting way of showing it." He attempted a light smile and cupped my face in his hand, once more kissing away my tears. "Shhh, Dara, don't cry. Not because of me. You've had too many tears in your life. I want to be the one who brings you joy and laughter, not tears."

"I drank too much wine, that's all it was," I insisted. He stared straight into my eyes and…he knew. I curled into him on the couch, leaning my head against his chest, and he held me, stroking my hair. "Maybe…I did this too soon," he pondered aloud. "I know we haven't been going out a long time, but…I suppose I thought, being that I was sure of you, you felt the same way. I'm sorry, Dara…. I didn't mean to pressure you."

"Uri, I *am* sure of you." And I was – though I was also sure that I was forever destined to carry an ache in my heart for Roni. I was likewise certain that my brain didn't operate in a normal manner. "Uri?"

"Yes?"

"Will you forgive me?"

"There's nothing to forgive."

"Then," I lifted my head from his chest and looked into his warm eyes, "will you marry me?"

He crinkled his brow, his eyes sweeping over my face. "I'd marry you tonight, if I thought it was what you really wanted."

"How can I convince you that it is?"

He considered that for a moment before answering. "Not throwing up might help," he half joked.

"Okay then. Ask me again, and I promise I won't throw up."

"My, that sounds…tempting," he laughed good-naturedly. "Every man's dream, I dare say."

I had to laugh too at how absurd I sounded.

"Dara, I want you to know something – when I bought this house, I bought it as an investment in my future. Not a monetary investment; rather, a life investment. I bought it with the intention that this would be the home I would share with my wife – where we would raise our children, and grow old together. I know that may sound…clichéd, but it's the truth. I've never…had any…women over in this house. I was saving it for someone special…for you."

I narrowed my eyes at him. "So…where did you take them?"

"Take whom?"

"Your women? Where did you take them?"

"Ha ha, of all the things you could say about what I just told you, you choose that?"

"You're avoiding the question."

"It's not important. They didn't mean anything to me. I merely wanted to point out that this home isn't tainted. As I thought I explained rather elegantly, I might add, it was built…waiting for you."

"How many were there?"

He sighed. "I honestly don't know. It's all a blur and I don't care to remember."

I pouted. I knew he had a life before me; I just didn't like knowing it was so *full*.

"Dara, are you actually jealous?"

"Maybe."

"Well, as much as I'm enjoying it, you needn't be…you're my one and only, forever." He kissed me tenderly. "Oh, and by the way, Dara, the little minidress number that you're wearing tonight didn't go unnoticed. You are one very bad girl." His hand worked its way up my leg.

"What are you waiting for, Uri?"

"If you must know…our wedding night."

"Really?" I asked, wide-eyed.

"Really." He shrugged. "I'm kind of a traditionalist in that way."

"I would never have guessed."

"Stick around, I'm full of surprises."

He took the ring from his pocket, "Shall I give this another shot and risk rejection for a second time tonight?"

"I never rejected you. I told you…it was the…"

"The wine – I know," he broke in. He gazed into my eyes and appeared to see something in them that made the smile return to his face. Taking my hand, he pressed his lips against it and then slipped the ring on my finger. It was a stunning, round-shaped diamond stone set on a platinum base, so elegant in its simplicity, and it fit…perfectly. "Dara, will you make me the happiest man on earth…be my wife…and let me spend the rest of my life trying to make you happy?"

"Yes, yes and you already do."

I stared at the ring on my finger. "It's simply beautiful, Uri."

He gazed down at my hand in his and studied it for a moment. "You are so delicate," he whispered.

"Mmm. Lucky for me that you prefer your woman to be delicate."

"So you concede," his tone oozed with smugness as his eyes bore into mine.

"I concede."

He broke into a broad smile. "Did I ever tell you that you have the most incredible blue eyes?"

"Tell me again," I murmured.

"I'd rather show you."

"That works for me."

"I had a hunch it would."

"You know, now that we're *almost* married…" I trailed off suggestively.

"You're killing me, Dara. You are absolutely killing me."

"Mmm." I nuzzled closer into him. "When do you want to get married?"

His hand traced up and down my body. "Tonight wouldn't be soon enough," he moaned and proceeded to smother me with gentle kisses.

Chapter 31

 "How is she, Yaniv?"

"She's...better. She's...finally moving on with her life."

"She met someone?"

"Uh...yeah, she did. He's a friend of mine. They're...getting married."

There was a long pause on the phone.

"That *was* what you wanted for her, wasn't it?"

"Yes...of course...that was what I wanted."

"Look, Roni...he's a quality guy. He'll be good to her."

"He'd better be."

"Are you going to be okay?"

"Yeah, *sababa*. When is the wedding?"

"In a couple of weeks."

Another long pause. "And where will they be living?"

"Down the road from me and Jenny, in Sde Dovid."

"So…you'll still keep an eye on her then…make sure she's happy – all right?"

"You know I will."

"Okay. So…uh…yeah…this is good…it's really…good. She deserves it."

"Yeah."

"You sure he's a decent guy?"

"Yes, he is."

"Good…good…that's all that matters then. Take care of yourself, Yaniv. I'll be in touch when I can."

"When do you think that might be?"

"You know how it is. It all depends when I can get to a secure phone."

"Right. Shalom, Roni, just…don't get yourself killed, all right?"

"Yeah, no problem. Shalom, Yaniv."

Berlin

A dark-haired, sturdy young man clad in a light-blue sports jacket with jeans and white tennis shoes – looking very much a tourist – walked casually out of the five-story walk-up on 13 Konstanzer Street. He crossed to the north side of the street and headed east toward Kurfurstendamm Boulevard, stopping at a corner kiosk to buy a pack of cigarettes. Lingering nonchalantly as he lit one, he then crossed back to the other side, walking south, leading to hotel row, where one can find Charlottenburg's most luxurious hotels. Passing by Kaiser Wilhelm Memorial Church, he eyed the vendors and South American musicians idle away their time on the church steps before making his way down the same street to the Hotel Concorde Berlin.

He navigated the elegant lobby adorned with contemporary artwork, passed the opulent hotel shops that vied for the wealthy tourists and hooked a right down the staircase leading to the conference room level. He found the men's room he wanted, entered a stall and removed his wig, facial hair, and clothing. Stepping up on the toilet, he reached to the ceiling to lift up the movable panel and retrieved a bag containing his regular clothing, along with credit cards and a driver's license that identified him as Eric Heller. He dressed and then in a meticulous manner, stored the first set of clothes back above the panel, flushed the toilet and stepped out of the stall. While washing his hands at the sink, he glanced into the mirror facing him. *Time for another damn haircut*, he thought as a hint of curl started to emerge from his short-cropped blond hair. A flashback of Dara entwining her fingers in his once-long mane stole into his thoughts. *Oh God, Dara, just be happy*. He splashed water on his face, grabbed a paper towel from the dispenser and wiped himself dry.

As Roni proceeded to the parking lot of the hotel, he rationalized his actions. There was no doubt that his assignment was critical for Israel's national security and had already borne fruit. Just several months ago, Israel's Navy SEALs stopped a shipment of arms, coordinated by Europe's neo-Nazi machine in collusion with Iran, bound for Arafat and his terrorist organization. He could think of two attempts at bombing Israeli embassies in the Netherlands successfully thwarted due to his diligence. And the firsthand intelligence he acquired on the Hezbollah and its rise over Lebanon was invaluable.

He knew his job, and he did it well – though the thought of spending an unspecified number of years in what he considered the most cursed country of the world turned his stomach. Knowing that he sacrificed having a life with the only woman he would ever love was slowly and painfully killing him with each year that passed. But he was determined not to ruin Dara's life. He would not have her sacrifice her own youth waiting years for him until he returned home. Yet, now that she was marrying another man, it felt as if someone had kicked him in the gut and ripped his heart from his chest. He knew that this day would come, and he knew that it would devastate him. But he was a man with a mission – a mission that was crucial to Israel's fight against the constant onslaught of terror, yet would grant him his own personal death.

Roni reached his car, turned the ignition and raced out of the parking lot toward Mitte, in the western district of Berlin. He had a meeting with Gerhard Kestel at his penthouse apartment on Ruedenshoff Boulevard, where Gerhard would often have drug and sex orgies taking place simultaneously. Gerhard Kestel was a man of many vices, and falling into his good graces was not difficult when you knew how to play his game in his world. Roni played the game – he had to – and it sickened him. He was able to circumvent taking drugs, but couldn't shun the women without raising suspicion. He loathed the German women and eyed them with contempt, wondering what role their parents had played as Nazis during World War II. He didn't want to touch them. To him, they were coarse and reeked of venom.

The ones that found their way to Kestel's penthouse came from society's upper echelon, which only made it worse when the nights were laced with anti-Jewish slurs amid the drinking, drugs and sex. They were people of influence – those that one needed to be wary of.

Roni turned into Auguststrasse, parked his car and entered a bar called The Pips. He would need a couple of drinks today before dealing with Gerhard. Not five minutes passed before an attractive, long-haired, blond woman sat on the stool next to his and attempted to strike up a conversation. "I've never seen you around here before. Are you new to the area?" He answered her curtly and stared straight ahead.

She leaned into him and put her hand on his arm. "Would you care to buy me a drink?"

The bile rose up in his throat. He downed a shot of scotch and closed his eyes. *Be happy, my sweet Dara. Be happy.*

Migdal, Israel

On instinct, I drove out to Migdal – to visit Roni's mother, Evaleen. I didn't call first. In fact, I respected Dalya's request and never contacted Evaleen and Shimshon. But now that five years had passed and it was just two weeks before I was to marry Uri, I felt an urgency to speak to Evaleen and allay my suspicions about Roni once and for all. I could not go into my marriage with half a heart. That would not be fair to Uri.

"Oh, Dara, what a surprise! It is so wonderful to see you after all these years. You are as lovely as I remember."

"Thank you, Evaleen. It's wonderful to see you as well."

"Please, come in. We'll have a nice cold drink and catch up."

I went into the salon with Evaleen and gazed at the surroundings. Nothing had changed since I was here last. Warm memories of the past flooded my mind as I recalled the day Roni brought me to meet his family for the first time. My eyes fell upon the large oak tree that stood outside the generously sized bay window. I felt the familiar ache and turned away. In one corner of the room stood a Bombay-style bureau that boasted an array of family photos. I moved toward it and took a closer look at a photo of Roni, tracing my fingers over his beautiful face.

"That picture was taken shortly after he met you. Following the Lebanon War, he never allowed us to photograph him. But everything changed once you entered his life." Evaleen said.

I smiled a bittersweet smile, remembering how Roni had told me that he was dead before he met me. I moved to the couch to sit with Evaleen. She took my hand in hers, her eyes filling with sadness. "I see that you are wearing another's engagement ring. Is that why you have come?"

I nodded and then chose my words carefully. "Evaleen, it took me a long time before I could even think of meeting another man. I have always had this feeling that Roni was still...alive, somewhere, somehow."

"I know how deeply you loved him."

"I still love him."

She hesitated and then said, "Roni is...gone now, and you must go on with your life, Dara. That's what he would want."

"Where was he killed, Evaleen? Please tell me what happened – I know nothing."

The pain was evident in her eyes as she looked into mine. I began to regret opening an old wound, but there were dozens of unanswered questions surrounding Roni's death which Dalya could not satisfy when I spoke to her upon my return to Israel. At that moment, Dalya walked through the door and Evaleen quickly answered me in a hushed voice. "I...I don't know any details. I'm sorry, Dara. Please...don't ask me."

"Dara!"

"Hello, Dalya." I stood up to give her a hug.

"This is such a surprise." Her eyes darted to her mother.

"Yes, for me, too," Evaleen put in. "It was so nice of Dara to drop in. She's...she's getting married."

"That's wonderful news, Dara. May your marriage be blessed with joy."

"Thank you, Dalya."

"So, who is this man that you're marrying?" Dalya sat down in an easy chair opposite Evaleen and me.

"His name is Uri. Uri Amrani."

"Amrani? The real estate Amranis?"

"Yes." I was uncomfortable with Dalya. The conversation I wanted to have with Evaleen would unfortunately have to come to an abrupt end. I had always felt that Dalya never cared for me and could never get out of my mind the picture of the way she looked at Roni when he announced our engagement. I never understood it. But now, I realized it no longer mattered. I would be moving on. My life was now with Uri.

"Well, I think I should be heading back to Jerusalem." I rose from the couch. "It's getting late and it's a long drive. Shalom, Evaleen. It was wonderful to see you again. Shalom, Dalya."

"Shalom, Dara, and good luck to you." Dalya answered more warmly than I expected.

Evaleen walked me to the door and embraced me before I walked out. "Be happy, Dara. That's all that Roni wants." I noticed how she spoke of him in the present tense. I gathered that she could not let go of him either. After all, she was his mother. I wanted to ask her if she too felt that he was still alive, but I stopped myself. I must have caused her enough pain by just showing up at her door. I left without saying another word.

Chapter 32

 *Israel, July 1990*

Four weeks after Uri proposed, we were wed. It was a small wedding set against the rolling waves on a private beach in Herzliya. The invitation list consisted mostly of Uri's family and friends. It was a great effort not to think about my parents, the circumstances of their deaths and their absence on this most special day of my life. I tried to free my mind from all the haunting thoughts and memories. I invited the old gang from the kibbutz, along with some university friends and some friends from work. Yaniv and Jenny walked me down the aisle. A woman in Jerusalem whom Jenny introduced me to had made my wedding gown from scratch. I dreamed of passing it down to the daughter I now hoped that I would one day have.

Jenny was fussing over me in the bridal room, making sure that my hair, dress and makeup were nothing less than perfection. "It's almost time," she said, as she brushed a last stroke of powder to my face. I stared at myself in the mirror, not really seeing myself. My mind was wandering – a dangerous venture for my wedding day. I hadn't seen Uri for the entire week before the wedding – a Jewish tradition that we both wanted to follow. It turned out to be more difficult than I expected. Uri had a way of keeping the destructive thoughts out of my head. Not seeing him all week left me with more time to think and ponder about things that I knew I shouldn't be thinking. "How are you doing?" Jenny asked, knowing well how my abnormal brain functioned.

"Fine," I answered impassively.

"*Fine?* Not exactly the answer I was hoping for."

I looked at Jenny's reflection in the mirror. She stood behind me with worry lines etched on her forehead. I could hide little from her. "Jenny, you don't have to look so concerned," I tried to reassure her and myself. "I'm more than fine. I love Uri and I know we have a bright future to look forward to."

"You're not very convincing, Dara," she frowned. "You're not excited – the way I hoped you would be – the way you *should* be."

"Jen," I sighed, and turned to face her, "I'm very excited about marrying Uri. It's just that…" I trailed off, deciding not to finish my thought. "Never mind."

"What is it, Dara?"

I hesitated for a long moment, not certain if I should let Jenny know the extent of my unhinged mind. In the end, I confided in her, allowing all my feelings to pour out of me – probably because I needed her to tell me how ludicrous and irrational I was. "Jen, before you start yelling at me, please, please, try to understand, I do love Uri…very much…but… at the same time, I know that when I stand under the canopy with him, I'll be saying my final good-bye to Roni – to a big part of me, a big part of my heart. And it's tugging at me, gnawing away at me. As much as I try, I can't stop it. You see," I went on, "for the past week, I've been haunted by these dreams that Roni is alive. I've been walking around wracked with guilt – guilt for betraying Uri with thoughts of Roni, and guilt for betraying Roni by marrying Uri. Oh Jen, I'm such a mess."

"You're right, Dara, you are a mess." She sighed loudly, putting her arm around me to comfort me. "But I'm not going to yell at you. Besides, I don't want to upset you, have you cry and ruin the perfect makeup job I just gave you," she tried to lighten the mood.

"You know, Dara," she said pensively, "Yaniv was also talking about you and Roni earlier today. It was very strange, really. He spoke of Roni as if he *were* still alive. But I understood – as close as Uri is to Yaniv, Roni was more like a brother to him. So, I suppose that it is only natural for Yaniv to think about Roni today. And…I suppose it's only natural for you to think about him as well. But Dara," she grasped me by the arms, "it has to stop now. Roni is *not* alive. And you have to get those destructive thoughts out of your head. *You must.* Uri is your life now, and he adores you."

"I know that. And I adore him." I slumped in my seat, shaking my head from side to side. "Perhaps it was not being able to see Uri this past week that caused all these harmful thoughts to affect me. I'm sure that must be it."

"Dara, look into the mirror," Jenny ordered in a stern voice. "Once and for all, say good-bye to the old Dara, to the old life and to the painful memories. You've been dragging around so much baggage for so long, I'm surprised your shoulders aren't hunched. Enough! All that's important is what is now and what will be tomorrow." I stared at Jenny, taken aback by her tone. "Go ahead," she insisted. "Look into the mirror and tell me what you see."

My eyes wandered back to the mirror, and for the first time that day I saw an unclouded vision of myself. "I see…a bride, Uri's bride," I smiled, "in a dream gown, looking…beautiful, thanks to my best friend standing next to me, who has always been by my side."

I knew I had much to be thankful for and much to look forward to. Of course Jenny was right. She was always right. *No more looking back!* I then looked her straight in the eyes. "You're right, Jen. It stops now. I'm marrying Uri today and that's all that matters. Don't worry." I felt I needed to set her mind at rest, as well as my own. "It will all be good. Oh, and by the way…great makeup job!"

"About time you noticed."

It was a lovely wedding. At least, I believed it was. The details eluded me; all I saw was the way Uri looked at me as I walked down the aisle. Every anxiety, every anxious thought, had scattered into the light summer's breeze as I thought of sharing my life with this amazing man. I didn't want to walk down the aisle – I wanted to run and leap into his arms.

The ceremony took place just moments before sunset. The weather couldn't have been more perfect had I ordered it myself, and there was joy-filled dancing and gaiety all around, thanks to Uri's brothers, who were quite the characters. It seemed they all possessed the daredevil bad-boy charm – each in his own way. To their parents' consternation, they conspired to break through the barrier separating the men from women on the dance floor. Uri's parents were very religious. There was to be only customary national hora dancing – gender separate. Nevertheless, by the end of the first round of dancing, somehow the tall floor plants separating the men and women vanished. I couldn't help but imagine how trying it must have been for their mother to raise four rambunctious boys. She did look tired, I thought.

At the close of the wedding and after saying good-bye to the last of our guests, Uri's family and Jenny and Yaniv saw us off as we drove away to begin our new life together. We traveled a short distance – just seven kilometers to Arsuf, where Uri's family owned a vacation cottage with a sea view. As we neared the property, I was awestruck at the "cottage" that awaited us.

Infinite floor-to-ceiling paned windows adorned a two-story structure. The shadows from the exterior house lights danced off its Spanish stucco walls. There was a generous courtyard, flanked in decorative painted glazed tiles, which boasted a broad stone staircase that invited us up to the intricately carved double wooden entry doors. It was magical. "I…I don't know what to say."

"You don't have to say anything, my lovely wife," Uri said, enjoying my wide-eyed reaction. He drew me closer to him and kissed me as we stood in the courtyard. I held on to him, not wanting to let go, just wanting to lose myself in his strong arms. I looked into his loving eyes and curled my fingers through his soft hair, bringing his face closer to mine, and he kissed me again, harder, pulling me tighter into him, his kiss growing more vigorous. My fingers sauntered down to his chest and I began to undo the buttons of his shirt. He peeled his lips from mine, "Uh, Dara? Right here, in the courtyard?"

"Is there a problem with that?" I worked my way down his shirt, kissing his chest softly. "Well, for one thing, the tiled floor may not be the best venue," he chuckled, taking my hands into his.

"How can you be so controlled?" I looked up to him, frustrated.

"Practice," he smirked. "Besides," he took in a deep breath, "you'll find out soon enough what I have planned for you tonight, Mrs. Amrani."

"Sounds ominous," I smiled. "Should I be frightened?"

"Very," he said wickedly, his hands trailing the contours of my body. "Come," he swallowed hard, "I'll show you around before I bring in our bags."

The front doors opened up to a storybook interior. There were sweeping archways, a wrought iron railing winding around a prominent staircase and heavy wood trim throughout, complementing the plush white furnishings and textured, pale-colored walls. It turned out to be a massive, private, beachfront luxury villa sitting on two acres of land – a rare find in Israel. The house itself was secluded and surrounded by palm trees. Crowning its crest was a huge deck that afforded a magnificent view of the Mediterranean Sea. It took my breath away. "Uri, this isn't a…cottage. This is…spectacular."

"My father has a discerning eye for quality," he shrugged with a smile.

"I can't believe that we get to be here for an entire week," I turned to him in childlike excitement.

"I didn't even show you everything." He took my hand and led me to the bedroom level. "I saved the best for last." There were four bedrooms, and he guided me to the one at the far end of the hall. It was like walking through to another world. The heavy textured walls of the bedroom, washed in a coppery tone, opened up to the floor-to-ceiling windows that stretched across the length of one wall, looking out to the sea. In the center of the room was a plush, four-poster bed of dark Italian wood with a mix of white, copper and ivory bedding, and the floors were of light crème marble. My mouth dropped open. I didn't know where to look first. "Uri, this is…the epitome of perfection."

"That's exactly what I was thinking."

I turned to him and caught his eyes busy undressing me. "I was talking about this room, Uri. It's magnificent."

"Magnificent, right." He raked his hand through his hair. "I must be superhuman," he muttered to himself and then took my hand, guiding me to one window, which opened to a small rounded balcony. "Look down." I did as he asked and gasped as my eyes met an oasis-like pool lit up by outdoor lamps, casting a golden glow upon the water. A small round table with two chairs stood at the side of the pool. On the table was a bottle of champagne chilling in a bucket of ice and two champagne flute glasses.

"You thought of everything," I breathed. "And just look at all the stars in the sky. This is like a dream."

"No, Dara," he lifted my chin to face him. "It's real – as real as you and me – as real as my love for you. But…I have to confess…I had nothing to do with the stars," he shrugged. "They came out on their own."

"Oh, Uri, I love you so much. All I need is to be in your arms." I snuggled into him.

"Is that all it takes?" He laughed lightly.

"Mmm hmm. I'm very low maintenance."

"And I'm very accommodating." He led me off the balcony, back into the bedroom. "Now, what do you say about getting out of this lovely wedding gown, Mrs. Amrani, and going for a starlight swim?"

"Sounds like a plan," I approved happily. "But…I'm going to need some help."

"I think I'm up for the task," his bad-boy look emerged.

"That's good to know," I smiled mischievously and turned around. "There are fifty-six buttons going down my back."

"Fifty-six?" I heard the shock reverberate in his voice.

"That's right."

"Fifty-six?"

"Repeating it won't make it any less, you know."

"Tell me something, Dara," he began unbuttoning the gown. "When you had this dress designed, the thought of a zipper didn't enter your mind?"

"I preferred buttons. I thought it was prettier."

"Dara…honey…love of my life…I'm trying really, really hard to make this an unforgettable, romantic night, but right now, I'm about a half second away from ripping the gown right off you and getting down to business."

"Mmm. It does sound enticing in a dramatic sort of way, but…I'd like to preserve the gown for our daughter."

"Of course...what was I thinking?" He continued unbuttoning my gown. "Fifty-six, eh? You're killing me, Dara. You're absolutely killing me."

"Oh, and please be delicate about it. They're very fragile."

"I'm nothing if not delicate."

"Yes...that was my first thought when I first met you...how delicate you were," I teased.

"So, what really was your first thought when you fell in love with me at first sight?"

"Love at first sight? I don't quite remember it that way."

"You know you were hot for me – it was so obvious." He kissed my back as he progressed with the buttons.

"Oh, is that what you think?"

"Need I remind you, Dara? I read you very well."

"Well, if you must know, I thought you were very smug."

"Smug, eh?" he chuckled. "That was only because I saw how you couldn't contain your raw passion for me."

"My *raw passion* for you?"

"You were oozing with it. You couldn't help yourself. Try as you might, you just couldn't hide it."

"Uri Amrani, are you done yet?" I asked, feigning annoyance. He sighed heavily. "I have about another thirty or forty more to go." He inched back to sit on the edge of the bed, moving me backward with him to continue the job. "Hmm..."

"What?"

"This task is becoming more interesting." He kissed me tenderly just above my waste and glided his tongue up and down my spine. "Mmm. I think I'm beginning to get a knack for this."

"You know, Uri," I decided to toy with him, "this is taking you a lot longer than I expected and we still have to bring our bags in."

"What's the rush?" he murmured. I took in a badly needed breath as his lips sauntered down to my lower back – now reaching the last few buttons. I could actually sense his smug satisfaction at my reaction. "Um…my bathing suit is… in my bag."

"You won't be needing one," he said casually.

"Oh? Is that how it's going to be?"

"That's exactly how it's going to be." He stood up, turned me around to face him and slipped my gown off my shoulders, letting it fall to the floor. His topaz eyes took me in, slowly, inch by inch. "My God, Dara," he whispered. "You're so beautiful." He whisked me up into his arms, gently laying me on to the bed. "Change of plans…the pool can wait."

Chapter 33

I awoke in Uri's arms to the sweet sound of chirping birds as we nestled atop layers of soft blankets spread about the grass lawn by the pool. Our first night together was far superior to any dream I could have imagined. I was glad Uri had us wait for our wedding night. It made it all the more special.

We went for a midnight swim, sipped champagne, made love again and fell asleep under the stars. I purred in contentment, stretching out under the thin sheet that covered us, beneath the warmth of the morning sun. *It doesn't get any better than this*, I thought.

"Someone seems happy and satisfied this morning," Uri said, propping himself up on one elbow as he gazed down at me.

"I am. Very happy," I said lazily. "But I'm afraid not entirely satisfied."

"Oh?" He raised an eyebrow.

"Mmm. No. I need more of you. I don't think I'll ever have enough."

"It appears I married a nymphomaniac," his eyes creased in amusement.

"Only where you're concerned."

"That's reassuring."

"You're not afraid of the challenge, are you?"

"Oh, I'm pretty sure I can handle it," he puckered his lips in that full-of-himself way of his.

"You'll have to prove it to me."

"I intend on spending my life proving it to you."

"So, how about starting now?"

"Well, my little nympho," he laughed lightly, "I suggest we wash up first and have something to eat. I had the caretakers stock up the kitchen before we got here, and trust me…you'll need all your energy."

"I'll need all my energy?" I crinkled my eyebrows. "What do you mean?"

"Oh, don't you worry about a thing, my dear." He wore a mock sinister look as he raised me up from our makeshift bed by the pool. "Hmm," his eyes roamed over me. "Better wrap you up in this bedsheet; otherwise, we'll never make it upstairs."

"Would that be so bad?" I asked suggestively as he draped the sheet around me.

He sighed contentedly. "I knew there was a good reason I married you," he moaned as his lips met mine, his hands trailing all the way down my back, squeezing me into him. "Oh, Dara," he pulled away from me, "don't get me started again," he begged off in a husky voice.

"Me? I'm not doing anything. I'm just standing here."

"Apparently that's all it takes." He edged away from me, turned toward the pool, and dived into the deep end, swimming its length and back until he emerged and wrapped a towel around his waist.

"Feeling better, Uri?"

"Better? No. More in control? Yes. Are you hungry?"

I smiled wickedly, moving toward him and traced my fingers down his chest.

"I meant for food," he smirked, taking my hand from his chest and holding it in his.

"If you insist," I frowned. "I suppose a little sustenance would be a good idea."

Uri smiled. "Good call. I actually have a full, meticulously planned itinerary for the day."

"Itinerary?"

His eyes gleamed with that naughty boy look of his.

"Exactly what do you have planned, husband of mine?"

"Let's just say I intend on fulfilling every fantasy I've had about you since the day I met you."

"That sounds like an interesting itinerary. And you say you've planned this out *meticulously*?"

"And methodically."

"Nothing like a methodical honeymoon."

"Oh, I promise you, Dara, you'll find that I can be very…innovative. You won't be disappointed," he said with an air of superiority. "Come on upstairs. We'll shower first."

"So…you have everything perfectly planned out, like a flawless equation, eh?"

"I always do," he answered with his usual smugness.

"Like clockwork," I agreed.

"It's just a matter of discipline."

"With no probability of variables, I suppose?"

"In this case, statistically improbable."

"I wish I could control myself the way you can," I said wistfully.

"Don't be so hard on yourself, Dara. You can't help finding me irresistible," he grinned and added, "It's irrefutably quantifiable."

"When you're right, you're right," I gave in. "But…" I trailed off.

"But what?"

"But first things first." I threw the sheet off me.

"Uh, Dara, what are you doing?"

"Introducing a variable into the equation, professor." I turned and dived into the pool, swimming beneath the water for a few moments before surfacing. "Mmm, that was *sooo* refreshing," I said as I popped up for air. I floated on my back for a moment or two and then turned and swam in a fluid motion to the opposite side. Once reaching the shallow end, I climbed up the steps in an unhurried stride and strolled leisurely back toward Uri.

"I know what you're trying to do," Uri said reproachfully, "but it's not going to work – I'm in complete control of myself."

"I'm not trying to do anything, Uri," I said. "Hmm…now where was that other towel? I don't want to go back into the house soaking wet like this." Uri rolled his eyes, picked up the bed sheet from the ground, intending to wrap it around me. "You are so transparent, Dara." His eyes roved up and down my wet body. "So…stop pretending that you don't know…what I'm…talking…about." He stood in place, distracted.

"Uri?"

"Uh-huh?"

"Are you planning to wrap that sheet around me anytime soon? I'm kind of dripping here."

"Uh, yeah, sure." He wrapped the sheet around me, attempting to knot it just above my chest, fumbling with the ends. The water dripping from my long hair quickly soaked through the thin white sheet now clinging to me. "Dara," he made an effort to smile in his attempt to maintain control, "your little plan to prove your point is not going to work."

"It isn't?"

"No," he breathed.

"So, I guess we won't be deviating at all from the 'itinerary'?"

"No reason to. Like I said, I planned it out perfectly."

"I believe you used the word *methodically*."

"I did, didn't I." He gave up trying to tie a knot and simply tucked in the ends of the sheet. "You know, you look like a Roman princess wrapped in this sheet," he entwined his hands in my hair.

"One of your fantasies?"

"You'll find out soon enough," he said in a mysterious manner. "Let's go take that shower now, and have some breakfast, shall we?"

Hmm. He's stronger than I thought. "Seems I underestimated your resolve, Uri. I can see that you're in complete control of yourself. I have to admit, it *is* an attractive quality."

"Don't do that."

"Do what?"

"Breathe that way."

"What way?" I had no idea to what he was referring.

"The way...that keeps me from thinking with a clear head."

"How am I breathing?"

"You...have this way...of.... But, it's not going to make...any...diff.... Aw hell, who am I kidding?" He wrenched the sheet off me and grabbed me at the hips. His lips swept over me in a wild rush as he pressed into me.

"Uri!" I gasped.

"Change of plans," he breathed roughly. "I have to have you now."

"But...your itinerary?" I suggested mischievously.

"What about it?" he mumbled, biting down between my neck and my shoulder, sending shudders through me.

"Um...I thought you wanted...to stick to your plan," I managed to puff out.

"Don't fret, my lovely wife," he murmured as his lips worked their way back up, brushing against my cheek. "You see, I neglected to mention the flexibility quotient. Hands-on perception always supersedes theoretical abstract." He inched downward, his warm breath on my chest as his tongue rushed over my skin.

"But," I protested feebly and then gave up the game as I could only think of how he was touching me.

"But what?" He slid his lips back up to mine, just faintly touching. "You wouldn't be questioning my expertise on the matter, would you?" His hands slithered deliberately back down, past my hips, grasping me firmly.

"No, Professor...of course not." I drew in much-needed air.

"Mmm, there's nothing like an obedient student. Now be a dear," he whispered into my ear, "and remove my towel. My hands appear to be otherwise occupied."

I couldn't hold back from pitching him one last tease. "Are you sure this won't throw everything you calculated off course?"

"Not a problem, my lovely temptress." He looked at me with a devilish glare as he assured me, "As long as the vertex is in focus."

"I gather...the vertex is...something good?"

"Always. In fact, it's the principle objective..." He edged me toward the bed of soft blankets and we fell back into them. "Now, pay attention, Dara...I'll be testing you on this...repeatedly."

The remainder of the week passed blissfully. Uri managed for us to accomplish everything he included in his "itinerary," although not quite in the exact order he initially envisioned. He didn't appear, however, to be disappointed with any of my revisions. For all his "methodical" talk, he was wildly imaginative, crazy and downright fun. True to his character, he smugly referred to his antics as ingenious and even took me by surprise one evening after we dined out for dinner, by pretending to kidnap me to his boat at the marina and hold me captive at sea. He had claimed he was "divinely inspired" and had no choice but to carry out his "mission."

"I'm going to miss this place," I said as we drove away, heading south to Sde Dovid. Uri glanced at me with a sly smile. "We can come back anytime you'd like. I still have a few ideas I wouldn't mind exploring."

"You're relentless," I flushed at a couple of quick flashbacks of the week.

"Let's just say, I'll never tire of making you blush – which, by the way, is no small feat considering your own amorous appetite."

"Are you looking for some kind of medal?"

"I think I deserve one, don't you?"

"You are so…"

"Pompous, I know," he laughed and then turned his attention back to the road and added casually, "For now, however, we have plenty to do when we get home."

"Like what?" I asked, unsuspecting.

"Oh, don't you concern yourself about it. I planned out everything perfectly."

"And methodically, I presume?" I caught on quickly.

"But of course," his eyes creased in a wicked smile.

"You have a one-track mind. Don't you ever get tired?"

"Why do you think I work out? It builds stamina."

"I thought you did it because it was a healthy thing to do."

"Think again."

After a pleasant drive, we arrived in Sde Dovid and parked the car in front of what would now be my new home with my new husband. A Welcome Home sign taped to the front door from Jenny and Yaniv greeted us as we walked up the short pathway to the house. *It is going to be great living so close to them,* I thought, *having all my family in one place.*

344 The Gilboa Iris

Uri unlocked the front door, and in the entry hall, a huge, stunning arrangement of white orchids sprinkled with red roses sat on the round accent table. I looked at Uri questioningly and he simply shrugged his shoulders, feigning ignorance. Inching closer, I found a card attached. It read,

> *Dara, my love,*
> *Now that you are home – in our true home in Israel –*
> *these rooms will at last blossom with joy.*
> *I will treasure you always, my lovely and delicate wife.*
> *Eternally, I'm yours,*
>
> *Uri*

"I'm not much of a writer…but…"

"Oh, Uri," I didn't let him finish. "You're wonderful. You really do think of everything." My eyes brimmed with tears, and I thought I would explode with all the love I felt for him. "I love you so much. I can't believe how lucky I am." I snuggled into him.

"No, Dara, I'm the lucky one." He lifted my face toward his and said softly, "Welcome home, Dara," and he leaned down to kiss me tenderly on the lips.

Chapter 34

Several months passed, and my life with Uri was a living dream. I was enjoying my new community in Sde Dovid; Uri, Jenny and Yaniv belonged to a close-knit group of friends that welcomed me warmly. In the meantime, Jenny and Yaniv had their first baby, a girl they named Liat. These were such happy times. Uri and I didn't encounter any of the typical difficulties that newlyweds have in the first year of marriage, and each day felt like another blessing. I couldn't have asked for more in a husband. He was easygoing, good-natured and incredibly loving. At times, my utter happiness worried me. I was scared of losing what I had. It all seemed too good to be true.

I was in the kitchen preparing dinner when Uri came home. Engrossed in my thoughts and in the process of frying onions, I didn't hear him come in. I jumped when he came up from behind me and put his arms around my waist, kissing me on the cheek.

"Whoa, why so jumpy?"

"Sorry, Uri, you caught me by surprise. How was your day?"

"Typical. But good news…we rented your house in Katamon at the price we wanted. So if there's anything you would want to take out of there before the tenants move in, this week is the week to do it."

"That is good news. I'll stop by there tomorrow and check if there's anything I need."

"Something smells good. What are you making?"

"I'm grilling steak. I started out making chicken, but I had to throw it out. It smelled funny. I think the butcher sold me old chicken."

"Well, we certainly can't let him get away with that. Wait here while I get my gun."

"You're crazy," I laughed.

"Just crazy for you. Hey," he furrowed his brows, "are you feeling all right, Dara?"

"Yes, why?"

"Your eyes…they're silver and you look a little pale."

"I'm fine. Maybe I'm just a little tired, that's all."

"Why don't you let me finish making the dinner and…"

"You're so sweet," I lifted my head up to kiss him, "but I'm almost done. Besides, I'm really fine."

"Okay, if you say so – I'll go wash up."

I turned back to the grill and flipped over the steaks. Then I moved to the wall oven and checked on the roast potatoes. *A few more minutes should do it*, I thought. The vegetables were ready for the salad and all that was left to do was make the dressing. While gathering the ingredients, I felt a sudden rush of heat to my head and a strange dizziness. Black patches started to form before my eyes, blocking out the light. Whatever I was holding in my hands crashed to the floor, and a second later, so did I.

"Dara?"

"Dara, did you drop something?"

"Dara?"

"My God! Dara!"

Shaare Zedek Emergency Room, Jerusalem

"I'm sorry, Uri."

"Sorry? Dara, you have nothing to be sorry about."

"You were so worried."

"More like terrified," he admitted. "But that doesn't matter. I just want you to be well."

"I am. The doctor said that my fainting was not unusual."

"Right. Easy for him to say."

"Oh, Uri, I'm fine. Really. I don't see why I have to remain in this bed."

"Humor me and stay put, my dear. And…just promise me you'll take it easy, okay?"

"Does that mean bungee jumping is out?"

"I'm afraid so."

"Mountain biking, too, I suppose?"

"Yeah, that, too," he smiled lightly, though his eyes looked pensive.

"What is it, Uri?"

"I never imagined that you could make me any happier than when you married me. And now, you proved me wrong." He placed his hand on my stomach. *"My cup runneth over.* I can't believe we're going to have a baby. I can't believe how lucky I am to have you." He paused, his brows crinkled in thought. "Dara?"

"Yes?"

"Are you happy?"

I brushed my fingers against his sweet face. "I'm ecstatic."

"Good," he whispered, taking my hand in his. "How are you feeling now? Do you still feel weak?"

I shook my head no. "I'm fine."

"That's what you said before I had to call the ambulance," he looked at me skeptically.

"I promise you, I'm okay. In fact, when can we go home? I'm hungry."

"It won't be long at all," he said, looking more relieved. "They're getting the paperwork ready to discharge you, and Yaniv is waiting outside to drive us back home." Uri turned silent as he continued to sit by my bedside, his golden brown eyes soothing in the severe surroundings of the hospital. I watched as his face brightened into a strange grin.

"What?" I smiled back at him.

"I was just thinking..." he tapered off.

"And...?"

"Well, I just realized that I never *made it* with a pregnant woman before. It's a whole new adventure."

"You're crazy," I smiled.

"Mmm. Crazy for you." His bad-boy look surfaced. "You *did* say you were feeling fine, right?"

The following day, on the way home from work, I stopped at my old place in Katamon. Once inside, I headed straight to the room off the kitchen, formerly my home office, and removed the framed Gilboa Iris from the bottom drawer of my desk. I hadn't taken it with me when I moved to Sde Dovid. But I couldn't leave it here any longer...not with strangers moving in.

I knew I shouldn't, but I opened the back of the frame where I had placed Roni's note and read it, as I had read it and reread it thousands of times before.

My Sweet Dara,
As is the Gilboa Iris,
You are light, you are perfection, you are life.
My life.

Roni

Even after marrying Uri, it was still impossible for me to believe wholeheartedly that Roni was dead. Something inside of me refused to accept it. Something inside of me would never let me let go of Roni. It didn't make any sense, and I often questioned my sanity. I wondered why I couldn't just put Roni to rest.

I loved Uri. I was madly in love with him. He was the one man who was able to reach me – to make me laugh, and make me love again, despite my longing for Roni. Yet although he was so good to me, and wonderful in every way, Roni would always be the love of my life. I went through my days filled with guilt over that, especially now that I was carrying Uri's baby. While I was thrilled about being pregnant and excited to build a family with Uri, it was as if I were cheating on him with what was most probably a ghost. I returned Roni's note to the back of the frame, fastened it carefully before placing it into my bag and walked out of the house.

Chapter 35

Ten Years Later – 2000

"Is she happy?"

"Yes, she is."

"And…he's still good to her?"

"Yeah. He's very much in love with her – treats her like a queen."

"Good."

"What about you? When are you coming back home?"

"Can't say."

"You can't stay away forever. One day, she's bound to find out. You really never thought this through."

"We've been over this, Yaniv. I did what was best for her."

"It took her a long time to get over you. She would have waited forever for you."

"That's exactly why I did what I did. She has a good life now — three kids and a husband who loves her. With me, she would have known only loneliness."

"And what about your life? What do you have?"

"That doesn't matter. I did what I had to do. I thought you understood that from the beginning."

"I merely respected your decision. I never agreed with it."

"Knowing that she's happy, I'm certain I made the right decision." Roni wanted to ask if Dara ever thinks of him now, but he thought better of it and held his tongue.

"Where are you off to now? Can you tell me this time?"

"Still tying up some loose ends here…after that, I don't know."

"Can you tell me for how long?"

"No."

"So it's just going to continue with one or two phone calls a year from you."

"It has to be that way."

"And what about your family?"

"They understand. Well…they accept it."

"I don't see how they can accept it when I don't."

"Yeah, I miss you, too, Yaniv. Look…uh…I have to go."

"Right."

"Take care now. And…*mazal tov* again on your fourth child."

"Thanks, Roni. *Shmor al atzmecha*, stay safe."

Yaniv hung up the phone with a heavy sigh. He did not immediately notice that he was not alone in the den. A cooing sound of a baby interrupted his thoughts and he looked up to see the shocked look on his wife's face. "Who…who was that on the phone?" Jenny asked in a hushed, shaken voice, her baby son wriggling in her arms.

He didn't answer.

"Yaniv, who was that on the phone?" she repeated in a voice that was now taking on a lilt of hysteria.

"What did you hear?" he asked in a quiet tone.

"That was Roni? Roni is alive? You were speaking to Roni?"

Yaniv rushed over to Jenny and took the baby from her trembling arms. "Sit down, Jenny," he calmly instructed her, leading her to the sofa. He set his son down in the playpen and sat down beside his wife. "Listen to me, Jen. First, calm down. There are things you don't understand."

"*There are things I don't understand?* Roni is alive! You kept this hidden – from me – from Dara! What is it exactly that I don't understand? What kind of horrible schemes have you and Roni plotted all these years?"

"Jenny, please…let me explain."

But she wouldn't listen. She rose from the sofa, her eyes bulging in outrage. "You spent sixteen years lying to me…and…I thought you cared about Dara. How could you…who are you?"

"Listen to me, Jen!" Yaniv rose to his feet and grasped her arms in a tight hold, staring firmly into her eyes. "I do care about Dara. That's *why* I kept Roni's secret. Look, I know this is a shock to you, but you must get a hold of yourself and allow me to explain."

"Fine, I'm listening. Now please explain before I explode."

Yaniv took a deep breath and blew out loudly. "Jen, while Dara was in America, before Roni knew what had happened to her parents, before any of us knew what she was going through, he was asked to…" he shook his head in frustration. "Look, I don't even know the details. It's classified stuff. Roni couldn't tell me everything. But what I can tell you is that I got a call from him sixteen years ago asking me to look after Dara. He had decided to have his sister inform her of his "untimely death" – killed in action in enemy territory. No one but his family and I knew that it wasn't true."

He put his arm around his wife and continued. "Jen, he did it for Dara. He didn't want her ruining her life over him – pining away for

him, waiting for who knows how many years till he'd be free from his…
assignment. It wasn't something he planned. He didn't want to do it.
He didn't want to lose Dara. He didn't want to take on that mission…
but he was…cornered into it…national security and all that…it was put
forward to him in such a way that he couldn't refuse."

"I don't understand." She pushed away from Yaniv, shaking her
head from side to side. "How could he have done this to her? How
could you have kept this from me? I'm your wife!"

"And you're also Dara's best friend. I *had* to keep it from you. I
wouldn't burden you with such a secret. It would have killed you all
those years before she met Uri to keep it from her. And telling her
would have done her no good. Whatever Roni did, he did out of love
for her. He was entirely selfless where she was concerned. He wasn't
going to doom her to a life of loneliness."

"She would have gladly waited for him."

"He knew that, Jen, but he wanted her to have a chance at happiness.
And…maybe he was right. I mean…look at Dara now. She's happy with
Uri. They have three beautiful children. She'd have none of that if Roni
had told her the truth."

"It wasn't his decision to make."

"Maybe not. I don't know. But he did, and I pledged my secrecy
and honored his decision. Jen…don't be so hard on Roni…he gave up
everything."

"Where is he now?"

"I can't say."

"Is that *assignment* over?"

"I'm not sure."

"So, what happens now?" Jenny's face contorted in distress.
"Yaniv…you don't understand something about Dara. As much as she
loves Uri, finding out that Roni is alive would pull the rug right out from
under her. It could destroy everything she has."

"That's right. That's why you'll never tell Dara what you now know," he said firmly.

"This whole thing is insane! When I think of all the pain she's been through. It took us five years to get her to even allow us to introduce her to another man!"

"All that doesn't matter anymore, Jen. That part of her life is long gone. It's over. She's with Uri now."

"You don't know Dara the way I do. She may have buried that part of her life – for Uri's sake – but it's just beneath the surface…she will *never* be over Roni."

"Then, she mustn't ever find out the truth. Promise me, Jen, that you will never utter a word of this to Dara."

"How could I keep this from her? It's a lie!"

"You must. It's for Dara's own sake – for her family's sake. Promise me, Jen! I want to hear you say the words. Promise me you won't tell her."

Jenny closed her eyes and breathed deeply, the truth weighing heavily upon her. "Yaniv, the truth always has a way of coming out. But all right, I promise."

"It's for the best, Jen," he wrapped his arms around her to comfort her.

Jenny looked up to her husband's face. "Then why do I have this gut feeling that Dara's world is going to explode right out from under her?"

Chapter 36

I felt Uri's gaze on me as I stretched out in bed, reluctant yet to open my eyes. There was no school today as it was the first day of Chanukah vacation, and not having to wake up early in the morning to get the kids ready was a real treat.

"Hey, sleepyhead."

"Hi," I smiled back at Uri, raising my eyelids only halfway. "What time is it?"

"Well, according to my expert calculations, we may have a full seven minutes before the kids come charging into our bedroom this morning."

"Mmm. Seven minutes, huh? I can see what's on *your* mind."

"I humbly offer you seven minutes of heaven."

"Humbly?" I giggled. "I didn't even know that you knew that word."

"I thought we'd have a replay of last night…" Uri's eyes creased in a playful smile.

"In seven minutes?"

"So, maybe just some highlights…"

"Hard to turn that one down, but, like you said, the kids may be jumping in here any minute. Sooo, I'm going to dash into a hot shower… got lots to do today for Gavriel's birthday party – I can't believe that he's turning ten!" I jumped out of bed and headed to the bathroom, leaving behind a frustrated Uri.

Uri tilted his head in thought as he heard the stream of the shower. *Hmm. Hot shower…sounds good to me.* He rolled off the bed and sauntered into the bathroom.

"Uri?"

"Just doing my part for water conservation, my dear."

❈

"Imma! Abba!" Ayala burst into our room just as Uri and I finished getting dressed. It was uncanny how she always managed to do that – as if she had radar. Ayala jumped into Uri's arms with tears running down her cheeks.

"Hey, what's wrong *katanchik*, my little one?"

"Matan said that I can't marry you when I grow up. That's not true, is it, Abba?"

"Well, I'm your Abba forever…and that's even better."

"But Imma said that she would share you with me."

Uri flashed me an amused look. "And Imma always tells the truth. So don't pay attention to Matan…he's just teasing you."

"Abba, don't you think it's about time you told Ayala how the world works?" Gavriel came strolling in, true to form in his older brother role, pretending to grimace as I gave him a big birthday kiss. "I mean, it's kind of weird to hear her talk about marrying you."

"Weird? Not at all, Gavi, my birthday boy." He wrapped his free arm around him. "I have that effect on females." He winked at me. "You'll see when you get older. It's the Amrani legacy."

"Sure, Abba, whatever you say." Gavi rolled his eyes.

"Scoff now, my son, but one day you'll thank me for the special Amrani charm you were born into," he smiled. "And don't worry about your little sister. What she's saying is normal – she'll grow out of it."

"No, Abba! I won't," Ayala pouted stubbornly. You're the best Abba in the whole world and I don't want to marry anyone else but you."

"Can't argue with that." He kissed her on the forehead. "You not only have beauty, you also have brains – just like your imma."

"Come with me, sweetie," I wrested Ayala from Uri's arms. "Time for breakfast, and then you and Matan can work on the decorations for Gavi's party while I run to the supermarket."

"Can I go with you, Imma?"

"Not this time. You'll stay home with Abba and the boys. Abba really needs your help to watch that Matan doesn't get into any trouble this morning, okay?"

"Can I help you bake a special birthday cake for Gavi when you come back?"

"I can't do it without you, sweetie."

"Dara, you're going to Jerusalem?"

"Yes, Uri. The supermarket there is larger and it has more of what I need."

Uri was uncomfortable with me driving on the highways ever since this past September when Yasser Arafat initiated the terrorist war, after the recently failed Camp David negotiations between him and Prime Minister Ehud Barak. The prime minister had offered Arafat 99 percent of what he demanded, yet rather than choose to negotiate over the remaining 1 percent, Arafat began a bloody war against the citizens of Israel. In an effort to reach a final agreement, Ehud Barak offered the most substantial concessions and far-reaching proposals, going beyond all the long-standing Israeli "red lines." When these terms were revealed in Israel, people were stunned at the extent of the concessions Barak offered, and it was unclear whether the Israeli public was prepared to support the deal. But the opportunity to endorse or reject the proposals was moot since Arafat rejected them out of hand – Israel, at any size, was unacceptable to the Arabs. It was never about the land, and we knew it.

While President Clinton laid the blame squarely on Arafat's shoulders, that didn't ameliorate the situation on the ground. Arab homicide bombers consistently targeted pizza parlors, buses and supermarkets. The local Arabs took pleasure in shooting at Jewish drivers on the road, that is, when they weren't hurling huge stones or Molotov cocktails at us. But I refused to become a prisoner in my own country and would not give in to their terror tactics. I never thought of myself as particularly courageous, but I felt that coming and going freely in my own land was elementary, and I would allow no one to rob me of that. Uri shared the same sentiments, though he couldn't help but worry each time I would travel the roads.

"Maybe you'll make do with the local markets today? It's very overcast," he urged. I knew what he was thinking, *easier camouflage for terrorists.*

"You worry too much. I'll be fine." I kissed him on the cheek and turned to leave the room with Ayala.

"You are so stubborn, woman." He grabbed my arm, his face blanketed in worry. He sighed in frustration and kissed me more affectionately.

"Aw, Abba," Gavriel protested. "Yuck, do we really have to see that?"

"Ooh gross, not again!" Matan had just then flown into the bedroom. "Talk about bad timing." I laughed at the usual way the boys reacted whenever they saw their Abba kiss me, but Uri wasn't laughing; he couldn't let go of his anxiety.

"Just keep your eyes open, Dara and…say the blessing for travelers."

"I always do, Uri."

Ten years! I reflected on the drive home from the supermarket in Jerusalem after picking up supplies for Gavriel's birthday party. It was often hard to grasp the many blessings bestowed upon me these past ten years. Uri – my kindhearted pillar of strength who taught me how to love again. My three beautiful children – Gavriel, my little drummer with jet-black hair and deep blue eyes; Matan, who just turned eight last summer and, like his father, is already proving to be quite the athlete; and Ayala, my five-year-old sweet angel, who has her Abba's light coloring and who is always so happy to be Imma's little helper.

My mind drifted to the other blessings in my life – my friends. Of course, Jenny and Yaniv, and the good fortune of having Lavi and Mikki move into our community last year. Ari and Adina were leaving the kibbutz on Gilboa and considered joining us as well. There were also two other couples in our circle of friends that I had become close with – Yael and Drory and Dina and Boaz. I was looking forward to the vacation down south in Eilat that our families had planned to go on just two days from now. That was always a highlight.

It was a dark, cloudy day with on-and-off drizzle. But rain is good in the Middle East. There was always a shortage of water in Israel. We never seem to have enough rain in order to rise above the red line in the reservoirs. I pondered this as my face broke into a smile over Uri's *efforts* this morning at water conservation.

My thoughts came to an abrupt end as I turned into the road

leading to my house. There was some type of commotion in front. From the top of the hill, I observed neighbors and friends crowding the street. Uri and the kids were conspicuously absent from this scene. I slowly descended the hill and spotted two ambulances, several army vehicles and police cars.

Jenny was there. I caught sight of her expression as she watched my car inching forward. I pulled over to the side of the street and I froze. I didn't want to exit the car. I didn't want to find out the reason for the devastated look in Jenny's eyes. A familiar sickening sensation filled the pit of my stomach. I knew that I was about to have my world crash down around my feet.

I don't remember getting out of the car, yet there I was, racing down the road toward my house. Jenny and Yaniv grabbed me before I could enter. "No, Dara. Wait! Don't go in there." Letting out a primal scream like a mad woman, I cut loose of their hold and stormed into my home.

I followed the din of activity into the den, where I immediately saw Uri's body riddled with bullets, a gun in his hand. Several feet away lay the body of an Arab, his Kalashnikov at his side. Further into the room, Gavi's body lay slumped over on the couch, and Ayala and Matan were facedown over the crafts table where they were making decorations for Gavi's birthday party. Each with bullet holes blasted throughout their small bodies, pools of blood coagulating on the floor around them. Paramedics were laying out plastic body bags. Members of Zaka entered to scrape off the blood and flesh from the walls for religious burial. Someone came over to speak to me. I don't know who it was or what was said. I sunk down to my knees, encircled in the massacre of my family. My eyes darted from one bloody limp body to the next – my Gavi, my Matan, my Ayala, my Uri. My life – zipped up in body bags. There were more voices, more noise. Someone took my pulse and someone else lifted me up. I did not want to be moved and all at once became enraged, letting out a bloodcurdling scream. This is *my home, my family! Don't move me! Don't touch me!* I wanted to cradle each of my children. I wanted to hold my husband. *Don't take them from me! Don't touch them! Don't take them from me!* More hands restrained me. *URI, STOP THEM! URI! URI! URIIII!* Soon, a slight sting in my arm, and then, blackness.

Chapter 37

I could not have walked from the car to the grave site at Kfar
Etzion on my own, and probably wouldn't have at all, had Jenny
and Yaniv not held me up from both sides. I did not want to go to the
funeral. I wanted to stay home and be with my children's souls, and with
Uri's soul. I had once heard that the souls of the dead hover for a full
year in the home in which they lived. My place was at home with them.

I did not want to hear the eulogies. They were meaningless, and
quickly forgotten. It was only the busload of disabled soldiers from
Tel Hashomer Sheba Medical Center that struck a chord. I could not
connect with Uri's three brothers, nor with his bereaved parents. I was
numb to all my well-meaning friends. I was dead to it all. I did not want
anyone's sympathy or pity. I did not want anything from this world. I
belonged to a new reality – of the walking dead. And the dead have no
friends and…no family. But God cursed me further with the need to

drink and eat, and I in turn cursed the food that entered my mouth, and my body complied by vomiting it out.

I did not want people coming to my home during the week of mourning to pay a condolence call. People I had never met came from all over the country. Apparently, the massacre of my family was all over the news. My eyes did not look up at anyone nor did my lips utter a word. However, on the last day, I spotted one unlikely visitor. He said nothing to me, and I nothing to him as he seated himself just inches away from me. Though it had been years, I remembered him right away. Dov Regev, of the Mossad — to whom I handed over my father's file. I lowered my eyes and did not speak. He respected my silence, as did everyone else. What was there to say, after all?

I recalled that over the years, I had met some mothers and wives who had lost their sons or husbands serving in the army, and others who had lost loved ones in terrorist attacks. They had accepted their loss stoically and bravely. *God had His reasons — though we may not always understand them.* Well, screw God's reasons! I wasn't interested in them, anyway. I would accept the slaughter of my family neither stoically nor bravely. The Arabs who did this were my enemy, and so was God. He was just as guilty.

Bless the True Judge. That is what Jews are supposed to say upon hearing of the death of someone. Bless the True Judge? I think not. My belief in God did not waver, however. Oh, I believed in Him all right. Moreover, I imagined a mutiny against Him, and trying Him for His ungodly performance.

Once the week of mourning was over, I kept to myself. I would not answer the door, nor would I answer the telephone. It was necessary to protect my friends from God's ways. He had killed every person I loved. I would not tolerate any more losses.

I refused to shed any tears. I sought no release and no relief. *Tears have never helped the Jewish people.* Roni's word's haunted me.

My phone rang incessantly. Jenny, Mikki, Dina, Yael and Adina as well left me many messages, begging me to answer the phone – until I had finally unplugged it. They came knocking at my door, but I ignored them. Jenny knew the code to my keyless door lock, and once tried to enter the house, but I had an extra bottom lock that Uri and I never used. I use it now. That lock required a key and Jenny didn't have a spare one and could not come in. She banged on the door determinedly, yelling for me to open it. Still, I did not answer. I was cold to her cries. The dead don't feel. *In time, they would forget about me. And they would be spared.* The same for Uri's family. They were better off without me. From now on, I would exist only for my ghosts – my family of ghosts.

It became routine for me to wander from bedroom to bedroom. I refused to clean out my children's rooms, leaving them just as they were the day God and his Arab accomplices took them from me. Every night I lay down in each of their beds breathing in their scent, clinging to their last traces – trying in vain to fill the empty shell that I had become. Mourning would never be over for me. There would be no *moving on*. How could I move on after having my insides gutted? I was the embodiment of desolation. I was barren. I was dead. Yet, not dead enough. Each breath I took fanned the flames of the agony burning inside me. There would be no respite until I would breathe my last breath.

Eventually I would make my way to my room, with the now huge empty bed. It was impossible to adjust to sleeping without Uri.

Oh, Uri. My dear, loving and wonderful Uri – he was larger than life. How could he be dead?

Mindful never to run into people I knew, I ventured outdoors only at night – to run. Uri had gotten me into running early on in our marriage. On the way home, I would pick up my mail. Though dead, I still had bills to pay, and the few groceries I required I had delivered. They learned quickly to leave the delivery outside on my doorstep.

Seven weeks after the massacre, there was one letter addressed to me in English in a distinctly American handwriting. There was no return address. I opened it and found that God apparently did not feel that my pain was deep enough.

> *Hey there, sweetness,*
> *Long time no see. Hope you're enjoying the calling card I left for you à la my Palestinian pals. I have to admit, it was not my intention to spare you, but with the circumstances turning out the way they did, I am relishing my revenge even more.*
>
> *Mace*

Chapter 38

 Berlin, Monday, Last Week of January, 2001

"He's a liability. He cost us many good people over the last decade. Once and for all, he must be taken care of."

"I agree, Gerhard."

"I didn't want to believe it, Eric, but that FBI report you got hold of on Devlin provides irrefutable proof that he caused some of our top people to get assassinated. As soon as that son of a bitch shows his face…"

"I have it all taken care of," Roni coolly broke in, confident in his role as Eric. He stared at Gerhard, his ice-blue eyes resolute.

"Yes, I know I can count on you, Eric. In the meantime, however, we just lost two major Swiss financiers of our gunrunning operation. I have no doubt that it was the Mossad who picked them off, just like the others."

"It certainly smelled like one of their ops."

"But, on the good side, our ties with Iran are strong, as well as with the Al Qaeda cell in Hamburg, and I see continued cooperation in the near future."

"Our boys also just had a successful training session in Syria together with Hamas and Hezbollah operatives," Roni added.

"Oh yes, Eric, that reminds me of what I wanted to tell you before I got sidetracked over Mace. As you know, I'm leaving tomorrow for Lebanon to meet with Hassan Nasrallah. We're going to discuss a joint operation against the Israeli embassy in France. I'll also be getting a bird's-eye view of the bunker system Hezbollah is building on the southern border. I'll only be gone for a few days, but I was thinking that you should come with me. Besides, Nasrallah asked about you. He's impressed with you from the last time the two of you met."

"Will do. What day is Mace expected to arrive in Mitte?"

"Thursday, February 5. We'll be back by then. But before we *resolve* the Mace problem, I would like to debrief him one last time."

"Of course."

"Now, what say you and I join the festivities in the next room? Clara has been asking about you. She was disappointed when you skipped out early at our last *gathering*."

"I'll just finish up my cigarette here and join you in a moment."

"I like your style, Eric. So aloof. If I didn't know better, I would think you hated women."

"Not at all. I just get bored easily."

Herzliya, Israel

Dov Regev showed me to a seat in his office. He knew better than to ask how I was. "Thank you for seeing me, Dov."

368 The Gilboa Iris

"Of course, Dara. It sounded urgent over the phone."

"I received this yesterday. It's from Mace Devlin." I handed him the letter. After reading it, Dov took a prolonged moment to contain his fury. I scanned his office while waiting patiently for his response. There wasn't anything of any personal nature that would mark this office as his own, save for one lone framed picture on his desk, otherwise piled high with a mountain of documents. It was of an attractive, dark-haired woman in her twenties holding a baby. *Must be an old photo*, I thought, as Dov looked to be about forty, his dark hair peppered lightly with gray at the temples.

"We knew he got out," he finally said, "and that he purchased a ticket to Germany for the first week of February – February 5 to be exact. We were wary that he would attempt to find you and take his revenge, but not until he met up with his contacts. In the past, he never made a move without the go-ahead from the top brass."

"And that top brass was located in Germany?"

"Still is – there, as well as in the United States, but his main connection was with this man called Gerhard Kestel who is based in Berlin. We suspected Mace was up to something but couldn't put a finger on it – no information was forthcoming that it had anything to do with you."

"What made you think he was up to something?"

"We were watching him. But Mace is no fool. Since his release from jail, he switches cell phones every day and never remains in one location long enough for us to locate him. On the other hand, he had created for himself plenty of enemies from the deal he made with the FBI. It wasn't illogical to assume he was just being extra careful to save his own skin. In the meantime, we had a man in Germany prepared to keep an eye on him and inform us if he planned any type of vendetta against you. But apparently, Mace decided to act alone. I can only now ascertain that, driven by his revenge, he sidestepped protocol. He's well connected, all the way up to Saddam Hussein of Iraq, who is a major backer of Yasser Arafat. And with Arafat now waging a full-blown terrorist war here in Israel…well, it must have been a cinch for Mace to arrange this revenge killing."

I sat in silence, taking in everything Dov said. My blood boiled for my own revenge. I wanted to rip Mace to shreds. My breathing became erratic and I was sure there must have been a crazed look in my eyes. I supposed I presented an alarming demeanor, and lacking anything better to say, Dov blurted out, "I'm…so sorry, Dara."

"Why? It's not your fault. And I didn't come here to point fingers at anyone." I tried to regain my composure, yet my tone was cold and detached. "Look, I just thought you should have this information." I rose from my chair to leave. Before exiting his office, I turned back around to Dov. "I want him dead."

"I assure you, Dara. He'll be taken of."

Now we fight back. Roni's words played in my head. I turned back to the door and left to return home to my ghosts.

Chapter 39

I would often spend hours sitting in my den, not doing anything in particular – staring at my family pictures on the wall as the hours flitted away, leafing through photo albums and watching family movies. Earlier, I had worked out on Uri's exercise machines, as I did each morning, imagining him there with me – or rather – feeling him there with me. That had become my usual routine. And…I started smoking. I knew Uri would have looked down on it, but I was dead anyway – what did it matter?

It was Friday afternoon, the eve of Shabbat. The weather outside was dark and dreary and there was a slight snowfall. Not anything that would stick, however. Snow was rare in Israel, except for up north, nearer to Mount Hermon. While gazing out the window at the few snowflakes, I noticed Dov Regev walking toward my house. *He must have news about Mace*, I thought, and I hurried to open the front door before he knocked.

"Hello, Dara."

"I saw you through the window. You have news for me about Mace?"

"No, I'm not here about Mace." He saw my confused look and added, "I'm staying by Jenny and Yaniv for Shabbat, and I wanted to come by and say hello."

"You know Jenny and Yaniv?"

"I met them some time ago…when I came to your house to pay a condolence call."

"I see."

"May I come in?"

Hesitant, I let him in. I didn't want any social visits.

"They miss you, and are very worried about you."

"Is that why you're here?"

"Pardon?"

"To persuade me, on their behalf, to reenter the world of the living?"

"I'm here on my behalf, Dara. I'm also concerned for you."

"You barely know me. Why should you be concerned?"

"I know enough."

"Look, Dov, I don't mean to be impolite, but I don't do social visits. The only reason I opened the door was because I thought you had news about Mace." His eyes looked past me into the dining room. "If you *don't do social visits,* why is your dining room table set for five?"

"That's none of your business." I knew it was harsh when I said it, but I didn't care. He was intruding in my world. It wasn't anything he or anyone would understand. They would think it insane that I set my table on Shabbat for my family. But it wasn't insane to me. It was now the only existence I knew. The only one I wanted. What should I have told him? That each Shabbat, I sit at the dining room table with the ghosts of Uri and my three children? *Yeah, that would go over well.*

Dov crinkled his brows in thought and stared down at me. "What are you doing to yourself, Dara?"

"You should leave now."

"No."

"No?"

"You need help."

I laughed. "I'm dead, Dov. And the dead do not require help."

"Dara, you know you're not dead."

"Do I?"

"Dara...please, you can talk to me. I know what you're going through."

"I doubt it. And...in any event, I have no desire to talk about anything. You see, the dead don't talk."

"Dara –"

"Look, Dov," I cut him off, "if it's not about Mace, there's no reason for you to be here. Now, please...just...go."

"Okay," he said quietly. "I'll leave – for now. But I'll be back." He turned and let himself out.

"How is she, Dov?" Jenny asked anxiously as Dov walked through her front door. Jenny was sitting with a group of friends gathered in the living room.

"Not good."

"Why isn't she speaking to any of us?"

"She considers herself dead, and the dead don't socialize. When she realized that I wasn't there to speak about Mace, she insisted that I leave."

"We just can't let things continue this way," Jenny said. "I'm so scared for her."

"Jen, doesn't this sound familiar to you?" Lavi asked.

"What do you mean?"

"Of course," Yaniv put in. "She's like Roni was after the Lebanon War."

"What are you talking about?" Yael and Dina asked together, as if in a chorus. "Who is Roni?"

"Roni was Dara's fiancé several years before she met Uri," Yaniv explained. "He…was killed in action back in December of 1984." Dov kept a straight face. This was a curious piece of information. Yaniv continued, "He went through his own hell in the Lebanon War, and… was pretty much dead when he came out of it…there's no other way to explain it. He, too, didn't want to socialize, or feel anything. That is… until he met Dara."

"So, now Dara…" Yael began putting it together.

"Yeah, she's become like Roni," Yaniv finished the thought. "Only much more extreme. Roni never let go of reality or cut himself off from the rest of the world."

"Well, what can we do about this?" Mikki asked.

"She needs time to heal," Dov interjected.

"She won't heal by playing dead," Jenny cried out.

"Don't push her into a corner. This is something you can't force. Trust me on this."

"I don't agree with you, Dov."

"Look, Jenny, let me have some more time. I think I can reach Dara. There's more to this than just pretending to be dead."

"What are you saying?"

"When I was over at her house, I noticed that her dining room table was set for the Shabbat meal…for five people."

"I don't understand. She's having…company?"

"Oh, my God," Yaniv thought aloud. "Poor Dara. She's lost it."

"What do you mean?" Jenny asked desperately.

"Five settings – she and Uri, Gavriel, Matan and Ayala."

Dov nodded. "Listen everyone, let me try to get through to her. I know what she's going through. Just give me some time."

"But Dov," Jenny threw in, "she won't speak to you unless you have news about Mace."

"I'm working on that."

⚘

The doorknob to the back porch off the dining room turned slowly. Someone was trying to jimmy open the lock. *Did Mace have second thoughts about leaving me alive?* I ran from the dining room to the kitchen to grab a knife. There was no time to get Uri's gun. *No Arab was going to take me down. Or, at the very least, I would take him down with me.* The porch door creaked open from the kitchen and I spun around.

"You! What do you think you're doing?"

"You ought to get a better lock on that door."

"How dare you break into my home!"

"Dara, what's with the knife?"

"Dov, I thought you were a terrorist!"

"And you imagined you would take down an armed terrorist with a kitchen knife?"

"There was no time to grab my gun. And I don't have to explain myself to you after what you just did! How could you?"

"Well, after our last conversation, you weren't likely to let me in through the front door."

"So, you thought it would be okay to break into my home and scare me to death?"

"Scare you to *death*? But...you're already dead, aren't you?"

"What do you want, Dov?"

"I don't want anything. I merely brought over dinner," he motioned to the insulated bag in his hand.

"I'm not hungry."

"You need to eat. You're looking too thin. And besides, it's Shabbat." His eyes darted to the plate settings on the table and then back to me. "You shouldn't be eating the Shabbat meal alone."

"I prefer it that way."

"Well, I'm not leaving until you sit down and have dinner with me."

"I don't want your pity, Dov. I don't need it."

"I don't pity you, Dara. I actually admire you."

"Admire me? Why?"

"All things considered, with everything you've been through in your life, one would imagine that you would have fallen to pieces by now. But you haven't. You're an unusually strong woman."

"If you believe I'm doing so well, *all things considered*, then why are you here?"

"You have a very worried group of friends. Actually, they're frantic over you."

"They'll get over it."

"If you think they're going to give up on you, you're mistaken."

"They don't have a choice in the matter."

"You're not a cold person, Dara. Why are you doing this?"

"Please, Dov, you're wasting your time – just leave. You...you can't be here," I pleaded with him. But he wouldn't listen. Instead, he opened the cooler and took out two settings of dishes, glasses and utensils in addition to a bottle of wine, and all the food necessary for the Shabbat meal. Jenny was very thorough, as always. After setting everything up on the opposite end of the table from where I had settings placed for my family, he pulled out a *kippah* from his pocket, placed it on his head, poured wine into his glass and recited the Shabbat benediction. As was customary, he poured some wine from his glass into mine. I watched him walk to the kitchen and wash his hands in the ritual manner with the special washing cup I had on my counter before returning to the dining room to cut the challah, the braided bread specifically eaten on Shabbat.

I waited until he finished the blessing over the bread and the ensuing tradition of taking a bite before being able to speak. "You're religious?"

"No. Just well educated." He motioned for me to sit down at the table, but I stood in place. "You don't really have much of a choice, Dara. I'm not leaving until you join me. Oh and... you can put the knife down now. I'm not a threat to you."

I hardly knew Dov, but I quickly learned that he was irritatingly persistent and quite adamant. I placed the knife down and seated myself at the table, hoping that my cooperation would facilitate dinner and his swift departure. He proceeded to fill my plate with food. I stiffened in anger. He made me feel like a child. Worse yet, he kept me from having the meal with my family.

"So, Dara, tell me, how do you spend your days?"

What, is he kidding me? Small talk?

"Besides visiting me at my office, do you ever go out?"

Now he sounds like a shrink.

"Are you planning on answering me anytime soon, Dara?"

"No."

"You're not eating anything."

I picked at the food with my fork. "Perhaps you would like to force-feed me?"

"Why are you angry with me?"

"I'm not angry. I just don't want you here."

"Why not?"

"Because I don't do dinner, I don't socialize, and I don't want to answer any of your questions," I blurted out.

"Why do you insist on pretending to be dead, or rather, something *like* dead?"

"Why do you insist on getting me to talk when I clearly don't want to?"

"Why *don't* you want to talk?"

"The only thing I will talk to you about is Mace. When you have some news on him for me, then you may speak to me. Otherwise, you're not welcome here."

"That's pretty harsh."

"I don't wish to be rude, but you're forcing me to be."

He put a forkful of food in his mouth, swallowed and unhurriedly drank some of his wine. "Jenny is a fine cook. Don't you think so?"

Why was he doing this to me?

He sighed deeply with an air of impatience and then leaned in toward me across the table. "You don't want to talk to me, Dara, because you're afraid that talking or having any kind of normalcy in your life will diminish your anger. And you don't want that to happen, do you? Diminishing your anger would weaken the presence of your family's souls in your home. And you want them here with you, don't you? You want them close to you. You want to bask in your anger and never let go. By doing so, in your mind, the souls will remain – the faces of your loved ones will never fade. You want to be able to see them every waking moment."

Stunned, my eyes burned into him. "Don't tell me you majored in psychology." My tone was nothing less than contemptuous.

"You don't learn this kind of stuff in a classroom."

I'm not interested where you learned it. I don't want to know anything about you. I'm not looking to make new friends. "Spare me your insights, Dov."

"Give it up, Dara. What you're doing won't last."

"It will."

"It can't. You'll only drive yourself insane. Is that what you want?"

"I don't care."

"You're still young, Dara. You still have a whole life ahead of you."

"If that's your way of trying to make me feel better, I assure you, it's the wrong ploy."

"Your friends are gearing to do an intervention."

"No! You tell them not to."

"Why would I do that?"

"Because, it won't work. I won't allow it."

"I won't be able to stop them, even if I wanted to. They'll never walk away from this."

"They will...in time."

"You're wrong."

"It's for their own good," I murmured under my breath.

"What was that?"

"Nothing."

He sighed heavily. "You know, I'm not going to leave until you eat something."

"I'm not a child."

"You're acting like one."

"Why are you involving yourself in this? You and I have nothing to do with each other."

"I wouldn't say that, Dara. I know all about you. Do you think I would have just let you walk out of my office all those years ago without giving a damn about what would happen to you? You were all alone in the world. I made sure to know how you were managing – up until you married Uri Amrani."

"You were *stalking* me?"

"Hardly," he smirked. "My *job*, shall we say, provides me with certain resources. I just made sure that you wouldn't be challenged by too many bureaucratic difficulties that new immigrants tend to have."

"What do you mean?"

"Well, for instance...when you went on an interview at the *Jerusalem Post*, I made a phone call to make sure you would get the job."

"You what?"

"I just wanted to make things easier for you. And that house of yours, which you bought in Katamon, I cut all the red tape involved in that as well. And lately, well…let's just say I've made certain that you'd be safe each night you go out running. You do reside in a pretty rough area, you know."

My mouth dropped open. The air seemed stuck in my throat. For a moment, I couldn't find my voice. But then I did. "Get out of my house now."

"Are you angry?"

"Angry? I'm livid!"

"But the dead don't get angry or…*livid*. The dead don't feel, Dara, isn't that right?"

I rose from the table, bolted to the kitchen and grabbed my pack of cigarettes out of a drawer. If he wasn't going to leave, I had to get away from him. I headed for the back porch to have a smoke.

After two cigarettes and still counting, Dov hadn't followed me out to the porch. I glanced at my watch – a full twenty minutes had passed. *Good.* He must have finally left. I put out my third cigarette and turned to go back into the house. Only Dov was standing there, right behind me, watching me. *How was it that I didn't hear him?* There was just one other person I knew who could move as stealthily as that. And he was dead, *of course.*

Dov began to speak in a casual manner as if we just finished a pleasant dinner. "I cleared away everything and packed it all up. I'll be heading back now to Jenny and Yaniv, but I'll return to visit you tomorrow. Unless…you'd like me to stay longer." I turned my back to him and lit another cigarette without answering.

"I thought you were kind of religious. You smoke on Shabbat?"

"When God returns my family to me, I'll stop smoking on Shabbat," I spit out without turning around.

"Fair enough. *Laila tov*, Dara, good night. Oh, one more thing… there isn't a lock I can't open."

I took in a deep drag of my cigarette and blew out heavily. *Why can't everyone just leave me alone?*

Chapter 40

"Mace will be here shortly. What do you have planned?"

Roni took a swig from his beer bottle, "I thought I might go for a drive with him – show him the countryside, perhaps…the Zehlendorf Forest. After all, it's been a while since he's visited our fine country."

"I like your style, Eric. I might be inclined to join you."

"As you wish, Gerhard."

"That weasel has been one massive headache for me. It is a shame – he once showed such promise. But now, after debriefing him, I am more furious at him than ever."

"Why is that?"

"Without first consulting with me, he decided to carry out a vendetta."

Roni had a sick feeling in his gut. "Against whom?"

"The girl who was instrumental in putting him behind bars for sixteen years."

His heart jolted to a stop. It took every ounce of training for Roni to mask the shock and the torment that exploded inside him. Keeping his voice even, he asked, "That American girl?"

"Yes, the Harow girl. Apparently, she moved to Israel some years ago. Mace tracked her down and arranged for some Arabs to waste her and her family."

His guts on fire, Roni rose from his chair and moved toward the window, his back to Gerhard. He needed to cover up any reaction that Gerhard would find suspicious. "I hate vigilantes," Roni spit out. "I like order. We don't have room for men like Mace in our organization."

"I agree." Gerhard chortled. "Of course, I have no qualms about killing Jews, but the dumb ass couldn't even get his revenge killing right."

Dara's alive? "What do you mean?" Roni turned around to face him, stone-faced, masking all emotion.

"It appears that the lucky Jew-bitch was out of the house when the operation took place. Her family was killed, but she's still alive. Ha! But I'm sure she wishes she *was* dead!"

"No doubt." Roni feigned disinterest, turning his face back toward the window pretending to gaze outside, but seeing only Dara's suffering. "At any rate, Gerhard, the fool will be finished by the end of this day."

"Yes, and then we can focus on our operation in France. This time we cannot fail."

"We won't. Besides, with our Al Qaeda connection it should run smoothly." Roni returned to his chair.

"Ah yes, how is it working with Zaid?"

"He's very proficient. I understand from him that something

very big is planned for the United States in September. He mentioned something about using planes as missiles. Sounds like a major suicide mission."

"Yes, the cell in Hamburg is involved. They have been planning it for some time now. It is going to change the world, Eric."

"I'm not surprised. Marwan al-Shehhi, Mohamed Atta…all of them good men – quiet, professional and very capable. What's the target?"

"Don't know. They're keeping a very low profile about it, which is best if it is to succeed." At that moment there was a buzz on the desk intercom. "Ah, Mace must have arrived. Yes, Mina."

"Herr Devlin is here to see you, sir."

"Thank you. Send him in."

Mace sauntered into the office, a self-assured smile on his face and not looking worse for wear after sixteen years behind bars. He eyed Roni – appraising him – and then turned his focus to Gerhard. "Good morning, Gerhard."

"Good morning, Mace. I'd like you to meet Eric Heller, my right-hand man. He'll be bringing you up-to-date today on a number of our operations."

"Of course. It's a pleasure, Eric. Gerhard has told me much about you." He offered his hand to shake Roni's. Roni reciprocated, nodded and offered a curt smile.

"Well, gentlemen, what say we start off our meeting with going out for brunch?" He turned to face Eric. "We can begin discussing *an appropriate place* for Mace and take it from there."

"Sounds good to me," Mace put in.

Roni smiled wryly. "Yes, it sounds good to me as well."

Chapter 41

 Sde Dovid, Shabbat, February 7

I awoke to Dov breaking into my house – again. There was no doubt in my mind that he would be true to his word about returning; I just didn't expect him this early. Having developed a habit of not going to sleep before the wee hours of the morning, rarely did I roll out of bed before ten or eleven o'clock. Without Uri by my side, I needed to reach complete exhaustion before finally plopping myself into bed, and even then, sleep did not come easily. I looked over at the clock on my nightstand. *Ugh. It was barely nine thirty!* I turned over under my blanket, facing away from the door to my room and attempted to ignore his approaching footsteps. Perhaps he would have the decency to leave me alone if he saw I was sleeping.

He didn't.

"Dara?"

I didn't respond, much less breathe. *Get out of my bedroom. Jeez! Is there nothing sacred?*

"I know you're awake, Dara."

How the hell does he know that?

"I warned you that I'd be coming over."

Not at this ungodly hour!

"You're not going to loll away in bed anymore. It's time to get up."

Hey, it's Shabbat — day of rest, remember?

"You didn't think I would give up so easily, did you, Dara?"

Don't you have any terrorists to hunt down, or something?

"Would you prefer me to physically force you out of bed?"

Just try it, pal, and you'll be prancing out of here as a soprano!

"One last warning, Dara. I *am* taking you out of that bed."

You had better not dare.

He dared. With one swift yank, he pulled my blanket off me. Appalled by his nerve, I glared up at him looking down on me. "I cannot believe you just did that!"

His eyes rolled over my scanty nightgown, one of Uri's favorites. "You may as well not be wearing anything," he observed, allowing himself a lingering look. At that, I sprung out of bed in a fit of fury, intending to strike Dov as hard as I could. He was fast though, and took hold of my wrists, twisted me around with my own arms, restraining me from behind in a straitjacket-like grip. "Dara, stop this nonsense and get dressed. I'll be waiting in the den." As soon as he loosened his grip, I turned and lunged at him a second time, and again he caught my wrists in a tight hold. "Don't try to fight me, Dara. You won't win." But I continued to struggle wildly out of his grasp until he pulled me into him, holding me in a bearlike clasp, preventing me from moving at all. I screamed in vain for him to let go of me.

"As soon as you calm down, I'll let you go," he said, unperturbed by my struggling. I tried to fight further, but it was no use. I had no more fight left in me.

I gave up, bowed my head, and began to sob uncontrollably. "Why are you doing this to me?" And it hit me that I hadn't cried once in the months following the murder of Uri and my children. But now it was as if the dam had burst and I couldn't stop the torrent of my despair. Dov gathered me up into his arms, carrying me to the armchair in the corner of my room, and sat down with me curled into him, shaking in a flood of tears.

"That's right, Dara," he said as he stroked my hair. "Let it out. You need to cry. Just let it out."

※

Cafe Morgenland, Skalitzerstrasse 35, Mitte, Berlin

"Ah, I sure did miss German cuisine," Mace said as he guzzled down the last drop of beer from his mug.

"I imagine the quality of food was lacking in prison," Roni offered dryly.

"You ever do time, Eric?"

"No."

"Well, it's brutal. Sixteen years without a woman...now that's cruel and inhuman punishment."

"I'm sure you will make up for lost time."

"Already started, my friend, already started. One thing is for sure though...it was anticipating the sweet taste of revenge that got me through it all."

"You're referring to the Harow girl?" Roni asked without a trace of emotion.

"Yeah...I'm just disappointed that I wasn't there to see her face when she came home to her dead husband and kids. It must have been pure poetry."

Roni envisioned the scene as well. He restrained himself from severing Mace's neck right then and there.

"The only regret I have is that I didn't take her when I had the chance," Mace continued to jabber on. "She was one hot piece of ass... kept thinking that she must have had some Aryan blood in her."

Roni quietly took a slug of his beer. *You're so right, Mace. Revenge is sweet — and it will be mine.*

"The hour is getting late, gentlemen," Gerhard announced and then spoke pointedly to Roni, "Eric, you and I have a meeting with Zaid. We should be on our way."

"Of course," Roni agreed. The three men rose to leave the restaurant. "Perhaps Mace would like to join us," Roni casually offered as they walked out to the street.

"That actually is a fine idea," Gerhard concurred. "Mace?"

"Sure, why not? I've got some time to kill."

Gerhard moved to sit in the backseat of Roni's car. Mace sat up front in the passenger seat. "You're not armed, are you?" Roni asked Mace as he turned the ignition.

"No, why?"

"Zaid prefers we come clean to the meetings." He floored the gas and raced the car down Skalitzerstrasse, heading southwest toward the Zehlendorf Forest.

For the duration of the drive, Mace regaled Gerhard and Roni with innumerable stories about prison, his female conquests and his obsession for revenge on Dara. As grating as his voice was, Roni was thankful that Mace kept talking rather than pay any attention to the road. It wasn't until he drove off the main artery leading to the outskirts of the forest that Mace took notice. "Hey, where are we? Why are we stopping here?"

"It's a shortcut," Roni said flatly. "We walk from here."

"There's nothing here but forest. What kind of meeting is this?"

Roni cut the engine and removed the keys from the ignition. He pressed a button that popped the trunk open, and then turned to face Mace. "Get out of the car, Mace."

"What? Here? Why?" He looked at Roni's ice-cold eyes, and his own suddenly filled with panic. Mace turned to Gerhard, sitting in the backseat. Indifference colored Gerhard's features as he lit a cigarette. "Gerhard? What's going on?" A blank stare was his only response. "What the hell is this?" Mace asked again, his voice taking on a desperate pitch.

With an air of nonchalance, Roni removed a 9-millimeter Glock from the holster beneath his blazer, attaching a silencer to it. He stepped out of the car, crossed over to the passenger side and pulled Mace out of his seat. "Walk toward the trunk of the car, Mace." Mace did as he was told. "Now, remove the shovel from the trunk," Roni ordered.

Mace took hold of the shovel with his trembling hands. His knees buckled and he began to heave, leaning on the shovel for support. "Why are you doing this?" he whimpered. But his cries only met Roni's cold and steady glare.

"Walk past the front of the car, farther into the forest," Roni instructed him further. "Fifty meters should do it." Roni trailed several feet behind him – his gun cocked and aimed at Mace's head. As Mace walked past the car, he looked into the backseat window at Gerhard, who was still enjoying his smoke. "Gerhard! I gave the organization the best years of my life! You can't do this to me!"

Gerhard looked ahead, impassive to Mace's desperate cries.

"Keep walking, Mace."

"After about ten meters, Mace whirled around to Roni, his face twisted in fear. "Why are you doing this?"

"I'm just *following orders*," Roni answered with a deadpan expression. "Keep walking."

Approximately fifty meters into the forest, Roni ordered Mace to stop. "Now, dig." With no alternative in sight, Mace began to dig, sniveling as he went about his gruesome task. Roni reflected how apropos it was for Mace to dig his own grave, as he thought of the countless Jews during World War II forced to do the same at the hands of the Nazis throughout the forests of Europe. *What goes around, comes around.*

"That's enough," Roni ordered down to Mace, standing four feet deep into the ground. "Now, slowly, place the shovel on the ground above the ditch."

"Eric...please...I don't deserve this," he whined as he let go of the shovel. His hair, matted in a nervous sweat, the snot running out of his nostrils, he clasped his hands in a begging mode.

"Lie down."

Mace fell to his knees and looked up at Roni. "How can you do this? I'm a fellow Aryan!"

Roni smirked. "*Ich bin ein Jude, Sie Schwiene.* Remember that on your way to hell."

Mace's eyes popped wide open. "You...you're a...Jew?"

Roni pumped six bullets into Mace's skull. One for each member of Dara's family that he murdered – her parents, her husband and her three children. *Now, that's poetry*, he thought. He set out to carry out the task of filling the grave with dirt, when he heard a gun cock from behind him.

"Put your gun down on the ground, and raise your hands above your head, Eric – if that's your real name. And please, do it carefully," Gerhard directed Roni. Roni did so, and then turned slowly around to face Gerhard, gaining a few strategic inches closer to him.

"What is this about, Gerhard?" he asked calmly.

"I was bored waiting in the car," Gerhard answered. "I thought to watch the finale. Imagine my surprise when I overheard you tell Mace that you were a Jew."

Roni chuckled, "Gerhard, you disappoint me, jumping to conclusions. I got bored as well," he acknowledged as he stole another few inches closer to his would-be killer. "I thought to amuse myself by having Mace think a Jew would be killing him. Surely, you can't believe that I'm..." Having no intention of finishing his "explanation," Roni aimed a swift kick to Gerhard's groin, effectively incapacitating him. Gerhard fell to his knees. Roni lunged at him, grabbing his head from behind, twisting his neck until he could hear the clear break. Hoisting Gerhard's limp body onto his back, he carried him the several yards to Mace's grave and dropped him on top of Mace. He retrieved his gun, and confirmed the kill before layering the grave with dirt, meticulously camouflaging the site with the generous foliage that his surroundings afforded. Proceeding deeper into the forest, he buried the shovel before returning to his car for the ride to the Mossad safe house in Charlottenburg.

Sde Dovid

My tears eventually subsided and I became all too aware of Dov holding me curled on his lap while comforting me. It was too close – much too close. Only Uri had that right. I removed myself from his arms and got up. It was an awkward moment until Dov said he would wait for me in the den while I dressed. I assumed he thought that my crying fest changed things. It didn't. *Tears never helped the Jewish people.* I would not make that mistake again. And I did not intend to allow my ghosts to fade.

They were my only true comfort.

As promised, Dov sat in the den, waiting for me. His eyes followed me as I sat down on the couch and gazed at the wall with my family pictures. "Perhaps you might consider coming for Shabbat lunch at

Yaniv and Jenny's house?" he asked.

"No. That's not possible. But *you* should have lunch with them. Don't come here."

"But Dara, I thought…" The sound of his beeper interrupted him. He glanced at the number, took out his cell phone and excused himself to the other room to make a call.

✤

"What's going on? Why are you at the safe house?" Dov spoke with a low voice into the phone.

"He's dead."

"Good. Complications?"

"I compromised my cover. I had to kill Gerhard."

"Any witnesses?"

"None. But I was seen earlier leaving a coffee shop with the two of them."

"Fine. Get the hell out of there before their absence is noticed. I'll see you back at my office."

✤

"Dara," Dov returned to the den after his phone call. "He's dead. Mace is dead."

I turned my face from my family pictures to Dov. "Are you sure?"

"One hundred percent sure."

"Good," I said quietly. The news of Mace's death did not bring any feeling of elation. I had not expected that it would. There was, however, some sense of gratification that he was on his way to hell. "So, I gather you were just on the phone with *your man* in Germany?"

Dov nodded.

"Was he the one who killed him?"

"What difference does it make?"

"Look, I just want to make sure that you got the news straight from the source. I think I have a right to know that there's no doubt whatsoever."

"There's no doubt."

"*Your man* in Germany then…he's that good – I can count on him?"

"He's…the best."

"Then, the next time you speak with him…can you…thank him from me?"

"Sure." He gazed at me with an uncomfortable look in his eyes.

"What are you holding back from me, Dov?"

"Nothing," he answered casually, and without missing a beat, said, "I just wish you would reconsider coming with me to Jenny and Yaniv."

"I won't."

"Then I won't stop them from trying to get to you. I won't allow you to continue barricading yourself in this house. I told you once before, there's no lock I can't open."

"Why are you doing this? What am I to you?"

"Let's just say, I feel responsible for you, and leave it at that."

"No. It doesn't make any sense. *Why* do you feel responsible for me?"

"Perhaps one day you'll understand. I just can't explain it to you now. You'll have to accept that."

"Well, I don't accept it. What is it…some more top-secret Mossad stuff? Something about my father? What?" He refused to answer. It was incredibly frustrating. "Fine. Don't answer me. I don't care. And I don't need you involving yourself in my life. If you try to get my friends to… I'll leave – without a trace – that even you won't be able to find me."

He laughed under his breath and responded in a condescending tone, "Dara, you know that's impossible. And you know you would never leave this house."

He was right. I would never leave – not permanently.

"Look, Dara," he sat next to me on the couch. "You have every right to mourn. But that's not what you're doing. You're building a life around ghosts. My God! You're setting the table for them! Don't you get it? You keep this up, and you'll spiral yourself down to a point of no return. I won't let that happen."

"Dov?"

"Yes, Dara?"

"Go to hell. And close the door on your way out." I turned my attention back to the wall of my family pictures.

Chapter 42

 Ben Gurion Airport, Sunday

Roni literally wanted to kiss the ground. Upon disembarking from the plane, he drew in a deep breath and immediately discerned the distinct sweet scent of Israel. The sound of Hebrew conversations, now all around him, was music to his ears. He had been so homesick that it hurt. All he desired at that moment was to shower the stench of Germany off his skin, but protocol demanded that he head straight to his handler, Dov Regev. He hailed a cab to Herzliya and got out a few blocks before his destination. The morning air felt refreshing. He needed it to get through the intensive debriefing with Dov.

When entering Dov's office, the two men shook hands and, uncharacteristically, Dov gave Roni a bear hug. "Great seeing you again after all these years, Roni. Please have a seat."

"Thank you, Dov. It's good to be home."

For the next several hours, the two reviewed a myriad of issues, checked and cross-checked data related to Roni's mission – gun-running to the PLO, Hezbollah, Hamas. Stats on Iran, Iraq, Al Qaeda, and terrorist plots against Israeli targets, most notably its embassies throughout Europe. "Okay, Roni, I don't know about you," Dov said, "but I'm beginning to see double. Let's break for lunch. We'll pick up where we left off at 1400. Ephraim will be meeting with you as well."

"The head honcho, huh? Fine. I'd like to move these proceedings as quickly as possible."

"I understand. Oh, by the way, Roni, the CIA never requested clarification after we passed along your information on the Al Qaeda cell from Hamburg."

"They're not taking it seriously?"

"I don't know what's going through their minds. All I know is that the information we provided them didn't elicit the reaction that it should have."

"Dov, my data is accurate. What about the list of Bin Laden's nineteen operatives that I gave to you? I provided concrete verification supporting all the facts."

"I know. Look, all we can do is pass the information to them. We can't shove it down their throats."

"Someone should."

"I wanted to recommend that you continue your surveillance on the cell while they're in Florida."

"Forget it, Dov. I'm done."

"What do you mean?"

"I think I made myself clear. I'm finished with this kind of work. No more. I gave sixteen years of my life. I'm done."

"I wish you would reconsider, Roni. I'd hate to lose you."

"There's nothing to reconsider. I never wanted Mossad. You knew that."

"It's because of Dara?"

Roni shot a curious look at Dov.

"Give me a break, Roni. We know how many times a day each of our operatives takes a leak. I knew you were once engaged to Dara Harow. What I *didn't* know is that you let her think you were killed in action. I just heard about that recently."

Roni rose from his chair and made his way to the door of Dov's office. "This is none of your business, Dov. Like you said, let's break for lunch."

"Maybe it is none of my business. But I made it my business."

Roni slowly turned to face Dov again. "Care to explain that?"

"When Dara first arrived in Israel, she came to my office bringing me her father's file. You know, the file Mace was after."

"Yes…I know. Get to the point, Dov."

"Well, let's just say I saw how much you sacrificed…. I felt responsible and made sure to look after her, from a distance, of course…she was never aware of my involvement, and it was only until she married Uri Amrani."

"So what do you want from me, Dov?" Roni's intoned angrily. "Heartfelt gratitude for looking after the woman you tore me away from?"

"No. I just want you to understand that Dara is not the same woman you left."

"No shit."

"I'm serious, Roni."

"So am I. Do you really think that I don't know what she's been through?"

"Then how the hell are you going to break the news to her that you're alive after all this time? She's in a very fragile state right now."

"I haven't figured that out yet. I just got off the damn plane." Roni was growing impatient with Dov.

"Why did you do it, Roni? Why did you have her think that you were dead?"

"You're *intelligence*. Figure it out." Roni's eyes then narrowed suspiciously at Dov. It didn't go unnoticed.

"Look, Roni, don't read too much into this. I only care because I've recently gotten to know Dara a little better. I also know from a personal perspective what she's going through. I'd like to see things end well for the two of you. You both deserve some happiness."

"Yes, well, it won't matter how I break it to Dara. She's going to despise me when she finds out the truth."

"Don't be so sure. She'll be angry as hell, but from what I've heard, she's still very connected to you."

"What are you talking about?"

"Don't look at me as if I'm crazy, Roni. Your friend Yaniv pointed it out to me."

"*You know Yaniv?* Sounds like you've been making yourself comfortable in my world."

"Relax. I met him and Jenny when I went to pay a condolence call to Dara. They approached me, wanting to know how I knew her. Anyway, it seems she's behaving similarly to the way you behaved after the Lebanon War in '82. She keeps to herself, refuses to talk to anyone. She considers herself dead. Sound familiar?" Roni didn't answer. He closed his eyes, rubbing his temples and sighing heavily. "She hasn't spoken to Jenny and Yaniv," Dov continued, "or to anyone in months. The only reason she spoke with me was to get updated information on Mace. Oh...and by the way...she thanks you for killing him."

Roni's eyes flashed up to Dov in surprise.

"She told me to convey her gratitude to *our man in Germany*."

"*Sababa*," Roni dripped with sarcasm.

"Look, Roni. The fact remains that I do feel responsible. I'd like to help in any way I can. Right now Dara has imprisoned herself in her house, because she…" Dov hesitated.

"She what?"

"She doesn't want to leave her…ghosts. You see, she –"

"You don't have to explain," Roni cut him off. "I get it."

"So what are you planning to do after the debriefing period?"

"I don't know. I need to think…maybe I'll go to my old kibbutz for a while…do some physical work. Perhaps the air up on the Gilboa will help clear my head…help me figure out the best way to approach Dara."

"I don't think you should wait too long. Things have a way of getting out. If she finds out before you had a chance to break it to her in your own way, she'll…" Dov paused. "Well, strong as Dara is, even she's got a breaking point. Roni…it'll drive her over the edge."

Roni nodded. "Look, Dov, in the meantime, if she'll still talk to you, just make damn sure she doesn't do anything…reckless. You owe me that. I'll see you back here at 1400."

Chapter 43

 Three Weeks Later – March 1, 2001

I lay in bed, staring up at the ceiling in shock. It had been a long time since I'd had any dreams. However, this morning I awoke with one so vivid, and so astounding and entirely incomprehensible. It played over in my head clearly, as if I personally witnessed it at the height of the day.

A shadow-like figure of Uri walked purposefully toward my bedroom dresser. Hidden at the bottom of my sweater drawer was my framed Gilboa Iris. Uri retrieved it, removed the crumbling dried flower from its aged and tarnished silver frame, and placed it into Roni's hand. Roni stood there looking as robust and alive as I remembered him. Once the Iris touched his hand, it became as alive as Roni appeared to be in my dream, its dried-out purple petals now vibrant, soft and moist with the morning dew.

Apparently, God was still torturing me. That, or Dov was right – I was driving myself insane. What other explanation could there be for such a dream? Something else then popped into my thoughts – an incident that occurred a few nights ago. It was two in the morning and I was getting ready for bed when, for no apparent reason, I was drawn to the window that faced the front of our house. I looked outside and noticed a strange car parked across the road from my front door. I took a double take. The man behind the wheel looked astonishingly like Roni. Had he long, blond curls, the resemblance would have been uncanny. But it was dark, I told myself. My mind was playing tricks on me. Obviously, it could not be Roni. Dov must have put one of his men on watch, though I couldn't fathom why. He still barged in on me every now and again, going through the motion of first ringing the bell, and after I would ignore him, he would jimmy open the lock and let himself in. It was exasperating, but I had no clue how to stop him. He wasn't exaggerating with his claim of there not being a lock he couldn't open.

I should go away for a few days, I decided. A change of scene wouldn't be a bad idea. Perhaps that may help keep me from dreaming. Yet, the thought of leaving my ghosts behind did not comfort me. Somehow, they would come with me. *Oh, God! I have lost my mind.*

March 2, 2001– Midnight

I can't take much more of this. Roni felt like a voyeur sitting in front of Dara's house night after night with the hope of catching a glimpse of her through the window. *I've lost my mind. I suppose sixteen years in Germany can do that. What the hell am I doing here? What was I thinking? I can't just show up at her door.*

Damn…. If I could just hold her again…. I'm so close to her…. So, what's stopping me?

I know what's stopping me.... All I've done is cause her pain. Why would I think that my being alive would be news that she'd want to hear? How could I be so selfish? Why can't I just leave her alone?

Because you're hopelessly in love with her, you idiot!

Okay...so maybe she would be angry at first.... What am I thinking? She'll hate me for what I've done. But then...maybe she'll forgive me. Maybe Dov's right – that she'd understand that what I did, I did for her. I couldn't destroy the best years of her life...or at least what I thought would be the best years of her life. Had it not been for Mace Devlin, she would still be happy. I could have lived with that, knowing that Uri was good to her, knowing that he loved her and that she had a good life with him.

Strange, but I feel some sort of bond with Uri. I'll always be grateful to him for bringing ten years of happiness to Dara. But now... she knows only pain. I can feel it as if it's my own. Because it is my own. My Dara, my sweet Dara. My *motek*. You are part of me.

Fine, call me selfish, but I can't let go of her a second time. I can't let her go again. God help me. I can't. I won't.

Roni remained in his car, keeping vigil over Dara's home. With the first sign of dawn, he turned the ignition and headed north, toward Migdal. On the way, he phoned his mother so as not to shock her when he walked through the door. The debriefing period was officially over and he could return home to his family. At least there, he knew to expect a warm homecoming. How he missed his family!

The long ride home to Migdal afforded him time to jump from one thought to another. He recalled his parents' heartbroken reaction when he told them how he was going to set Dara free from him – but how they also agreed that it was best for her. They had always supported him unconditionally. He likewise knew they would support his decision to confront Dara with the truth. The confidence Roni had in his own family just brought it closer to home that Dara had no one. His heart

ached knowing how alone she was. She had no family to count on. She
was forsaken…by life, by God and…*by me.*

His mind traveled back years, vividly summoning up how he once
told her that *he* was her family after her own parents let her know they
would disown her should she marry him. *For God's sake!*

Suck it up, Roni! No more vacillating. You're going back to Dara
and never leaving her.

Chapter 44

 Migdal

"Oh, bless God! Roni *yikari*! My dear Roni!" Evaleen broke down crying at the sight of her son she hadn't seen in sixteen years, clinging to him as he clung to her.

"I missed you, Imma. It's good to be home," Roni said softly, as he held her in a loving embrace.

Evaleen stepped back to get a good look at him. "Don't you ever do that to me again! Do you understand?" she admonished him and clung to him once more.

Roni smiled. "Don't worry, Imma. I'm not going anywhere." He noticed how his mother's once strikingly dark hair had turned gray – the worry lines around her eyes, more profound. He knew much of it could be attributed to him. Just then, Shimshon entered the house. He didn't say a word. His eyes said it all. He slowly stepped toward his son, taking in every inch of him before finally wrapping him in a lingering bear hug. "Abba," Roni murmured.

Gilad and Margalit, Dalya and Natanel came through the front door at that moment. Uncharacteristically, none uttered a word as they joined Shimshon and formed a huddle around Roni.

Gilad was the first to speak. "So, you big loser, have you seen Dara yet?"

"Smooth, Gilad. Real smooth."

"Leave him alone, Gilad." Evaleen said sternly. "Roni will do what is right, in his own time."

"Thanks, Imma. I appreciate that."

"Of course, Roni. Just…do it soon."

"I will, Imma." Roni said with a good-natured smirk.

"She will forgive you. I know she will," Evaleen encouraged her son.

"I hope you're right."

"Of course Imma is right. Have you ever known her to be wrong?" Shimshon bellowed proudly.

Roni considered that for a moment. "Actually…no."

"Come, Roni, first have something to eat."

"Thanks, Imma, but I'm not hungry."

"Then have some cinnamon croissants at least. They're fresh! I made them especially for you."

"But I just called you from the road. When did you have time?"

"Roni, we are Ben-Aris – people of action! Where do you think you get it from?"

Roni's eyes creased in a smile. "You're so right, Imma. Besides, how can I say no to your croissants? That and a quick coffee, and then…I'm going to Dara."

"Just remember one thing," Evaleen said as the family moved into the kitchen. "Be patient with her. You may just have to sweat a little to win her back."

"Ha!" Gilad roared. "This could be your toughest mission yet!"

Roni let out a deep breath. "I'm afraid you're right."

"Want me to go along with you, bro? I bet she still likes me!"

"Hush, Gilad! Let your brother enjoy his croissant in peace."

Roni glanced at Dalya, who moved to sit next to him at the kitchen table. She was unusually quiet and her eyes were bright with fresh tears. "Hey, *yehiyeh b'seder*," Roni assured her. "It'll be okay. I don't regret what I did. And...I don't blame you." Dalya could only nod.

Chapter 45

 *Sde Dovid*

Can't wait to get on the road. I tossed one small suitcase into the trunk of my car, before going back into the house to get my shoulder bag. *That should do it.* After all, I'll only be gone for three days.

There was just one more thing I had to do. I went into the den, toward the wall where Uri and I hung all our family pictures. There was one of Uri and me sitting on the grass with Gavriel, Matan and Ayala playfully climbing all over us. Yaniv had taken it during a barbeque that he and Jenny had in their backyard last summer. Such happy faces. It was from another world. I took it down to take with me. In a last-minute decision, I ran to my bedroom and unburied another photo that I wanted to take. I didn't want to leave any ghosts behind.

Back to the entry foyer, I took in a deep breath as I reached for the doorknob. This would be the first time since the massacre that I would be leaving the house for any length of time. I just needed some distance – a change of scenery, I told myself. I needed to escape from my dreams that inexplicably became more frequent. And they were always the same. A ghost of Uri – Roni...alive – and my Gilboa Iris. I needed to be somewhere where I could be alone and anonymous.

I opened the front door to head out to my car and came upon Dov crouched down in the midst of working the front lock – my friends standing behind him. He almost fell into my front hallway. I gasped as I reflexively shut the door, locking the bottom lock once more, knowing well that Dov would easily open it. *No! Not now!* I was trapped. Jenny pleaded with me to open the door. *Don't feel, Dara! Don't feel!* I ran to the back porch, hoping to loop around to the front of my house toward my car as they entered inside.

The air was hot and heavy outside as I made my way around the backyard. The Middle Eastern weather would at times be unpredictable. We were in the midst of an early *sharav* – a desert heat storm. As I emerged from the side garden, Yaniv caught me completely by surprise. While everyone else was already inside the house, he waited for me and grabbed me before I could reach my car. "No, Yaniv! Let me go!" Hearing my screams, Lavi and Mikki opened the front door, helping Yaniv force me inside.

"You don't know what you're doing!" I yelled at all those I once considered my closest and dearest friends.

"Dara, you're going to listen to us now. You have no choice," Jenny eyed me firmly.

"You're wasting your time...Yaniv, let go of me!"

"Sit down, Dara," he said while pulling me to the dining room table and plopping me down on a chair. The entire gang was here for the "show." Dina, Boaz, Lavi, Mikki, Yael and Drory and even Ari and Adina joined Jenny and Yaniv around the table. *When did they move in?* Dov pulled up a chair as well. I felt like a caged animal.

Jenny was the first to speak. "Listen Dara. We're all here because we love you." She leaned in closer to me as she continued. "We don't want to lose you, Dara. You are so dear to us…you're irreplaceable." Jenny was choking up with emotion and I couldn't listen to it. I moved to get up from my chair, but Yaniv stood behind me and placed his hands on my shoulders, impelling me to back down.

"We're not going to allow you to continue like this," Jenny went on. "You can't keep isolating yourself, Dara. While everyone has his or her own personal way of mourning, what you are doing is simply not normal and not healthy. It's downright crazy. And if you're not crazy yet, that's exactly where you're headed. I won't let that happen to you. None of us will. You need help, Dara. You need help to get over everything you've been through."

"I *don't* need help. You just don't get it," I hissed.

"Then explain it to me, to us."

"No."

"Why not?"

"Because you won't understand." I didn't want to get over it, dammit!

"Try us!"

I didn't answer her. All I could think of was how to escape.

"Dara," Lavi interjected, "you're building a life around ghosts, creating a fantasy, ignoring the real world around you. You are not *you* anymore. You've turned yourself into Roni…only you're going about it more drastically. He never cut himself off from the world. He never let go of reality."

I shot a look at Lavi. No one had ever brought up Roni's name to me since the day I married Uri. "What do you know about reality?" I said through gritted teeth. "There are things you can't possibly understand, and I don't wish to explain them. Now, you can all talk about this till you turn blue, but I have somewhere else I need to be right now, so…"

"You're not leaving, Dara," Yaniv said, his hands still firmly on my shoulders.

"You can't keep me here."

"We'll do whatever it takes."

The others took their turns speaking to me, but I closed my mind to them. What was I going to say to them? That I was trying to save them from God's wrath? How He was out to kill everyone I cared for? Or that I didn't want my ghosts to fade? That I wanted to live out the rest of my life or death sentence, as it were, surrounded by my ghosts?

Dov didn't take a moment's rest from staring at me – staring at me with pity in his eyes. Above all else, *that* would drive me mad – not my self-imposed isolation or my ghosts. The rage rumbled inside of me. "Enough!" I said. "Face it! I...am...dead! I will have nothing to do with any of you! Accept it." In a fury, I pushed back Yaniv's attempt to keep me seated and darted for the door, but he jumped ahead and blocked my way. Everyone else rose from their chairs and surrounded me.

"Step away, Yaniv."

"No, Dara, I won't," he replied firmly. Jenny stood beside him. There was no use in appealing to her. I turned to Dov and eyed him angrily. He, after all, had unlocked the door for them. It was clear that I would receive no help from him. I turned to Yaniv once more. "Get out of my way. You have no right to do this."

"The hell I don't, Dara. You and Roni are family to me and I promised Roni I would look after you till he returns!" The words escaped from his mouth, and it appeared as though he regretted them. Jenny shot him a quick look, as did Dov. Yaniv responded to Dov's look with a curious look of his own.

I glanced from one to the other in total confusion. "Why are you speaking as if Roni is alive? What do you mean *till he returns?*"

Yaniv backtracked. "Well, you know. I told you a long time ago that while you were still in America... before he left on his last mission – he had me promise to look after you until his return, or in the worse-case scenario...if he never made it back."

"And you, Dov? Why did you give that look to Yaniv?"

"What look?" he said casually.

"I know what I saw, Dov. What do *you* know about Roni?" The moment I heard the question leave my lips, I gasped. It all became clear. The reason why Dov suddenly appeared in my life after my family's murder – the reason he looked after me from a distance when I arrived in Israel sixteen years ago. He felt responsible...obligated. "Oh, my God! You...you were the one who..."

"Dara!" Dov tried to stop me.

"Do you really think I give a damn about your cover? You sent Roni out on the mission that killed him!" I blurted out. "That's why you feel so damn responsible for me!" Still, there was much that remained unclear. Why did Yaniv refer to Roni in the present tense? And...Roni wasn't with the Mossad...or at least, I didn't know he was. I noticed Yaniv and Jenny looking at Dov, trying to put it all together as well. But I couldn't think. I only knew I had to get away from all of them.

"Well, I'll let you off the hook, Dov," I said. "And you, too, Yaniv. I don't need *anyone* to look after me!"

"Dara," Dov stepped closer to me, his voice calm and even, "I came to see you after you lost your family because I knew what it felt like to lose a family." My mind flashed back to Dov's office. The picture of a young woman holding a baby blazed across my memory.

"No! Don't!" I yelled out, taking a step back. "I don't want to hear it!" But he continued, ignoring my cry. "Back in 1978, my wife and baby girl were riding on a bus going down the coastal road when an Arab terrorist attacked the bus."

"No!" I covered my ears with my hands.

"They were killed along with dozens of others," he went on. "So yes, Dara, I know what it's like to lose a family."

"Stop it. Damn you. I don't want to know. I don't want to feel."

"But you do feel, Dara," Jenny mixed in, grabbing me by my arms. "You do feel, because you're not dead." I stared Jenny straight in the eyes. I was beyond anger now – beyond fury – beyond rage. She looked at me with alarm, unsettled by my seething temper. "Why, Dara?" she asked in a hushed, frightened voice. "Why are you being so stubborn?"

It was then I finally exploded in a piercing octave I didn't recognize. "I DON'T WANT YOU TO DIE, TOO!" My outburst stunned everyone and stunned me as well. But I had mere seconds to exploit the window of opportunity and lunged for the front door. I raced to my car and fumbled with my keys before finally starting the ignition. Blinded by my own tears, I quickly tried to dry them before speeding off. The gang burst out of the house after me, and then stopped dead in their tracks. Their attention went toward another car that raced passed me, skidding to a stop. I didn't see who it was, nor did I care, and drove out of there as fast as I could.

The driver of the other car spun around, glancing for a second at the group of friends piled on the front path of the house, before racing after Dara.

"Who was that?" Boaz asked.

"That was…Roni," Lavi answered in disbelief, staring after the dust of Roni's now vanished car. "But I thought he was dead…" he trailed off as he turned to Yaniv for an explanation, as did everyone else.

Yaniv smiled faintly and murmured under his breath. "Go get her, Roni."

Chapter 46

I checked into my room at the Dan Accadia Hotel in Herzliya – a luxury suite with a large terrace facing the Mediterranean Sea. It was perfectly beautiful. Only, the beauty of such a place made me feel more alone than ever. I imagined how impressed my *sophisticated* Gavriel would be by such a room, how Uri would have to keep Matan from climbing on the wrong side of the terrace rails and how Ayala would be smitten by the tranquillity of the sea. From my bag, I removed the family picture I had taken from the den prior to leaving, as well as an old picture of Roni and me on the kibbutz, and I placed them on the dresser. Now all the ones I loved were with me...at least in spirit.

The sadness and loneliness I felt was overpowering. I had thought that a change of scenery might do me some good, but leaving the familiar walls of my secluded existence turned out to be more than I could handle. The emotions that I had kept under a firm restraint were breaking through my not-too-strong facade. I didn't want to break down. I didn't want to cry. This "getting away" was clearly not a good idea. The thought of returning to Sde Dovid, however, was out of the question…at least for today. No doubt, Yaniv and Jenny as well as the others would be watching for my return in order to pounce on me once more with their form of therapeutic intervention. Without any viable alternative in sight, I decided to go down to the beach. I changed into a bathing suit and grabbed my iPod; perhaps I'd feel more in control after a good run.

Just as I was ready to leave my room, there was a knock at the door. I opened it to a bellhop holding a small rectangular box, claiming the package was for me. There was something awfully familiar about the box. I thanked him, closed the door to the room and hesitated before opening it. No one knew I was here. Unless…Dov had me followed. I lifted the lid of the box and separated the tissue paper within. The vibrant purple petals of the Gilboa Iris caught my breath. I gasped for air and groped my way to the couch before my knees gave out. There could be only one person who would have given me this, and that person was dead. But the box…it was the same as the one Roni had given me when I left for America after our year together on kibbutz. My hands shook as I turned it over to check for a label I suspected would be there. I was not mistaken. The label was there, clear as day – *Gifts by Evaleen*. Roni's mother had a small gift shop in the Galilee, not far from Migdal.

I raced to the elevator, pressed the button for the lobby, and headed toward the front desk of the hotel with the box in hand. A man and a woman were on duty. I instinctively opted to speak with the woman. "This package was sent to my room. There wasn't any note. Can you tell me who sent it?"

"Oh, yes," her eyes brightened with her recollection. "That was sent by another guest by the name of Roni Ben-Ari." My knees felt once more as if they were going to buckle under me, and I held onto the counter for support. "Mrs. Amrani, are you all right?"

I nodded yes and managed to choke out another question. "Would you happen to know where Mr. Ben-Ari is at the moment?" Her eyes darted right past me. Before she could answer, a voice I never imagined I would ever hear again called out softly, "He's standing right behind you."

My heart jumped out of my chest. I spun around and the crystal-blue eyes that had haunted my thoughts for so many years met mine. "Oh my God," I struggled for breath. "Roni...my Roni."

"I'm here, Dara."

"I'm not imagining this, am I? You're here, you're real. You're alive."

"Yes, Dara. I'm here. I'm alive." He curled his fingers in my hair in the exact way I remembered, and in that moment, I was no longer dead. His eyes blazed into mine and I lifted my hands to touch his sculptured face to make sure he *was* real. He seemed just as shocked to be holding me, as I was to be holding him.

"No. This is just another dream. It has to be. I'm going to wake up any moment, and you'll be gone."

"No, Dara. This is no dream. And I'm not going anywhere. I'm here to stay." But I couldn't believe it. I couldn't trust my own senses. *Oh God. Is this what losing one's mind feels like? I finally went over the edge.*

"How can I be sure that you're real?"

He held my face in his hands, "My Dara, my *motek*." He kissed me, his warm, sweet breath meshing with mine, literally taking my breath away as I felt myself crumble into unconsciousness.

"Dara, Dara, open your eyes." I heard Roni's voice through my dazed state. "Don't be afraid." But I was afraid – afraid to awaken from my dream – afraid to lose Roni yet again – afraid to open my eyes to the emptiness of my life – afraid of more pain.

"I promise you, Dara, I will never leave you again. Never."

"This isn't a dream?" I asked with my eyes still closed.

"No, *motek*."

I opened my eyes to find Roni kneeling beside me – his beautiful, sparkling eyes dazzling into mine. He had carried me to one of the couches in the hotel lobby and a circle of curious onlookers gathered around. The woman from behind the front desk handed me a glass of orange juice. "Don't be embarrassed," she whispered in my ear. "Any woman would faint to be kissed by him." I knew then that I wasn't dreaming. I allowed myself to gaze upon Roni. He was just as beautiful as I remembered him. His features, though, were hardened, and there were lines around his eyes I did not remember. I imagined he must have suffered a great deal before he was able to free himself from whatever hell he had endured.

"Roni?"

"Yes, *motek*," he helped me to a sitting position and the small crowd began to dissipate.

"I have so many questions."

"I know."

"Can we go somewhere to talk?"

"Of course. Drink a little more juice and then we'll go. Can't have you fainting in my arms again." His smile was too good to be real.

We walked toward the beach, our eyes fixed on each other in amazement as the rolling waves whipped in the background in a soft rhythm. It reminded me of our last days together at the Kinneret. We had no trouble finding a quiet spot to sit, as it was nearly sunset and most of the hotel guests were packing up to get ready for dinner.

We sat on the sand and Roni spoke first. "Forgive me, Dara. I know you have a great deal of questions to ask me, but…I just can't help but stare at you." He brushed the back of his hand against my cheek. "I never thought I would see you again. You're more beautiful than the day I met you…if that's even possible." He paused and took my hand in his. "I…I know what you've been through. I know how much you've suffered – how much you've lost. I wish to God that I could remove your pain. I'm so sorry I wasn't there for you."

"Roni…it seems we've both been through a lot these sixteen years. You have nothing to apologize for."

"You may feel differently after you hear what I have to say." His eyes washed over my face. "But I need you to know that what I did, I did out of love for you."

"W-what do you mean? What did you do?"

"I realize you must be assuming that since I'm alive, I must have been missing in action till now…taken prisoner…or something to that effect."

"Well, yes. I mean, that's the only logical explanation. Isn't it?"

"I wasn't missing in action, Dara…nor was I taken prisoner. I was…on a…long-term…mission."

"I don't understand. Your unit handled short-term operations – one, two, three weeks at the most."

"That was true. That is, up until my commanding officer assigned me to a mission coordinated together by Special Ops and the Mossad. I refused it…at first. I recognized instantly what the operation entailed – requiring years to reach the position they needed me to reach in order to be effective. I didn't want any part of it. I didn't want to lose you. And I knew that accepting that mission meant at least ten or fifteen years out of the country, and…out of touch with you."

"But you did go," I breathed, horrified at what he was leading up to.

"Yes. I had to, Dara. They had no one else who was qualified enough to handle the job. It was crucial for Israel to carry out that mission, and it was something that I was specifically trained for…in every way. In the end…I couldn't refuse to go. There was just too much at stake."

I felt the blood drain out of my head. Not because Roni stepped up to take on the mission – not because it was long-term. I knew Roni. I could have told him – before he even knew – that he would shoulder the burden and sacrifice himself for Israel and for his people. That was who he was. That was who I fell in love with. Only, in that instant, I grasped what he was about to tell me and I couldn't bear to hear it, I couldn't bear to imagine that he would... *Oh God!* I staggered to my feet, feeling the wind knocked out of me, and backed away from him.

"Dara." Roni got up and moved toward me.

"You...you...had Dalya write me that you were dead! That you were killed in action!"

"I had to."

"You...had...to?"

"I wasn't going to destroy your life, Dara. I saw what it did to my sister, and I couldn't do that to you."

"Your sister? Dalya? W-what are you talking about?"

"Do you remember wondering why Dalya was always so sad? Why you never got to meet her husband?"

I nodded, still confused. Roni inched closer to me, grasping my arms in each of his hands as he stared into my eyes, willing me to understand what he could not say outright. "Dalya's husband was rarely home. She would only get to see him a mere few weeks out of the year. She was lonely and miserable. It changed her entirely. It turned her into a bitter woman. I wasn't going to do that to you. And with me, it would have been worse. We wouldn't have been able to see each other at all...not until the mission was completed, and it was impossible to predict when that would be. I wouldn't rob you of the best years of your life."

"I would have waited for you, no matter how long it took."

"I knew that. That's why I had to let you think I was dead. I wanted you to have a chance at a happy life."

"It wasn't your decision to make!" I cried out, traumatized by his confession.

"I wasn't going to destroy your life, Dara!"

"It wasn't your decision to make," I repeated, bursting into tears – sobbing. "How could you do such a thing? And your family was all behind it? Your parents?"

"They didn't like it, although they understood it would be better for you. Please, Dara, try to understand, I only did it because I loved you so much. I was away for sixteen years! I couldn't curse you to a life filled with pain and longing."

At that, I began to laugh in a mad hysteria as the tears streamed down my face. I pushed his hands from me and took another step back from him. "You didn't want to give me a life filled with pain? That's all my life has been! You thought you would shield me from it? You played God with my life – you played God with my heart, and you had no right!"

"Dara, it would have been nothing less than selfish to keep you chained to me. It would have been cruel. I knew the only way to get you to go on with your life was to have you think I was dead. And... the truth was...that without you...I *was* dead. The only thing that kept me going was the hope that one day you would find some happiness."

"You were my life, Roni. *You* were my happiness."

"And you were mine. That never stopped. You hold my heart, Dara."

"You held mine. And you crushed it."

"Believe me, that wasn't what I wanted. But it was the only way for you to forget about me."

"Forget about you? How could you think that I could ever forget about you?" I wailed through my tears.

"Dara, it was the only way for you to be able to meet someone else. And you did. You married Uri. As much as it hurt for me not to be the one to share your life, I was glad you did marry him. Yaniv told…"

"Yaniv? Oh, my God! Of course. He knew! He knew all along that you were alive."

"Outside of my family, he was the only one. He didn't agree with my decision, but he did agree to respect it."

"Jenny kept this from me?"

"No, Yaniv never told her. Please don't be upset with him. He loves you like his own sister."

I fell to my knees, the weight of the truth too heavy to come to terms with. Roni knelt down to me, "Listen to me, Dara. Giving you up was the hardest thing I ever had to do in my life. Still, I was grateful that you and Uri found each other. He was good to you. You had a family. You were happy. That's all I wanted for you. Had it not been for Mace Devlin…"

"H-how do you know about…?"

"I know about it all. I know…everything," he admitted.

"Of course you do," I said, exhausted from the intense emotions that swept through me. "Dov Regev," I whispered to myself. "You were…*the…man…in…Germany*, weren't you?"

"Dara…I…"

"No. No, Roni. There's nothing more you can say. Because there was one thing you *didn't* know. I never could truly believe that you were dead. I even went to see your mother, days before my wedding, to find out the truth about what happened to you – to see if there was some validity to my suspicions, to some kind of gut feeling that you were still alive, somewhere, somehow, before I committed myself to Uri. Only… she kept your secret for you. Your horrible secret. Still, as much as I loved Uri, you remained alive in my heart. Uri knew it as well. But yes, Roni, you were right about one thing – the only thing. Uri *was* good to me. He loved me and was able to look past it. He accepted it. He understood what you did not – how deep my love was for you."

"You're wrong, Dara. I did what I did precisely because I understood how deep your love was for me."

I bowed my head and in between my sobs I cried out, anger coloring my tone so that I no longer recognized my own voice. "Well, the bottom line is…Uri was a better person than I – because I *can't* accept what you did. I'm not that *motek*, that *sweet Dara* you knew sixteen years ago."

"Dara, no matter what, no matter where you are, no matter what you do, you will always be my sweet Dara." Roni grabbed me and tried to soothe me – enveloping me in his arms, but I could not be soothed. I shook my head no and once more broke down sobbing, pounding my fists against his chest in anger and in frustration. He remained in place, taking it, his eyes glazing over with tears – something I never thought I would see. Though seeing his pain did not stop me from lashing out at him further.

"That *sweet* Dara is dead! You killed her when you killed yourself. You wanted to keep me from becoming bitter? You wanted to prevent me from getting hurt? Well, guess what, Roni. You failed!" And then I saw his own tears escape from his eyes – crystals of agony trailing down his etched features. I imagined how my words must have pierced him like a dagger. I immediately wanted to comfort him, but something stopped me. It was as if an invisible glass wall stood between us – impenetrable. I couldn't let go of my anger or the sting of my own deep pain.

"Forgive me, Dara. Forgive me," I heard him murmur through my wailing. He held my face in his hands, gently wiping my tears away with his thumbs, paying no mind to his own. I almost succumbed to his soothing voice and to his tender touch. *Almost.*

I tore away from him and ran back to the hotel.

Chapter 47

I returned to my room broken. How much loss and how much betrayal can one person endure? And yet, ridding myself of the last vision I had of Roni at the beach was hopeless – the agony in his eyes, impossible to get out of my mind. In addition to my own pain, I ached for his. I grabbed a cigarette and went out to the terrace to light it.

The sun had just set, and the sky was bright red. In my depressed state, it looked like the entire horizon was bleeding. And then, I noticed him. Roni was still at the beach, where I had left him, gazing out at the sea. I wanted to run back to him, to hold him, to be held by him, but I couldn't let go of the hurt. I couldn't find the strength to forgive. It was too raw. I must have stood there watching him for hours, until he finally lifted himself from the sand and walked slowly back to the hotel.

There would be no sleep for me tonight as I lay awake in bed trying to understand why he had done what he had done. I was shattered, beyond repair.

The next morning I decided to check out of the hotel early. There was no point in staying. I couldn't even recall the reason why I had decided to come here. But going home didn't seem like the answer. I didn't know where I belonged anymore. With no plan of action, I drove around aimlessly for hours until I found myself following the road to Beit She'an, the valley at the foot of the Gilboa Mountains.

It was already getting late in the day, and I realized I had not yet eaten. I stopped at a falafel place on the side of the road and tried to figure out my next move. I thought about how I had not once visited the kibbutz on Gilboa since I had stayed there all those years ago, and the notion of returning there now seemed more palatable. It seemed… to make sense. *Why not?* I would return to work the land, even if just for a short time – to do something useful – to give of myself instead of wallowing in despair. Yes. I would return to Gilboa.

I drove home with my new game plan in mind and wondered if the kibbutz had changed much in sixteen years. After a long two-hour drive, I finally reached Sde Dovid, but on impulse, passed my street and drove my car up the road toward Jenny and Yaniv's house.

Her children's voices were perceptible through the front door. She had four now, her baby son crying amidst the din of his siblings. The cry of life. I remembered that once my home, too, embraced the cry of life before becoming a den of death. I shook the morbid thoughts from my head before ringing the doorbell. *What a pitiable person I had become.*

"Dara!" Jenny opened the door, a bright yet cautious smile on her face. I entered her home without a word and saw Lavi and Ari sitting in the living room with Yaniv, their eyes darting up to me in surprise. "Dara!" they called out in choir form. Mikki and Adina zipped out of the kitchen. "We heard what happened with you and Roni," Jenny said awkwardly. "He came by earlier."

"I trust you all had a pleasant reunion." My sarcasm was evident and the response was an uneasy silence. My gaze flitted from one to the other and finally rested on Jenny. "You didn't know?"

"No, Dara. I …"

"If you're going to be angry at anyone," Yaniv broke in and moved toward me, "be angry at me. I kept the secret from you, from Jenny, from everyone."

"Why, Yaniv? Why?"

"I gave him my word. You know that Roni is like a brother to me. I couldn't do otherwise."

I turned to leave. *What did it matter anyway?* I thought. Nothing mattered.

Apparently, however, it mattered to Yaniv. "Look, Dara, he did what he did with the best of intentions. The only thing that motivated Roni was his love for you. I had to respect his wishes. And at the time, if you recall, none of us knew what you were going through in America. You didn't tell anyone about your parents and Mace until after you returned to Israel. And by then, Roni was long gone and you had already received Dalya's letter."

"What are you saying?"

"I'm not all that sure Roni would have gone through with the charade had he known that you had just lost both your parents. He didn't find out about that until much later. But, in any case, Dara, *you know* Roni. There is no one less selfish than he is. He would sacrifice his own life…but he wasn't going to ruin yours."

"Dara," Jenny added, "you both have been through hell. It's time to end it."

Does hell have an end? On some level, I found it somewhat amusing that Jenny would assume that my hell reached bottom. Hell was as constant as my shadow. It followed me wherever I went. It was my trusted companion. I moved toward the door to leave. "Wait! What are you going to do now?" Jenny asked.

"I...I was thinking of returning to Gilboa, to the kibbutz – for a short while, at least."

A curious smile brightened Jenny's face.

"Did I say something funny?"

"No, of course not. I'm just glad you won't be barricading yourself inside your home. Spending time on the kibbutz sounds like a good idea for you."

I glanced at Ari and Adina, who had just recently moved to Sde Dovid from Gilboa. "Is Moti still in charge of the work detail?"

"Yes, he is. You know what, Dara?" Ari offered. "Let me give him a call for you, and I'll set it all up – one less thing for you to think about."

Feeling emotionally spent, I nodded. "Thank you. That would be helpful."

"In fact," Ari took out his cell phone from his pocket, "I'll call him right now." He stood up. "Uh...bad reception here," and stepped out to the terrace.

With the onset of April, I returned as a volunteer to the kibbutz. Many of the old faces were still there, while there were a number of new members and volunteers as well. My first day of work brought me back to the cotton fields. Though it had been sixteen years since I had done any field work, I was confident I could handle it. Thanks to Uri, I had kept myself in shape. Our home gym had state-of-the-art equipment, and I worked out regularly in addition to running five miles every night.

Moti met me outside the dining hall and drove me down to the *radrah*, where we had a chance to catch up on each other's lives. I didn't need to tell him much about mine, since the murder of my family had been plastered all over the papers. The terrorist war was raging throughout Israel, and there were many casualties among the civilian population. Terrorist infiltrations, homicidal bombers and shooting at cars on the highways throughout Israel were constantly making the news.

"For the most part, things have been relatively peaceful in this area," Moti said. "But we must always be vigilant. Jenin is nearby and it's a hotbed of terrorism, and unfortunately, the orchards are easy targets."

"I agree. We can never let our guard down."

"I noticed you're armed."

"It was my late husband's gun. I don't go anywhere without it now."

"You're comfortable with it?"

"Yes. Uri made sure that I knew how to use it. In the Judean Hills, one strongly feels the impact of the terrorist war." *Now there's an understatement.* I changed the subject and asked him about his children. It wasn't too long before we reached the *radrah* and Moti informed me that I'd be working on the irrigation system for the cotton fields. "You remember how it's done, don't you?"

"I'm sure it'll all come back to me. Are there many volunteers these days?"

"A few. It's not like the old days. Wait here, Dara. I'll go check if the truck is ready with all the equipment."

I leaned against the jeep, taking in the view of the sprawling fields. It felt good to be back here. I was looking forward to working in the fields and to the tranquillity it provided, when suddenly I heard a not-too-unfamiliar outburst coming out of the *radrah.*

"Are you kidding me? What is *she* doing here? Forget it, Moti, I might as well just work the fields alone."

My God! What was *he* doing here?

"Roni, she knows what to do just as well as you do. Now, suck it up and don't give me hassles!" Moti then called out to me. "Dara, go with Roni to the truck. It's all loaded up."

Roni stormed out of the *radrah* and without giving me so much as a fleeting look, he walked several paces ahead of me, his anger oozing out of every pore of his body. He jumped into the cab of the truck and slammed his door shut. *For God's sake, he was thirty-eight years old! Don't men ever grow up? It was 1983 all over again.* I climbed in on my side and thought it best to clarify that I was not hounding him. "I hope you don't think that I followed you here, because that's not the case at all."

He clenched his jaw without saying a word. We drove in silence to the cotton fields.

More than running into him on the kibbutz, his anger took me completely by surprise. I had often heard the cliché that there's a fine line between love and hate, though I never truly comprehended it – until now. It seemed that every muscle in his body tensed with loathing. I tried to see things through his eyes. There was never a question in my mind that whatever he did, he did from his heart – either for me or for our people – never for himself. Yet, I couldn't get past him having me think he was dead, though I knew it was done out of selflessness. All he wanted was for me to be happy, while he, himself, sacrificed sixteen years living a wretched, lonely existence – putting his life on the line as a Mossad agent in Germany. No doubt, he was disappointed and thoroughly disillusioned with me. He must have thought that I was entirely self-absorbed. And I was – entirely absorbed in my own pain and my own anger.

Not once did he glance at me throughout the ride to the fields. He acknowledged my presence only with a cold and stony demeanor. But why should I have expected more than that after I had rejected him, refusing to forgive him? I had thought that he would attempt to contact me again after our first encounter at the hotel – give me time to digest all that he told me. He never did, though. Now I knew why. Roni detested me.

We reached the cotton fields and Roni jumped out of the truck, walked toward the back and began unloading the pipes and the rest of the supplies that we would need. I went over to help.

"What are you doing?" He didn't bother to hide his annoyance.

"What do you *think* I'm doing?"

"I got this, Dara. You just chill."

"You chill," I answered and continued unloading the pipes.

He clenched his jaws again as his eyes gave me the once-over. "You're packing a pistol?"

"It's a 9-millimeter Glock."

"I know what it is, Dara," he smirked. "Why the hell do you have it?"

"I suspect for the same reason you have yours."

He laughed arrogantly under his breath as he continued to unload the pipes. "Like you would use it," he mumbled.

"If I had to, I would."

"Still trying to be so tough!"

"And you're still an arrogant boor!"

We stood in place facing one another, staring each other down. Roni spoke first, not flinching from his stance. "Do you need me to explain how to put the system together, or do you remember?"

Damn! I didn't remember where all the parts went! "If it's not too much trouble, a quick explanation would suffice," I said as haughtily as I could. His eyes unexpectedly softened and he slowly went over the procedure, patiently explaining how to put together all the different parts. But his manner remained formal. "Any questions, Dara?"

"No…I got it."

"Then, let's get to work." And so we did – moving up and down the rows of the cotton field, carrying out our task in utter silence.

We continued in this fashion for the next several days until we finished covering three fields. There were too many moments where I just wanted to run into his arms, too many moments where I wanted him to reach out to me and hold me in his strong embrace. Only, something always stopped me – my own stubbornness, I supposed. And Roni was altogether aloof. On one occasion, I had come very close to breaking through the wall I had built, only to look into his eyes and see…nothing.

On the final afternoon at the cotton fields, the truck wouldn't start when it was time to return to the *radrah* and catch the ride back to the kibbutz. "That's strange," Roni murmured to himself and got out to check under the hood. I followed him out of the truck and looked on as he checked the engine.

"Lose your touch, Roni?" He ignored me and took out his cell phone to place a call. "Moti, the engine on my truck is dead. Someone messed with it while I was in the fields. What's going on here?" He furrowed his brows at whatever Moti was telling him. "I know engines, Moti. Someone went into the panel and deliberately blew out the ignition fuse…. Look, just get another ride for Dara and me…. What do you mean everyone left the *radrah*? It's only one o'clock…. Did you not notice that Dara and I weren't back yet?... What? How long?... You can't be serious, Moti.... She won't be able to handle that."

"What won't I be able to handle?" I piped in.

Once again, he ignored my question and continued talking on the cell phone. "Look, Moti, she put in an eight-hour day from four thirty this morning. She's tired – it's hot as hell out here – she'll never make it back to the *radrah* on foot – you're talking about twelve kilometers with the sun at its peak…. Yes, there's still water in the jerry can, but… What kind of sick game are you playing, Moti?…

"Great, *sababa*! Yeah, later." He shut the phone, blowing out heavily in frustration.

"What's going on?" I asked.

"We'll have to walk back to the *radrah*," he answered as he went to the back of the truck to retrieve the jerry can. He poured some water into a cup. "Here, Dara, you'll need to drink."

"I don't understand. Why can't Moti just send someone for us?"

"Because he mysteriously can't get hold of another driver, and he himself is *unavailable* for the next few hours. Now, please, just drink."

I drank the water, and he then poured me another cup. "Drink some more."

I did as he asked, and after drinking a cup of water himself, he strapped the jerry can to his back. "Come on. Let's start walking."

"Roni, you can't walk twelve kilometers in this heat carrying that heavy jerry can."

His lips curled into an arrogant smirk. "Let's go, Dara."

After hiking for what must have been at least an hour beneath the Beit She'an sun, my feet began to drag. Roni periodically stopped to have me drink. I prided myself at being fit, but having been up since before dawn, and putting in a full day of physical labor in the fields, I was wiped. Even though Roni slowed his pace for me, I had a difficult time keeping up. Each step I took was a great effort, and I had to concentrate extra hard on not tripping over the small stones that lined the dirt road. They appeared to be jumping out at me while everything else around me began to look fuzzy. *Was I no longer walking straight?* Roni put his arm around my waist in an attempt to steady me. "Stop here, Dara."

"But we just stopped a few minutes ago. We should keep going." I thought I heard my speech slur. He brought me to a sitting position on a large stone by the side of the road. "Don't argue with me." He crouched down to me, removed the jerry can once more from his back, poured water into the cup and poured it over my hair. He repeated this again and again, gently splashing water on my face and, after hesitating for a moment, he poured water down the front and back of my T-shirt. "I have to get you out of the sun, Dara, before you succumb to heatstroke. You're not perspiring and your body is overheating." I thought I detected some kind of emotion in his eyes, but I couldn't be sure, since I was no longer seeing too clearly. "Come, Dara, we have to keep moving." There was an apologetic tone to his voice. I wasn't hallucinating. *At least he didn't hate me that much to want me dead.*

He helped me to my feet and wrapped his arm securely around my waist, pretty much carrying me the rest of the way. I looked up to his face. His eyes focused straight ahead and the sweat poured down his chiseled features. Roni was still quite the Nordic god. His golden hair had grown out since I last saw him, and the curls were taking shape. I lifted my hand to his face and wiped away his sweat. He looked back at me with his crystal-like gaze and I felt that once-familiar tingle down my spine. Maybe I was wrong. Maybe, I ventured, he didn't hate me after all. *My Roni.* It was so surreal seeing him again. It was wonderful and it was painful all at once.

"We're almost at the *radrah*, Dara," he reassured me.

"How long have we been walking?" I asked weakly.

"About three hours."

"I'm sorry."

"For what?"

"If not for me, you would have reached the *radrah* long ago."

"I'm fine, Dara. It's you I'm worried about."

You are? "I'll be fine. Like you said, we're almost at the *radrah*." I tried to smile, but I had an odd loss of control over my face. I imagined my head floating away. He tightened his grip around my waist. "Remind me to kill Moti when I see him," he said only half jokingly.

"Why would he do this to us?"

Roni narrowed his eyes at me in thought. "Did you happen to mention to any of our friends about your plans to volunteer on the kibbutz?"

"Yes. Ari called Moti to arrange things for me."

"I see."

"What do you see?"

"Ari knew I was at Gilboa. They all knew. They didn't tell you I was here?"

"No, they didn't." I at once recalled the strange smile on Jenny's face when I told her of my plans to return to Gilboa.

"I suppose they meant well. Still, Moti is a fool. Some things never change," Roni noted under his breath. "Well, there it is, Dara. Just up ahead. We'll be there shortly."

Completely exhausted at this point, I could barely keep my eyes open.

"Dara?"

"Nnhmm."

Roni raised my arms, placing my hands around his neck. "Hold on to me, Dara." He lifted my limp body in his arms and carried me the rest of the way.

Once inside the *radrah*, he sat me down on a chair by a table and had me drink more water. Feeling queasy, I bent over, heaving up what I just drank. He held me, wiping my face down with cold water. Again, he gently poured water over my hair and down my T-shirt. Our eyes met, and for a moment I caught the tenderness in his that I had long ago committed to memory. He furrowed his brows, remembering himself, and quickly averted his gaze and muttered, "You need some sugar. I'll go into the kitchen and find something for you."

Several minutes passed and Roni came back with a pitcher of orange juice, a bowl of fruit, pita and hummus. "Not much to choose from, but this should do it." He pulled up a chair next to me and filled my cup with juice. "Please, Dara, try to drink this." I sipped the juice slowly and managed to keep it down. "Are you feeling a little better now that you're out of the sun?"

I nodded faintly, though my head pounded.

"Hmm. I'll believe you when your eyes turn back to blue," he smiled lightly as he handed me a plum. "I'll tell Moti to take you off work detail tomorrow."

"That won't be necessary. I'll...be fine."

"Dara, we're in the middle of an unseasonable heat wave. It won't hurt for you to take a day off, especially after what Moti just put you through."

"Will you be taking the day off as well?"

"No, of course not."

"Well, then, why should I?"

He looked at me incredulously. "Because you have all the signs of heat exhaustion. You're dizzy, you can't walk a straight line, you're nauseous, your speech is slurred. You should be taking the next day off to rest and drink fluids to ward off dehydration. As for me, *I* am fine. *You* are not."

"If you can work, so can I."

"Are you actually going to compare yourself to me? Why do you always have to prove how tough you are?"

"Why do you always feel you need to protect me?"

"Why do you always have to be so stubborn? I'm just talking about taking one day off, Dara. You can go back to being the savior of the kibbutz movement one day later."

"I will make my own decisions!"

"Fine, Dara. Make your own decisions – because you're so damn good at it!"

"What is that supposed to mean?"

"I heard how you've been...coping – if you can call it that. You isolated yourself, broke off contact with all your friends and with Uri's family. You cut yourself off from the world and pronounced yourself dead, and...you won't let your dead rest. Look, Dara," he paused, shook his head in frustration as he looked to the ground and then flashed his eyes back to me. "I'm...worried about you."

"I don't need you to worry about me." My obstinacy took over once more.

"Too late, because I'll never stop worrying about you." His harsh tone didn't match his words. "You may despise me, but dammit, I'll always love you – and there's nothing you can do to change that," he spit out.

"And you show your love by letting me think you're dead?"

"I explained why I did that!"

"Well, it wasn't good enough!"

The muscles in his face and neck tensed as he took out a pack of cigarettes from his pocket and lit one, all the while staring me down with his eyes that looked like shards of ice against his bronzed skin. I could almost see him counting to ten in his head before deciding to speak to me again. "Bottom line, Dara, you had ten years of a loving marriage, ten years of beautiful children...ten years of bliss! That's more than many people on this earth ever have. Believe me – I know. What would you have had with me? I'm not minimizing your pain and your loss, but maybe – just maybe – instead of drowning yourself in death and bitterness, you can try to find some solace in the blessings that you did have in the last decade. I know damn well what God took from you, but do you know what He *gave* to you?"

I opened my mouth to respond, but Roni cut me off right away. "No, Dara, I'm not done. Had I not let you think I was dead, you would never have known the joy of giving birth to three babies, the joy of hearing their laughter, and the joy of tending to their cries. Nor would you have had the good fortune of being in a real, healthy and loving marriage. Yes, I know...it was short-lived. Much too short. But that was beyond anyone's control. The only thing under our control is how we weather the storm. If you want to continue the rest of your life in anger, I can't stop you. But that's not you, Dara. At least that's not the

Dara I know. And wallowing in anger doesn't make you tough. It just makes you sad. Sad and alone. Trust me…I know about that as well."

"How dare you tell me how I should feel!" I rose from my chair finding renewed strength, fueled by my rage. I went off in a tirade, not even fully realizing what I was saying, or if I was making any sense. I accused him of not knowing what true pain is – of not knowing what true love is – castigated him for choosing to abandon me to play cowboy in Germany. I was being irrational, but I couldn't stop myself from lashing out at him. Throughout my raving and ranting, inside I knew every word I had said was unjust. I was mad at myself really, and frustrated, and I took it all out on Roni. In the midst of it all, Roni stood up and walked back to the kitchen. "Don't you walk away from me when I'm yelling at you, Mr. Ben-Ari. I still have a lot more I need to say to…" He returned with a bucket of cold water and poured it over my head. I screamed at the shock of it.

"You need to cool off, woman." He tossed the empty bucket to the side.

"You…you… Unnhh! I hate you!"

He stood in place with his arms folded over his chest, his lips arching to one side in a taunting grin. "Mmm. I must say, how propitious it is that you're wearing a white T-shirt today."

"I hate you, Roni Ben-Ari. I will always hate you."

"I know, my sweet Dara, I know." His tone was gratingly patronizing. "Now, if you don't mind, I think I'll partake of a bit of pita and hummus before I hijack a jeep from here and drive us back to the kibbutz. I'm ravenous. Care to join me?"

I stood there drenched, dripping on the floor, wavering until I decided I, too, was hungry. Grudgingly, I sat back down, grabbed a pita and ate with him. He poured orange juice into a cup and handed it to me. "Drink."

Chapter 48

 I didn't work in the fields the next day – forced to admit that Roni was right, as I was indeed suffering from heat exhaustion. My alarm was set as usual to rise before dawn, but I was too weak to lift my head from my pillow. Roni had quietly entered my room before heading down to the *radrah*. He brought a pitcher of juice along with a plate filled with fresh fruit and breakfast Danishes from the kibbutz kitchen and placed them on my dresser. I pretended to be asleep. He crouched down beside me at the head of my bed and felt my forehead with his palm, and then tenderly stroked my face with the back of his hand. He then left as quietly as he came in.

The weeks turned into months, and Moti – most certainly at the behest of the gang back at Sde Dovid – was still attempting to play Cupid as he continued to assign us both to the same work detail. It was ridiculously obvious. Roni and I, however, kept our distance from one another – speaking to each other only when it was necessary. Although he had professed that he still loved me that day at the *radrah*, he didn't attempt to improve our cold-war state. It was completely frustrating – though I had no one to blame but myself. I was the one who put up the wall between us. I was the one who could not forgive him. The nights, when I didn't see him, were insufferably long. Roni was right. I was stubborn.

That was not the only thing he made me realize. One night I walked over to Roni's room and knocked on his door. "Come in," he called out calmly. He was sitting at his desk reading an Arab newspaper, and when he turned to see me enter his room, he masked his surprise expertly. *He was always good with that stuff.*

"I wanted to show you something," I said and moved toward him, handing him several photos. "These are pictures of my children." All at once, the mask Roni wore came off. "This one here, on top, was Gavriel. We called him Gavi. He had glistening black hair and… intelligent eyes…always deep in thought. He played the drums. He was very talented and…my oldest. It was his tenth birthday, when…" I began to choke up and fought the surge of tears straining to come out. My throat felt raw and I paused to swallow before I could find my voice again. "Well, sometimes…Gavi acted as if he were twenty…the way he would look after his younger sister and brother.

"And this one," I pointed to the next photo, "this was Matan. He was the spitting image of Uri and was very athletic…and…he had a wonderful sense of humor, like his father. He was always getting into some kind of trouble." I managed to chuckle feebly. My mind then drifted to what seemed like some long-ago memories. After a moment or so, I returned to the present, feeling Roni's gaze upon my face. "This photo is of my Ayala." An involuntary gasp prompted me to pause once more, pressing my lips together to regain control…to find my breath. "She was just five here – the last picture I ever took of her. An angel. So very, very sweet. Always friendly…always smiling. She was my little helper, and of course…her Abba's little girl." The soreness in my throat became more painful. I struggled with each breath, and the tears ultimately escaped silently down my cheeks. I wiped them away and continued. "They were all so very good-natured – each had a kind soul – like their father. This last photo is of Uri."

Roni looked down at all the pictures, and then slowly back to me, and I saw my agony swimming in his eyes. He rose from his chair and without a word, wrapped me in his arms. I felt him straining to catch his breath in an attempt to regain his composure, as we both clung to each other, my tears soaking his shirt. I lifted my head from Roni's chest, backing away slightly, and gazed up at him, his eyes floating in a pool of tears. "I should go now…I…just wanted to tell you…you were right, Roni. They *were* blessings." I swallowed again, and then let go of him. "*Laila tov*, good night. I'll…see you at work tomorrow."

"Dara," he managed in a hushed tone before I walked out the door.

"Yes?" I turned back to face him.

"Don't go."

"I…I…I can't." I ran from the room, back to mine.

Chapter 49

The comfort of the kibbutz routine welcomed another new dawn and I was at the *nadrah* the next day. I wasn't sure what mood to expect from Roni after last night.

"We'll be weeding today." He handed me working gloves as he guided me to a jeep, looking irritated. Even though I more than proved myself in handling strenuous field work, he still didn't like that I insisted on toiling at such arduous work – his reasoning, I was certain, motivated by his machismo mind-set. Secretly, however, I despised weeding. It was tedious and backbreaking work. When we reached the field, he insisted I drink from the jerry can. "But I'm not thirsty now. The sun has barely risen," I protested.

"You're right, Dara. The sun *has* barely risen and you're already arguing with me. Just do me one little favor this morning and humor me." He handed me a cup of water, and I drank it without another word.

During the course of the morning, we both proceeded up and down the fields pulling weeds, and as in the past, many of them were huge and deeply embedded in the ground. It was only a matter of time until I reached one impossible for me to budge. I dug my feet in, grabbed a firm hold and pulled with all my might, but to no avail. I sat on the ground, grabbing hold of the part nearest to the roots and persisted in my effort when I noticed Roni standing parallel to me in the next row, arms folded against his chest, watching me with an amused look on his face. "What is so funny?" I called out to him through clenched teeth.

"You," he answered simply. I decided to ignore him and focus on my stubborn bush weed. He moseyed over to me but didn't offer any assistance.

"Are you just going to stand there and gawk, or do you plan on helping me out?"

"I'm quite content gawking at you." He drew off his work gloves and crouched down next to me, skimming the back of his hands against my arms as I tugged firmly at the weed. *Great. So now he's teasing me.* "Roni, I'm trying to concentrate."

"Oh? Do I distract you?"

Yes, damn you. "No. Of course not."

"Your arms are very toned."

I made the mistake of turning toward him, catching his eyes floating over me. A rush of yearning for him pulsated through me. I tried to push those thoughts out of my head. "Are you going to help or not?"

With what I thought was a devious look on his face, he positioned himself behind me, draping his hands around my arms and slowly gliding them down toward my hands. "Mmm. You always did have such soft skin...like velvet. Remember how I would tell you that?"

"Um...yes."

"And your hair," he brushed his lips against it, "is like a long, delicate scarf of raven silk."

"Roni…"

"Yes?"

"Nothing."

He uncurled my hands from their grip around the trunk of the bush, replacing them with his, gave two swift tugs, and successfully yanked the weed from the ground. His hands gingerly inched back up my arms, caressing them tenderly. I closed my eyes, forgetting myself, leaning back into his chest, as he squeezed my arms in a tighter hold.

"Dara?"

"Yes?"

He curved me around to face him, our eyes locking into each other's. "We should finish the field."

"Right. We should…finish."

He let go of me, stood up and started walking back to his row. "Oh, Dara," he stopped and turned to face me once more.

"Yes?"

His face broke into a self-assured grin. "You're still hot for me." He put his gloves back on his hands, and meandered back toward his part of the field.

"Roni Ben-Ari, you are…"

"Right," he called over his shoulder.

"If you were the last man on earth, I wouldn't let you touch me!"

"You didn't have any trouble with it a moment ago."

"You're…despicable! I don't know how I ever let myself fall in love with you. I must have been insane!"

"You were," he whirled around to face me again, "and still are. Insanely in love with me, that is."

"You are *so* wrong! Your arrogance has made you delusional. You…" All of a sudden, Roni jumped over to me, pushing me to the ground. "Shhh, Dara, did you hear that?" he whispered.

"What?" I struggled to get up.

"Stay down!" he covered me with his body.

I then heard it – gunshots. There was no mistake about it. "It's coming from the orchards just beyond our field," Roni murmured. At that moment, his pocket two-way radio went wild with messages screaming about the situation at the orchards. Arab infiltrators, at least four of them, were holding our workers at bay with gunfire. Only one of our men was armed. Roni looked at me. "I can't leave you alone here but I must get over there. Run with me to the jeep, Dara. You'll drop me off near the gate and then I want you to continue to the kibbutz immediately."

"I'm staying with you," I said as we jumped into the jeep. "I have a gun, I can…"

"Are you crazy?"

"I can help!"

"Forget it, Dara. No way! Start driving!"

As soon as we neared the orchards, Roni turned to me. "Go straight to the kibbutz, Dara! Don't do anything stupid!" I slowed the jeep and Roni jumped out before I could come to a full stop.

Dvir, another kibbutz member, met Roni at the gate and handed him an M16, and they both disappeared into the foliage. They followed the path according to the coordinates received over the two-way radio.

The scene was utter chaos. Volunteer workers, most of them female teenagers, were shrieking in panic as the bullets were flying, ricocheting off the trees and the metal ladders, making it difficult to ascertain from which direction the enemy was shooting. It was déjà vu, only this time there were more than two terrorists involved.

There were now three armed Israelis, and as the moments passed, Roni and the other two members were hitting their targets. "Three down," Roni calculated.

"Crap!" One by the name of Adiel shouted and fell back from the force of a bullet that ripped through his arm. It struck me how easily it could have been Roni, and my heart pounded with the sheer terror of it. I saw Roni turn swiftly, shooting into the trees on his left, ending the barrage from that direction. "That's four.... Adiel!" he called out.

"It's okay, Roni. It's just my arm." Taking advantage of the lull, Dvir ran over to Adiel and began administering first aid.

"Dvir, cover my back!" Roni proceeded to check for further infiltrators. I heard the sound of a fresh magazine loaded into a gun. Roni rolled to his back, shooting upward to a position high atop the branches. The terrorist fell to the ground, dead. "That's five," he counted.

From my spot of cover, I watched as Roni made his way over the dirt road toward the next row of trees. He moved agilely, gracefully, as if in a dance. A quick flash of the sun's reflection caught my eye. It hit an object hidden behind the thick branches of one tree just several yards from my position. Focusing harder, I strained to discern the hidden silhouette. The breath caught in my throat as I witnessed an Arab taking aim at Roni's back. The sun once again flashed off his wristwatch, disclosing his position. There was no thinking, no deliberating. I aimed my own gun and took the shot. Roni spun around to see the Arab tumble out from his hiding place into the dirt – blood oozing from his head – and then he saw me, gun in hand, still frozen in the shooting position. He rushed over to me, took the gun out of my trembling hands, put it on safety, and returned it to my holster. Just then, reinforcements arrived on the scene and began combing through the orchard. Pulling me to a safer position behind a thicker tree, he stared at me with astonishment and lifted his hand to my face in a tender caress. "You're crazy, you know that?" he said softly.

"I thought I was going to lose you again," I cried.

"But you didn't," he said soothingly, stroking my hair. "You saved my life, Dara."

"I can't lose you again! I can't!" My body was wracked with sobs, and I threw myself at him, clutching onto him for dear life. "I can't lose you again!"

"Shh, Dara, it's okay, it's okay." He clasped me in a tight embrace. "You won't lose me, Dara. I'm never letting you go. Never."

"I can't take any more losses." I clung to him. "Promise me, Roni. Promise me."

"Dara," he took hold of my arms, "look at me, Dara! Look at me!" I lifted my head from his chest and his eyes blazed into mine. He marked each word with a burning intensity, "I promise. I will *never* let you go."

"Good! Because I'm not *letting* you let me go."

"Good. Because there's nowhere else I would want to be." He pulled me closer to him, kissing me with an urgency as we adhered fiercely to each other. We clung to one another until our hearts beat as one, and our frenzied coming together ensued into calmness. For a time we stood quietly holding on to each other, staring into each other's eyes, recognizing the long and painful journey that led us to this moment. The edge to his features softened as he tenderly brushed the back of his hand against my cheek. "Dara," he whispered.

"Yes, Roni?"

"You're one hell of a shot." His crystal eyes creased in a glorious smile.

⚜

Later that day, I came out of the shower and found Roni waiting in my room, sitting on my bed. He extended his hand to me and I moved toward him, placing my hand in his, and sat beside him. "What is it, Roni?"

"I'm not sure how to say this, so, please, just try to bear with me, okay?"

I nodded. He took in a deep breath and exhaled loudly. "When I was in Germany and heard from Yaniv that you were engaged to be married to Uri...I...well...part of me felt like I had the wind knocked out of me. On one hand, I was devastated, and yet...another part of me, felt...relieved – thankful – that you were able to love again, finally getting the happiness that you deserved. It was all I wanted for you. It pained me to know that you were mourning over me for so long. So... even though I didn't know Uri personally...I was grateful to him – for giving you the joy that *I* couldn't give you. On some level, I felt close to him...almost like a brother. I felt...indebted to him, because he was taking care of the love of my life."

He paused for a moment before continuing. "Yaniv told me how good Uri was to you...how deeply he loved you. I want you to understand, Dara, that the one thing that kept me going was knowing that you were surrounded by...a band of angels...Uri, Gavi, Matan and Ayala – all of them...shielding you with their love." He stopped to wipe away the tears that rolled down my cheeks. "I..." he trailed off, looking down and crinkling his brow, struggling to find the right words. "I will always be grateful to your family. I will always love them for taking care of you, for loving you – for giving you joy. And I promise you this, Dara. I won't let Uri and your children down. I won't let you down. I will use every moment of my life to deserve your love for me. I love you, Dara. That never stopped. Not for a moment." He reached behind him and handed me a freshly picked Gilboa Iris. "As is the Gilboa Iris, you are light, you are perfection, you are life...my life."

I bowed my head on Roni's shoulder, and he held me as I cried – tears for all I had lost, tears for all I had found, and I lifted my eyes to his and traced my hand over his face, smiling at him through tears of triumph, for life goes on.

One Year Later, Spring 2002

I never returned to my job at the *Jerusalem Post*. Roni had encouraged me to do something positive in memory of Gavi, Matan, Ayala and Uri. He reminded me how it was once a dream of mine to have a house filled with children playing all sorts of different musical instruments and motivated me to turn the home that Uri and I shared into a music therapy center for children. It felt right – the perfect answer to the Arab terror that felled my family – building something positive in the wake of evil, and I dedicated my time to its success. True to his nature, Roni insisted we live in Sde Dovid so that I could be near the center, even though this meant a very long commute for him back and forth to work. Roni had decided to return to the Mossad – not as a field agent but rather as a coach for operatives, in addition to serving as the chief expert on Arabic documents.

Not that we needed any convincing to cherish what we had with each other, but with the bombing of the World Trade Center last September, it brought a sense of how fragile and vulnerable the entire world was. Roni said that 9/11 was just the tip of the iceberg of global jihad. That it was not just a matter of a few fringe extremist elements seeking global domination. "It's in full gear now," he said, "an offensive war waged by radical Muslims against all non-Muslims to convert them to Islam – and to impose Shariah law." Israelis were no stranger to Arab terror. But now, the rules of the game had changed for the world at large. We were on the precipice of something huge – too ominous to fathom, and too colossal to control by mere human endeavors. It frightened me.

I very much needed to find that tiny ray of hope that somehow passes from one generation to the next, radiating the spirit to persevere, defy the odds and dare to flourish. I needed it now – more than ever. I needed it for Roni. I needed it for us.

One evening after dinner, I stood out on the balcony of our bedroom, when Roni came out to join me. "There you are. Are you trying to hide from me?"

"Never," I leaned back into him as he wrapped his arms around me, his hands cradling the new life inside of me.

The night was warm and serene and our breathing was in sync with one another as we stared up at the stars. "You seem deep in thought, Dara," Roni observed. As always, Roni was tuned in to my mood. "I thought I was the brooder between us," he added lightheartedly.

I tried to change the subject – I knew he had an important meeting in Jerusalem tomorrow with Dov at the Prime Minister's Office, and I didn't want him to worry about my state of mind. "Perhaps we could meet in Jerusalem after your meeting, and go out for an early dinner?" I offered. "I'm sure I'll be done with my doctor's appointment by the time you finish."

"That sounds like a good idea. But I really hate missing going to the doctor with you."

"You've been to every appointment so far," I laughed lightly. "Dov will have a conniption if you don't show up for that meeting."

"It's worth it just to see him go ballistic," Roni chuckled.

"Hmm. Seeing Dov go ballistic – that would be entertaining," I smiled. "Anyway, it's just a routine visit."

"All right, Dara," he kissed me gently on my cheek and returned his attention back to the energetic life growing inside of me.

Jerusalem

My fingers shook as I fumbled for Roni's number on speed dial. "Roni?"

"Perfect timing, Dara – just got out of the meeting. How did the doctor's appointment go?"

"I need you to come with me to the Mount of Olives before we go out to dinner."

"The Mount of Olives? What's this all about, Dara? Is everything okay?"

"Yes, I just need to go to the Mount of Olives."

"Dara…what's wrong? You sound…"

"Just trust me."

"I do, but…"

"Please, Roni."

"Okay, Dara. Stay where you are – I'll pick you up in a few minutes."

The Mount of Olives

"Do you believe there is still hope, Roni?" I asked as I looked out on the Jerusalem hills from the Mount of Olives.

Roni turned me around to face him, narrowing his eyes at me. "What happened at the doctor's office, Dara?"

"Roni, I'm fine – the…baby…is fine. I promise. Just, please tell me, do you believe there is still hope?"

"Then I take it you mean, hope for civilization?" Roni asked, obviously confused by my behavior.

I nodded.

"There's always hope, Dara," he answered softly, "down to the final human breath."

"You sound so sure."

"Ironically, I learned that on the battlefield. Hope thrives in the trenches."

I thought about that for a moment. "I want to hope. Although…I can't help but feel frightened. Everything seems to be…insurmountable. Even in the face of global terror, the world refuses to recognize radical Islam for what it is."

"Is *that* what you're worried about? Dara, it's not surprising, you know that," Roni said almost flippantly. "It's much easier to target us. They fear offending the offenders. But," his manner then turned more serious, "it will come with a heavy price – much heavier than 9/11."

"Then, where is there room for hope when we have to fight the entire world?"

"I suppose that's where our faith comes in," Roni said simply.

I didn't expect that kind of answer from him. I looked at him curiously, his golden curls blowing carefree in the wind – an image so contrary to his serious posture. He smiled at me, knowing what I was thinking. "I never lost my faith, Dara. I was angry with God…for a long time, but that didn't diminish my belief in Him."

"I haven't lost faith, Roni. Still…I don't know if I believe in miracles, and that's exactly what we'll need."

"Look, Dara, I'm not saying that God is going to save Jerusalem for us in one swooping miracle. I believe that there's a partnership between man and God. We have to do our part to protect our land and our people."

"I'm so scared of what's brewing."

"My tough Dara? Scared?" he said with a smile.

"Maybe…I'm not so tough after all."

"Now, now…I won't have you talking about my wife like that," he smiled as he edged behind me, snuggling me in his arms, and tenderly kissing my hair.

"Roni, I need to know where you get your strength. I want to be strong, too."

"We don't have much of a choice." I heard the smile in his voice.

I turned around and clung to him. He looked down at me, his eyes washing over my face. "I think you should leave the brooding to me. I'm much better at it."

"I think you're right."

"Dara, you do realize that right now it's normal for you to feel more apprehensive than usual."

"I suppose so. Still…it all seems so…hopeless."

"You should be thinking about yourself and our baby at this time – not world events."

"But that's just it, Roni. I *am* thinking about our baby."

He crinkled his brow, looking at me thoughtfully. "Look, Dara, it may seem like it's us against the world," he said, as he gently stroked my hair, "but we're not alone." With a mock dramatic flair, Roni continued. "According to the prophecies, *Jerusalem will be a cup of poison* to all those who attempt to besiege Jerusalem and take her from Jewish hands. *All those who participate in it, will suffer from it.*"

"Hmm, all mocking aside…do you believe in the prophecies?"

"Yes…I do. We're already witnessing it. From all four corners of the earth, the rest of the Jewish people are steadily returning home to Israel."

"Then…you don't have any fears of what's yet to come?"

"No. But the final battle *will be* over Jerusalem and we must be ready for it."

"Pops used to say that if enough of us do good deeds, it could prevent the horrible war in the end of days, and that the Messiah would come through peaceful means."

Roni didn't answer. He continued to stroke my hair while gazing into my eyes.

"I suppose you don't believe that, do you?" I asked softly.

He cupped his hand to my cheek. "Our enemies are many, Dara. No…I don't believe they will simply disappear. But," his eyes burned with resolve like a true warrior of Israel, "they will never take Jerusalem from us. Never again."

The Jerusalem air whipped about us and he tightened his hold around me to shield me from the mounting winds. He creased his brow in curiosity as he saw the worry in my eyes. "What is it, Dara? Why did you want to come to the Mount of Olives today?"

"This is the place we believe will be the final battle, right?"

"Right, Dara, but…"

"But the olive branch is also a universal symbol of peace, right?"

"Right, but…"

"So, even here, on the Mount of Olives, at the site of the final battle, there's hope."

"I'm…not sure I follow you, Dara."

"I wanted to come here…finding hope. I…needed to be sure that *you* have hope…in our future."

"I do, Dara. You know I do. I promise you, I will never let go of that. But," he smiled broadly, trying to reassure me, "I don't think we're quite at that point of the *final battle*."

"So, you don't think it's all futile?"

"To hope? No, Dara. Hope is never futile. It's the hope that gives us the wherewithal to go on, against all odds. It's the hope that maintains the fight in all of us — to hold on to what we cherish and to protect it with our very lives." He studied my face. "You're like me in many ways. You carry the burden of the world on your shoulders. But," he stroked my cheek tenderly, "I know there's something more going on in that beautiful head of yours. What are you trying to tell me, Dara?"

"Roni…I had a sonogram today. They found…two heartbeats. We're having…twins," I smiled faintly.

Silence. His lips parted but no sound came out, and his luminous eyes stared at me in a glittery trance.

"Roni?"

I watched Roni's stunned look gradually give way to a smile. He lowered his eyes to my stomach and cautiously placed his hand over it.

"Of course the doctor couldn't be absolutely sure from the sonogram, but he thinks, also with the differing heart rates, one might be a girl and one a boy," I quietly added and watched his smile grow wider as his eyes shot back up to mine.

"My *motek*," he murmured as his eyes dazzled into mine, "how can you have any doubts, when hope blossoms inside of you?" Then without warning, he whisked me into his arms and spun me around, heartily laughing into the wind. "And you say you don't believe in miracles! There are two miracles growing inside you, my beautiful wife!" Roni's laughter was infectious and I found myself laughing with him.

"Roni?"

"Yes, *ahuvati*, my love?"

"I'm feeling a little dizzy. C-can you put me down now?"

"Oh. Sure." He wore a silly grin on his face. "So...twins, eh?"

I nodded.

"I'm better than I thought." His eyes twinkled.

"Oh, you..." I shoved him playfully away. "You *would* take all the credit for it!"

"Ha ha! I am insanely in love with you!" Forgetting himself, he grabbed me, lifted me up and whirled me around once again. "Let's go home and celebrate," he gushed as he set me down. He was like a little boy who had just received his first shiny, new bike.

"Celebrate, huh. And exactly *how* would you like to celebrate?" I laughed. His giddiness was contagious.

"Trust me," he pursed his lips with his devilish glare. "I'll...come up with something."

"Oh, I see..."

"Unless you have a better idea...?"

"Hmm," I considered. "None that I can think of."

"Wow. You really *are* a lot like me," his eyes sparkled in a huge grin. "First things first, though." He turned to face the direction of the Temple Mount, in the way Jews have done for some three thousand years, and for the first time since I've known Roni, he prayed. To my surprise, he knew the words of our ancient prayers by heart, giving thanks and homage to God for our two new blessings. I, too, took the few minutes to meditate, thank God and appreciate the good fortune I hoped to share with Roni.

What a long, difficult and painful, winding road it had been. I wondered where I found the strength to go on, but deep down, I knew. Even when I thought Roni was gone, his inner strength helped me to move forward. It was his courage and his unrelenting hope that urged me on.

And now, here I was, together with my Roni, ready to take another chance at life, ready to begin again and ready to make our mark in the destiny of our people – in our land. I looked up at the sky, closed my eyes and saw the faces of Uri, Gavriel, Matan and Ayala – my band of angels. Yes, there was the familiar ache of yearning for them that I would forever carry with me, but then, a warm, peaceful feeling draped its way around my heart and enveloped me – their blessings for me and for Roni all but tangible.

My eyes opened to Roni wrapping his arms around my waist as he stood behind me, his silken curls against my cheek as he leaned down and nestled his head on my shoulder. I turned my face toward his and met his brilliant gaze that never ceased to take my breath away. We stood, lingering on the hilltop of the Mount of Olives, looking out upon our enchanting city.

"Roni?" I broke the silence.

"Mmm." He tightened his embrace.

"I already thought of two names…if it's all right with you."

"I'm certain that anything you choose will be perfect. What are they?"

"Well, for the girl…I thought, Alana. And…for the boy…Uri."

He gently kissed my hair. "That sounds just right," he whispered.

End

Acknowledgments

The list is long. I've been blessed with eager "first readers," some my best of friends and others my best of critics, and those who shine among the professionals, all to whom I owe a debt of gratitude.

Marilyn, Noa and Merav Adler, along with Michaella Schmit and Mindy Orlinsky, for their scrupulous review of the initial draft, their sound and honest advice, spectacular feedback and consistent encouragement and enthusiasm, virtually holding my hand from the very start as each chapter came alive.

Aron Adler, for his logistical advice based on his own experience as an Israeli combat soldier and paramedic for a paratroopers commando unit.

David and Rommi Englard, my two combat soldier sons, for being my sounding board when brainstorming and for advising me on Israeli army specs.

Nili Englard, my teenage daughter, for approaching my writing mania with her youthful wit.

Gelah Goldberg, Nomi Keil and Lorraine Krell for their genuine interest, bedrock support and constructive input.

Eve Harow, for believing in me more than I do myself, and for her generosity in allowing me to "borrow" her family name for the main character.

Estee Kreisman, for her incredible book cover design that captured the essence of the story.

Chemi Mor, I'd be lost without you...literally!

Deborah Mor, for her unending kindnesses, constantly at the ready to assist me.

Shelly Sanders, for her invaluable proofreading of the original manuscript.

Jordana Sipzner, my eldest daughter, for her spectacular vision as a fellow writer and "no-holds barred" critique.

Michele Wechsler for her dynamic insight that helped me smooth out some kinks and for her animated excitement that spurred me on.

Gefen Publishing House, notably Ilan Greenfield and Michael Fischberger, for trusting in this project, enabling me to see it through and making it all possible. A special acknowledgment to the two people instrumental in all levels of production: projects coordinator Lynn Douek and my editor, Ita Olesker, who really "gets me"!

About the Author

A native of New York, Zahava England lived in Teaneck, New Jersey, before moving with her family to Israel in 2006. An outspoken activist in the United States on behalf of Israel, Zahava has worked to advance awareness and raise funds on behalf of the humanitarian and security needs of Jewish communities throughout Judea, Samaria and Gaza. She served as trustee on the executive board of One Israel Fund and, in the year preceding her immigration to Israel, served as its executive director.

Presently, Zahava lives in Efrat, Gush Etzion, has one married daughter, two sons currently serving in the army, and another daughter attending high school in Gush Etzion. She is a member of Women in Green and the Raise Your Spirits Theatre Group. Zahava is also a freelance writer and lectures as a guest speaker in the United States and Israel about her books, Jewish activism and her passion for Israel's well-being. She is the author of *Settling for More: From Jersey to Judea* (Urim Publications). *The Gilboa Iris* is her first novel.